John Russell

The Life and Times of Charles James Fox

John Russell

The Life and Times of Charles James Fox

ISBN/EAN: 9783337094485

Printed in Europe, USA, Canada, Australia, Japan

Cover: Foto ©Raphael Reischuk / pixelio.de

More available books at **www.hansebooks.com**

THE
LIFE AND TIMES

OF

CHARLES JAMES FOX.

BY

EARL RUSSELL.

VOLUME II.

" Et vitam impendere vero."

LONDON:

RICHARD BENTLEY, NEW BURLINGTON STREET,

Publisher in Ordinary to Her Majesty.

1866.

[The Author reserves the right of Translation.]

PREFACE

TO

THE SECOND VOLUME.

It has been my object, in this volume, rather to give a sketch of the Times of Mr. Fox, than to follow minutely his Life. The next volume, if I should be able to complete it, will be more biographical, and less historical.

CONTENTS.

THE LIFE AND TIMES

OF

CHARLES JAMES FOX.

CHAPTER XVIII.

THE COALITION MINISTRY—THE INDIA BILL—EXPULSION OF
THE MINISTRY.

ALTHOUGH Lord Shelburne resigned on the 24th of February, it was not till the 2nd of April that the Coalition Ministry was admitted to office. The delay was almost entirely occasioned by the repugnance evinced by the King to submit to the rule of the Whig party. Meeting Lord North's father, Lord Guildford, who was Chamberlain to the Queen, the King said to him : " Did I ever think, my Lord Guildford, that Lord North would have delivered me up in this manner to Mr. Fox ?" Lord Guildford replied, that he was sure it was not Lord North's intention to do what was disagreeable to his Majesty, but he understood his Majesty had got over any difficulty on that head by his sanction of the interview between Mr. Fox and Mr. Pitt.

It is said that the Lord Advocate advised that Mr. Pitt should be made Prime Minister ; and that, on the morning of the 27th of February, Mr. Pitt had consented for a short time to stand on that perilous eminence. If this account was true, his boldness was but for a moment. Thoughts of placing Lord Gower at the Treasury, and other ineffectual schemes, together with the desperate resolution of going to Hanover, fluctuated in the royal bosom. At length, on the 4th of March, the King sent for Lord North, and endeavoured to prevail on him to return to the Treasury. But Lord North, though weak in character, was too much a man of honour to recede from his engagements. On the 8th, in the evening, the King saw Lord North again.* He then consented that the Duke of Portland should be at the head of the Ministry, according to the plan Lord North had proposed, but said that, as he should not like to change again, he desired the basis might be broad enough. The meaning of this intimation was, that the King wished Lord Thurlow to remain Chancellor. He also told Lord North to desire the Duke of Portland to send him his arrangement in writing. This was positively refused by the Duke, who sent word that if the King condescended to employ him, it would be necessary that he should see his Majesty. It had been a common practice of the King, from the beginning of his reign, to obtain a list of persons proposed to fill Cabinet offices from the statesmen charged by him to form a Ministry, and then to work on the resentments of those who had been omitted. In this way he had, in 1764, inflamed the anger of the Duke of Bedford against Mr. Pitt, and induced him to become President of the Council in the Grenville Ministry. In the same way he now endeavoured to work on the feelings of General Conway, whom it was not intended to place in the new Cabinet. But Conway, being of a calm temper and unambitious character, was not irritated, nor even displeased, at this omission. The King likewise endeavoured at various times to sow jealousy between Lord North and Mr. Fox. But these attempts to work on the tempers of two men, both of them

* Fitzpatrick to Lord Ossory: " Correspondence," vol. ii.

devoid of envy or jealousy, were entirely unsuccessful. Indeed, Mr. Fox observed in the House of Commons, that there had been, it was true, some slight difference between the members of the Coalition; but that out of five weeks, it only took up ten hours, and was then finally and conclusively settled.

The difference here alluded to arose on the question of the office to be held by Lord Stormont. It seems to have been intended by Lord North that Lord Stormont should be Secretary of State for the Home Department. But this arrangement not suiting the views of the Whigs, who dreaded fresh complications from the appointment of two Secretaries differing so widely in opinion as Mr. Fox and Lord Stormont, it was agreed on the 14th of March, between the Duke of Portland and Lord North, that Lord Carlisle should be Secretary of State, and Lord Stormont should be President of the Council, or Privy Seal. But Lord Stormont declined both these offices; and the King, on his part, insisted that, in order to form the Administration on a broad bottom, Lord Stormont should be Secretary of State, and the Chancellor should retain his office. These differences were at length adjusted; the King did not insist on the retention of the Chancellor, Lord North took the office of Secretary of State, and Lord Stormont consented to be Lord President. The list finally presented, and agreed upon for the Cabinet, was as follows:—

First Lord of the Treasury . Duke of Portland.
Secretaries of State . . . C. Fox and Lord North.
Chancellor of the Exchequer . Lord John Cavendish.
Lord President . . . . . Lord Stormont.
Lord Privy Seal . . . . Lord Carlisle.
First Lord of the Admiralty . Lord Keppel.

Had Lord John Cavendish been Secretary of State with Mr. Fox—Mr. Pitt, Chancellor of the Exchequer—Lord North, President of the Council—and had Mr. Burke, as Paymaster, been admitted to the Cabinet,—a really strong government would have been formed. As it was, the King, irritated but not dismayed, cast about him for means and opportunity to overthrow his *new tyrants,* as he was said to call them. Mr. Pitt, relieved from all obligations to Lord Shelburne, was at liberty to combine the discontented followers of Lord North and Mr. Fox, with the King's friends, and thus rally a beaten army upon a strong position. The favour attendant upon the son of Chatham, the bright and rising flame of his eloquence, the confidence with which he confronted Fox, gave a reputation to this new party which Dundas and Jenkinson, with their suspicious connexions and corrupt antecedents, could never have acquired. The *stirpis Achilleæ fastus* emboldened this young orator, scarcely three-and-twenty years old, to meet in debate the united strength of the leaders of the two parties who for nine years had divided the admiration and the allegiance of the House of Commons.

Internally the Ministry was united; Lord North, always indolent, and seeking present ease, yielded in everything, with a passing remark (often sagacious and prophetic), to the genius and energy of Mr. Fox. In foreign politics Mr. Fox was of course supreme; on the affairs of Ireland he wrote to the Lord Lieutenant in the language of a master; in finance alone he abandoned the direction to his colleague who was charged with that department.

The Great Seal was put in commission, and Lord Loughborough was placed at the head of the commission. In this situation he was not formidable to the Minister as a rival, but neither was he so useful an assistant as he might have been had he held the office of Lord Chancellor. When Mr. Fox kissed hands on his appointment, Lord Townshend, an observing and caustic old man, said he saw the King turn back his ears and eyes just like the horse at Astley's, when the tailor he had determined to throw was getting on him. Yet Mr. Fox was treated with civility; Lord North, with manifest coldness and dislike. In fact the King had never felt any attachment to Lord North, and from the moment he ceased to be a convenient tool, his easy, benevolent good-nature provoked a master who was fretting with pride, anger, and resentment. To Lord North himself he owned that, although on former occasions he had commanded his temper, he now was unable to restrain it. To others he had spoken more openly. To Mr. William Grenville his Majesty gave a description of the characters of Lord North and Mr. Fox: "The first, he said, was a man composed entirely of negative qualities, and actuated in every instance by a desire of present ease at the risk of any future difficulty. This he instanced in the American War, and in the riots of 1780, of which he gave me a very long detail. As to Fox, he allowed that he was a man of parts, quickness, and great eloquence; but that he wanted application, and consequently the fundamental knowledge necessary for business, and above all was totally destitute of discretion and sound judgment."*

Mr. Fox immediately applied himself with the diligence he had before displayed to the duties of his office. His simple and direct manner of transacting business—his friendly kindness to all employed under him, whether at home, or

---

* " Court and Cabinets of George III." vol. i. p. 213, March 23rd, 1783.

abroad, were generally acknowledged. Above all, perhaps, the satisfaction felt at seeing the Foreign office filled, for the first time since Lord Chatham, by a man of transcendent abilities,—pervaded all the courts of Europe except those of France and Great Britain.* His letters and dispatches were often communicated to the Sovereign and Ministers of the respective countries, and were generally admired, especially by the King of Prussia and the Empress Catherine, for the ease and grace of their language, the simplicity and soundness of their views, and for the artless and conciliatory exposition of designs favourable to the preservation of peace and the independence of the nations of Europe. M. de Vergennes, however, could only remark, " C'est un fagot d'épines que ce M. Fox."

George III. shut himself up in a cold and sullen reserve. When Mr. Fox tried to improve the preliminaries of peace in the definitive treaty, the King said that, having agreed to the preliminaries, he could not take any further interest in the matter. When Mr. Fox urged the importance of endeavouring to unite Russia and Prussia in a system of counterpoise against France, the King observed that it was best to await passively the course of events. With the tenacity of a little mind, he constantly taunted Mr. Fox with the vote of February, 1782; and said that, since we had so lowered ourselves, it was no wonder that other nations slighted us. Yet, in fact, nothing but his own obstinacy had led to that extreme use of the right of remonstrance by the House of Commons. If the King was unable to see this, he might have remembered that his late Ministers, Lord Shelburne, Mr. Pitt, and General Conway

* Lord Holland.

(the mover of the vote) had been quite as active in the matter as Mr. Fox himself.

Thus opposed and thus discouraged, Mr. Fox could not effect any positive and permanent change. Frederick the Great, who in other days had expressed his joy when William Pitt took the direction of the war, now manifested his approbation of the character and views of Mr. Fox, and acknowledged the advantage of having in England what he said he had long regretted the want of—a Ministry on whose honour and abilities he could rely; but he stated frankly his opinion that affairs were not in his opinion ripe for an entire change of system. Catherine of Russia, with views of ambition turned to Poland and to Turkey, was only solicitous of alliances which would facilitate her projects.

In the definitive treaties with France and Spain Mr. Fox obtained the settlement of some points which had been omitted, or left doubtful, in the preliminaries. No care had been taken for the protection of the British inhabitants of Tobago, which was ceded to France : this omission was now supplied. The limits within which the gum trade in Africa was to be carried on were clearly laid down and defined; the vague term, " ancient possessions," applied to the possessions of our allies in India, was defined to mean the state of possession in 1776. Besides these improvements, an ambiguity respecting a treaty of commerce with France was removed by stipulating that the treaty was to be made within two years from January, 1784; and in case the negotiations should fail, the treaty of Utrecht was to revive and be in full force. The definitive treaties were finally signed at Versailles on the 3rd of September, 1783. In the letter to Mr. Fox, by which the King acknowledged the arrival of the definitive treaty, he proceeds to make some remarks on the hostility of the Dutch, and ends by the remark, "in states, as well as men, where dislike has once arose, I never expect to see cordiality."

This remark is exemplified in the King's whole treatment of the Coalition Ministry. Indeed, such was his hostility, that on the question of an allowance to the Prince of Wales he was on the point of dismissing them. The allowance proposed was 100,000*l.* a year, which, although considered extravagant by Lord John Cavendish and Lord North, was acquiesced in by the Cabinet, and apparently assented to by the King. But a few days afterwards it appeared that the King was by no means disposed to sanction the proposed allowance, and indeed was ready to push his resistance to extreme consequences. Happily, the difficulty was removed by the waver on the part of the Prince of any claim to which his father did not freely assent, and by the consent of the King to pay 50,000*l.* a year from the Civil List, and make over to the Prince the Prince's own property in the Duchy of Cornwall, which he had hitherto withheld. The income of the Duchy was supposed to be equivalent to 12,000*l.* a year. The following extracts from a letter of Mr. Fox to Lord Northington, and the journal of Lord Temple, will show the opposite views taken by the King and his Minister:—

"I am sure you have too much consideration for the various plagues and troubles of my situation to attribute my silence to any neglect of you; but the truth is that, busy as I have been, I should before this time have fulfilled my promise of explaining to you the business of the Prince of Wales's establishment, if I had not understood that the Duke of Portland had written to you freely on the subject. As to the opinion of our having gained strength by it, the only rational foundation for such an opinion is, that the event has proved that there subsists no such understanding between the King and Lord Temple as to enable them to form an Administration; because, if there did, it is impossible but they must have seized an occasion in many respects so fortunate for them. They would have had on their side the various cries of *paternal authority, economy, moderate establishment, mischief-making between father and son*, and many other plausible topics. As therefore they did not avail themselves of all these advantages, it seems reasonable to suppose that there is as yet nothing settled and understood amongst them; and in this sense, and inasmuch as this is so felt and understood in the world, I think we may flatter ourselves that we are something stronger than we were; in every other view I own I think quite otherwise. The King has certainly carried one point against us, and the notoriety that he has done so may lead people to suppose that he might be successful in others, if he were to attempt them. Everybody will not see the distinction between this and political points so strong as the Ministers have done. Perhaps I do not myself, but yet no man was more convinced of the necessity of yielding than I. The truth is that, excepting the Duke of Portland and Lord Keppel, there was not one Minister *who would have fought with any heart in this cause.* I could see clearly from the beginning, long before the difficulties appeared, that Lord North and Lord John, though they did not say so, thought the large establishment extravagant; and you will, I am sure, agree with me, that to fight a cause where the latter especially was not hearty, would have been a most desperate measure. Indeed all the advantages we have hitherto derived, and are every day deriving, from the deserved and universal good opinion which is entertained of Lord John Cavendish, would not only have been flung away, but his name would have been used against us; for it is quite certain (at least it appeared to me), that his sentiments would have been known enough to have this effect.

" Under all these circumstances there appeared to me no alternative in common sense but to yield with the best grace possible, if the Prince of Wales could be brought to be of that mind. I believe he was naturally very averse to it; but Colonel Lake and others whom he most trusts, persuaded him to it, and the intention of doing so came from him to us spontaneously. If it had not, I own I should have felt myself bound to follow his Royal Highness's line upon the subject; though I know that by so doing I should destroy the Ministry in the worst possible way, and subject myself to the imputation of the most extreme wrong-headedness. I shall always therefore consider the Prince's having yielded a most fortunate event, and shall always feel myself proportionally obliged to him, and to those who advised him.

" With regard to the conduct of the Cabinet Ministers, you will easily collect from what I have said, that there was nothing of that kind of division to which you and others naturally looked. Lord North was perfectly disposed to make *cause commune* as much as man could do. Lord Stormont kept himself, I think, rather more distinct, but not more than I expected; nor was there the least suspicion that he had any greater share of the King's confidence upon this occasion than the rest of his Ministers. I do not think I have omitted anything that can serve to throw light on this affair. I need not point out to you that I have written all this in the utmost confidence. There are parts very unfit to be known by anybody, and especially what relates to Lord John; for though there have been surmises in the world relative to his opinion, and though Pitt even alluded to them in his speech, yet the true state of the case is not generally known, nor is it fit it should, for many obvious reasons. The same observation holds in regard to the manner · of the Prince's yielding. In short, the only thing that ought to be said is, that it was not a point upon which Ministers ought to dispute his Majesty's pleasure, and that they were the better enabled to yield by the generosity of the Prince, who was most ready to give up his own interest rather than be the cause of any confusion, or appear to be wanting in duty to the King. Well, but this matter being over, what is now our situation? I will tell you fairly what *I believe*, I mean it literally, for I should not be at all surprised to find myself mistaken : I believe the King is neither pleased nor displeased with us; that he has no inclination to do anything to serve us, or to hurt us; and that he has no view to any other Administration which he means to substitute in lieu of us."

Now let us see in Lord Temple's account the reverse of the medal : " Upon my return to England," he says in his Journal, " I was honoured with every public attention from his Majesty, who ostensibly held a language upon my subject, *calculated to raise in the strongest degree the jealousy of his servants.* In the audience which I asked, as a matter of course, after being presented at his levee, he recapitulated all the transactions of that period, with the strongest encomium upon Mr. Pitt, and with much apparent acrimony

hinted at Lord Shelburne, whom he stated to have abandoned a situation which was tenable, and particularly so
after the popular resentment had been roused. This was
naturally attended with strong expressions of resentment
and disgust of his Ministers, and of personal abhorrence of
Lord North, whom he charged with treachery and ingra-
titude of the blackest nature. He repeated, *that to such a
Ministry he never would give his confidence, and that he would
take the first moment for dismissing them.*"

Lord Temple then discussed with the King the proposal
for an allowance of 100,000*l.* to the Prince of Wales.
" His Majesty declared himself to be decided to resist
this attempt, and to push the consequences to their full
extent, and to try the spirit of the Parliament and of the
people upon it. I thought it my duty to offer him my
humble advice to go on with his Ministers, if possible, in
order to throw upon them the ratification of the peace,
which they professed to intend to ameliorate, and to give
them scope for those mountains of reform which would
inevitably come very short of the expectations of the
public. From these public measures, and from their probable dissension, I thought that his Majesty might look
forward to a change of his Ministers in the autumn; and
that, as the last resource, a dissolution of this Parliament,
chosen by Lord North and occasionally filled by Mr. Fox,
might offer him the means of getting rid of the chains
which pressed upon him. To all this he assented; but
declared his intention to resist, at all events and hazards,
the proposition for this enormous allowance to his Royal
Highness, of whose conduct he spoke with much dissatisfaction. He asked what he might look to if, upon this
refusal, the Ministry should resign; and I observed that,

not having had the opportunity of consulting my friends, I could only answer that their resignation was a proposition widely differing from their dismissal, and that I did not see the impossibility of accepting his Administration in such a contingency, provided the supplies and public bills were passed, so as to enable us to prorogue the Parliament. To all this he assented, and declared his intention of endeavouring to gain time, that the business of Parliament might go on, and agreed with me that such a resignation was improbable, and that it would be advisable not to dismiss them unless some very particular opportunity presented itself."*

Such was the precarious position in which the Coalition Ministry was placed; the King only watching for an opportunity to overthrow the Ministers he hated. In the multitude and complication of public affairs, such an opportunity was sure to arise. Ireland was by no means in a satisfactory state. The concessions of the past year were considered by the English Government as the final settlement of a long-disputed question; by Irish agitators as the beginning of a struggle for national independence.

The Bishop of Derry and Mr. Flood were the leaders of this new movement. The Bishop was at the head of the Volunteers, the largest armed body in Ireland; Mr. Flood was one of the most powerful and eloquent of the many able and eloquent orators of the Irish Parliament. There were not wanting some plausible reasons and some favourable circumstances to colour and instigate their proceedings. The settlement of the former year had conceded in substance rather than in express terms the legislative independence of Ireland. A decision of Lord Mansfield, re-

* " Court and Cabinets of George III." vol. i. p. 303.

versing a judgment pronounced in Ireland, had, in the opinion of Lord Shelburne's Government, made it necessary to introduce a bill into the British Parliament "For removing Doubts concerning the exclusive Rights of the Parliament and Courts of Ireland in Matters of Legislation and Judicature." "Was it not desirable," it was argued, "to remove all such doubts, and to place the relations of the two countries upon a clear and permanent footing?"

While such was the *ratio justificatoria* of the Irish malcontents, their *ratio suasoria* was not less strong. They had seen Great Britain foiled by colonies whose force she had despised; they had seen her yield inch by inch till she had abandoned the whole ground not only of her modern pretensions but of her ancient sovereignty. In the same manner the claims of the Irish had been met first with neglect, then with contempt, and lastly with deference and ample concession. Forty thousand Volunteers were still in arms, flushed with the victory of the preceding year—the servants of yesterday, perhaps the masters of to-morrow.

Great Britain was still pale, worn, and exhausted, from the effects of her struggle with America. Could there be a more auspicious moment to strike a blow?

On the other hand, there were inherent causes of weakness in the new movement. The essential objects of legislative self-government and judicial independence had been gained. To attempt to push the victory further might rouse the pride of Great Britain. "A nation which tries to humiliate another is a foolish nation" was the dictum of Grattan. Let us add to this that Lord Charlemont and Mr. Grattan · brought the lustre of pure patriotism and unsullied character to the cause which they led. Lord Bristol and Mr. Flood had no such halo round their heads.

An armed body, which cannot deliberate without violating the Constitution, nor act without violating the law, can only be kept together by a Cæsar or a Cromwell, whose sword must make his way to a throne or a tomb.

Lord Bristol was not prepared to encounter such a risk, or fitted to reach such an eminence. Besides, dissensions were sure to creep in. For instance, hitherto the spirit of national union had prevented the mischief of religious jealousy, and a body of Roman Catholic Volunteers had fired a salute after marching round the statue of King William with as much readiness as the Protestants.*   But this suppression of well-founded grievances could not be expected to last. Had the Roman Catholics put forward their claims, Lord Charlemont was ready to appear as their decided opponent.

In this state of affairs the following letter was addressed by Mr. Fox to Lord Northington. Written with all the ease of familiar correspondence, it appears to me to show as much administrative power and practical wisdom as was ever evinced in a document of more form and pretension :—

MR. FOX TO LORD NORTHINGTON.

"St. James's-place, Nov. 1st, 1783.

" DEAR NORTHINGTON,—I believe it is a better excuse, and I am sure it is a truer one, for having so long postponed my letter to you, to say that it is owing to my idleness rather than my business. The few moments of idleness one has just before the opening of the most terrific session of Parliament that ever was held, are too valuable to be employed in anything that looks so very like business as writing a letter. I was ten days at Newmarket, Norfolk, &c., which came under the description of perfect idleness;

* From Lord Wellesley, who told me he saw it.

and since my return I have put off writing from day to day, in order to be more perfectly master of those topics upon which I mean to write to you, and which are of infinite importance not only to the credit of our Administration, but to the well-being of the country.

"And first with respect to the Volunteers and their delegates. I want words to express to you how *critical*, in the genuine sense of the word, I conceive the present moment to be. Unless they dissolve in a reasonable time, Government, and even the name of it, must be at an end. This, I think, will hardly be disputed. Now, it appears to me that upon the event of the present session of your Parliament this question will entirely depend. If they are treated as they ought to be, if you show *firmness*, and the firmness is seconded by the aristocracy and Parliament, I look to their dissolution as a certain and not very distant event. If otherwise, I reckon their Government, or rather their anarchy, as firmly established as such a thing is capable of being; but your Government certainly is completely annihilated.

"If you ask me what I mean by firmness, I have no scruple in saying that I mean it in the strictest sense, and understand by it a determination not to be swayed in any the slightest degree by the Volunteers, nor even to attend to any petition that may come from them. This sounds violent, but I am clear it is right; for if *they* can pretend with any plausibility that they have carried any one point, it will be a motive for their continuing in their present state, and they will argue thus: 'We carried this this year; let us go on as we have done, and we shall carry some other point in the next.' Immense concessions were made in the Duke of Portland's time, and those concessions were declared by an almost unanimous House of Commons to be sufficient.   The account must be considered as having been closed on the day of that vote, and should never again be opened on any pretence whatever.   It is true that the bill we passed here last year does not agree with my system; but you know the history of that bill, and the stage in which it was when we came in, otherwise I am satisfied it never would have been passed—at least I am sure it would not without the strongest opposition from the Duke of Portland and me.

"It is possible that I may be told that these are fine *words*, but that to act up to them is impossible.   It may be so, but every information I have had from Ireland leads me to think that the spirit and firmness of the aristocracy will depend entirely upon the degree shown of those qualities in the Castle.   Recollect that this is a crisis.   Peace is the natural period to the Volunteers, and if they are encouraged to subsist for any considerable time after this period, all is gone, and our connexion with Ireland is orse than none at all.   I have so high an opinion of Grattan's integrity and love of his country, that I cannot persuade myself that he can see the present situation in any other light than that in which I do.   Volunteers, and soon possibly Volunteers without property, will be the only Government in Ireland, unless they are faced this year in a manful manner; and there is no man in conscience and honour so much bound to face them as Grattan himself. He has employed a dangerous instrument for honourable purposes; now that those purposes are answered, fully answered, by his own declaration in the vote before alluded to, is he not peculiarly bound to take care that so dangerous a weapon should no longer remain in unskilful or perhaps wicked hands, to be employed for objects as bad as his were just and honourable? England justly relied much on his opinion that they would be satisfactory, in making the concessions in 1782, and he is therefore bound to England for the Irish part of the bargain, which was nothing more than to be satisfied.

"I heard with great satisfaction from Serjeant Adair that Grattan, though a friend to the parliamentary reform, would take a wise distinction upon the manner in which it comes to the consideration of Parliament, and oppose it steadily upon that ground; but from what the Duke of Portland read me from Pelham's letter, I do not think this appears quite so certain. I know your natural inclination is to firmness, perhaps much more than mine is, and therefore I hope all I have said upon the subject is superfluous; but I am so perfectly convinced that this is the crisis of the fate of Ireland, that I cannot help dwelling upon it. The Volunteers never were, depend upon it, so considerable as they were represented. Their having chosen a madman for their head, of whose honesty, too, there is no opinion, and their having laid their chief stress upon a point upon which there is so much real difference of opinion in both countries, and which militates as much against the interests of the prevailing influences in Parliament, are circumstances which must have weakened them. If they are resisted, I am satisfied they will be defeated, and I cannot bring myself to think that much is risked in the trial; for if they are suffered to carry their points by timidity and acquiescence, it is as much over with English government, in my judgment, as if they had carried them by force. All other points appear to me to be trifling in comparison of this great one of the Volunteers; but I will trouble you with a few observations upon some others.

" In regard to annual sessions, I own I do not think them very material, and in some respects, perhaps, I see some advantages arising to Government from them. You must have misunderstood Lord North, if you consider yourself as precluded either from consenting to them, or even from proposing them by your friends in Parliament. The propriety of such a measure was meant to be left to your discretion, but it was the mentioning of them in the speech that was objected to, and I own I concurred in this objection; but if I had imagined that you thought this form of proposing them to be as material as I now suspect you did, I should have been of another opinion. I wish, therefore, for the future, when you write for instructions on material points, that you or Pelham would write a private letter to the Duke of Portland or me, letting us know how far you consider each point as important to your plans and arrangements; if we had conceived that you considered the mention of this point in the speech to be of this nature, I have no doubt but your instructions would have been agreeable to your wishes. With respect to some other points which have been discussed among us to-day, perhaps the same observations will hold. I own I think the production of Pinto's paper to the House formally, a very exceptionable measure; but if you upon the spot judge it necessary, my opinion will alter. However, I must say that it would be a very dangerous precedent, and tend very much to embarrass persons in my situation in all future negotiations. You will understand, however, that my objection is entirely to the formal production of it. I have none whatever to Pelham's informing the House correctly of all that has passed, and even reading Pinto's memorial as a part of his speech, if he choose it. My objection is to the grounding of a proceeding upon a memorial of a foreign Minister, which, in my opinion, ought never to be done, except in the cases of going to war or of censuring a Minister. However, this may be given up to a very pressing conveniency, though certainly it ought not to be done. But no conveniency in my opinion would justify the laying before the Irish Parliament the definitive treaties, preliminaries, &c. If they are once produced, who can say that they shall not be discussed, that addresses shall not be moved upon them, and that the opinions of the two kingdoms, upon the conduct of the Ministers who made them, may not be diametrically opposite? The responsibility of Ministers here can only be to the British Parliament; and to lay treaties before an assembly to whom we are not responsible would only be an idle compliment at best; but might be in the end productive of some of the worst consequences, which are to be feared from the very peculiar relation in which the two kingdoms now stand one to the other.

"What you propose about beer is so reasonable that there can be no objection of a public nature; but the intention which there is in the Treasury of laying a very heavy tax upon that article (which, by the way, ought not to be mentioned), makes one wish, if possible, to avoid doing anything which our brewers will complain of. The prudence of listening to this objection will depend upon the degree of advantage you expect from the measure you propose, and of this you must be the judge.

"I hope, my dear Northington, that you will not consider this long letter as meant to blame your conduct; but I think I owe it as much to my friendship for you as to the public to give you fairly my opinion and advice in your most arduous situation; and I will fairly own that there is one priuciple which seems to run through your different dispatches which a little alarms me; it is this: you seem to think, as if it were absolutely necessary, at the outset of your government, to do something that may appear to be obtaining boons, however trifling, for Ireland; aud what I confess I like still less is, to see that this is in some measure grounded upon the ampleness of former concessions. Now I see this in quite a different light, and reason that because those concessions were so ample, no further ones are necessary. If because the Duke of Portland gave much, you are to give something, consider how this reasoning will apply to your successor. I repeat it again, the account must be considered as having been closed in 1782. Ireland has no right to expect from any Lord Lieutenant to carry any more points for her. Convenient and proper regulations will always be adopted for their own sakes, and stand upon their own ground; but boons, gifts, and compliments Ireland has no right to expect. She has more to fear from us than we from her. Her linen trade, which is her staple, depends entirely upon the protection of this country. I do not mean by saying this that menace ought to be used; but neither ought we, in our present situation, to pay her too much court.

"This country is reduced low enough, God knows; but depend upon it we shall be tired if, year by year, we are to hear of granting something new, or acquiescing in some-thing new, for the sake of pleasing Ireland. I am sure you must feel as I do upon this subject; but, situated as you are, among Irishmen who, next to a job for themselves, love nothing so well as a job for their country, and hardly ever seeing any one who talks to you soundly on our side of the question, it is next to impossible but you must fall insensibly into Irish ideas more than we do, who see the reverse of the picture; and who, of course, are much more sensible to the reproaches of this country than of that. Ireland appears to me now to be like one of her most eminent jobbers, who, after having obtained the Prime Serjeantry, the Secretaryship of State, and twenty other great places, insisted upon the Lord Lieutenant's adding a major's half-pay to the rest of his emoluments.

" It would be most unconscionable, after this very long letter, to trouble you with anything of a private nature, so that I will defer till my next letter the few things I have to say of that sort. I hear many of our friends disapprove of the idea of advancing Scott and Fitzgibbon. You know I am no enemy to coalitions; but all I say is, take care when you are giving great things, to oblige those to whom you give them, and that you do not strengthen an enemy instead of gaining a friend. I repeat it again, my dear Northington, that if there should appear in this long and hastily-written letter some shades of dissatisfaction, I hope you will attribute it to the earnest manner in which I am used to write and speak, and to the sincerity and openness which I owe to you. I have no doubt but you will have done what is best; but the times are so very critical, that I cannot help speaking anxiously and eagerly upon points which must, in my judgment, decide the future happiness of both kingdoms. I am, very sincerely, my dear Nor-thington,

" Yours ever,

" C. J. Fox.

" I congratulate you upon the excellent accounts I hear of Pelham from all quarters."

Lord Northington answered the material parts of this letter in a very satisfactory manner. He expressed his conviction that there was no danger in allowing the Convention to meet; "friends of all denominations, new and old, agree that no consequences are to be feared. That it will end in confusion, and contempt will attend its fall." After various suggestions, he then makes the following important remarks :—

"I have a most difficult task. The country is full of disorder, madness, and inconsistency, deriving much of its inclination to disquiet and vexation from a notion of the instability of Government at home, and the influence of a *secret hand* attempting to undermine Government here; I mean a secret hand from a high quarter. I will more particularly state this matter to you in my next.

"In addition to all this, I must confess it is a very wrong measure of English Government to make this country the first step in politics, as it usually has been; and I am sure men of abilities, knowledge of business, and experience ought to be employed here, both in the capacity of Lord Lieutenant and Secretary, not gentlemen taken wild from Brooks's to make their *dénouement* in public life. I feel very forcibly the truth of this observation in my own instance, and wish heartily it was better supplied. However, as I am in this predicament, I will not shrink from the collar, and will manage as well as I can; I depend upon assistance from yourself and the Duke of Portland, and particularly for *support in the objects* I recommend."

Lord Northington was not mistaken in his anticipations. The Committee of Convention having finished their plan, instructed Mr. Flood and Mr. Brownlow to introduce it in Parliament. The Government immediately called a meeting, at which they declared to their friends and supporters that they meant to oppose giving leave to bring in the bill for reform of Parliament, upon the ground of the plan originating in an assembly unconstitutional and illegal, endeavouring to awe and control the Legislature. Grattan could not concur in this vote, but in other respects he agreed with the Government. The Government had a large majority, and the question was set at rest.

I now arrive at that question which from the first was full of danger to the Government, and which ultimately led to their overthrow. The state of India had for many years occupied the attention of Parliament. Two men of very opposite characters, of very different kinds of talent, but both of great ability, Edmund Burke and Henry Dundas, had applied themselves to this vast and intricate subject with great industry and masterly comprehension.

Lord Shelburne and Mr. Pitt, Lord North and Mr. Fox, had all concurred in the necessity of providing a remedy for the violation in India of all the established maxims for the government of dependencies. Mr. Dundas had moved in the House of Commons a resolution that it was the duty of the Directors of the East India Company to recall Mr. Hastings from the government of Bengal. The House assented, and the Directors made an order accordingly. But thinking it necessary before sending out this order, to consult the Court of Proprietors, that body resolved to rescind the order of the Directors. The Directors, obeying this new impulse, proposed dispatches desiring Mr. Hastings to remain Governor-General; but Mr. Townshend, then Secretary of State, interposing, refused to allow these dispatches to go to India.

It was impossible to permit this confusion of powers to

continue. Lord Shelburne, during his Administration, had advised the King to use the following language in his speech to Parliament :—

" The regulation of a vast territory in Asia opens a large field for your wisdom, prudence, and foresight. I trust that you will be able to frame some fundamental laws which may make their connexion with Great Britain a blessing to India; and that you will take therein proper measures to give all foreign nations, in matters of foreign commerce, an entire and perfect confidence in the probity, punctuality, and good order of our Government."

Whatever these latter words may signify, the intention of framing " some fundamental laws, which may make their connexion with Great Britain a blessing to India," must evidently point to some large system of policy in contrast to that which had been hitherto. pursued. In order that the reader who has not studied the history of India, may have a conception of the magnitude of the evils to be encountered, it may be useful to trace an outline of some of the most striking of the events which in the course of a few years had crowned the British nation with the brightest glory, and sunk her in no common infamy. Lord Clive and Warren Hastings may be considered as the Cortez and Pizarro of our Indian empire. But if, like the Spanish adventurers, they had a mild and unwarlike race to contend against, they had obstacles to overcome which did not embarrass the conquerors of Mexico and Peru. They had to meet European enemies in the field, and they had to satisfy a corrupt and craving corporation at home. They accomplished both these objects; they defeated the foreign enemy and bribed the domestic master; but in doing so they tarnished the good name of England.

It is with Warren Hastings only that we are now concerned. He had been sent from Westminster school, "the best scholar of his year," to enter the civil service of Bengal. He had there been noticed by Lord Clive, and had made progress under Mr. Vansittart. He learnt with rapidity the languages of Bengal, and as quickly made himself master of the prevailing weaknesses of the rulers and people of India. His own wants were few; he was abstemious in his diet, regardless of the pomp which others deemed necessary to captivate Eastern imaginations: plain English broadcloth was his dress; and a few horsemen his retinue. With indomitable courage and unshaken perseverance he soon acquired by his energy in council that sway which Clive had won by his sword in the field. Returning to Madras in 1769, he was appointed to Bengal in 1772 as first member of the Council. His measures of policy, his destruction of the Rohilla country, the infamous treaty of Chunar, the cruelty used towards the Begums of Oude, the torture of the eunuchs, will be best described when we arrive at the story of his impeachment.

The treaty of Chunar had been signed in September, 1781; the torture of the Begums and their servants took place during the year 1782. But an avenger was at hand. In 1781 the House of Commons named two committees; one a Select Committee, in the usual form, to consider the state of administration in Bengal; the other "Secret," to inquire into the causes of the war in the Carnatic.

The Secret Committee was presided over by Henry Dundas, Lord Advocate of Scotland. In April, 1782, he displayed to the House the information collected by the committee in an able speech of three hours. A few weeks later he moved a resolution for the recall of Hastings, "he having, in sundry instances, acted in a manner repugnant to the honour and policy of this nation."

The Select Committee brought to light a story showing the state of the internal government of Bengal, not less wonderful than that which the Secret Committee had revealed regarding the foreign policy of the Governor-General.

In the month of October, 1774, General Clavering, Colonel Monson, and Mr. Philip Francis, a clerk in the War-office, arrived in the Ganges with the appointments of members of the Council of Bengal. These gentlemen were intent upon thwarting the Governor-General, and they willingly listened to the accusations brought against him by Nuncomar, a very rich and powerful Hindoo. A public trial, curious disclosures, a solemn inquiry into the acts of the Governor-General were expected; but while the Indian world were gazing in anxiety for the issue of this process, Nuncomar was suddenly arrested for a forgery committed some years before, tried, convicted, and hanged. The consternation spread among the Hindoos by this rapid execution was extreme. To Englishmen it might be said that forgery was by the laws of England a capital offence, that the trial had been a fair one, and that no reason appeared for the interposition of mercy. But to Hindoos the sudden execution of an enemy of Hastings for a common and as they deemed it a venial offence, appeared no otherwise than a fatal warning to all who should venture to oppose the will of the Governor-General.

Sir Elijah Impey, the first judge of the Supreme Court, declared he had done no more than apply the law. But some years afterwards this impartial judge obtained from Hastings an appointment of 5000l. a year of a *quasi* judicial nature, to be held *during the pleasure* of the Government.

The Select Committee which ascertained these facts reported them, and their chairman moved, in May, 1782, an address to the King, praying that he would recall Sir Elijah Impey "to answer to the charge of having accepted an office granted by and tenable at the pleasure of the servants of the East India Company, which has a tendency to create a dependence in the Supreme Court of Judicature upon those over whose actions the said Court was intended as a control." Nothing could be said against this motion, and accordingly it passed without debate or division.

Such was the deep-seated disease for which Mr. Fox was called upon to find a remedy. It could hardly fail to be either useless from its inadequacy or dangerous from its efficiency.

It may be remembered that the King had agreed with Lord Temple that a resignation of his Ministers was improbable, and that it would be advisable not to dismiss them unless some very particular opportunity presented itself. The opportunity of the affairs of India now presented itself, and the King was not slow or unskilful in taking advantage of it.

One ineffectual attempt was made during the recess to reconcile the King and his Ministers. It was proposed to give the Great Seal to Lord Thurlow, and as an inducement to the Ministers, they were to be allowed on his accession to office to bestow some peerages on their friends. But it was evident that Thurlow would have entered the Cabinet rather as a Court spy than a trusty colleague, and the bonus held out of creating peers by the permission of the King and Lord Thurlow, was in itself humiliating to the apparent advisers of the Crown.　The proposal was rejected.　Parliament met on the 11th of November.　Definitive treaties of peace with France and Spain were announced.　The King proceeded to say :—

"The objects which are to be brought under your deliberation will sufficiently explain my reasons for calling you together after so short a recess.　Inquiries of the utmost importance have been long and diligently pursued, and the fruit of them will be expected.　The situation of the East India Company will require the utmost exertions of your wisdom to maintain and improve the valuable advantages derived from our Indian possessions, and to promote and secure the happiness of the native inhabitants of those provinces."

The King called the attention of Parliament to frauds in the collection of the revenue.　He declared to the House of Commons that the reduction made in the establishments had brought them as low as prudence would admit "At the end of the war," he went on to say, "some part of its weight must inevitably be borne for a time. I feel for the burthens of my people, but I rely on that fortitude which has hitherto supported this nation under many difficulties, for their bearing those which the present exigencies require, and which are so necessary for the full support of the national credit."

This honest and manly language seems to have produced a good effect.　Mr. Pitt, it is true, indulged in some sneers on the congratulations upon a treaty which had been censured by a former vote, but reserved his opposition for the India Bill.

On the 18th of November, Mr. Fox moved for leave to introduce his India Bill.　He dwelt at length on the embarrassed state of the Company; upon the debt of eight millions which they were unable to discharge; on the mal-administration in India; on the resolution of the House of Commons that Mr. Hastings should be recalled; the con-currence of the Court of Directors; the dissent of the Court of Proprietors, and their vote of thanks to the very Governor whom the House of Commons thought unfit for his position. Not content with pointing out the anarchy and confusion which had thus arisen, he showed how it was that the proprietors of East India Stock were unfit to be trusted with the government of a great empire. Mr. Fox then proceeded to develope his measure :—

" His plan was to establish a Board, to consist of seven persons, who should be invested with full power to appoint and displace officers in India, and under whose control the whole government of that country should be placed; the other class to consist of eight persons, to be called assistants, who should have charge of the sales, outfits, &c., of the Company, and in general of all commercial concerns, but still be subject to the control of the first seven. The Board he would have held in England, under the very eye of Parliament; their proceedings should be entered in books for the inspection of both Houses. Their servants abroad should be obliged to make minutes of all their pro-ceedings, and enter them into books to be transmitted to Europe; and if ever they should find 'themselves under the necessity of disobeying an order from the Board (and he was ready to admit that cases might occur when not only it would not be blameable to disobey orders, but when disobedience would be even meritorious), a minute should be entered, stating the reason of such disobedience: and on the same principle he meant to oblige the Council at home to make minutes of their reasons as often as their orders should not be complied with and they should not immediately recal the servant who had disobeyed their instructions. This, he was aware, was new, when applied to the common course of business, but the long practice of it by the India Company had proved its utility.

" He meant to lodge a discretional power with the council, which their responsibility would require. If it appeared to them that a servant of the Company had acted in disobedience of orders from home, from the immediate exigency of affairs, or that he had an obvious good intention in so doing, or that it was for other reasons inexpedient to recall him, they should be obliged to assign in a minute, as short as they pleased, why they did not recal him, and thus avow what they would justify as the expedient grounds of their conduct. This would ensure security to the Commissioners, and oblige them to act on motives of necessary precaution. The Company's servants abroad were already in the habit of entering minutes, and it was a custom of infinite utility; for, if no such custom had existed, India would have been unavoidably lost to us, for we never should have been able without these minutes to trace the melancholy effects up to their true causes.

" For the present, he intended that Parliament should name all the persons who should sit at this Board; but then it should be only *pro hâc vice:* he felt already the inconvenience of parliamentary appointments; for at present the Governor-General of Bengal, deriving under an Act of Parliament, seemed to disavow any power in the Court of Proprietors, Directors, or the King himself to remove him. He would have the Board to be established for three or five years; or for such a length of time as should be thought

sufficient to try the experiment how far this new establishment might be useful. When that should be known, if
experience should have proved its utility, then he proposed
that in future the King should have the nomination of the
seven first. If any of the eight assistant counsellors should
die, the vacancies should be filled up by the Court of Proprietors. A learned gentleman (Mr. Dundas) in the Bill
he brought into Parliament last year, proposed to give the
most extraordinary powers to the Governor-General of
Bengal; he at the same time named the person who was to
fill that office. The person was Earl Cornwallis, a noble-
man whom he [Mr. Fox] named now, only for the purpose
of paying homage to his great character; the name of such
a man might make Parliament consent to the vesting of
such powers in a Governor-General : but certain he was,
that nothing but the great character of that noble lord
could ever induce the Legislature to commit such powers to
an individual, at the distance of half the globe. In this
plan the greatest powers might be entrusted with the
Board, because the members of it would be at home, and
under the eye of that House, before whom their proceedings
must be laid. The learned gentleman had entrenched his
bill behind the character of Lord Cornwallis, but he [Mr.
Fox] would not mention a single name that he intended
to insert in his bill : not because he was afraid they
should not be found most respectable; but because he
wished the bill might rest for support on its own merits,
and not on the characters of individuals. . . .

" He requested that his bills might be considered apart
from the merits or demerits of Mr. Hastings. He said he
was aware that the measure he had proposed was a strong
one; he knew that there was great risk in it; but when he

took upon himself an office of responsibility, he had made up his mind to the situation and the danger of it."

Mr. Pitt, on the address in answer to the King's speech, had called upon the Minister to bring forward without delay some plan for securing and improving the advantages that might be derived from our possessions in the East : "a plan not of temporary palliation, of timorous expedients, but vigorous and effectual, suited to the magnitude, the importance, and the alarming exigency of the case."

Mr. Fox's measure, to whatever objections it might be liable, did not fall short of the magnitude, the importance, and the alarming exigency of the case. The first of his two bills has been already described. By the second bill a number of regulations, to prevent corruption and check ambition, were to be enacted by Parliament. The Governor-General of India was to be prohibited from making war upon any native prince or state, unless upon certain intelligence, allowed to be so by the majority of the Council, that such prince or state was about to make war upon the territories of the Company. Various other provisions were made for controlling and preventing the abuses of power, of which instances had occurred in India. Above all, the Governor-General and Council in Bengal were to be bound to obey the orders of the Court of Directors. The directions for drawing these bills were given by Mr. Burke; the bills were drawn by the Solicitor-General, Mr. Lee. When the draft was completed it was submitted to Lord Loughborough, the Duke of Portland, and Lord North.

Lord North writes to Mr. Fox on the morning of the day when the bill was read a first time : "Influence of the

Crown, and influence of party against Crown and people, are two of the many topics which will be urged against your plan. The latter of the two objections will not be sounded so high and loudly in the House of Commons, *but it may be one of the most fatal objections of your measure.* It certainly ought to be obviated as much as possible." Lord North's sagacity was prophetic; his advice was disregarded.

It has been said that the India Bill was the work of Mr. Burke; and this is so far true, that the draft of the measure was certainly derived from Mr. Burke's instructions. But it is necessary to distinguish between the two bills which Mr. Fox introduced. The first of these bills was a measure described to Lord Northington by Mr. Fox as " a vigorous and a hazardous one, and," Mr. Fox adds, " if we get that well over, I have very little apprehension about anything else here."

It is scarcely possible that such a measure should not have received the full attention, and have been approved by the deliberate judgment of Mr. Fox. Nor do those who wish to relieve that great man from responsibility do justice to his conscientious sense of public duty. He wished to relieve the people of India from intolerable cruelty, rapacity, and oppression; he was prepared to risk power and popularity to attain that object. It may be said with truth that he did not guard with sufficient caution against the abuse of the powers that he gave; that by naming Commissioners of a political character, he laid himself open to the accusation of setting up a rival to the Crown; that he miscalculated the influence and personal enmity of the King, and the strength of the harpies disturbed in their repast. But he fought for the happiness of millions, and there can be little doubt that his bill would have secured it. Seven Commissioners of high character, responsible to Parliament for their conduct, would have prevented any scandalous perversion of the powers of government in India.

The second bill was of a different kind. It contained an attempt to control the government of a territory at the distance of a six months' voyage from England by a number of regulations which could hardly have been enforced in the Channel Islands. Varying circumstances, overpowering emergencies, European enemies, might from time to time render impossible or destructive the application of rules framed at Westminster for the guidance of Calcutta. It is very possible that, in framing this bill, Mr. Burke, from his acquaintance with the history of past abuses, may have been allowed the most ample discretion. It does not appear that the King made any objections to the measures before they were brought in. As was usual with him, he appears to have concealed his opinions from his Ministers, while he concerted with their opponents the means of making them prevail. The advice which Lord Temple, a leading member of Opposition, had given the King in the spring of the year was not forgotten.

Leave was given to bring in the bill; but two days afterwards, when Mr. Fox introduced it and proposed to read it a second time on that day se'nnight, all the batteries of Opposition were opened against him. Mr. W. Grenville declared that the bill made an attack on the most solemn charters, violated all the ties which bind man to man, and was fraught with the most pointed mischief against national power. Mr. Jenkinson, unfurling the banner of the Court, stated the proposed commission as the setting up within the realm of a species of executive government independent of the Crown; he wondered at the boldness of men who could venture to propose a measure which threatened such ruinous consequences to British liberty, and declared that the influence of Ministers would be such as to endanger the rights of every free Englishman. Mr. Fox must have known by this time what he had to expect. He did not, however, change or modify his purpose; and, on the 27th of November, he moved the order of the day for the second reading. This was agreed to, and the bill was read a second time. In moving that the bill be committed, Mr. Fox entered at length into the financial situation of the Company, which had been stated as one of solvency and security.

Mr. Pitt having moved the adjournment of the debate, the House divided, for adjournment, 120; against, 229.

Mr. Fox having thus shown that the majority of the House of Commons supported him, did not renew his motion to commit the bill till the 1st of December. On that day the Opposition displayed all their forces. Mr. Pitt, Mr. Dundas, Mr. Powys, Mr. Ord, and other members, brought to bear every argument that could affect the minds either of courtiers, or of friends of liberty against the bill.

. The report of the speech of Mr. Fox on this occasion is so full, and contains so able a defence of a measure on which he risked and lost his power as a Minister, that I shall give it entire in the Appendix.*

I will give here the splendid encomium on Mr. Fox pronounced by Mr. Burke :—

" And now, having done my duty to the bill, let me say a word to the author. I should leave him to his own noble

* See Appendix A.

sentiments, if the unworthy and illiberal language with which he has been treated, beyond all example of parliamentary liberty, did not make a few words necessary; not so much in justice to him as to my own feelings. I must say, then, that it will be a distinction honourable to the age, that the rescue of the greatest number of the human race that ever were so grievously oppressed, from the greatest tyranny that was ever exercised, has fallen to the lot of abilities and dispositions equal to the task; that it has fallen to one who has the enlargement to comprehend, the spirit to undertake, and the eloquence to support so great a measure of hazardous benevolence. His spirit is not owing to his ignorance of the state of men and things; he will know what snares are spread about his path, from personal animosity, from court intrigues, and possibly from popular delusion. But he has put to hazard his ease, his security, his interest, his power, even his darling popularity, for the benefit of a people whom he has never seen. This is the road that all heroes have trod before him. He is traduced and abused for his supposed motives. He will remember that obloquy is a necessary ingredient in the composition of all true glory; he will remember that it was not only in the Roman customs, but it is in the nature and constitution of things, that calumny and abuse are essential parts of triumph. These thoughts will support a mind, which only exists for honour, under the burthen of temporary reproach. He is doing, indeed, a great good; such as rarely falls to the lot, and almost as rarely coincides with the desires, of any man. Let him use his time. Let him give the whole length of the reins to his benevolence. He is now on a great eminence, where the eyes of mankind are turned to him. He may live long, he may do much;

but here is the summit.   He never can exceed what he does this day.

" He has faults ; but they are faults that, though they may in a small degree tarnish the lustre, and sometimes impede the march of his abilities, have nothing in them to extinguish the fire of great virtues.   In those faults there is no mixture of deceit, of hypocrisy, of pride, of ferocity, of complexional despotism, or want of feeling for the distresses of mankind.   His are faults which might exist in a descendant of Henry IV. of France—as they did exist in that father of his country.   Henry IV. wished that he might live to see a fowl in the pot of every peasant in his kingdom.   That sentiment of homely benevolence was worth all the splendid sayings that are recorded of kings. But he wished perhaps for more than could be obtained, and the goodness of the man exceeded the power of the king.   But this gentleman, a subject, may this day say this at least, with truth, that he secures the rice in his pot to every man in India.   A poet of antiquity thought it one of the first distinctions to a prince whom he meant to celebrate, that through a long succession of generations he had been the progenitor of an able and virtuous citizen, who, by force of the arts of peace, had corrected governments of oppression, and suppressed wars of rapine :—

> 'Indole proh quantâ juvenis, quantumque daturus
> Ausoniæ populis ventura in sæcula civem.
> Ille super Gangem, super exanditus et Indos,
> Implebit terras voce ; et furialia bella
> Fulmine compescet linguæ.'

" This was what was said of the predecessor of the only person to whose eloquence it does not wrong that of the mover of this bill to be compared.*   But the Ganges and

---

* The passage is from Silius Italicus, and describes a supposed ancestor of Cicero.

the Indus are the patrimony of the fame of my honourable friend, and not of Cicero. I confess I anticipate with joy the reward of those whose whole consequence, power, and authority exist only for the benefit of mankind; and I carry my mind to all the people, and all the names and descriptions that, relieved by this bill, will bless the labours of this Parliament; and the confidence which the best House of Commons has given to him who the best deserves it. The little cavils of parties will not be.heard where freedom and happiness will be felt. There is not a tongue, a nation, or religion in India, which will not bless the presiding care and manly beneficence of this House, and of him who proposes to you this great work. Your names will never be separated before the throne of the Divine Goodness, in whatever language, or with whatever rites pardon is asked for sin, and reward for those who imitate the Godhead in His universal bounty to His creatures. These honours you deserve, and they will surely be paid, when all the jargon of influence, and party, and patronage are swept into oblivion.

"I have spoken what I think and what I feel of the mover of this bill. An honourable friend of mine, speaking of his merits, was charged with having made a studied panegyric. I don't know what his was. Mine, I am sure, is a studied panegyric; the fruit of much meditation; the result of the observation of near twenty years. For my own part I am happy that I have lived to see this day. I feel myself overpaid for the labours of eighteen years, when at this late period I am able to take my share, by one humble vote, in destroying a tyranny that exists to the disgrace of this nation, and the destruction of so large a part of the human species."

At four o'clock the House divided; for the bill, 217; against, 103. Thus the palm of parliamentary victory seemed to rest with Mr. Fox.

But the scene of conflict had been changed. The centre of Opposition to the King's Minister was in the King's closet. On the very day when Mr. Fox was battling his enemies in the Commons, when he and Mr. Burke were fighting in the open day with the weapons of argument, and imploring justice to the millions subject to our sway, Lord Thurlow delivered to the King the following memorandum. Who, besides himself and Lord Temple were parties to it, does not appear :—

"Dec. 1st, 1783.

"To begin with stating to his Majesty our sentiments upon the extent of the bill : viz.,

"We profess to wish to know whether this bill appear to his Majesty in this light; a plan to take more than half the royal power, and by that means disable (the King) for the rest of the reign. There is nothing else in it which ought to call for this interposition.

"Whether any means can be thought of, short of changing his Ministers, to avoid this evil.

"The refusing the bill, if it passes the Houses, is a violent means. The changing his Ministers, after the last vote of the Commons, in a less degree might be liable to the same sort of construction.

"An easier way of changing his Government would be, by taking some opportunity of doing it; when, in the progress of it, it shall have received more discountenance than hitherto.

"This must be expected to happen in the Lords in a greater degree than it can be hoped for in the Commons.

"But a sufficient degree of it may not occur in the Lords, if those whose duty to his Majesty would excite them to appear, are not acquainted with his wishes, and that, in a manner which would make it impossible to pretend a doubt of it, in case they were so disposed.

"By these means, the discountenance might be hoped to raise difficulties so high as to throw it (out), and leave his Majesty at perfect liberty to choose whether he will change them or not.

"This is the situation which it is wished his Majesty should find himself in.

"Delivered by Lord Thurlow, December 1st, 1783.

"NUGENT TEMPLE."

The opening line and the note at the foot are in the handwriting of Lord Temple, the substance is probably in the handwriting of Lord Thurlow.

A representation to the King on the part of two statesmen, one of whom had been recently his Lord Chancellor, and the other his Lord Lieutenant of Ireland, that a bill before Parliament was "a plan to take more than half the royal power, and by that means disable (the King) for the rest of his reign," was calculated to produce the strongest impression on the royal mind. When it is added that the authors of the plan were men whom the King considered his tyrants, and whom he thoroughly disliked, it may well be conceived that this plot was likely to succeed. In fairness and in justice, however, the King's feelings ought to have been communicated to the Ministers; they might have altered their bill, they might have given way to the real advisers of the Crown. But this plain course did not suit the dark contrivers of this intrigue; the Ministers were allowed to send the bill to a committee, to insert the names of the Commissioners, to read the bill a third time in the Commons, and to send it to the House of Lords, without any apparent marks of displeasure on the part of the Sovereign. But the curtain was soon drawn up, and such a scene exhibited as has never been seen before or since. The names of the proposed Commissioners inserted in the bill were:—

> Earl Fitzwilliam.
> Right Hon. Frederick Montague.
> Lord Lewisham (afterwards Earl of Dartmouth).
> Hon. George North.
> Sir Gilbert Elliot, Bart.
> Sir Henry Fletcher, Bart.
> Mr. Robert Gregory.

On the 9th of December, Mr. Fox, attended by a great number of members, presented the bill at the bar of the House of Lords. On the first reading Lord Thurlow, Lord Temple, and even the Duke of Richmond, denounced the bill. Lord Thurlow went the whole length of defending the financial position of the East India Company and the moral purity of Warren Hastings. All three spoke of the bill with abhorrence. The second reading was fixed for the following Monday. This conversation took place on the Tuesday. On the Thursday, Lord Temple had a long audience with the King; he came out, saying, on the part of his Majesty, " that he should deem those who should vote for the bill not only not his friends, but his enemies, and that if Lord Temple could put this in stronger words, he had the King's authority for doing so." It would seem that the Duke of Portland had but one course to pursue, and an excellent precedent for pursuing it. During the progress of the bill for repealing the Stamp Act, Lord Rockingham heard that Lord Strange had used the King's name for asserting that the King was not for repeal, but for modification. Lord Rockingham instantly resolved to obtain the King's authority for the repeal, or to resign. Accordingly he asked for an audience, and on that occasion, or on various occasions, obtained three papers in the King's handwriting, declaring that the King was for the repeal as against enforcing.* Thus armed, Lord Rockingham went on with the bill, and carried it by a large majority through the House of Lords. The Duke of Portland did not take this plain and manly course. Lord North was flattered by the belief that his partisans would be firm, and the Archbishop of Canterbury, in particular, was said to be "more than friendly." Lord North did not like this awkward phrase. In fact, the political friends of Lord North were the friends of the prerogative, and when the two objects of their attachment, the Crown and Lord North, could not be followed together, they clung to the Crown as the true idol of their worship. Thus, on the 15th, Fitzpatrick writes to his brother: "The bishops waver, and the *Thanes fly from us;* in my opinion the bill will not pass; the Lords are now sitting," &c. Lord John Townshend writing, in 1830, to Lord Holland, says: "Boreas' troops deserted him by dozens; very few, excepting his brother, the Bishop of Winchester, Loughborough, Sandwich, my father (who by the way was personally canvassed by the King), and Lord Stormont, remained firm and stout. . . . Your uncle,

* "Rockingham Papers," vol. i. p. 300. The three papers are all somewhat equivocal, and Lord Rockingham doubted as to resignation; but the result showed he was right to remain.

too, I must own, was strangely deceived into a belief that, after our great majority in the Commons, there was no danger whatever from the Lords."

On the 16th the second reading was moved in the House of Lords.

On this occasion a very curious discussion took place on the subject of the King's alleged interference.

The Duke of Portland, First Lord of the Treasury, adverted to a rumour, which he said was of a very extraordinary nature indeed. " In that rumour, the name of the most sacred character in the kingdom had been aspersed, and the name of one of their lordships, he hoped, abused : but certainly such was the complexion of the rumour, that he should be wanting in regard to his own character, wanting in that love and zeal for the Constitution, which, he trusted, had ever distinguished his political life, wanting in the duty he owed to the public as a minister, if he did not take an opportunity, if it turned out to be true, of proposing a measure upon it to their lordships that would prove they felt the same jealousy, the same detestation, and the same desire to mark and stigmatize every attempt to violate the constitution, as he did."*

It will be observed that the Duke of Portland did not pretend to have any authority to contradict the rumour which he denounced. Lord Temple's answer was equally remarkable: " That his Majesty had honoured him with a conference was a matter of notoriety. It was not what he wished to deny, nor what he had it in his power to conceal. He said that it was the privilege of peers, as the hereditary councillors of the Crown, either individually or collectively, to advise the Crown. He had given his advice;

* " Parliamentary History," vol. xxiv. p. 152.

what that advice was he would not then say, it was lodged in the breast of his Majesty; nor would he declare the purport of it without the royal consent, or till he saw a proper occasion. But, though he would not declare affirmatively what his advice to his Sovereign was, he would tell their lordships negatively what it was not. It was unfriendly to the principle and object of the bill,"* &c.

It does not appear clear whether the Duke of Portland made any answer to this extraordinary statement. The Duke of Richmond said very absurdly that, with respect to a bill pending in Parliament, it was as unconstitutional in a Minister of the Crown to give advice to the King as for any other person to do so, &c.

Earl Fitzwilliam mentioned the " rumour, which they must all have heard, that a noble earl, in his eye, had declared that he had been empowered by a great person, whose sacred name should never be heard as interfering in the progress of a bill, to say that that person was hostile to the bill." But when challenged by Lord Temple for his authority, he merely referred to the facts "as matter of rumour." The consequence that might have been expected followed. An adjournment was carried by 87 to 79, thus leaving Ministers in a minority of 8. It was clear that Lord Temple had a constitutional right as a peer to go into the closet and give advice to the King. But it is equally clear that if that advice was, as Lord Temple avowed, unfriendly to a bill brought forward by the King's Ministers, it was necessary for the Duke of Portland to obtain from the King a disapproval of that advice, or to retire from his service. The course he took of appearing as a Minister to denounce a rumour which he could not contradict, exposed

* " Parliamentary History," vol. xxiv. p. 154.

him to defeat, and almost to disgrace. On the other hand, the King, by giving his confidence to Earl Temple, while he gave his apparent countenance to his Ministers, left the broad path of the Constitution and joined in an intrigue to undermine his ostensible servants.

Such was the fatal consequence of a departure from that plain and open way of dealing which the example of Lord Rockingham had recommended.

Two days after the vote of the House of Lords, Mr. Baker moved in the House of Commons, "That it is now necessary to declare, that to report any opinion, or pretended opinion of his Majesty upon any bill or other proceeding depending in either House of Parliament, with a view to influence the votes of the members, is a high crime and misdemeanour, derogatory to the honour of the Crown, a breach of the fundamental privileges of Parliament, and subversive of the Constitution of this country." This motion gave Mr. Pitt an opportunity of blaming the Ministers for their base attachment to their offices, when, upon their own statement of the case, it was clear they had lost their power, and no longer possessed the confidence of the Sovereign. It must be owned that Mr. Fox's position at this moment was an untenable one. No one denied that the rumour in question had been spread, and that the name of Lord Temple had been connected with it. The Ministers had by virtue of their offices access to their Sovereign. If Lord Temple had used his name without his authority, Mr. Fox could at once, by a denial on authority, have destroyed the rumour and its author. If, on the contrary, the King himself was the source of the report, how could Mr. Fox, the servant of the Crown, concur in a vote which became, in that case, a censure upon his Sovereign? Everything shows, therefore, that, before taking part in the debate of the 17th of December, Mr. Fox should have tendered his resignation.

"I remember a saying," he stated, "of an able statesman, whom, though I differed with him in many things, I have ever acknowledged to be possessed of many eminent and useful qualities. The sentence I allude to I have always admired for its boldness and propriety. It was uttered by the late George Grenville in experiencing a similar treachery; and would to God the same independent and manly sentiments had been inherited by all who bear the name! 'I will never again,' said he, 'be at the head of a string of Janissaries, who are always ready to strangle or despatch me on the least signal.'"

Now, whose was the similar treachery? To whom was it imputed? To whom but the King, whose Minister Mr. Fox still was, when he uttered this reproach?

This circumstance apart, the complaints of Mr. Fox were natural and manly. "It is not in the human mind," he said, "to put forth the least vigour under the impression of uncertainty. While all my best-meant and best-concerted plans are still under the control of a villainous whisper, and the most valuable consequences, which I flattered myself must have resulted from my honest and indefatigable industry, are thus defeated by secret influence, it is impossible to continue in office any longer, either with honour to myself or success to the public. The moment I bring forward a measure adequate to the exigency of the State, and stake my reputation, or indeed whatever is most dear and interesting in life, on its merit and utility, instead of enjoying the triumphs of having acted fairly and unequivocally, all my labours, all my vigilance, all my expectations,

so natural to every generous and manly exertion, are in-
sidiously and at once whispered away by rumours, which,
whether founded or not, are capable of doing irreparable
mischief, and have their full effect before it is possible to
contradict or disprove them."

The motion was carried by 153 to 80. But on this very
day the India Bill was rejected by the House of Lords by
95 to 76. At midnight Mr. Fox and Lord North received
orders by a messenger to deliver up the Seals of their
offices, and send them by the Under-Secretaries to the
King, as a personal interview would be disagreeable to
him. Thus ended for a long period the ministerial life of
Mr. Fox. He did not again receive the Seals till January,
1806, when his health was declining and the seeds of a
fatal disease had been laid in his constitution.

The India Bill, which was the immediate cause of Mr.
Fox's dismissal, was far from being the dangerous measure it
was represented. So far as India was concerned, it was a
violent but effectual remedy for a malignant disease. So
far as the British Constitution was concerned, it would
have been more prudent to have named Commissioners un-
connected with party. But the power of Mr. Fox's Commissioners would have been as a small taper compared to
the rays of royal favour and the broad beams of ministerial
patronage. Nor is there any reason to believe that, during
the four years to which their power was limited, Lord
Fitzwilliam and his colleagues would have exercised an
influence greater than that which Commissioners of Excise
and Customs appointed by one Ministry apply during the
sway of a succeeding administration.

CHAPTER XIX.

ON Thursday night, the 18th of December, Mr. Fox was dismissed from office. On the following day (the 19th), Mr. Pitt was made First Lord of the Treasury and Chancellor of the Exchequer. Upon the same day the House of Commons met. At three o'clock Lord North entered the House and took his seat on the Opposition Bench. Mr. Fox, who soon followed, finding Mr. Dundas on the same bench, jocularly took him by the ,arm, saying, "What business have you on this?—go over to the Treasury Bench." This incident raising a laugh, in which both parties heartily joined, was a good-humoured prelude to one of the most violent party contests of modern times.

Mr. Arden then moved a new writ for Appleby, in the room of William Pitt, appointed First Lord of the Treasury and Chancellor of the Exchequer. So little were the Opposition prepared for what was to follow, that this motion was received with laughter, and the utmost confidence and cheerfulness prevailed among the party expelled from office.

Mr. Baker having proposed that the House. should adjourn till Monday, Mr. Dundas moved, as an amendment, that the House should meet on the Saturday—the following day. This he did on the ground that the Land Tax Bill would speedily expire. But Mr. Fox said that as the Land Tax Bill would not expire before the 5th of January, and it was now only the 19th of December, it was idle to suppose that the delay of two days would prevent its passing. He moreover assured the House that neither he nor his friends had any intention to obstruct the progress of a bill necessary for the maintenance of public credit.

The House having met on the 22nd, the Land Tax Bill was accordingly read a third time. Mr. William Grenville on the same day announced the resignation of Earl Temple, in whose hands the seals of Secretary of State had been placed on the dismissal of the Coalition Ministry. Mr. Fox intimated that as there was no evidence of the interference of Earl Temple, he had no intention of bringing any charge against him. Yet the House had voted, only a few days before, " that to report any opinion, or pretended opinion, of his Majesty upon any bill or other proceeding depending in either House of Parliament, with a view to influence the votes of the members, is a high crime and misdemeanour, derogatory to the honour of the Crown, a breach of the fundamental privileges of Parliament, and subversive of the Constitution of this country."

It seems strange that so much smoke should be followed by no fire, and that no inquiry should be instituted either by a Select Committee or otherwise, in order to ascertain who had committed a crime and misdemeanour, said to be subversive of the Constitution of the country. This seems the more strange when it is considered that Earl Temple was generally named as the author of the report in question, which was said to have influenced many members of the House of Lords, some of them holding office in the King's houschold. Nor did Earl Temple seem very solicitous to deny the correctness of this report. The truth is, that either the resolution in question ought never to have been moved, or ought to have been followed up by inquiry. But from the outset of this unhappy business, the Opposition seem to have aimed their blows at the King's secret influence without adopting the means of making those blows effective.

Had the House of Commons traced to Earl Temple advice given to the King against measures which his authorized Ministers were pursuing, and had they asked the King to dismiss him from his presence and councils for ever, they would have pursued a bold, perhaps a dangerous, but assuredly a constitutional course. Had they confined themselves to a resolution that the existing Ministry did not possess their confidence, they would probably have weakened it so far as to force Mr. Pitt to resign. But by striking at the prerogative, and founding their resolutions on a point affecting the King's personal conduct, they alarmed the public mind and prepared their own defeat. On the same day (December 22nd), Mr. Erskine moved an address to the King, humbly beseeching him to allow them to proceed on the business of the session without prorogation or dissolution, "and that his Majesty will be pleased to hearken to the advice of his faithful Commons, and not to the secret advices of particular persons, who may have private interests of their own, separate from the true interests of his Majesty and his people." These last words were copied from an address to William III.

Mr. Bankes assured the House, on the part of Mr. Pitt, that he had no intention of dissolving Parliament. But this assurance not satisfying Mr. Fox, the address was carried without a division. In the course of this debate,

Lord North spoke of the coalition to the following effect :—

"Our intimate connexion was founded on principles of honour; when the great points on which we differed were no more, we thought we might act together with cordiality and without inconsistency. We were not mistaken; we tried the experiment and it succeeded : no meanness, no dishonour, no jealousy discovered itself; all was inviolable adherence to honour and good faith on one part, all was confidence on the other. No mean concessions were made on either side; I appeal to my right honourable friend, if ever I sacrificed any one opinion which I formerly seriously held upon principle, unless where reason and argument might have pointed out the propriety of it; and, in justice to my right hon. friend, I must declare that he never sacrificed to me any principle which he ever held when in Opposition to the Government of which I was the head. The necessity of the State called for that coalition, which has been so often denominated a cursed coalition; nay, the very circumstances of the present day demonstrate that necessity; for where could an administration be formed without a coalition ?"

It was in the same debate that, alluding to an expression of Mr. Martin, he observed: "It was said on a former day that a starling ought to be placed in the House to repeat the words 'Coalition! coalition! cursed coalition!' But admitting the patriotic spirit which caused this proposal, I submit that this House is in possession of a Martin, who will serve the purpose quite as well." The House laughed, and was content to be amused. But the country required more substantial reasons to justify the coalition.

The King's answer to the address acknowledged the importance of the subject which required the attention of Parliament, but limited the royal pledge to an assurance that the King would not interrupt their meeting after such an adjournment as the present circumstances may seem to require by any exercise of the prerogative, either of prorogation or.dissolution.

Mr. Fox felt the insufficiency of this answer, but no more could be obtained by persisting. He therefore moved an adjournment, at first to the 8th, but ultimately to the 12th of January. When the House met on the 12th of January, Mr. Fox rose at half-past two o'clock to move the order of the day for the House resolving itself into a Committee on the State of the Nation. He was interrupted by the swearing in of the members who had accepted office, which lasted till near four o'clock. He then rose, but was again interrupted by Mr. Pitt, who said the reason for his rising was to present to the House a message from the Crown. Mr. Fox, however, being in possession of the House, was first heard, and moved the order of the day. Mr. Pitt did not again refer to the message from the Crown, but asked the House to allow him to bring in a bill on the affairs of India, which was one of the subjects upon which the House had grounded their prayer to the Throne, to be allowed to deliberate without interruption. He therefore opposed the order of the day.

Mr. Powys attacked the Opposition. He said: " Was it the Minister to whom they objected? Why did they not say so? They ought not to have suffered a day to pass without declaring that he had not their confidence." There was truth in this remark. It is the prerogative of the Crown to appoint its Ministers. It is the privilege of the House of Commons to refuse their confidence to any

Ministers whom they consider incompetent or unfaithful. In the present case the House of Commons would have been justified in declaring their opinion that a young man of twenty-three, with only one colleague of eminent ability, ought not to exercise the whole executive power of the State, to the exclusion of Mr. Fox, Lord North, Mr. Burke, Mr. Sheridan, and the able statesmen who followed the Whig standard.

By fighting the battle on the weak ground of prerogative, instead of the strong ground of privilege, Mr. Fox lost the victory, which at one moment appeared to be in his hands.

Mr. Fox, in answer to Mr. Pitt, declared he was ready to go into the consideration of his India Bill, but the House could not do so with the danger of dissolution hanging over their heads.

" But why not," he said, " suffer the right honourable gentleman to move for his bill first, and go into the Committee on the State of the Nation afterwards? For the clearest of all possible reasons. Because, if they were suffered to pursue this course, they feel the pulse of the House, and finding it is disagreeable to them, the next day dissolve the Parliament; whereas, by going into the committee measures might be taken to guard against a measure so inimical to the true interests of the country."

Here, again, we find Mr. Fox disputing the prerogative, and attempting to defeat its exercise by the advisers of the Crown. But if the two Houses could not agree upon an India Bill, there would surely arise a constitutional occasion for a dissolution. On the other hand, the power of dissolution could hardly be wrested from the Ministers, or even suspended by the House of Commons, without a violent encroachment on the ordinary functions of the Crown. Nor was the example of the Long Parliament an encouraging precedent to the lovers of our balanced Constitution. Mr. Pitt saw clearly the advantage to be derived from the conduct of an Opposition who did not venture to attack the interference of Lord Temple, and thus force him to defend an unconstitutional course or abandon a powerful friend; and who yet contrived to mix the expression of their legitimate discontent with oblique attacks on the undoubted rights of the Crown. Yet, with a caution and foresight beyond his years, the young Minister forbore to precipitate a rupture with the House of Commons, and waited with patience till public opinion should condemn their violence and applaud their dismissal.

While Mr. Fox proposed to make a dissolution impossible, Lord North spoke with justice and truth on the subject of secret influence :—

" Secret influence, which might formerly have been problematical, was now openly avowed. A peer of Parliament had given secret advice and gloried in it. He would not say that a peer or a privy-councillor had not a right to advise the Crown, but he would contend that the moment he gave such advice, he ought to take the Seals and become a Minister, in order that advice and responsibility might go hand in hand."

This was sound doctrine, and ought to have been used to censure Lord Temple. Equally sound in conclusion, though there is probably some error in the expressions reported, was Lord North's view of the prerogative of dissolution :—

" The prerogative of the Crown to dissolve Parliament was unquestionable, but prerogative could receive efficacy only from the support and confidence of Parliament (query aud the people?). Without these it would be a scarecrow prerogative, and without them the King would be nobody; but when the prerogative was supported by the confidence of the nation, it made the King somebody—it made him the greatest prince in the world; and whoever would attempt to make him great without the support of Parliament and his people, would only deceive his Majesty and disappoint themselves."

The question in suspense, however, was, on which side would Parliament and the people ultimately decide? Mr. Pitt courted this appeal, Mr. Fox tried to prevent it, and therefore on popular as well as on prerogative grounds Mr. Pitt was on this occasion the true champion of the Constitution. In the present debate, Mr. Pitt, after an unwarrantable attack on Lord North, proceeded to say :—

" With regard to the questions put to him as to the dissolution, it did not become him to comment on the words of a most gracious answer of the Sovereign delivered from the throne; neither would he presume to compromise the royal prerogative, or bargain it away in the House of Commons." He vehemently denied the charge of secret influence, but carefully abstained from any reply to the pointed distinction drawn by Lord North.

On the question for reading the order of the day the House divided.

Ayes 232
Noes 193

Majority for Mr. Fox 39

When the House had resolved itself into a committee, Mr. Fox moved first for a return of the issues of public money, and secondly, that no further issues should be made till the return should be on the table. This second motion was withdrawn by Mr. Fox upon hearing it alleged that public inconvenience might ensue. Mr. Fox then moved that the Mutiny Bill should be read a second time on the 23rd of February, saying at the same time that this resolution would allow ample time for passing the Bill into a law before the subsisting act should expire.

Lord Surrey then moved that it is peculiarly necessary that there should be an administration which has the confidence of this House and the public.

All these resolutions having been carried after some discussion, the Earl of Surrey moved,—

"That it is the opinion of this committee that the late changes in his Majesty's councils were immediately preceded by dangerous and universal reports that his Majesty's sacred name had been unconstitutionally abused to affect the deliberations of Parliament, and that the appointments made were accompanied by circumstances new and extraordinary, and such as do not conciliate or engage the confidence of the House."

The debate lasted till seven in the morning, when the House divided.

> For adjournment 142
> Against 196
> ———
> Majority 54

The resolution was then carried, the House resumed, the resolutions were reported and agreed to. Mr. Pitt then brought up a message from the Crown, which was found to refer to the landing of some Hessian troops, and at half-past seven in the morning the House adjourned.

On reviewing these proceedings of Mr. Fox and his

majority, they seem to be wanting at once in vigour and in moderation. Had the majority felt themselves strong enough in public support to impose terms on the Crown, they might have inquired into the interference of Lord Temple, and have censured his unconstitutional conduct. They might at the same time have refused their sanction to any issues of public money, and have declined to proceed with the Mutiny Bill until an administration should be formed entitled to the confidence of the House of Commons. In this manner they would have given a warning to all future statesmen who should form a clandestine connexion with the Court in order to overthrow the ostensible Ministers of the Crown. They would also have reduced the King to accept the resignation of his present advisers, and form a Ministry having the confidence of the majority.

If, however, the majority of the House could not be brought to support so strong a measure, Mr. Fox might have contented himself with moving resolutions of want of confidence, and have left the issues of public money and the stages of the Mutiny Bill to follow the ordinary course. He would thus have accepted the arbitration of the country, and have boldly met the appeal to the people on the India Bill and the Coalition. The nation would have appreciated the manliness and fairness of this willing resort to the judgment of the people at large. Mr. Fox, unhappily for himself and his party, took a line which had the demerits of each of these two courses. By declaring that he meant to prevent a dissolution, he seemed to usurp for the House of Commons a supreme power over the prerogative of the King and the independence of the House of Lords, while at the same time he took no step to make that control effectual. Thus the dissolution of Parliament which he seemed to dread, took place in spite of his efforts to prevent it.

On the other hand, the vague denunciations of Lord Surrey's resolutions, while they failed to convict Lord Temple, appeared to threaten the person of the King. Thus Mr. Pitt, instead of being left to assume the odium of setting his own ambition in the scale against the public welfare, was placed in a position where he was bound to defend the Sovereign whom he had consented to serve. He could not acquiesce in his own condemnation; still less could he surrender, unless at the expense of his honour, the dignity of the King. He was hemmed up in a citadel, which he could not yield except to force or to famine. Mr. Pitt himself put this point very well, when in a subsequent debate it was suggested that he might resign and come in again as a member of a new Ministry.

"The honourable gentleman who spoke last had talked of the fortress in which he was situated, and had declared that he did not wish him to march out of it with a halter about his neck. The only fortress he knew of, or desired to have a share in defending, was the fortress of the Constitution. . . . With what regard to personal honour or public principle could it be expected that he should consent to march out of it with a halter about his neck, change his armour, and meanly beg to be re-admitted and considered as a volunteer in the army of the enemy? To put himself into such a predicament, and to trust to the foe to loosen and take off from his neck the halter he was expected to march out with, was a degree of humiliation to which he never would condescend," &c.

Thus situated, being unable to impose on the Crown humiliating conditions, and unwilling to return to office without them, Mr. Fox was sure to be ultimately defeated. The alleged usurpation of the House of Commons formed a capital topic for the House of Lords, was discussed in every public meeting, and finally was the theme of general condemnation. While this process was going on, and public opinion was gradually forming into a compact mass, Mr. Fox consumed himself and his party in vehement but vain efforts to displace his rival.

On the 14th of January Mr. Pitt opened his plan for the government of India. In the exordium of his speech he made this remarkable admission: "Any plan which he or any man could suggest for the government of territories so extensive and so remote must be inadequate; nature and fate had ordained in unalterable decrees that government, to be maintained at such a distance, must be inadequate to its end. In the philosophy of politics such a government must be declared irrational; it must be declared at the best to be inconvenient to the mother and supreme power, oppressive and inadequate to the necessities of the governed." This language showed at once that Mr. Pitt did not contemplate, as Mr. Fox had done, a large scheme of government which should neither be oppressive. to the persons, nor inadequate to the necessities of the governed.

Mr. Pitt then proceeded to develope his plan :—

1. The administration, civil and military, and the commerce, to be left in the hands of the Company.

2. A Board to be established, consisting of Privy Councillors with a Secretary of State, and the Chancellor of the Exchequer, to be appointed during the pleasure of the Crown, to control the policy of the Court of Directors, to possess a veto on its nominations to the chief offices, and to institute prosecutions against great offenders.

3. A revision to take place of all the establishments in India, to see where retrenchments might be made.

4. A new tribunal to be created, to consist of the principal judges in Westminster Hall, of certain members of the two Houses of Parliament, and some civilians. The functions of this new tribunal were to be most extensive. " They should be directed to question, to arraign; they should determine the nature of offences, and in offences he would reckon the disobedience of orders, acceptance of presents, oppressions of the natives, monopolies, rapacity; and all the train of offences which had tainted the national character in India." They were to inquire into the personal fortunes of the delinquents; to admit evidence which Westminster Hall would not receive, and to have the power of inflicting any punishment short of capital. Mr. Pitt concluded by asking for leave to introduce his bill.

Mr. Fox immediately rose and commented on the proposed plan. In stating the objects to be desired, he said : " What were the regulations or establishments required by the wishes of the House and of the country? Were they not humanity to the natives of that extensive territory which has been wrested from its original owners ; safety to the whole proprietary of the greatest trading company in the world; the justice, equity, and liberality of the English law to all who participate of the English Government; a restraint put on iniquitous contracts, and gross peculation of every sort; a system of responsibility and obedience, that master and servant, in this strange and absurd system, might continue no longer synonymous and convertible terms?"

Mr. Fox proceeded to object to the bill on the following grounds : 1. That it set up a double Government of discordant powers. 2. That the Board of Superintendence would always be under the influence of the Ministers of the Crown. 3. That the Governor-General of India would still be able to defy the authority at home.

In comparing the two schemes, it may be allowed that the plan of Mr. Pitt avoided the objections against a violent interference with the chartered privileges of the Company, and the creation of a body with vast power and patronage, independent of the Crown. On the other hand, the welfare of the natives of India was less adequately provided for, and indeed seemed to be an object of subordinate concern to Mr. Pitt. It was not till Mr. Burke brought the Governor of India before the bar of the House of Lords, and fulmined over the world, in words of burning eloquence, that cruelty was arrested in its career, and malversation checked in its source.

On the 23rd of January Mr. Pitt's bill was read a second time. But on the motion that it be committed, a long debate arose. Mr. Fox, in a masterly speech, recapitulated all his arguments against the plan; he said it would leave the Company subservient to its servants in India, and the Board of Control subservient to the Ministers of the Crown; thus perpetuating the evils which had desolated India, and introducing a new element of corruption into the Constitution. Mr. Pitt retorted on the bill of Mr. Fox. If, he said, the proposed Commissioners for India were to be independent of the Crown, a new power would be introduced into the Constitution; if they were to be removable by majorities of the two Houses concurring in the wish of the Crown for their removal, how is the system called permanent to survive amid all the changes of Administration? He declared that Lord Fitzwilliam would, by

Mr. Fox's bill, have had the power to involve the country in war with France or Holland, not only without the direction, but without the privity of the Government of this country.

The bill was rejected by 222 to 214. The small amount of this majority should have taught the Coalition that their hold over the House of Commons was already much weakened. But Mr. Fox, confident in his powers, would accept of nothing short of the unconditional surrender of the Court. For a long period debates followed each other in an unceasing stream.

On the 16th of January Lord Charles Spencer moved a resolution, stating that the appointments of the present Ministers of the Crown were accompanied by circumstances new and extraordinary, and such as do not conciliate the confidence of the House; and that their continuance in office was contrary to constitutional principles, and injurious to the interests of his Majesty and his people.

In commenting on this resolution, Mr. Dundas said that by its terms Ministers constitutionally chosen by the King were instantly turned out. " Sir, is it therefore for their incapacity and insufficiency that you overthrow them? (Hear! hear!) Then, sir, I insist that their incapacity and insufficiency shall be named as the ground upon which you deny them your confidence." This demand was a fair one, and ought to have been complied with. But to censure the mode of appointment, without naming any one, was in effect to censure the King. Mr. Powys having hinted that Lord North might be sent to the House of Lords in order to remove an obstacle to the union of parties, Lord North said he had no wish to be kicked up-stairs; he should be sorry to stand in the way of any arrangements that might be useful to the country; but, nevertheless, he would not go to the House of Peers.

The House divided.

For the resolution 205

Against 184

Majority 21

On the 20th of January, Mr. Rolle having put off a motion of which he had given notice on account of the prevailing rumours of a negotiation for a union of parties, Mr. Fox declared that there was no truth in the rumour so far as he was concerned, and described the existing struggle as a contest between privilege and prerogative, or rather between prerogative and the Constitution. Yet, in order to give time for Ministers to consider their position, he postponed the order of the day till the Monday following. Mr. Drake, Mr. Grosvenor, and Lord Frederick Campbell testified their joy at the cessation of arms, and their hopes of a general pacification. Lord Frederick Campbell, indeed, expressed some fear of a dissension of the two Houses on the subject of the India Bill, but said he understood that Mr. Fox would not obstinately defend every provision of his bill, and that, provided the Commissioners were made irremovable for a given number of years, and that their control over the servants of the Company in India should be absolute, he would not be stubborn as to the other regulations. Mr. Fox in reply said that this was not on his part a struggle for power, and that unless a real union on principle could be established, it was better that the contest should be carried on openly in that House than secretly in the Cabinet Council. In this sentiment Mr. Pitt cordially concurred.

As to the contest thus spoken of, there was not, after all, any material difference of opinion on the question of prerogative and privilege between Mr. Fox, Lord North, and Mr. Pitt. Mr. Fox admitted that the King had a right to appoint and dismiss his Ministers; Mr. Pitt allowed that the King could not attempt to maintain Ministers who had not the confidence of the House of Commons. The difference between them related to fact rather than principle; Mr. Fox held that the existing House of Commons fairly represented the people; Mr. Pitt considered that the nation differed from their representatives.

On Friday, the 23rd, Mr. Pitt's India Bill was thrown out, as we have already related. Immediately after its rejection, Mr. Fox rose to bring in his bill for the regulation of the affairs of the East India Company. He said there were only two principles from which he could not depart—one that the system should be permanent, the other that the Government should be at home. Having said this, Mr. Fox put a direct question to Mr. Pitt, whether the House was to be allowed to discuss his India Bill, or was to be dissolved. Mr. Pitt sate still, members from different sides calling upon him in vain to rise. This silence on the part of the Minister gave rise first to an angry debate, and finally to a scene of confusion.

General Conway on this occasion spoke in the strongest terms against the conduct of Mr. Pitt. He said that after the representatives of the people of England had declared that they had no confidence in him and his colleagues, the Ministers had endeavoured by every mean, sinister, and unworthy art to keep their places, although they knew that they were incapable of serving their country by any one act by their continuance in office. Mr. Pitt replied that he had not been long accustomed to the violence of that House, nor to its harsh language, but he had been long enough accustomed to it to assure the House that neither unsupported slander nor intemperate invective should discompose his mind. He would not condescend to answer interrogatories which he did not think gentlemen entitled to put to him.

Mr. Fox in these circumstances showed great calm and self-control. At two in the morning he moved that the House should adjourn till the next day (Saturday) at twelve, in order that the Minister might consider his situation, and the House, if necessary, take measures to vindicate its honour and assert its privileges.

On the following day the House met at twelve, which appears to have been its usual hour. Mr. Powys, who was so affected that he shed tears while he was speaking, said that the scene of confusion to which he had been last night a witness had so haunted his mind, that it had never been absent from it since. He thanked Mr. Fox sincerely for having interposed his influence with the House to prevent it from proceeding to any resolutions in the temper of mind in which they appeared when they broke up last night. He then asked Mr. Pitt whether the House might expect to meet again on Monday. Mr. Pitt, after some delay, replied that he had laid down to himself a rule, from which he did not think that he ought in duty to depart, which was not to pledge himself to the House that in any possible situation of affairs he would not advise his Majesty to dissolve the Parliament. He was, however, ready to say that he had no intention of preventing the meeting of the House on Monday.

Monday, the 26th of January, brought an explanation from the two parties of the position they respectively occupied. Mr. Eden moved a resolution that the King's answer on the subject of dissolution contained assurances upon which the House could not but most firmly rely, that the King would not interrupt their deliberations on the affairs of India by prorogation or dissolution. Mr. Pitt immediately rose to speak to a motion which concerned him personally. The motion implied that the true construction of the King's answer was that his Majesty had promised not to interrupt their deliberations while the affairs of India, and the support of public credit, continued the subjects of their consideration. To such an indefinite promise he would not subscribe, because he knew that when he advised the words in which the King's answer was conveyed, he never had such an indefinite sense of them in contemplation. In the present situation of affairs he thought a dissolution could not but be attended with great detriment and disadvantage, and therefore he would not advise any such exercise of the prerogative.

Mr. Fox said that the declaration of Mr. Pitt on the subject of dissolution was perfectly satisfactory; but, had he made that declaration a fortnight sooner, he would have spared the House and the country a great deal of anxiety. But, said Mr. Fox, there was a part of Mr. Eden's argument which had not been noticed; Mr. Pitt must be expected to give an account of the reasons which had induced him to remain in office after the House had expressed their disapprobation of his doing so. The honour of the House could not be satisfied while the present Administration remained in office, and they would establish a most dangerous precedent if they allowed it to continue.

Mr. Pitt's position was at this moment a most difficult one. He had in effect determined to disregard the resolution of the House, but it was obvious that to avow this determination would have appeared like a defiance, and would have brought upon his head a worse storm of indignation than he had hitherto endured. He therefore spoke with an appearance of humility. To suppose that he held himself as superior to the House of Commons, or that he disregarded numbers, and these so reputable, was what no man in his senses could conceive. Much less could it be thought that he held the resolutions of the House in contempt, or regarded them with indifference. He had the profoundest respect for the House, the utmost reverence for their resolutions, being perfectly aware that the House had it in its power to take measures that could not fail to render them effectual. He owned he stood in a situation perfectly new, but the circumstances were extraordinary; he was bound not to leave office to make room for an Administration in which the Crown, the Parliament, and the people could not equally repose confidence. He owned that a Minister holding his office against the consent of the House, would in all probability be made to repent his levity, and to attempt to do so without the strongest reasons possible would be rash, imprudent, and unjustifiable.

Having conciliated the House by these marks of deference for their resolutions, and the confession of their power, Mr. Pitt avowed the true reasons why he had not bowed to their authority. Had he resigned after the division of Friday night, he should have let in Ministers who he believed, however they might enjoy the confidence of that House, *had not the confidence of the nation.* Even in that House the majority against him had gradually decreased. Mr.

Pitt finished as he had begun, by trusting that he had held constitutional language, and had said nothing disrespectful.

Mr. Fox urged that the Minister had set his own private opinion against that of the House of Commons, and held himself superior to the whole House. He argued with much force and acuteness on the inconvenience to the public caused by a Ministry which had no power to carry its measures through the House of Commons. There could be no doubt of the truth of these arguments. But Mr. Pitt had evidently, though cautiously and respectfully, appealed to the nation against the House of Commons. Had Mr. Fox felt strong in popular support, he ought to have accepted this appeal, and have welcomed that dissolution which he so earnestly deprecated. The motion was carried without a division. Mr. Fox postponed the Committee on the State of the Nation till Thursday, the 29th, and on that day again proposed an adjournment to the Monday. He did so in order to give time for negotiation. "He trusted the well-meant endeavours of such as wished to produce something like a union, might not again prove abortive. But he was bound in conscience once for all to declare, that while the present Ministry retained their situations, every effort of that kind must be useless and unavailable."

There appears some weakness in this conduct. If Mr. Pitt was to be driven out by resolution, a fortnight had elapsed since a vote of want of confidence had been passed. If he was to be wheedled out by the country gentlemen, his declarations that he would not retire had bound him in honour to remain in office, and such an attempt would be hopeless. Mr. Fox ought either to have proceeded to stronger measures, or have given up his Committee on the

State of the Nation, and have left Mr. Pitt to dissolve a House in which he had not a majority.

In the course of this debate Lord Nugent asserted that Mr. Fox had no better right to advise his Majesty on the great political concerns of the country than Earl Temple. To this assertion Mr. Fox replied: "Did the noble lord recollect that at the period when the advice to which he had alluded was given by the noble earl, when that secret influence had been employed which had excited the attention and drawn down the indignation of the House, he was acting as the responsible Minister of the Crown, the authorized adviser of Majesty; and as such, had he not an official title superior to the noble earl, or to any other person, to advise his Majesty on the great concerns of the realm? He was confident there was no person who attended to these circumstances but would admit their truth, and allow that the conduct of the noble earl to whom reference had been made was an encroachment on the privileges, and a direct invasion of the rights of Ministers." There can be no doubt that Mr. Fox was right on this point; but if so, why had not the personal conduct of Lord Temple been directly censured by the House of Commons?

The real reason for the adjournment of the Committee on the State of the Nation soon appeared. On the 26th of January a meeting of nearly seventy members of the House of Commons, anxious to promote a union of parties, took place at the St. Albans Tavern. They came to a resolution calling for a union of parties, and asking the several leaders to communicate with each other on the arduous situation of public affairs, trusting that by a liberal and unreserved intercourse "every impediment may be removed to the co-operation of great and respectable characters, acting on the same public principles, and entitled to the support of independent and disinterested men." Both parties gave a nominal assent to this proposal, both gave a real negative. The Duke of Portland said he could have no intercourse with Mr. Pitt so long as he held his official situation; Mr. Pitt on his side refused to resign his office as a preliminary to negotiation. With a view to obtain the concurrence of the House of Commons in the views of the meeting, Mr. Thomas Grosvenor, their chairman, moved, on the 8th of February: "That it is the opinion of this House that the present arduous and critical situation of public affairs requires the exertion of a firm, efficient, extended, and united Administration, entitled to the confidence of the people, and such as may have a tendency to put an end to the unfortunate divisions and distractions of this country."

This proposal led to one of the most interesting debates which ever took place in Parliament. Sir Edward Astley opposed any attempt to bring the coalition, which he said stank in the nostrils of the nation, again into office. Sir George Cornewall and Mr. Powys supported the motion. Mr. Martin opposed it. Sir Cecil Wray spoke in favour of the Ministry, and Sir Peter Burrell against it.

Mr. Fox, unwilling to offend the respectable body of country gentlemen from whom this motion proceeded, declared that he heartily adopted it. The constitutional doctrine he laid down in such a manner that no one could deny it : "He was sorry it had so happened during this important debate that the distinction which the Constitution had established between a free and an absolute monarchy had required so often to be stated. He declared that consummate ruin would be the inevitable and immediate consequence of carrying any of those prerogatives which distinguished the respective estates of the Constitution to excess. . . . . . Many were the privileges of the Commons, but who would affirm that these were intended to act in a manner opposite to, or inconsistent with, the public welfare? It was precisely the same case in both. His Majesty had undoubtedly the power of choosing his own Ministers, and the House of Commons of assigning the supplies. But were the one to take into his service any men, or set of men, most agreeable to the royal inclination, without any regard as to how such appointments might operate on the public, might not the House, with the same propriety, withhold the purse of the people? Both extremes ought to be avoided, because equally injurious to the public welfare and to that Constitution which depends on the tendency of all its separate and combined virtues to one great and substantial object."

No one can deny that this was moderate and just language. He further said :—

"But why had this House so much interest in the choice of Ministers? And why were all the operations of the Constitution endowed with this public tendency? The reason, which to his mind was perfectly satisfactory, was that, as the business of the public consisted of so many acts of confidence and trust, the Minister was consequently under the necessity of possessing their good opinion in a very eminent degree, in order to be qualified for guiding an active and vigorous Government. In voting for the army extraordinaries — in voting especially for the navy — in voting for a variety of other things, he considered the House as voting literally, and, in every sense of the word, so much credit."

With regard to an actual union with those at present in

office, Mr. Fox, however, was far from conciliatory. He admitted, indeed, "that the right honourable gentleman meant nothing unconstitutional in his own favour;" he said that " he had never, at any time of his life, dealt in a general proscription ; it had always been a maxim of his that when the cause of animosity ceased, there should be an end of animosity.

"Many who now held offices under the Crown, might still hold them in a manner more honourable to themselves, as well as more beneficial to the public. Among these the right honourable gentleman would always occupy a capital department with every Administration to whom he could attach his talents and exertions."

Still there were difficulties. Their opinions on Indian affairs were not identical. The influence by which the present Minister had seized the reins of government could only be discussed subsequent to the resignation of Ministers.

" Surely the House could never forget that the present contest was not against men, but against Ministers unconstitutionally called into office. It was the systematic influence of an undue tendency that he had ever struggled against, and which he would continue to struggle against while he had a seat in that House."

Referring to the example of Lord Chatham, he said :—

" Surely if this pernicious evil was ever to be redressed by an individual, the right honourable gentleman's noble father was equal to the task. He at least had more popularity, more talents, more success than any other Minister this country ever had; and he would undoubtedly have done much but for one imperfection which he (Mr. Fox) had always deemed his greatest. He trusted too much to his own superior abilities, which, transcendent as they were, were completely overcome at last by that secret influence which had since done so much mischief."

Mr. Pitt, on his side, was cold upon the subject of union, and owned that he was perfectly satisfied in his own mind that the sense of the people was in favour of the present Ministers. "With regard to a resignation before a treaty for a union should take place, he said he would repeat what he had so often said before, that he foresaw the greatest evils to the nation if his Majesty's present Ministers should give up their offices. Still, if he could see a prospect of a strong and well-connected Government ready to succeed him, he would cheerfully retire without the least desire of forming part of such a Government."

The question was put, and carried without a negative, but the chances of union were apparently very small. The Opposition seem to have been pre-determined not to allow even these small chances to remain.

As soon as Mr. Grosvenor's motion had been agreed to, Mr. Coke of Norfolk moved :—

"That it is the opinion of this House that the continuance of the present Ministers in their offices is an obstacle to the formation of such an administration as may enjoy the confidence of this House, and tend to put an end to the unfortunate divisions and distractions of the country."

It was evident that if there had been any desire to form a union, this motion would not have been made. The former resolution, unanimously agreed to, contemplated the formation of " a *firm, efficient, extended, and united* Administration," which should " have a tendency to put an end to the unfortunate divisions and distractions of this country." It was obvious that no such Ministry could be formed without putting an end to the existing Administration. It

would, however, have been terminated and supplanted by
the appointment of another without any sacrifice of the
honour, the pride, and the dignity of the King or of Mr.
Pitt.   Whether Mr. Pitt should negotiate as actual Chancellor of the Exchequer, or as holding office only till a new
Ministry could be appointed, was surely not a question upon
which a man of Mr. Fox's grasp of mind, had he been
anxious for union, could have hesitated for five minutes.
If a compromise was to be made at all, it could only be
made on terms honourable to both parties.

There was, however, a further question upon which Mr.
Fox might well be reluctant to enter.   It was understood
that the King meant to stipulate that four members of the
Cabinet—viz., the Lord Chancellor, the Duke of Richmond,
Mr. Pitt, and Lord Gower, should be members of the
united Administration.*   They would have remained avowedly as the King's friends, to protect his prerogative and
espouse his opinions.   One of these opinions, espoused by
Lord Thurlow and Mr. Pitt, was adverse to the whole
principle and design of Mr. Fox's India Bill.   Mr. Fox
had already felt the evil of being opposed by a majority in
the Cabinet enjoying the favour of the King.   He was
naturally unwilling to make a sacrifice even in terms in
order to enter a Government in which he would have been
thwarted, undermined, and probably forced either to sacrifice his character or break up the Ministry.

In fact, the time for union was gone by.   Too much
jealousy had been roused, too much violence had been
elicited, to allow of a union which should be solid and
durable.   Mr. Fox could only stand on his majority in the
House of Commons to give him a present triumph; Mr.

* Walpole.

Pitt could only rely on the opinion of the public as the source of future victory. Mr. Dundas accordingly intimated this appeal to the public in his answer to Mr. Coke: "The Ministry, now the objects of a motion for their removal, are confided in, loved, and caressed by the people. There is no society of a hundred persons in the country out of which ninety-nine are not their firm and avowed friends. In what a dilemma, then, must an address for the removal of such favourites of the people place the Sovereign?" Mr. Fox met this assertion boldly:—

"They [the Ministers] court the affections of the people, and on this foundation they wish to support themselves, in opposition to the repeated resolutions of this House. Is not this declaring themselves independent of Parliament? Is not this separating the House of Commons from its constituents, annihilating our importance, and avowedly erecting a monarchy on the basis of an affected popularity, independent of and uncontrollable by Parliament? Such a scheme I can view under no other aspect than as a system of the basest tyranny, and calculated to accomplish the ruin of the liberties of this country."

Had the King, like Charles II. in 1680, or Charles X. of France in our own days, repeatedly dissolved Parliament, and then attempted to govern in defiance of them, Mr. Fox would have been justified in this invective. But George III. never contemplated, and Mr. Pitt certainly never would have executed, such a scheme. Mr. Fox concluded with animation, saying:—

"I have been charged with ambition; but on what grounds have these accusations been made? Have I ever set myself in defiance to this House? Have I ever sought power through the means of base corruption or dark intrigue? . . . I have never sacrificed my principles to popularity or ambition. I have ever acted openly and fairly. I would rather be rejected, reprobated, and proscribed; I would rather be an outcast of men in power, and the follower of the most insignificant minority, than prostitute myself into the character of a mean tool of secret influence. I call, therefore, on the country gentlemen to stand aloof from a Ministry who have established themselves in power by means so unconstitutional and destructive."

It was obvious that such language forbade the bans of union. Mr. Pitt accordingly "begged the House to consider the present question as it really was, and to ask themselves if it was at all likely to further the purpose of the motion that had been voted that day? For his part he must consider it as an effectual bar to the union so much desired by the respectable and independent gentlemen who had called for such a measure." It was on this night that he declared, as has been before noticed, that he would not march out with a halter about his neck and meanly beg to be re-admitted as a volunteer in the army of the enemy.

The House divided:—

  For 223
  Against 204
           ———
  Majority for Mr. Coke's motion . 19

On the 3rd of February Mr. Coke moved that the two resolutions which had been passed on the previous evening should be laid before his Majesty by such members of the House as were of the Privy Council.

Mr. Wilberforce took this occasion to declare his support of Mr. Pitt and to attack the coalesced statesmen; he said, however, that, of the two, Mr. Fox was undoubtedly the most

popular and respectable.   It had been hitherto averred that
the assertion that Lord Temple had given advice to his
Sovereign was an assertion without proof; but Mr. Wilberforce took the more manly ground of praising Lord Temple
for giving his advice openly, and therefore, in his opinion,
fairly.

Mr. Sheridan also spoke in this debate, and described the
part he had taken in reference to the Coalition.   When the
idea was first started he said " he had advised Mr. Fox not
to accept it.   His right honourable friend had great popularity, which he might lose by a coalition—respectable
friends whom he might disgust, and prejudices of the
strongest nature to combat."   But, seeing the necessities of
the times, and the honour, fairness, openness, and steadiness
of Lord North and his friends, he rejoiced that the Coalition
had taken place even against his own advice.

There has been much question as to the part which Mr.
Sheridan took on the formation of the Coalition; and Lord
John Townshend, an intimate friend of Mr. Fox, has denied
that Mr. Sheridan opposed it at the commencement.   Yet
it is difficult to disbelieve the evidence of Mr. Sheridan's
own speech, made in the presence of Mr. Fox, and relating
to a fact so recent.

Mr. Sheridan in the same speech attacked the coalition of
the Anti-coalitionists.   In truth, while Lord North, the
unwilling instrument of the King in carrying on the
American War, was made to bear the whole blame of that
disastrous policy, the earnest and obstinate supporters of
the Court during that war, had, to the number of upwards
of one hundred, rallied round Mr. Pitt, and cheered his
invectives against the " infamous Coalition."   Thus it was
that Mr. Pitt, the son of Lord Chatham the Whig and the

Reformer, became virtually the head of the Tory party, and the ally of Mr. Jenkinson, the child and champion of secret influence. Mr. Coke's motion was carried by 211 to 187, a majority of 24.

The position of Mr. Fox became by this success only the more difficult and embarrassing. He was already loaded with the unpopularity of the Coalition and the India Bill; if to these two subjects of misconception and sources of odium he should add the obloquy of attempting to stop the supplies, and found power on a narrow majority of the existing House of Commons, it was easy to foresee that all the timid would be alarmed, all the moderate alienated, and the great mass of the country fly for refuge to the Throne. Yet from this extreme imprudence Mr. Fox did not refrain.

Before any further steps could be taken, however, the Earl of Effingham thought proper to bring to the notice of the House of Lords the resolutions already agreed to by the House of Commons. He founded himself on a resolution of the House of Lords of the year 1704, to the following effect :—

"That it is unconstitutional and contrary to law for any one branch of the Legislature to assume to itself a right of making any resolutions which should impede or put a stop to the executive power of Government as by law established."

Lord Effingham then referred to the resolutions of December 24th, 1783, and January 16th, 1784, and proceeded to move, first, that an attempt to supersede the execution of law is unconstitutional; and, secondly, that "the undoubted authority of appointing to the great offices of Executive Government is solely vested in his Majesty, and that this House has every reason to place the firmest reliance on his Majesty's wisdom, in the exercise of this prerogative."

It seemed to be the object of this motion to commit the House of Lords to an opinion contrary to that expressed by the House of Commons. With regard to the constitutional point, Lord Loughborough stated the whole truth when he admitted " the undoubted right of the Crown to name its own Ministers ; but that the House of Lords or Commons had an equal right to advise his Majesty to dismiss them."

The nature of the prerogative, and the co-extensive right of the Houses of Parliament to advise the Crown upon its exercise was fully elucidated upon a motion for a Select Committee of Inquiry moved for in the House of Commons by Lord Beauchamp. It appeared from the report of this committee that from June, 1660, the year of the Restoration, to June, 1782, a period of one hundred and twenty-two years, there were numerous precedents of resolutions agreed to by the House of Commons containing advice on the discretionary exercise of the prerogatives of the Crown. Lord Beauchamp then moved six resolutions, of which the two first were to the following effect :—

" 1. That this House has not assumed to itself any right to suspend the execution of law.

" 2. That it is constitutional and agreeable to usage for the House of Commons to declare their sense and opinions respecting the exercise of every discretionary power which, whether by Act of Parliament or otherwise, is vested in any body of men whatever for the public service."

The House, after a long debate, divided on the previous question, when there appeared 157 against and 187 for putting the resolutions.   The resolutions were then carried without a division.

On the 9th of February Mr. Fox again proposed to adjourn the Committee on the State of the Nation.   This was agreed to.

On the 11th of February, upon a new discussion on the union of parties, Mr. Fox showed a great disposition to make concessions upon the India Bill, and Lord North declared that if he formed any obstacle, he was ready to give up any claim to hold office in the united Government. These declarations produced great satisfaction on the part of the country gentlemen, and Mr. Marsham, as their organ, called upon Mr. Pitt to resign.   This call, however, he declined to answer, and the conversation dropped.

The gentlemen who met at the St. Albans Tavern had not yet given up their patriotic endeavour to form a united Ministry.   They suggested that the Duke of Portland might be commanded by the King to confer with Mr. Pitt on the formation of a new Ministry.   Mr. Pitt accordingly signified the King's commands to the Duke of Portland, " that he should have a personal conference with Mr. Pitt for the purpose of forming a new Administration."   Had the letter stopped here, the Duke of Portland could not have refused to meet Mr. Pitt, and the real obstacles to a union would at least have been clearly explained.   But Mr. Pitt added the words, " on a wide basis, and on fair and equal terms."   The words " wide basis" were probably intended to include Lord Thurlow, as on a former occasion, and the words " equal terms" meant obviously an equal share of seats in the Cabinet.

I have already stated the reasons why Mr. Fox objected to such an arrangement.   The Duke of Portland, therefore,

while he admitted the term "fair," required an explanation of the term "equal," which he said would seem to
imply the idea of having equal numbers of each party in
the Cabinet, rather than mutual confidence and unity of
principles. Mr. Pitt dryly answered, that the word could
be explained at the conference. The Duke of Portland then
proposed either that the message he had received should be
construed as a virtual resignation, or that he should receive
a message directly from the King. Both propositions were
declined, and all hopes of an arrangement were at an end.
It is obvious that neither party was really desirous of agreement. For it was clear that the formation of a new
Ministry implied the extinction of the existing Administration, and that the demand of the Duke of Portland on
the one hand, and the refusal of Mr. Pitt on the other,
showed a determination not to agree to the union proposed.
The St. Albans meeting closed their labours with an expression of their regret that all further progress towards
union had been stopped by a doubt respecting a single word.
Many persons thought, and thought justly, that the efforts
of the country gentlemen to produce a combination of parties,
though well meant, tended only to complication and delay.

On the 18th of February, upon the order of the day for
receiving the report of the Committee of Supply, Mr. Pitt
declared that his Majesty had not yet, in compliance with
the resolutions of the House, thought proper to dismiss his
present Ministers, and that his Majesty's Ministers had
not resigned. This much he thought necessary to say prior
to any discussion on the subject of supplies. This declaration on the part of Mr. Pitt seemed to be intended to provoke Mr. Fox into some violent course on the subject of
supplies. The country was so sensitively loyal upon this

matter, that the Minister might confidently anticipate a diminution of his adversary's strength, should he be tempted to obstruct the public service. Mr. Fox did not wholly gratify the probable expectations of Mr. Pitt. He began, indeed, with stating, that he had heard the declaration of the right honourable gentleman with the greatest astonishment and concern; it was in his opinion such language as the House had not heard since the Revolution, or, at least, since the accession of the House of Hanover. He treated Mr. Pitt's statement as amounting to a determination to govern in contempt of the opinion and advice of the House of Commons, and he declaimed with eloquent indignation upon this theme. But at the end of his speech he said he was happy to find that the particular species of supply now moved for was not immediately indispensable, and that no material disadvantage could accrue, at least for the very short space to which he wished the House to adjourn. He shuddered at the thought of debating a proposition of such magnitude, *Tempus inane peto requiem spatiumque furori.* He concluded with moving that, instead of " now," the report be received " on Friday."

Mr. Fox's position was unfortunate. He had upon a former occasion expressed an opinion that the House of Commons had lost the power of refusing supplies, though not of delaying them. But the power of delaying supplies can only be effectively exerted as a significant hint that, if not attended to, the refusal will follow. If the Minister can feel confident that the supplies, though postponed for a time, will be voted as soon as they become indispensable to the public service, he may smile at the threat implied in the postponement.

Had Mr. Fox enjoyed the confidence of a large majority

of the House of Commons to such an extent as to have been able to say that on the Friday the supplies would be refused, the King must at once have yielded. But, as he could not do that, as he could only speak, argue, remonstrate, and declaim, he was, when opposed to a man so resolute and courageous as Mr. Pitt, already beaten. He could only excite alarm without effect, and create a dread of his violent intentions, while, in fact, he was preparing for retreat. Mr. Pitt, however, insisted that the moderate proposal of Mr. Fox was in fact a motion for stopping the supplies. It was evidently his wish to force his opponents to that extreme and unpopular step.

Lord North spoke strongly for union. He said that the India Bill was out of the way, his own pretensions were out of the way, and on what ground could Ministers insist on the retention of their offices? But it clearly appeared, in the course of this debate, that Mr. Pitt had now obtained in his own opinion that popularity in the country which would give him a majority at a general election, and that, far from wishing to unite with Mr. Fox, he was intent only upon seeking a pretext for destroying his influence in the House and the country.

On the 20th of February Mr. Powys moved a resolution :—

" That this House, impressed with the most dutiful sense of his Majesty's paternal regard for the welfare of his people, relies on his Majesty's royal wisdom that he will take such measures as may tend to give effect to the wishes of his faithful Commons, which have already been most humbly represented to his Majesty."

This motion might have passed with general concurrence had not Mr. Eden proposed, as an amendment, to insert after the word measures, " by removing any obstacle to the formation of such an Administration as this House has declared to be requisite in the present critical and arduous situation of public affairs."

Sir William Wake, in opposing the motion, said that the tide of popularity unquestionably ran in favour of Mr. Pitt; that the House of Commons, indeed, was against the Minister; but what was a small majority of that House compared with the other two branches of the Legislature and the voice of the people?   It would be a fatal dignity indeed, if the House should adhere to its resolutions.

The amendment having been inserted, Mr. Marsham, as chairman of the St. Albans Meeting, with the leave of Mr. Pitt and Mr. Fox, stated what had passed on the subject of the India Bill.   Having waited on Mr. Fox by desire of the meeting, to learn his intentions respecting the new India Bill, Mr. Fox told him that, provided Mr. Pitt would consent that the Government of India should be in this country, and permanent for at least a given number of years, he would leave it entirely to that right honourable gentleman to settle the article of patronage as he pleased. With this information he waited on the Minister, who told him that the article of patronage being thus given up, an opening was so far made to a negotiation.

Mr. Fox afterwards explained that he had not entirely given up the article of patronage to be dealt with according to the pleasure of Mr. Pitt, but that he had said that there could hardly be any arrangement of the patronage suggested to him to which he should not be willing to consent.

In the debate on the main question Mr. Fox made one of his finest speeches :—

" With regard to the argument that stopping the supplies would be attended with confusions and distractions, that depended entirely upon his Majesty's Ministers; good Ministers, who wished well to the peace and quiet of their country, would always prevent them by resigning before the House had proceeded to such a vote. Upon this ground he was convinced it was that the present Lord Camelford (then Mr. Thomas Pitt) had acted two years ago, when he proposed stopping the supplies; but the Ministers of that day knew their duty too well to suffer such a motion to pass—they prevented it by a timely resignation."

With regard to Lord North, he said that if his declaration was supposed to mean "that he would quit a scene in which he formed so material and important a character, there was no person who would blame such a conduct more than he should, because he knew that such a conduct would take away a great and principal means by which a strong, vigorous, and effectual Government could alone be formed in this country."

Referring to the public meetings which had taken place, he said :—

" Allusions had been made in the course of the debate to the battle of Westminster, the battle of Hackney, and the battle of Reading. These inglorious tumults, he was persuaded, did no good whatever. Of such petty warfare it might be said,—

> " ' Cumque superba foret Babylon spolianda tropæis
> Ausoniis, umbrâque erraret Crassus inultâ,
> Bella geri placuit nullos habitura triumphos.' "

Mr. Pitt, after pointing out the mischief which would accrue from a refusal of the supplies, said :—

" By what I am now going to say, perhaps I may subject myself to the invidious imputation of being the Minister and friend of prerogative; but, sir, notwithstanding those terms of obloquy with which I am assailed, I will not shrink from avowing myself the friend of the King's just prerogative. Prerogative, sir, has been justly styled a part of the rights of the people, and sure I am that it is a part of their rights which the people were never more disposed to defend, of which they never were more jealous than at this hour. Grant only that this House has a negative on the appointment of Ministers, and you transplant the executive power to this House. Sir, I shall call upon gentlemen to speak out, for there is nothing more dangerous among mixed powers than that one branch of the Legislature should attack another by means of hints and auxiliary arguments, urged only in debate, without daring to avow the direct grounds on which they go, and without stating in plain terms on the face of their resolutions what are their motives and what are the principles which lead them to come to such resolutions. Above all, sir, let this House beware of suffering any individual to involve his own cause, and interweave his own interests in the resolutions of the House of Commons. . . . The right honourable gentleman is possessed of those enchanting arts whereby he can give grace to deformity: he holds before your eyes a beautiful and delusive image; but, as sure as you embrace it, the pleasing vision will vanish, and this fair phantom of liberty will be succeeded by anarchy, confusion, and the ruin of the Constitution."

Following up this argument, he said:—

" Where is the independence—nay, where is even the safety of any one prerogative of the Crown, or even of the

Crown itself, if its prerogative of naming Ministers is to be usurped by this House, or if (which is precisely the same thing) its nomination of men is to be negatived by us without stating any one ground of distrust in the men, and without suffering ourselves to have any experience of their measures? Dreadful, therefore, as the conflict is, my conscience, my duty, my fixed regard for the Constitution of our ancestry, maintain me still in this arduous situation. It is not any proud contempt or defiance of the Constitutional resolutions of this House—it is no personal point of honour—must less is it any lust of power, that makes me still cling to office; the situation of the times requires of me, and I will add, the country calls aloud to me, that I should defend this castle, and I am determined, therefore, · I will yet defend it."

During the month which elapsed from this time till the dissolution of Parliament, the majority confined themselves to resolutions and addresses, while they showed, both by their language and conduct, that they were quite ready to vote the supplies of the year. Indeed, upon one occasion, the Opposition declared they had been ready to vote the navy estimates to a further extent than the Ministers had asked them.

In the argument which was carried on between the contending parties, the Opposition had the advantage of holding the more constitutional doctrine. Mr. Pitt, unable to use the true defence of his position,—namely, that the ultimate appeal was to the people at large,—seems to have been drawn on by the rays of royal and popular favour to the assertion of doctrines which Lord Chatham would have blushed to hear from the lips of his son. The King, in an answer to the address of the Commons of the 25th of

February, was made to say : "That no charge or complaint had been suggested against his present Ministers." It was obvious that this doctrine tended to restrain within a very narrow compass the functions of the House of Commons, who are, as Mr. Burke truly said, "a council of wisdom and weight to advise, and not merely an accuser of competence to criminate."

Had Mr. Pitt's doctrine prevailed, the King might have named any weak Court favourite his Minister, with the Lords of the Bedchamber for his colleagues, and the Commons would have had no redress ; for, according to another opinion of Mr. Pitt, the House were bound to vote supplies for the public service, however little they might trust those by whose hands those supplies were to be distributed.

Another passage in the King's answer much objected to was one in which he stated "That numbers of his subjects had expressed their satisfaction at the change he had made in his councils." This preference of addresses got up by partial meetings to the legitimate organ of the people, the House of Commons, was justly reprobated as an imitation of the Court practices in the days of Charles II., when the country was canvassed to send addresses with a view to overthrow the authority of Parliament.

But while Mr. Fox had the advantage in the abstract discussion, Mr. Pitt was advancing by large strides towards the practical object of his policy. Every hostile resolution was followed the same evening by a vote in supply. The majorities against the Minister were obviously decreasing. On the 20th of February the address moved by Mr. Powys, and amended by Mr. Eden, in favour of a united Administration, and the removal of any obstacle to its formation, was carried by a majority of 21. Upon the King's refusal, a second address was agreed to on the 1st of March, but only by a majority of 12. On the 4th this address was presented to the King, whose reply was firm, explicit, and decided. He said that he had been desirous of taking every step conducive to the formation of an extended Administration, and that he remained in the same sentiments, but that he continued equally convinced that it was an object not likely to be attained by the dismission of his present Ministers. That no charge, or complaint, nor any specific objection, had yet been made against any of them. That if there were any ground for their removal, it ought to be equally a reason for not admitting them as a part of an extended and united Administration. That he did not consider the failure of his recent endeavours as a final bar to the accomplishment of the purpose he had in view, if it could have been attained on those principles of fairness and equality without which it could neither be honourable to those concerned nor lay the foundation of a strong and stable Government. That he knew of no further steps which he could take that were likely to remove the difficulties which obstructed that desirable end.

Nothing could be plainer than this language. The refusal to dismiss his Ministers, and the repetition of the word equality, with the intimation that no further step could be taken, showed that the King had finally determined to remain on the ground he had hitherto occupied.

Mr. Fox moved, on the 8th of March, a long address in reply to the King's answer, which, in order to mark its adverse character, he styled a representation. In this address Mr. Fox repeated the sense of the former resolutions of the House, and ended with casting the responsibility upon those who had disregarded the opinions and neglected the admonitions of the representatives of the people. The address was carried by a majority of 1 only—191 to 190.

This division seems to have sunk altogether the spirits of the Opposition. A few days before they had spoken confidently of a short Mutiny Bill, limited in point of time, so as to prevent the possibility of a dissolution. But, on the 10th of March, a Mutiny Bill, for the usual period of a year, went through committee, Mr. Fox declaring that he yielded his opinion on this subject to that of others. It was pretended indeed that, as no Appropriation Bill had passed, the issuing of public moneys for the services that had been voted, would be a high crime and misdemeanour, and subversive of the Constitution. But Mr. Pitt, now confident of a majority in the new Parliament, and a bill of indemnity for any irregularity, could afford to remain silent amidst the pointed questions, the severe taunts, and the personal invectives of his opponents.

On the 24th of March the King summoned the Commons to the House of Lords, and thus addressed his Parliament :—

" My Lords and Gentlemen,—On a full consideration of the present situation of affairs, and of the extraordinary circumstances which have produced it, I am induced to put an end to this session of Parliament; I feel it a duty which I owe to the Constitution and to the country, in such a situation, to recur as speedily as possible to the sense of my people, by calling a new Parliament.

" I trust that this measure will tend to obviate the mischiefs arising from the unhappy divisions and distractions which have lately subsisted ; and that the various important objects which will require consideration may be afterwards proceeded upon with less interruption and with happier effect.

"I can have no other object but to preserve the true principles of our free and happy Constitution, and to employ the powers entrusted to me by law for the only end for which they were given, the good of my people."*

On the following day the Parliament was dissolved.

The success of the measure of dissolution was not long doubtful. The popular current set in strongly in favour of the King and Mr. Pitt, and against Mr. Fox and the Coalition. Everywhere the members of the late majority found their conduct severely reprobated, and in many cases they failed in their attempts to be re-elected. The agents of men of property attached to the Coalition were in several instances found acting openly and avowedly against their employers.

The Dissenters espoused warmly the part of Mr. Pitt. Mr. Wilberforce, attacking the Coalition, in Yorkshire, said that it bore the features of both its parents—the corruption of the one, and the violence of the other. "Upwards of 160 members lost their seats; and of those almost the whole number were the friends of the late Administration. So complete a rout of what was looked upon as one of the strongest and most powerful parties that ever existed in Great Britain is scarcely to be credited."†

Such is the testimony of the "Annual Register," at this time under the direction of Mr. Burke. In that publication an attempt is made to account for this result by alleging various circumstances. The question of the government of India, it is said, related to the administration of a remote dependency, respecting which the

* "Parliamentary History," vol. xxiv. p. 774.   † "Annual Register."

people at large could not be expected to take a lively interest. In regard to the privileges of the House of Commons, those privileges being of the nature of delegated power, excited envy and jealousy, feelings which it had been the care of the Court to nurture and to cherish. During the contest in Parliament, the majority, anxious to prevent a dissolution, had neglected their general interests in the nation, and their particular connexions as representatives. Add to these considerations the mystery in which Mr. Pitt had veiled his plans, and his apparent intention, amounting almost to a public pledge, to allow public business to proceed without resorting to a dissolution. Hence the measure burst at length upon the Opposition totally and universally unprepared.

It seems to me that these reasons entirely fail to account for a rout so complete of "what was looked upon as one of the strongest and most powerful parties that ever existed in Great Britain."

There are, however, causes not far to seek which appear to me sufficient to account for this great political defeat :—

1. Mr. Fox, after leaving Lord Shelburne, instead of keeping up his connexion with the Duke of Richmond, Lord Camden, General Conway, and other opponents of the American War, including Mr. Pitt himself, had made a close alliance with Lord North, the Minister of that war, and the weak tool of the Court. It might be said by those who knew Lord North, that neither his head nor his heart had ever sympathized with the Court on the American War, and that the quarrel being over, he would act, as in fact he did act, in easy and cordial subordination to Mr. Fox. But in politics it may almost be said, *De apparentibus, et de existentibus eadem est ratio.* The ostensible chief of the

Ministry during the American War was Lord North; the ostensible representative of high Tory doctrines in the House of Commons was Lord North; such a coalition was sure to be condemned by public opinion. Nor is it true, as Mr. Fox seems to have more than once thought, that by combining the chief leaders of weight in debate and experience in affairs, a body might be formed of sufficient power to overcome all resistance, and defy all competition. Where there is a public sentiment, especially if that sentiment is shared or inspired by the Sovereign, there will not be wanting in this country, nurse as it is of free discussion, men capable of becoming the organs and the leaders of a popular and powerful party. Thus, Mr. Pitt, in 1783 and 1784, without a colleague in the House of Commons, defied Mr. Fox, Lord North, Mr. Burke, Mr. Sheridan, and Mr. Erskine. Thus, Mr. Perceval, in 1807, defeated the coalition of Lord Grey and Lord Grenville, and led his fanatical majority with undaunted spirit and unquestionable success. Eighteen years of power consolidated the victorious party of Mr. Pitt; twenty years of Tory administration followed the triumph of Mr. Perceval.

2. The Coalition might, perhaps, have reconciled the King by temper and concession, and slowly have established themselves in public favour. Had the Great Seal been given to Lord Thurlow, and Mr. Pitt entrusted with the management of the finances, important public objects might have been accomplished. But a measure of so unusual a character as the India Bill afforded an obvious ground for alarm, and the most plausible reasons for asserting that Mr. Fox would be satisfied with nothing less than the sway of a dictator. In the last days of the Parliament, a basis for agreement on the India Bill was arrived at by the opposite parties. Had this

concession been made earlier, had even the Board of the Seven Kings, as they were called, been composed of men remote from party connexion, known by their experience in the affairs of India, or equally divided between the followers of Mr. Fox and those of Mr. Pitt, the impression made by the India Bill would have been very different. But when it was proposed to transfer the whole power, patronage, and revenues from the East India Company to seven persons intimately connected with one or other branch of the Coalition, it was no wonder that an alarm was created in the country, and jealousy infused into the King. It appeared as if, by the side of the Crown and the two Houses of Parliament, a new body was to be placed in authority which might defy the Executive, and corrupt the legislative body. The head of the proposed commission, Lord Fitzwilliam, though a most respectable man, was only known to the country as the successor of Lord Rockingham, and had no special qualification for the government of India.

3. With the odium attaching to the Coalition, and the India Bill hanging about him, Mr. Fox attempted to reduce the Court to surrender to the majority of the House of Commons. But, while he was undoubtedly right in maintaining that no Ministry could conduct public affairs with advantage to the country unless they had the confidence of that House, he failed to perceive or chose to be blind to the truth that there is a wide difference between the House of Commons existing at any particular moment and the House of Commons as a part of the Constitution. He always argued as if Mr. Pitt were defying the authority and advice of the House of Commons when he was only refusing to acknowledge the supreme power of the House of Commons elected in 1780. Had

the result of a dissolution been to confirm the decisions of that House, there can be no doubt that Mr. Pitt would and must have retired.

To the people, or rather to the electors of Great Britain, lay that ultimate appeal which was to close the dispute between the King, his Ministers, and the Lords on one side, the Coalition and the House of Commons on the other. The evident wish to avoid such an appeal only increased the unpopularity of that party which pretended to overlook the supreme tribunal of the nation, and thus appeared to set up an authority in the House of Commons independent of those from whom their sole title was derived.

Nor ought it to have been forgotten that the most decisive success obtained in Parliament could not have been effectual unless it had been ratified by national approbation. For instance, had the King yielded to the address of the House of Commons and removed his Ministers, the Duke of Portland and Mr. Fox must have carried the supplies and the Mutiny Bill; but they could not have prevented the King from either dismissing them or forcing them to a resignation during the recess, and then appealing to his people by a dissolution.

While such were the errors in policy committed by Mr. Fox, there is no reason to doubt that he sought great public objects, and that he displayed the highest abilities in the parliamentary contest. The good government of India, the punishment of oppression and fraud in her rulers, the check of corruption at home, a government favourable to liberty at home and abroad—such were his objects. All his opponents and the great body of the country gentlemen bore their testimony to the extent and

depth of his views—to the force of his oratory—to the
fertility of his arguments. "Fox," said Dr. Johnson to
Boswell, "is a most extraordinary man," describing him in
strong terms of objection in some respects, "who has
divided the kingdom with Cæsar; so that it was a doubt
whether the nation should be ruled by the sceptre of George
III. or the tongue of Fox."*

While such was the position and such the genius of Fox,
his adversary derived many advantages from the circumstances which attended his dawning power. He was young,
and could neither be reproached by the enemies of the
American War nor hated by its abettors, for he had neither
caused its disasters nor opposed the King. If he appeared
more arrogant than became his years, and more confident
than his want of eminent colleagues seemed to justify, such
haughtiness might be excused in a son of Chatham. Again,
while he enjoyed the support, and was entitled to the gratitude of the Court, he could not be considered, like Lord
Bute, as a mere reflexion of royal favour, or, like Lord
North, as a Minister defending a policy which his judgment
did not approve. Indeed, the circumstance that there was
no overt act of mal-administration which could be charged
against him, while it was not decisive of his merits, told
prodigiously in his favour. With a just appreciation of
public duty and a sound estimate of the spirit of the time,
he rejected the "shabby" advice of Lord Thurlow to
take the great sinecure of Clerk of the Pells for himself,
and by conferring it on Colonel Barré, saved a pension
of 3000*l.* a year to the State. His reward was an immense
popularity. The public in general, so far from looking
upon him as the creature of secret influence, expected

* Boswell's "Johnson," 1784.

from his enlightened understanding and just estimate of
the national resources a recovery from the late ruinous and
corrupt waste of the public revenues, and a restoration of
the British name to its pristine honour and reputation.
While Mr. Fox, therefore, revived by his Coalition the
blasting memory of the American War, Mr. Pitt, by
standing alone, gave new hopes of an age of reform,
economy, and peace.

CHAPTER XX.

WESTMINSTER ELECTION—MR. FOX'S POSITION—"ROLLIAD."

OF all the elections of the year 1784, that which attracted most public attention was the election for Westminster.

At the end of the second day's poll Mr. Fox was in a majority over Sir Cecil Wray of 139; at the end of the tenth, he was in a minority of 318; on the twentieth, this minority was reduced to 84; on the thirtieth, Mr. Fox had a majority of 166; and on the fortieth, when the poll finally closed, Mr. Fox's majority was 236, the numbers being—

Lord Hood	6694
Mr. Fox	6234
Sir Cecil Wray	5998

The processions, the fights, the bribery, and the drunkenness which took place during this election disreputably mark the manners of that day. The Duchess of Devonshire canvassed for Mr. Fox, and contributed greatly, by her charms, her activity, and her zeal, to gain electors to his side. She was in revenge libelled in the grossest manner by the advocates of the Court candidates.

In the course of the election a man was killed, and the Court party accused the other of causing or effecting his murder. A trial took place at Guildhall on the 1st of

June, when Patrick Nicholson and three others were indicted for the wilful murder of Nicholas Casson. Great violence was proved to have been used against the unfortunate deceased; but whether by Nicholson, or one of his own party, or some one else, did not appear. Mr. Erskine examined for the defence, and Mr. Sheridan gave evidence of the disorder caused by the constables. All the prisoners were acquitted.

At the end of the election there was an immense crowd collected for the chairing of Mr. Fox. Mr. Fox mounted a car; an immense procession followed, which was closed by the state-carriages of the Duchesses of Portland and Devonshire, drawn by six horses each. Mr. Fox descended from the car at Devonshire House, where the Prince of Wales and the Duke and Duchess of Devonshire were assembled on a temporary scaffold to receive him. He dined at Willis's Rooms, where he made a warm speech on the subject of the election. On the same day, the Prince of Wales, after attending the King at a review at Ascot, rode up St. James's-street in his uniform, and afterwards went to dine at Devonshire House, wearing Mr. Fox's colours and a laurel-branch for victory.

On the following day more festivities took place. The Prince of Wales gave a grand breakfast, which lasted from noon till six o'clock in the evening.

Although Mr. Fox obtained a tardy and hard-won victory at Westminster, the defeat of his party and the popularity of his rival must have been mortifying to his ambition and depressing to his spirit. For nine years he had fought against the Court and the general voice in favour of the cause of America. That cause had at length triumphed, and the independence of America had been acknowledged. But Mr. Dundas, Mr. Jenkinson, and a great portion of the party which had followed Lord North on Tory principles, now formed the strength of Mr. Pitt's majority. After resisting Mr. Dunning's resolution and Mr. Burke's retrenchments, these accommodating politicians returned to power in the guise of friends of economy and admirers of financial reform.

Nor was the result of Mr. Fox's efforts in behalf of India less discouraging. In concert with Mr. Burke, he had devised measures for arresting the march of rapine, and giving to the millions of our Indian subjects the benefits of a just rule and the shield of public integrity; not only had these measures been defeated, but the motives of their authors were assailed, and an outcry raised on the false allegation that they intended to subvert the throne and substitute their own supremacy in its place. It might add something to the bitterness of this reflection, that their successors were in effect aiming at the destruction of the body they pretended to uphold, and the elevation of that influence of the Crown which they pretended to deprecate.

It is no wonder that Mr. Fox was fatigued and dispirited by the injustice and ill-fortune he had sustained. In a letter to the Duke of Portland, from St. Ann's, of July 27th, 1784, he says, among other things :—

" With regard to the idea of a general attendance in the House, I must beseech you to re-consider it before I can adopt it in direct contradiction to my own full conviction. . . . With respect to my inclination, I know it ought to give way, but yet, if any one else had done all I have for these last eight months, and was as completely tired out with it, body and mind, as I am, I believe he would think he had some right to consult it. I cannot express to you how fatigued I was with the last day's attendance, and how totally unequal I feel myself in point of spirits to acquit myself as I ought to do, either for the good of the party or for my own reputation.   However, I must submit to your judgment and to theirs, if you persist in your opinion.   But I am sure you will not repent it, if you will so far trust me as to believe that I know the House of Commons as well, and myself something better, than those who differ from me."*

While Mr. Fox, thus wearied with strife, was inclined to recruit his strength in the delightful shades of St. Ann's, the followers of the mighty warrior covered his retreat with the sharp missiles of wit and fun.   A cloud of arrows flying around made the supporters of the Minister smart with pain, at once triumphant and ridiculous.

The "Rolliad," or "Criticisms on the Rolliad," as it is more properly called, is the quiver of this squadron of wits.   Mr. Rolle, member for Devonshire, was a warm Ministerial supporter, who showed his zeal by interrupting and coughing down Mr. Burke.   The genealogy of John Rolle, Esq., from the records of the Heralds' Office, is an amusing parody of the labours of genealogists.

"We find in Camden that the race of the Rolles fell into adversity in the reign of Stephen, and in the succeeding reign, Gaspar de Rolle was an ostler in Denbighshire.   But during the unhappy contests of York and Lancaster, the Venerable Bede, and, indeed, the 'Chronicle of Croyland,' have it that the Rolles became Scheriffes of Devon —'Scheriffi Devonienses Rolli fuerant,' and in another passage, 'Arrest averunt debitores plurimi Rollorum;' hence a doubt in Fabian whether this Rollo was

* "Memoirs," &c., vol. iv. p. 230.

not Bailiff, *ipse potius quam scheriffus.* From this period, however, they gradually advanced in circumstances. Rollo, in Henry the Eighth, being amerced in 800 marks for pilfering two manchetts of beef from the King's buttery, the which, saith Selden, *facillime payavit."*

Mr. George Ellis, the author of this pedigree, was the writer of some of the best verses in the " Rolliad." From the landing of Rollo, when,—

> "Wrapt in a close great-coat, he plods along,
> A seeming smuggler, to deceive the throng,"

the critic proceeds to the sixth book, "in which Rollo, almost despairing of success, descends into a night-cellar to consult the illustrious Merlin on his future destiny." Then describing the future heroes who were to be co-temporaries of Mr. Rolle, the same pen gives us a portrait of Mr. Pitt :—

> " Pert without fire, without experience sage,
> Young with more art than Shelburne glean'd from age,
> Too proud from pilfer'd greatness to descend,
> Too humble not to call Dundas his friend,
> In solemn dignity and sullen state
> This new Octavius rises to debate!"

By Mr. George Ellis, too, were the lines descriptive of Mr. Prettyman, the future Bishop of Winchester :—

> " Prim preacher, prince of priests, and prince's priest,
> Pembroke's pale pride, in Pitt's *præcordia* placed,
> Thy merits shall all future ages scan,
> And Prince be lost in Parson Prettyman."

Again, in reference to his squinting :—

> " Argus could boast an hundred eyes, 'tis true,
> The Doctor looks an hundred ways with two,
> Gimlets they are, to bore you through and through."

Again of Mr. Pitt :—

> " Above the rest, majestically great,
> Behold the infant Atlas of the state,

> The matchless miracle of modern days,
> In whom Britannia to the world displays
> A sight to make surrounding nations stare,
> A kingdom trusted to a schoolboy's care."

From Mr. George Ellis, too, came those admirable verses on the Marquis of Graham, who had incautiously said, in the House of Commons: "If the hon. gentleman calls my hon. friend Goose, I suppose he will call me Gosling." Loud assenting cheers welcomed this sally, and the Marquis of Graham, being soon after elected Chancellor of the University of Glasgow, is thus addressed:—

> "If right the bard, whose numbers sweetly flow,
> That all our knowledge is ourselves to know,
> A sage like Graham can the world produce,
> Who in full senate call'd himself a goose?
> Th' admiring Commons from the high-born youth
> With wonder heard this undisputed truth;
> Exulting Glasgow claim'd him for her own,
> And placed the prodigy on learning's throne."

The position of the Speaker is thus described:—

> "There Cornwall sits, and oh! unhappy fate!
> Must sit for ever through the long debate!
>
> . . . . . .
>
> Painful pre-eminence! he hears, 'tis true,
> Fox, North, and Burke, but hears Sir Joseph too."

During the French revolutionary war Mr. George Ellis took the part of the Government, and wrote in the "Anti-Jacobin." Supping one night with Mr. Pitt, his new friends asked him to tell them the story of the composition of the Rolliad. Mr. Pitt, hearing the request, leant forward, and said:—

> "Immo age, et a primâ dic hospes, origine nobis,"—

He left to be implied "casusque tuorum, *Erroresque tuos.*"*

* "Æneid," lib. 1.

Another distinguished author of the " Rolliad," whose contributions perhaps exceed in number those of any other, was Dr. Lawrence, the very learned civilian.   His are the lines :—

> " Crown the froth'd porter, slay the fatted ox,
> And give the British meal to British Fox.
> But for an Indian Minister more fit,
> Ten cups of purest Padre pour for Pitt,
> Pure as himself ; add sugar, too, and cream," &c.

Dr. Lawrence did not forget the present of an ivory bed to the Queen from Mrs. Hastings, the divorced wife of Imhoff, a German artist.

> " Above, in colours warm with mimic life,
> The German husband of your Warren's wife,
> His rival's deeds should blazon and display,
> In his blest rule the glories of your sway."

Colonel Fitz-Patrick, another of these authors, with more wit than humanity, turned to account the circumstance of Alderman Brook Watson's having lost a leg by the bite of a shark while bathing in the sea :—

> " ' One moment's time might I presume to beg,'
> Cries modest Watson, on his wooden leg ;
> That leg in which such wondrous art is shown,
> It almost seems to serve him as his own.
> Oh ! had the monster who for breakfast ate
> That luckless limb, his nobler noddle met,
> The best of workmen and the best of wood
> Had scarce supplied him with a head so good."

Richardson, Lord John Townshend, and Tickell were, with Lawrence, Ellis, and Fitz-Patrick, the chief authors of the " Rolliad."   Sheridan had no part in it.   The Greek, Latin, and Italian verses, supposed to be intended as inscriptions upon the column where Rolle went to school, are very amusing.   The Latin begins :—

> " Hic ferulæ dextram, hic virgis cædenda magistri,
> Nuda dedit patiens tergora Rolliades,"—

and concludes :

> "I, puer, I forti tolerando pectore plagas
>   Æmula Rolliadæ nomina disce sequi."

The Italian is a sort of dialogue :

> " A chi sta questa colonna?   Al Rolle,
>   Che di parlar apprese in questo loco
>   Greco e Latino no, ma Inglese—un poco—
>   Basta così.   Chi non sa il resto è folle."

The Greek recording that here

> " πρωτα ΔΕΒΩΝΙΖΕΙΝ απεμανθανε παις ποτε ΡΩΛΛΟΣ,"—

is a fair hit at Mr. Rolle's Devonshire dialect.

CHAPTER XXI.

NEW PARLIAMENT—MR. PITT'S FINANCIAL AND COMMERCIAL
POLICY FROM 1784 TO 1788.

ON the 17th of May the High Bailiff of Westminster, instead of making a return, sent to the Crown Office a statement of the numbers on the poll for the respective candidates, and an allegation that he had granted a scrutiny, which was then proceeding. But Mr. Fox was not thereby excluded; he was returned to this Parliament for Orkney.

The Parliament met on the 18th of May. Upon the choice of a Speaker Mr. Fox called attention to the fact that the numbers of the House were not complete, but on Mr. Pitt's objecting that until a Speaker was chosen, the return for Westminster could not be before the House, the question was postponed.

Before the address was moved, Mr. Lee called attention to the circumstances of this case, and moved that the High Bailiff ought to have made an immediate return. Sir Lloyd Kenyon, Master of the Rolls, defended the High Bailiff, and opposed the motion, on the ground *audi alteram partem*. It was clear that the motion was no censure of the High Bailiff, but a decision upon the right of a returning officer to delay a return for any period—

perhaps for the whole seven years of the Parliament. Mr. Scott, afterwards Lord Eldon, said there was no instance of a power to delay a writ, returnable on a certain day. Yet Mr. Pitt was not ashamed to protect the High Bailiff in his violation of his duty as returning officer; and Mr. Lee's motion was rejected by 233 to 136. Yet the sequel justified his proceeding.

On the 8th of June, Mr. Welbore Ellis moved, " That it appeared to this House that Thomas Corbett, Esq., Bailiff of the Liberty of the City of Westminster, having received a precept from the Sheriff of Middlesex for electing two citizens to serve in Parliament for the said city, and having taken and finally closed the poll on the 17th day of May last, being the day next before the day of the return of the said writ, he be now directed forthwith to make return of his precept, and of members chosen in pursuance thereof."

On this occasion Mr. Fox delivered one of the most memorable of his speeches. The opening passages afford a happy instance of his promptitude and skill as a debater.

" Mr. Speaker, before I enter upon the consideration of this question, I cannot help expressing my surprise that those who sit over against me (the Ministry) should have been hitherto silent in this debate. Common candour might have taught them to have urged whatever objections they have to urge against the motion of my honourable friend before this time, because in that case I should have an opportunity of replying to their arguments; and surely it would have been fair to allow me the slight favour of being the last speaker upon such a subject. But, sir, I have no reason to expect indulgence, nor do I know that I shall meet with bare justice in this House."

In consequence of a murmur from the other side, Mr. Fox paused and said :—

" Mr. Speaker, there is a regular mode of checking any member in this House for using improper words in a debate, and it is to move to have the improper words taken down by the clerk, for the purpose of censuring the person who had spoken them. If I have said anything unfit for this House to hear or for me to utter, if any gentleman is offended by anything that fell from me, and has sense enough to point out and spirit to correct that offence, he will adopt that Parliamentary and gentleman-like mode of conduct; and that he may have an opportunity of doing so, I again repeat, that I have no reason to expect indulgence, nor do I know that I shall meet with bare justice in this House.

" Sir, I am warranted in the use of these words by events and authorities that leave little to be doubted and little to be questioned. The treatment this business has received within these walls, the extraordinary proceedings which have sprung from it, the dispositions which have been manifested in particular classes of men, all concur to justify the terms I have adopted and to establish the truth of what I have asserted.

" If the declaration I have made had happened not to have been supported by the occurrences I allude to, the very consideration of Mr. Grenville's Bill is of itself sufficient to vindicate what I have said. That bill, sir, originated in a belief that this House, in the aggregate, was an unfit tribunal to decide upon contested elections. It viewed this House as every popular assembly should be viewed—as a mass of men capable of political dislike and personal aversion; capable of too much attachment and too much animosity; capable of being biassed by weak and by wicked motives; liable to be governed by ministerial influence, by caprice, and by corruption. Mr. Grenville's Bill viewed this House as endowed with these capacities, and judging it, therefore, incapable of determining upon controverted elections with impartiality, with justice, and with equity, it deprived it of the means of mischief, and formed a judicature as complete and ample, perhaps, as human skill can constitute. That I am debarred the benefits of that celebrated bill is clear beyond all doubt, and thrown entirely upon the mercy, or, if you please, upon the wisdom of this House. Unless, then, men are to suppose that human nature is totally altered within a few months—unless we can be so grossly credulous as to imagine that the present is purged of all the frailties of former Parliaments—unless I am to surrender my understanding, and blind myself to the extraordinary conduct of this House, in this extraordinary business, for the last fortnight—I may say, and say with truth, ' that I expect no indulgence, nor do I know that I shall meet with bare justice in this House.'

"There are in this House, sir, many persons to whom I might, upon every principle of equity, fairness, and reason, object, as judges, to decide upon my cause, not merely from their acknowledged enmity to me, to my friends, and to my politics, but from their particular conduct upon this particular occasion. To a noble lord (Mulgrave) who spoke early in this debate, I might rightly object as a judge to try me, who, from the fulness of his prejudice to me, and predilection for my opponents, asserts things in direct defiance of the evidence which has been given at your bar. The noble lord repeats again, that ' tricks ' were used on

my side in the election, although he very properly omits
the epithet which preceded that term when he used it in a
former debate; but does it appear in evidence that any
tricks were practised on my part? Not a word. Against
him, therefore, who, in the teeth of the depositions on your
table, is prompted, by his enmity towards me, to maintain
what the evidence (the ground this House is supposed to go
upon) absolutely denies, I might object with infinite propriety as a judge in this cause.

"There is another judge, sir, to whom I might object
with greater reason, if possible, than to the last. A person
evidently interested in increasing the numbers of my adversaries upon the poll, but who has relinquished his right as
an elector of Westminster, that his voting may not dis-
qualify him from being a judge upon the committee to
decide this contest;—a person, too, sir, who in the late
election scrupled not to act as an agent—an avowed, and
indeed an active agent—to my opponents."

Lord Mahon took this to himself; but Mr. Fox went on
thus :—

"Is there any interruption, sir? I hope not. I am but
stating a known fact, that a person who is to pronounce a
judgment this night in this cause, avoided to exercise one
of the most valuable franchises of a British citizen, only
that he might be a nominee for my adversaries, concluding
that his industry upon the committee would be of more
advantage to their cause than a solitary vote at the election. This, sir, I conceive, would be a sufficient objection
to him as a judge to try me.

"A third person there is, whom I might in reason
challenge upon this occasion. A person of a sober demeanour, who, with great diligence and exertion in a very

respectable and learned profession, has raised himself to a considerable eminence [the Master of the Rolls] ; a person who fills one of the first seats of justice in this kingdom, and who has long discharged the functions of a judge in an inferior but very honourable situation. This person, sir, has upon this day professed and paraded much upon the impartiality with which he should discharge his conscience in his judicial capacity as a member of Parliament in my cause. Yet this very person, insensible to the rank he maintains, or should maintain, in this country, abandoning the gravity of his character as a member of the senate, and losing sight of the sanctity of his station, both in this House and out of it, even in the very act of delivering a judicial sentence, descends to minute and mean allusions to former politics, comes here stored with the intrigues of past times, and instead of the venerable language of a good judge and a great lawyer, attempts to entertain the House by quoting, or by misquoting, words supposed to have been spoken by me in the heat of former debates, and in the violence of contending parties, when my noble friend and I opposed each other. This demure gentleman, sir, this great lawyer, this judge of law, and equity, and constitution, enlightens this subject, instructs and delights his hearers, by reviving this necessary intelligence, that when I had the honour of first sitting in this House for Midhurst, I was not full twenty-one years of age ; and all this he does for the honourable purpose of justifying the High Bailiff of Westminster in defrauding the electors of their representation in this House, and robbing me of the honour of asserting and confirming their right by sitting as their representative. Against him, therefore, sir, and against men like him, I might justly object as a judge, or as judges to try my cause; and it is with perfect truth, I once more repeat, 'that I have no reason to expect indulgence, nor do I know that I shall meet with bare justice in this House.'

"Sir, I understand that the learned gentleman I have just alluded to (I was not in the House during the first part of his speech) has insinuated that I have no right to be present during this discussion, and that hearing me is an indulgence. Against the principle of that assertion, sir, and against every syllable of it, I beg leave, in the most express terms, directly to protest. I maintain that I not only have a right to speak, but a positive and clear right to vote on this occasion; and I assure the House that nothing but the declaration I have made in the first stage of this business should prevent me from doing so. As to myself, if I were the only person to be aggrieved by this proceeding, if the mischief of it extended not beyond me, I should rest thoroughly and completely satisfied with the great and brilliant display of knowledge and abilities which have been exhibited by the learned gentleman who appeared for me and for my constituents at your bar. If I alone were interested in the decision of this matter, their exertions, combined with the acute and ingenious treatment this question has received from many gentlemen on this side of the House, whose arguments are as learned as they are evidently unanswerable, would have contented me; but a sense of duty, superior to all personal advantage, calls on me to exert myself at this time. Whatever can best encourage and animate to diligence and to energy, whatever is most powerful and influencing upon a mind not callous to every sentiment of gratitude and honour, demand at this moment the exercise of every function and faculty that

I am master of. This, sir, is not my cause alone—it is the cause of the English Constitution, the cause of the electors of this kingdom, and it is in particular the especial cause of the most independent, the most spirited, the most kind and generous body of men that ever concurred upon a subject of public policy: it is the cause of the electors of Westminster, the cause of those who, upon many trials, have supported me against hosts of enemies, of those who, upon a recent occasion, when every art of malice, of calumny, and corruption—every engine of an illiberal and shameless system of government—when the most gross and monstrous fallacies that ever duped and deceived a credulous country, have been propagated and worked with all imaginable subtlety and diligence, for the purpose of rendering me unpopular throughout the empire—have with a steadiness, with a sagacity, with a judgment, becoming men of sense and spirit, defeated all the miserable malice of my enemies, vindicated themselves from the charge of caprice, changeableness, and fluctuation, and, with a generosity that binds me to them in every tie of affection, supported me through the late contest, and accomplished a victory against all the arts and powers of the basest system of oppression that ever destined the overthrow of any individual. If by speaking in this House (where many, perhaps, may think I speak too much), I have acquired any reputation, if I have any talents, and that attention to public business has matured or improved those talents into any capability of solid service, the present subject and the present moment beyond any other period of my life, challenge and call them into action; when added to the importance of this question, as it bears upon the English Constitution, combined with the immediate interest I feel personally in the fate of it, I am impelled by the nobler and more forcible incitement of being engaged in the cause of those to whom the devotion of all I have of diligence or ability would be but a slight recompence for their zeal, constancy, firm attachment, and unshaken friendship to me upon all occasions and under all circumstances."

Mr. Fox then proceeded to argue the question in two leading points of view,—the first, whether the High Bailiff had sufficient evidence to justify him in granting a scrutiny; the second, whether he could by law grant a scrutiny which could not commence till after the day on which the writ was returnable.

With regard to the first point, Mr. Fox showed that the High Bailiff had proceeded on insufficient and contradictory grounds. On the 'second point, he examined the four grounds of positive statute, of precedent, of legal analogy, and, lastly, of expediency and common sense. All these grounds he traversed with wonderful acuteness, and concluded that on none of these grounds could the conduct of the High Bailiff be justified. To one argument of his opponents, which at least was plausible, he thus replied :—

" To that argument—if it deserves the name of argument—that we are inconsistent in desiring the High Bailiff to make a return, when we contend that all his authority under that writ is completely defunct, it is almost unnecessary to reply, because it evidently defeats itself. In contending that the High Bailiff was *functus officio* on the 18th of May, we are fortified by law, and in desiring he would make some return, we are justified by precedent.

" We contend—and contend with truth—that the writ under which the High Bailiff carried on the election being returnable on the 18th of May, on that very day deprived the bailiff of all judicial authority, and divested him of all legal power under that writ. To proceed with a scrutiny is a great act of authority; to tell us who have in his opinion the majority of legal votes, is not. That this House should order a returning officer to commence a scrutiny several days after the positive day on which his writ was returnable, cannot be paralleled by a single case in all the history of Parliament—that it should order a returning officer, who tells you he proceeded to an election, carried on a poll for a sufficient time, and that he then closed that poll of his own authority, to make a return, has happened again and again. We do not desire him to exercise any jurisdiction under that writ now, we only desire him to acquaint us with the fruits of the jurisdiction which he has exercised under it. 'I have done so and so,' says the High Bailiff. 'Tell us what you mean,' is all we say. 'I have, on such a day, proceeded to an election,' says he; 'I have carried on a poll for forty days; I have, on the day before the return of the writ, closed that poll of my own authority.' All this we understand—in all this you did your duty—only tell us who are the candidates chosen upon this long poll? We do not mean to say you have at present any authority to do anything under that writ; all we want to know is, what you have done when you had authority under it? Let the House reflect upon this fair and reasonable distinction, and they will see the paltriness of those quibbles, the misery of those low subterfuges, which imply that we would bring 'a dead man to life,' and which imply an inconsistency between the motion and the arguments advanced in support of it."

He then touched in the following terms on the question of expense :—

" Having said so much as to the real authors of this measure, there remains another consideration with which I am desirous to impress the House; it is a consideration, however, which in policy I ought to conceal, because it will be an additional incitement to my enemies to proceed in their career with vigour; but it will nevertheless show the extreme oppression and glaring impolicy of this scrutiny— I mean the consideration of expense.

" I have had a variety of calculations made upon the subject of this scrutiny, and the lowest of all the estimates is 18,000*l.* This, sir, is a serious and an alarming consideration. But I know it may be said (and with a pitiful triumph it perhaps will be said) that this is no injury to me, inasmuch as I shall bear but a small part of the burden; but this, sir, is to me the bitterest of all reflections.

" Affluence is, on many accounts, an enviable state, but if ever my mind languished for and sought that situation, it is upon this occasion—it is to find that, when I can bear but a small part of this enormous load of wanton expenditure, the misfortune of my being obnoxious to bad men in high authority should extend beyond myself; it is, when I find that those friends whom I respect for their generosity, whom I value for their virtues, whom I love for their attachment to me, and those spirited constituents to whom I am bound by every tie of obligation, by every feeling of gratitude, should, besides the great and important injury they receive in having no representation in the popular legislature of this country, be forced into a wicked waste of idle and fruitless costs, only because they are too kind, too partial to me. This, sir, is their crime; and for their adherence to their political principles and their personal predilection for me, they are to be punished with these complicated hardships."

He concluded by a warning to Mr. Pitt:—

"To the right honourable gentleman over against me I will beg leave to offer a little advice. If he condemns this measure, let him not stoop to be the instrument of its success. Let him well weigh the consequences of what he is about, and look to the future effect of it upon the nation at large. Let him take care that when they see all the powers of his administration employed to overwhelm an individual, men's eyes may not open sooner than they would if he conducted himself within some bounds of decent discretion, and not thus openly violate the sacred principles of the Constitution. A moderate use of his power might the longer keep people from reflecting upon the extraordinary means by which he acquired it. But if the right honourable gentleman neglects his duty, I shall not forget mine. Though he may exert all the influence of his situation to harass and persecute, he shall find that we are incapable of unbecoming submissions. There is a principle of resistance in mankind which will not brook such injuries, and a good cause and a good heart will animate men to struggle in proportion to the size of their wrongs and the grossness of their oppressors. If the House rejects this motion and establishes the fatal precedent that follows that rejection, I confess I shall begin to think there is little to be expected from such a House of Commons. But let the question terminate as it may, I feel myself bound to maintain an unbroken spirit through such complicated difficulties, and I have this reflection to solace me, that this unexampled injustice could never have succeeded but by the most dangerous and desperate exertions of a Government which, rather than not wound the object of their enmity, scrupled not to break down all the barriers of law, to run counter to the known custom of our ancestors, to violate all that we have of practice and precedent upon this subject, and to strike a deep blow into the very vitals of the English Constitution, without any other inducement, or temptation, or necessity, except the malignant wish of gratifying an inordinate and implacable spirit of resentment."

Mr. Pitt in reply had little of argument to allege. He again affirmed that, if the High Bailiff made a return, it would be made with a dead man's hand; he called Mr. Fox "an apostate," and spoke of him as "a candidate whose conduct and principles had rendered him detestable to the public." Mr. Sheridan very properly reprehended Mr. Pitt for his "severity of epithet, redundancy of egotism, and pomp of panegyric upon administration."

The House divided.

> For the motion 117
> Against 195

The High Bailiff was then, upon the motion of Lord Mulgrave, ordered to proceed with the scrutiny with all practicable dispatch. Yet if the House had no right to interfere with the High Bailiff, it is difficult to see how they could be justified in giving him this direction.

The remainder of the history of the scrutiny fully justified those who wished the High Bailiff to act in conformity to all former usage. At the commencement of the year 1785, Mr. Welbore Ellis moved that the High Bailiff should attend at the bar of the House. On inquiry, it appeared that the scrutiny had only been completed in one parish—that of St. Ann. In that parish, Sir Cecil Wray had objected to seventy-one votes, of whom twenty-five were struck off, while Mr. Fox had objected to thirty-two, of whom twenty were struck off. In the parish of St. Martin, where the scrutiny was still proceeding, Mr. Fox had lost eighty, and Sir Cecil Wray sixty votes. Thus in eight months the poll had been only altered by twenty-five votes, while only one-fourth of the electors had been subjected to the scrutiny. At this rate, and with similar results, the scrutiny would still last two years, and Mr. Fox would at the close still have had a majority of upwards of a hundred votes.

At this stage a motion for an immediate return was lost by a majority of nine only, and on the 4th of March, a similar motion made by Alderman Sawbridge was successful. Mr. Pitt having moved as an amendment that the House should adjourn, was defeated by 162 to 124, and the original question passed without a division. On the 5th, Lord Hood and Mr. Fox were returned as members for Westminster.

Mr. Pitt had thus the mortification to see his majority desert him, and public opinion strongly pronounced against him, upon this question. The reputation of the Master of the Rolls as a lawyer suffered greatly, and the "Rolliad," being soon after collected into a volume, was dedicated to Sir Lloyd Kenyon, Bart., Master of the Rolls, and the engraver's likeness of him on the title-page thus celebrated:

> " Behold the engraver's mimic labours trace
> The sober image of that sapient face:
>
> .   .   .   .   .   .

> See him each nicer character supply—
> The post no meaning puckering round the eye;
> The mouth in plaits precise, demurely closed;
> Each order'd feature and each line composed;
> Where wisdom sits a-squat in starch disguise,
> Like dulness couch'd to catch us by surprise."

The whole affair was discreditable to the Minister, who showed himself devoid of magnanimity, and disgraceful to the Crown-lawyers, who endeavoured to substitute chicanery for law.*

Let us now turn to other subjects.

The large majority which the country returned in favour of Mr. Pitt, enabled that minister to carry into effect any plans his understanding could devise for the restoration of the strength of the country from the depression and lassitude of the late disastrous war. Placed in command of a noble though shattered castle, it was his duty to repair the ruins, to plan new works to supply the place of the parts which had been destroyed, and to take advantage of the interval of peace to restore to its pristine strength an ancient and famous fortress.

This task the young Minister performed with great ability.

The state of the nation was one which required all the exertions both of the Minister and of the people. The public debt had increased during the late war from one hundred and fifty to two hundred and fifty millions; commerce had been crippled by severe and repeated losses; the treaty of peace had registered and ratified the losses of the State; thirteen flourishing colonies torn from the parent stem and erected into an independent republic; Minorca, our only colony in the Mediterranean, restored to Spain;

* Adolphus. Lord Campbell: " Lives of the Chief Justices."

losses in the West Indies of great importance—were the symbols of our defeat, and apparently the steps of our decline; yet Great Britain rose from her fall more powerful than ever.

One of the first of Mr. Pitt's measures was a commutation of the duty on tea. He stated to the House of Commons that the quantity of tea consumed annually amounted to 13,000,000 of pounds, while the quantity which paid duty only amounted to 5,500,000 pounds. With a view of defeating the smuggler, he proposed to reduce the duty to twelve and a half per cent. on Bohea teas, and a higher duty on the finer kinds, rising to thirty per cent. on Congou. He reckoned that the produce of the duty would fall from 700,000*l.* to 169,000*l.* The deficit he proposed to cover by a graduated duty on windows, rising up to 20*l.* on a house of 180 windows, in addition to the existing duty on houses and windows. He reckoned the produce at 700,000*l.*

On the 30th of June Mr. Pitt brought forward the budget. The current services of the year he stated to be, navy, 3,159,690*l.*; ordnance, 610,149*l*; army, 4,064,594*l.* The unfunded debt he stated to be 14,000,000*l.* It had been his wish to fund the whole of this sum, but he found the money market would not bear a loan to that extent on good terms, so he satisfied himself with funding 6,600,000*l.* Having then to provide for 6,000,000*l.*, he had settled that the lenders should receive 100*l.* of three per cents., 50*l.* four per cents., 5*s.* 6*d.* of long annuities, and two-thirds of a lottery-ticket. He thus gave five per cent. at present and about four and a half per cent. in perpetuity to the lenders, besides the long annuity and the lottery-ticket. But while Mr. Pitt in this respect followed from necessity, as he alleged, the vicious practice of his immediate predecessors, he did justice in his speech to the true principles of finance.

"It was always his idea that a fund at a high rate of interest was better for the country than those of low rates— that a four per cent. was preferable to a three per cent., and a five per cent. better than a four. The reason was, that in all operations of finance we should have in our view a plan of redemption. Gradually to redeem and extinguish our debt ought ever to be the wise pursuit of Government, and every scheme and operation of finance should be directed to that end, and managed with that view."

Happy would it have been for the country if Mr. Pitt had persisted in these prudent and well-considered opinions. The rest of his long speech related to the taxes. Those he proposed to impose were very numerous and various :— 1, hats; 2, ribbons and gauzes; 3, coals; 4, horses; 5, printed and stained linens and calicoes; 6, candles; 7, licences to dealers in excisable commodities; 8, bricks and tiles; 9, qualifications for shooting; 10, paper; 11, hackney coaches. The whole he estimated at 930,000*l.*

It might have been conjectured that proposals comprehending so many fresh burthens would have afforded a large field for the objections of a leader of Opposition. But Mr. Fox contented himself with praising Mr. Pitt for funding so large a portion of the unfunded debt, and for getting the loan on the best terms he could procure. The only part of the taxes he criticized was the estimate of the produce of the tax upon ribbons.

Mr. Pitt readily acknowledged that Mr. Fox had spoken in a manner perfectly liberal and candid, and professed his desire to give him and the committee every satisfaction in his power.

There was not much discussion afterwards on any of these taxes, but Mr. Fox opposed the Commutation Bill on the ground that it obliged those who did not drink tea to pay for those who did. There was little force in this objection, and on a division the commutation was carried by 143 to 40.

This measure was thoroughly successful.

In the following year the King in his speech from the throne spoke of "the success which has attended the measures taken in the last session towards the suppression of smuggling, and the improvement of the revenue." Subsequent experience justified these congratulations.

In the following year (1785) Mr. Pitt brought forward his famous commercial propositions for regulating the intercourse between England and Ireland. By the settlement recently made, each country was left free to impose any restrictions or prohibitions on the trade with the other, but each was at liberty to trade directly with the colonies and with foreign countries. Mr. Pitt proposed:—1. That the produce and manufactures of America and Africa might be imported through Ireland to Great Britain, paying the same duties hitherto payable on direct importation. 2. That the produce and manufactures of Great Britain and Ireland should not be subject to prohibition on their importation from the one to the other. 3. That the duties on such importation should be the same, and not very high in amount. 4. That Ireland should pay for this advantage by a contribution to the support of the navy.

These propositions were open to different kinds of objection. As propositions for free trade they did not go far enough, for Mr. Pitt relied on the system he seemed to undermine. For instance, he founded the security of our woollen manufacture on the prohibition to export wool. But if the Irish had chosen to import Saxon wool, and to foster their woollen manufactures by bounties, as they had done their linen trade, this security would have been of little value. Mr. Pitt, therefore, in upholding the system generally of prohibition and restriction, cut the ground from under him, and exposed himself to all the narrow objections which were founded on the prevalent notions of monopoly, and the maintenance of the Navigation Act, as the foundation of our commercial and maritime greatness.

In the next place, the proposed plan could not be adopted without binding the Irish to the commercial policy of the empire. And although this would have been a great advantage, both to the empire collectively and to Ireland separately, yet it offended too directly the newly-acquired sentiments of Irish legislative independence to be viewed with favour by the patriots and people of Ireland. They had just acquired the right of wearing a sword, and they were asked to subscribe to a condition to keep it in the scabbard. Thus, this half-measure of Mr. Pitt, which combined principles of free trade with adherence to a system of monopoly, and union in legislation with disunion of legislatures, was exposed to the mingled storm of commercial prejudice, and of national jealousy without any solid footing in liberty of commerce, or consolidation of parliaments. Thus it was that this plan, though framed with the most benevolent intentions, and affording glimpses of the most enlightened views, was opposed by the manufacturing jealousy of England and the susceptible pride of Ireland. A petition from Manchester signed by eighty thousand persons was presented to the House of Commons. The plan was attacked and ridiculed by Mr. Fox, Lord North, and Mr. Sheridan. The Minister, indeed, contrived to carry his resolutions after long debates and frequent divisions.

But when the resolutions went over to Dublin, a fresh flame broke out, and the eruption of the Irish volcano sent forth burning lava over the land.

On the 12th of August, when Mr. Orde proposed to bring in a bill to carry into effect the resolutions, a violent debate arose. Mr. Grattan's speech was one of the finest he ever made.

On a division, Mr. Orde's motion was only carried by 127 to 108. Mr. Pitt considered this majority as not sufficient to ensure the success of the measure. The bill was introduced, printed, and withdrawn.

On the 11th of July Mr. Fox wrote to Lord Ossory:—

" We are going to-day to the last debate of the year. Was there ever a history of folly like this Irish business? When you are in Ireland, you will see the ridicule of this plan to conciliate your countrymen still more strongly."

On the 9th of March, 1786, the House of Commons appointed a committee to examine a report on the annual income and expenditure, and the Committee having reported the chief facts, Mr. Pitt on the 29th brought forward his plan for the reduction of the National Debt.

He began with adverting to the importance of their deliberations, and the extent of the national resources.

" To you do the public turn their eyes, justly expecting that from the trust you hold you will think it your duty to make the most serious efforts, in order to afford them the long-wished-for prospect of being relieved from an endless accumulation of taxes, under the burthen of which they are ready to sink. . . . Yet not only the public of this

House, but other nations, look to the business of this day, for by the establishment of what is now proposed, our rank will be established among the powers of Europe. To behold this country emerging from a most unfortunate war, which added such an accumulation to sums before immense, that it was the belief of surrounding nations, and of many among ourselves, that our powers must fail us, and we should not be able to bear up under it; to behold this nation, instead of despairing at its alarming condition, looking boldly its situation in the face, and establishing upon a spirited and permanent plan the means of relieving itself from all its encumbrances, must give such an idea of our resources and of our spirit of exertion, as will astonish the nations around us, and enable us to regain that pre-eminence to which we are on many accounts so justly entitled."

This extract gives a fair sample of the magniloquent style of Mr. Pitt. Let us now look to his practical measures.

The amount of the revenue, from the 1st January, 1785, to 1st January, 1786, Mr. Pitt stated, from the report of the committee, at 15,397,471*l.* The expenditure he stated at 14,478,181*l.*, including 1,800,000*l.* for the navy and 1,600,000*l.* for the army; but which last sum he hoped, by reductions of the army, to diminish. Deducting the whole of the expenditure from the annual income, there would remain a surplus of 900,000*l.* This sum he meant to raise by additional small taxes to 1,000,000*l.* He proposed to place this surplus of a million in the hands of commissioners, to be laid out annually in the purchase of stock. Mr. Pitt thus stated the expected results of his scheme:

" If this million to be so applied is laid out, with its growing interest, it will amount to a very great sum in a period that is not very long in the life of an individual, and but an hour in the existence of a great nation; and this will diminish the debt of this country so *much as to prevent the exigencies of war from raising it to the enormous height it has hitherto done.* In the period of twenty-eight years, the sum of one million, annually improved, would amount to four millions per annum. Every sinking-fund hitherto established, Mr. Pitt remarked, had been misapplied by the minister of the day, whenever it suited his convenience. This mischief he would for the future prevent by the appointment of commissioners.

"A minister could not have the confidence to come to this House and desire the repeal of so beneficial a law, which tended so directly to relieve the people from their burthens."

Such was the theory and such the promise of Mr. Pitt. Let us now examine the theory and inquire into the practical effects of a measure so pompously proclaimed. The notion of applying a surplus of revenue in time of peace, under the denomination of a sinking fund, in order to expunge a debt created in time of war, was not new or extraordinary. Sir Robert Walpole had extinguished a part of the national debt of his day by means of a sinking fund, until for political reasons he thought fit to suspend its operation. But it is obvious that while at a time when revenue exceeds expenditure, a sinking fund extinguishes debt, yet when expenditure, as in time of war, exceeds income, it can have no such effect. Mr. Fox, with his usual good sense, put the case of a necessity for a loan of six millions when the sinking fund produced one, and he proposed a clause to which Mr. Pitt assented, whereby in such a case the commissioners might lend to the State, and thus, by diminishing the loan to be raised in the market, enable the Minister to obtain the loan on better terms. This clause was afterwards struck out to please the money-dealers, but the reason upon which it was founded is indisputable. The only way in which the debts of a state, like those of an individual, can be extinguished, is by a surplus of income over expenditure. If, for instance, twenty millions are required for the purposes of the State beyond its revenue, there is no advantage in borrowing thirty millions and using ten millions to pay off a former debt borrowed at the same or a lower interest. Indeed, it is probable that this payment, by increasing the amount of loan to be raised, and multiplying transactions in the money-market, will only make the case of the borrower more onerous than it would otherwise have been.* Yet, in this supposed inviolability of the Sinking Fund, working at compound interest, consisted the whole merit and originality of Mr. Pitt's measure. As to the boast that this measure would prevent the debt ever rising, during war, to the height it had previously done, facts have converted these rosy tints of eloquence into the sombre colours of national encumbrance. The American War left this country charged with a debt of two hundred and fifty millions; Mr. Pitt's French war left it indebted to the amount of eight hundred millions. Some advantage was derived by stock-jobbers from the weekly purchases of the Commissioners of the National Debt, but the nation required every year larger loans, and had to pay an additional bonus to the lenders.

On the 12th of February, 1787, Mr. Pitt brought forward

---

* See especially Mr. Hamilton's work on the National Debt, and Lord Grenville's pamphlet on the Sinking Fund.

the important question of the commercial treaty he had made with France. As the measure was one of the most beneficial in its scope and intent which any minister ever proposed, so the speech was one of the most masterly which Mr. Pitt ever pronounced.

He began with contrasting the reception of the treaty with that which had been given to the Irish propositions. On that occasion the propositions were evidently opposed by the manufacturers of this country. But in the present case the manufacturers had taken no alarm. The woollen trade had manifested no species of apprehension. The manufacturers of cambrics, of glass, the distillery, and other members and branches of our domestic trade, though in fact particularly affected by the treaty, had made no complaint, much less had Ministers received notice from the manufacturers of hardware, pottery, and other branches, of any objection. So far were the public from entertaining any dislike or even doubt concerning the merits of this treaty, that from the very best information he could assert, in the presence of many members of the great commercial towns, that they looked with sanguine wishes to the speedy ratification of it.

It would be necessary for the committee to take into their consideration the relative state of the two kingdoms. France had the advantage in the gift of soil and climate and in the amount of her natural produce; Great Britain was, on her part, as confessedly superior in her manufactures and artificial productions. In point of natural produce, therefore, France had greatly the advantage in this treaty. Her wines, brandies, oils, and vinegars were of such value as to destroy all idea of reciprocity. But was it not clear that Britain in its turn possessed some manufactures exclusively her own, and that in others she had so completely the advantage of her neighbour as to put competition at defiance? Having each its own and distinct staple, having each that which the other wanted, and not clashing in the great and leading lines of their respective riches, they were like two great traders in different branches — they might enter into a traffic which would prove mutually beneficial. A market of so many millions of people, a market so near and prompt, a market of expeditious and certain return, of necessary and extensive consumption, thus added to the manufactures and commerce of Britain, was an object to which we ought to look with eager and satisfied ambition. To procure this advantage we ought not to scruple to give liberal conditions.

The surrender of revenue for great commercial purposes was by no means new in the history of Great Britain, but here we enjoyed the extraordinary advantage of having it returned to us in a threefold rate, by extending and legalizing the importation of the articles we most required. Increase by means of reduction, he was obliged to confess, appeared a paradox, but experience had now convinced us that it was practicable. After explaining the commercial provisions of the treaty, Mr. Pitt turned to its political aspect, and thus summed up his policy and his hopes.

" Considering the treaty in its political view, he should not hesitate to contend against the too frequently advanced doctrine, that France was and must be the unalterable enemy of Britain. His mind revolted from this position as monstrous and impossible. To suppose that any nation could be unalterably the enemy of another, was weak and childish. It had neither its foundation in the experience of nations, nor in the history of man. It was a libel on the constitution of political societies, and supposed the existence of diabolical malice in the original frame of man. But this absurd tenet was taken up and propagated—nay, it was carried further; it was said, that by this treaty the British nation was about blindly to throw itself into the arms of this constant and uuiform foe. Men reasoned as if this treaty was not only to extinguish all jealousy from our bosoms, but also completely to annihilate our means of defence; as if by the treaty we gave up so much of our army, so much of our marine; as if our commerce was to be abridged, our navigation to be lessened, our colonies to be cut off or to be rendered defenceless ; and as if all the functions of the State were to be sunk in apathy. What ground was there for this train of reasoning? Did the treaty suppose that the interval of peace between the two countries would be so totally unemployed by us as to disable us from meeting France in the moment of war with our accustomed strength? Did it not much rather, by opening new sources of wealth, speak this forcible language—that the interval of peace, as it would enrich the nation, would also prove the means of enabling her to combat her enemy with more effect when the day of hostility should come? It did more than this; by promoting habits of friendly intercourse and of mutual benefit, while it invigorated the resources of Britain, it made it less likely that she should have occasion to call forth those resources. It certainly had at least the happy tendency to make the two nations enter into more intimate communion with one another, to enter into the same views even of taste and manners; and while they were mutually benefited by the connexion and endeared to one another by the result of the common benefits, it gave a better chance for the preservation of harmony between them, while, so far from weakening, it strengthened their sinews for war.

That we should not be taken unprepared for war was a matter totally distinct from treaty. It depended in no degree on that circumstance, but simply on the watchfulness and ability of the administration for the time being. He had heard of the invariable character of the French nation and of the French Cabinet, her restless ambition and her incessant enmity and designs against Great Britain, and he noticed the particular instance of her interference in our late disputes, and the result of her attack at that time. That France had, in that instant of our distress, interfered to crush us, was a truth over which he did not desire to throw even the slightest veil.

" Oppressed as this nation was, however, during the last war, by the most formidable combination for its destruction, France had very little to boast of at the end of the contest, which should induce her again to enter deliberately into hostilities against this country. In spite of our misfortunes, our resistance must be admired, and in our defeats we gave proofs of our greatness and almost inexhaustible resources, which perhaps success would never show us.

> " ' Duris ut ilex tonsa bipennibus,
> Nigræ feraci frondis in Algido;
> Per damna, per cædes, ab ipso
> Ducit opes animumque ferro.'

" Indeed, whilst he recollected the whole of that dreadful controversy, he could deduce arguments from it to reconcile the present conduct of France with more equitable and more candid principles of policy than gentlemen seemed willing to attribute to our rival. May we not suppose that when France perceived that, in that dreadful contest, when with the enormous combinations of power against us it might be truly said that we were struggling for our existence, we not only saved our honour, but manifested the solid, and he might also be tempted to say, the inexhaustible resources of the land; that reflecting that, though she had gained her object in dismembering our empire, she had done it at an expense which had sunk herself in extreme embarrassment; and reflecting also, that such a combination of hostile power against us, without a single friend in Europe on our side, can never be imagined again to exist; may we not be led to cherish the idea that, seeing the durable and steady character of our strength, and the inefficacy as well as the ruin of hostility, France would eagerly wish to try the benefits of an amicable connexion with us?   It was a singular line of argument which he had heard, and which he saw was also propagated out of doors, that the treaty would prove objectionable, if it should be found that, though advantageous to ourselves, it would be equally so to them. It was ridiculous to imagine that the French would consent to yield advantages without an idea of return: the treaty would be of benefit to them; but he did not hesitate to pronounce his firm opinion, even in the eyes of France, and pending the business, that, though advantageous to her, it would be more so to us.   The proof of this assertion was short and indubitable.   She gained for her wines and other produce a great and opulent market; we did the same, and to a much greater degree.   She procured a market of eight millions of people, we a market of twenty-four millions. France gained this market for her produce, which employed in preparation but few hands, gave little encouragement to its navigation, and produced but little to the State.   We gained this market for our manufactures which employed many hundreds of thousands, and which, in collecting the

materials from every corner of the world, advanced our
maritime strength, and which, in all its combinations, and
in every article and stage of its progress, contributed largely
to the State. France would not gain the accession of
100,000*l.* to her revenue by the treaty, but England must
necessarily gain a million. This could easily be demon-
strated. The high price of labour in England arose chiefly
from the excise, and three-fifths of the price of labour were
said to come into the Exchequer. The produce of France,
on the contrary, was low in the staple, and less productive
to the State in the process. Even the reduced duties were
so proportionably high, that France could not send to us
500,000*l.* of brandies but we must gain cent. per cent. by
the article. In this view, then, though France might gain,
we must be comparatively so much more benefited, that we
ought not to scruple to give her the advantages; and
surely ought not to fear that this very disproportionate gain
could be injurious to us in case of a future contest. It was
in the nature and essence of an agreement between a manufacturing country and a country blessed with peculiar
productions, that the advantages must terminate in favour
of the former ; but it was particularly disposed and fitted
for both countries. Thus France was, by the peculiar
dispensation of Providence, gifted, perhaps, more than any
other country upon earth, with what made life desirable, in
point of soil, climate, and natural productions. It had the
most fertile vineyards, and the richest harvests; the greatest
luxuries of man were produced in it with little cost, and
with moderate labour. Britain was not thus blessed by
nature; but, on the contrary, it possessed, through the
happy freedom of its constitution, the equal security of its
laws, an energy in its enterprise and a stability in its exer-

tions which had gradually raised it to a state of commercial grandeur; and not being so bountifully gifted by Heaven, it had recourse to labour and art, by which it had acquired the ability of supplying its neighbour with all the necessary embellishments of life in exchange for her natural luxuries. Thus standing with regard to each other, a friendly connexion seemed to be pointed out between them instead of the state of unalterable enmity, which was falsely said to be their true political feeling towards one another. In conclusion, he remarked that, with respect to political relation, this treaty at least, if it afforded us no benefits, brought us no disadvantages. It quieted no well-founded jealousy; it slackened no necessary exertion; it retarded no provident supply; but simply tended, while it increased our ability for war, to postpone the period of its approach."

The measure of Mr. Pitt was opposed by Mr. Fox in a speech of great ability. He was supported by Mr. Burke, Mr. Sheridan, Mr. Windham, Mr. Flood, and, in a maiden speech of striking eloquence, by Mr. Charles Grey. The whole staple of their argument consisted of political distrust of France, as a ground for refusing commercial confidence, and what Mr. Burke called a partnership of capital. But the division gave a majority of two to one to the Minister. Happy, had it been possible by this treaty, so wisely conceived and so powerfully defended, to extirpate the animosities it was intended to assuage, and to obliterate those passions of national rivalry which seven years afterwards precipitated the two countries into the most deadly struggle they had ever waged against each other!

On the 27th of February Mr. Pitt brought forward a plan for the consolidation of the several duties of customs, excise, and stamps. These duties were complicated to an incredible extent. Different duties were assigned to pay the interest of various loans ; and articles imported from abroad, being charged with a penny under one act, a halfpenny under another, three farthings under a third, and so on, through twenty or thirty acts of parliament, merchants were unable to tell to what duties their goods were liable, and obliged to rely on the assistance of a clerk of the customs. Mr. Pitt proposed to bring all these various duties upon one article into one integral sum, and so charge the whole debt upon the aggregate of the whole duties to be collected together under the name of the Consolidated Fund. In order to avoid any charge of breach of faith, he proposed to give time to the national creditor, with an option to refuse the new security, and to add to that security the taxes imposed for the service of the year. In order to simplify these numerous duties, no less than three thousand resolutions were required.

Mr. Fox and Mr. Burke gave their hearty approbation to this plan.

Thus, in the course of little more than three years from Mr. Pitt's acceptance of office as First Lord of the Treasury, great financial and commercial reforms had been accomplished. By laying on a sufficient amount of taxes to meet the expenditure of the year, public credit had been raised and confirmed. By just economy a surplus of a million had been secured on the balance-sheet, and this sum had been strictly appropriated to the diminution of the national debt. Commerce and manufactures had been promoted by a treaty with France, founded on principles mutually beneficial. For the further benefit of trade, a dark and confused chaos of duties had been penetrated by the light of order and simplicity. The nation, overcoming its difficulties, and rising buoyant from its depression, began rapidly to increase its wealth, to revive its spirit, and renew its strength.

Such was the work of Mr. Pitt, now no longer the Minister of the Court, but of the nation. The cry of secret influence, and the imputation of his being the organ of an unseen power, was heard less and less as the resources of his powerful understanding developed their energies and ripened their fruits. During this period the conduct of Mr. Fox, though not wanting in ability and in eloquence, betrayed the deficiencies of a mind ready for the debate of the day, but not stored with the reasonings of economical writers, or directed by an enlarged view of the liberal policy of a mercantile people. Whether, while embracing the prejudices of manufacturers, he opposed the Irish propositions, or, while listening to national animosities, he denounced the commercial treaty with France, he displayed on either question a mind whose notions of commerce were erroneous, and whose patriotism fostered national jealousy, in place of cultivating national friendship.

The time was yet to come when Mr. Pitt should sound the trumpet of war to inflame the ancient animosities of two great nations, and Mr. Fox should invoke in vain the sacred principles of peace and goodwill among men.

CHAPTER XXII.

IMPEACHMENT OF WARREN HASTINGS.

1786 — 1787.

MEMORABLE among modern trials is the impeachment of Warren Hastings. For ten years he had exercised supreme power in Bengal. Often opposed, sometimes thwarted, he had contrived to carry his own plans into effect, to dispose of territories, to distribute sovereign power, to aid his friends and depose his enemies with an energy which no man since Clive had displayed. Defeating every effort for his recall, he had voluntarily retired, and on his return to Europe was attended to his vessel by the respect of the native princes, and the attachment of the people at large. But there was one man who had watched his conduct, and for five years had made it his peculiar study. He rose from that study, convinced that Mr. Hastings had overstepped all the limits of conventional law, and broken the bonds of primitive morality. That man was Mr. Burke. He justified his animosity by alleging the patience and perseverance of his inquiries. He was not actuated, he said, by ignorance, inadvertency, or passion. "Anger, indeed, he had felt, but surely not a blameable anger; for who ever heard of a digesting anger, a collating anger, an examining anger, a deliberating anger, a selecting anger?" Yet this plea is not quite conclusive; Mr. Burke kindled his anger by the perusal of bulky documents, and heaped up the fuel of his indignation by poring over a vast mass of dispatches. Governed in a great degree by his imagination, a worshipper of ancient dynasties, and the ceremonies of a national religion, he was inflamed almost to fury against Mr. Hastings, and as eager to punish the violators of an Indian zenana, as he afterwards was to revenge the cause of an insulted Queen. He was accustomed to speak of the followers of Budh, and the worshippers of Vishnu, as he had formerly spoken of the assemblies of New England, and as he afterwards spoke of the ancient nobility of France; the nature of his mind led him to revere institutions, dynasties, and aristocracies, and that which he revered he dressed up in the gorgeous robes of fancy, and worshipped on his bended knee the idol which his own imagination had purified and exalted. With these tendencies of his mind was joined a temper by no means gentle, soon heated by the ardour of pursuit, easily roused to opposition, and scarcely ever softened to forgiveness.

The next chief actor in this matter was a man of extraordinary qualities, and no less extraordinary defects. Richard Brinsley Sheridan represented an Irish family, which, from the days of Swift, was eminent among the aristocracy of talent. He had, at an early age, produced two comedies, which, if not the most skilful in plot, are yet, for brilliancy of dialogue and humour of character (perhaps the chief characteristics of good comedy), the best on the English stage. His own marriage with Miss Linley— beautiful, bright, and gentle, the St. Cecilia of Reynolds— had been a sort of romance in itself. Thus fortunate in literature and love, he still burnt for the distinction of a great orator and successful statesman. Having obtained at some cost a seat in Parliament, he made a speech not altogether adequate to the expectations of his audience.   The thick and indistinct mode of his delivery contributed much to mar the effect of his matter.   After he had spoken, he went up to Woodfall in the gallery, and asked him what he thought of his first attempt.   Woodfall answered, " I am sorry to say, I do not think this is your line; you had better have stuck to your former pursuits."   Sheridan rested his head upon his hand a few moments, and then exclaimed, " It is in me, however, and by G---d it shall come out."   In fact, he soon became a frequent, and even a very brilliant speaker.   It was his habit to prepare much, and sometimes so to cover the texture of his discourse with the embroidery of ornament, that the staple of his argument was concealed in figures and in fringe.   Yet, when Mr. Pitt ventured with juvenile insolence to suggest, that " the elegant sallies of his thought, the gay effusions of his fancy, his dramatic turns, and his epigrammatic point," should be reserved for their proper stage, Mr. Sheridan, after some remarks on the taste of this sarcasm, happily retorted : " But let me assure the right hon. gentleman that I do now, and will at any time he chuses to repeat this sort of allusion, meet it with the most sincere good humour.   Nay, I will say more, flattered and encouraged by the right hon. gentleman's panegyric on my talents, if ever I again engage in the compositions he alludes to, I may be tempted to an act of presumption, to attempt an improvement on one of Ben Jonson's best characters, the character of the Angry Boy in the ' Alchymist.' "*   Yet, like the Wharton of Pope, Sheridan, with the eloquence of Burke, and the wit of Charles Townshend, the husband of a lovely and affectionate woman, the prodigy of his time, forfeited character,

* Moore's " Life of Sheridan."

happiness, and permanent fame for the indulgence of an insatiate vanity, the triumphs of successful gallantry, and the applause of convivial carousers:

> "Though wondering senates hung on all he spoke,
>   The club must hail him master of the joke;
>   Shall parts so various aim at nothing new?
>   He'll shine a Tully, and a Wilmot too."

A character so showy, and a vanity so irritable, could have little in common with Fox, who was always simple, sincere, and in earnest. Accordingly, although they acted for many years together, there never seems to have been a very cordial or intimate friendship between Fox and Sheridan.

While Mr. Fox led the Whigs to the prosecution of Hastings, with the aid of these two eloquent Irishmen, Mr. Pitt was assisted by the advice of a Scotchman, less brilliant as an orator, less accomplished as a scholar, but far more versed in the ways of the world, and fully able to guide the young minister through all the changes and chances of political fortune. Henry Dundas, of the great northern family of Dundas, born in 1742, had served as Lord Advocate of Scotland under Lord North, and adhered to him with unswerving fidelity, until he saw that the American War was a failure, and the Minister was sinking. He then gave it to be understood in the House of Commons, that he should be glad to assist in overthrowing his chiefs. He remained Lord Advocate during the Administration of Lord Rockingham, and was active in support of Lord Shelburne. He endeavoured, as we have seen, to procure for that Minister the support of Lord North, while Mr. Pitt attempted to gain that of Mr. Fox.

Upon the failure of these efforts, he attached himself to

the rising fortunes of Mr. Pitt, and carried to the standard of the young chief not only the experience of a shrewd politician of forty years of age, but a large number of those who had followed Lord North when support of the American War was the road to place and patronage.

He was by nature and constitution a jolly, genial companion in a drinking party; not much attached to any cause, nor very scrupulous, either in public or in private life. Yet no one could deny that he was shrewd, able, and bold beyond any of his contemporaries. Accordingly he appears to have been the only man to whom Mr. Pitt gave his unreserved confidence.

Upon the question of India, Mr. Dundas was thoroughly well informed. In 1782 he had been Chairman of the Select Committee to inquire into Indian Affairs. In that capacity he had made a very powerful speech of three hours, and concluded with moving, " That Warren Hastings, Esquire, Governor-General of Bengal, and William Horneby, Esquire, President of the Council at Bombay, having in sundry instances acted in a manner repugnant to the honour and policy of this nation, and thereby brought great calamities on India, and enormous expenses on the East India Company, it is the duty of the directors of the said Company to pursue all legal and effectual means for the removal of the said Governor-General and President from their respective offices, and to recal them to Great Britain."

Mr. Dundas was now ready to denounce Mr. Hastings or to absolve him, to censure or to praise him, as the interest of the Ministry might require. He was himself at the head of the Board of Control, and he seems to have early perceived the advantage of an intimate union with the Directors, and the benefits to be derived from the rich Iudian patronage. In the mean time, he watched the game of less cautious players, and was prepared to check Mr. Burke or to excite him, to follow Mr. Pitt or to turn him round, with all the dexterity of which his shrewd understanding and cool temper gave him the command.

On the 17th of February, 1786, Mr. Burke commenced his charges against Mr. Hastings, by moving for some papers. Mr. Dundas on this occasion blamed Mr. Hastings, but said he had never been able to affix criminality on his conduct.

Various discussions took place on this and other motions for papers, Mr. Pitt sometimes granting, and sometimes refusing, the documents that were moved for. At length, being repeatedly urged by the friends of Mr. Hastings to bring forward a tangible charge, Mr. Burke, on the 4th and 5th of April, produced articles of impeachment. The principal of these were comprised in what were called the Rohilla charge, the Benares charge, and the Oude charge.

The Rohilla charge was the first considered. The substance of this charge was, that whereas the Court of Directors had directed their servants in Bengal not to engage in any offensive war whatsoever, and had laid it down as an invariable maxim, that they were to avoid taking part in the political schemes of any of the country princes, Warren Hastings, after the most solemn professions, that no object or consideration should either tempt or compel him to pass the political line which the Directors had laid down for his operations with the Nabob of Oude, did nevertheless, in September, 1773, enter into a private agreement with the said Nabob, for a stipulated sum of money, to be paid to the East India Company, to furnish him with a body of troops for the express purpose of " thoroughly extirpating the nation of the Rohillas." That the sole pretext of this agreement was, that the Rohillas owed the Nabob forty lacs of rupees, but that no explanation was asked from them, nor any mediation offered. That the object avowed, and the motives put forth by Warren Hastings for extirpating the Rohillas, were thus stated by himself: " the acquisition of forty lacs of rupees to the Company, and of so much specie added to the exhausted currency of our provinces; that it would give wealth to the Nabob of Oude, of which we should participate; that he, the said Warren Hastings, should be always ready to profess that he did reckon the probable acquisition of wealth among his reasons *for taking up arms against his neighbours;* that it would ease the Company of a considerable part of their military expense, and preserve their troops from inaction and relaxation of discipline; *that the weak state of the Rohillas promised an easy conquest of them;* and finally, that such was his idea of the Company's distress at home, added to his knowledge of their wants abroad, that he should be *glad of any occasion to employ their forces which saved so much of their pay and expenses."* That the said agreement was carried into effect by making war in a barbarous and inhuman manner, " by an abuse of victory," " by the unnecessary destruction of the country," "by a wanton display of violence and oppression, of inhumanity and cruelty," and " by the sudden expulsion and casting down of a whole race of people, to whom the slightest benevolence was denied." That the families of the Rohilla chiefs were reduced to utter ruin, and the country brought to a state of decay and depopulation.

On the 1st of June, 1786, Mr. Burke brought this charge before the House of Commons, and after much discussion upon the form, moved that Mr. Hastings should be impeached for a high crime and misdemeanour. The debate being adjourned, Mr. Grenville on the following day made a set defence of Mr. Hastings. He said that it was necessary for the safety of the Nabob that a frontier territory should be held by a friendly tribe, and not by the allies of his enemies, the Mahrattas; that although the debt of forty lacs of rupees was the cause of war, it was not incumbent on the Nabob to confine his demands after victory to the redress of that grievance; and he quoted to this purpose the peace of 1763, in which we had obtained far more than satisfaction for the frontier dispute which had been the cause of the war.

This sophistry was torn to pieces by Mr. Fox, who made on this occasion one of his most powerful appeals to the principles of justice and humanity. It is said he urged, "That if we guaranteed the Nabob, we are bound to follow him to the extent of what he proposed, and that there was no medium between forfeiting our faith as guarantees, and joining with him in the destruction of the Rohillas. This is, indeed, horrid policy! Instead of acting the part of an equitable umpire and moderator, what is it but to countenance and assert barbarous vengeance and rapacity? . . . A noble lord (Lord Mulgrave) has most sagaciously asked what, in such a situation, is a governor of India to do—is he to consult Puffendorf and Grotius? No; but I will tell him what he is to consult—the laws of nature, not the statutes to be found in those books before us, or in any books, but those laws which are to be found in Europe, Africa, and Asia—that are to be found amongst all mankind—those principles of equity and humanity implanted in our hearts."

With regard to the guarantee, he said: " Sir Robert Barker, who signed the treaty alluded to, had no powers for this purpose. He himself thought it no guarantee. The Board of Directors thought it no guarantee. . . . With regard to the justice of the war, it is impossible, in my opinion, that any human mind can feel that it is not highly unjust in every respect, and in the most extensive degree. No principle that could tend to justify it was ever defended until this period, and that, too, in a British House of Commons! Much difference has arisen about the policy of restricting servants in Asia from entering into offensive war. I must own that I am on that subject entirely of the opinion of the Directors. I think that the reputation of equity and moderation is so necessary to the preservation of our possessions in India, that if the rich dominions of the Rohillas had been annexed to our territory, the acquisition could not have made up for the loss of character we have sustained. I think nothing that was possible to be proposed could make up for it. The principle upon which Mr. Hastings acted was horrible; it was the principle upon which the most insignificant mercenary States form their measures. What a principle for a great nation— the English nation! It was no less than this in the most express terms: You must pay me, and I will exterminate them. This was the language held by the man who was entrusted with the government of the greatest territory belonging to the British empire, or perhaps to any empire: Give me the forty lacs of rupees, and I will break through the orders I have received from my masters, and you shall make use of their army to exterminate the

Rohillas, and take possession of their country."*   Mr. Fox
read letters from Colonel Champion, the agent of Hastings
in the war.   The following are a few extracts :—

"My hands have been tied up from giving protection or
asylum to the miserable.   I have a deaf ear to the lament-
able cries of the widow, of the fatherless, and shut my eyes
against a wanton display of violence and oppression, of
inhumanity and cruelty."—"I could not help compassion-
ating such unparalleled misery, and my requests to the
Vizier to show lenity were frequent, but as fruitless as the
advices which I almost hourly gave him regarding the
destruction of the villages, with respect to which I am now
constrained to declare that, although he always promised as
fairly as I could wish, yet he did not observe one of them,
nor cease to overspread the country with flames till three
days after the fate of Hafez Rhamet was decided. . . . .
The reputation of the British name is in his hands, and the
line which has been laid down for me is clear."†

"'Consider, my friend,' says his Excellency, the Vizier,
repeatedly to Mr. Hastings, 'that it was my absolute
determination to extirpate the Rohillas, and that I requested assistance of the English for that purpose.'

"However well it is known," continued Mr. Fox, "that
his Excellency is equal to the barbarous design for which
he thus publicly and daringly avows that he solicited the
aid of the English, is it possible we can believe that the
respectable gentleman here traduced could have been privy
to so horrid a purpose?   Could he have so entirely overcome the feelings of humanity?   Could he have been so

* "Fox's Speeches," vol. iii. pp. 228-9.
† Extract of a Letter to the Governor-General and Council, dated
Jan. 30th, 1775.

lost to every sense of honour as to prostitute the English troops, and to stain the glory of the British name, by subscribing to a preconcerted massacre? What is not his Excellency capable of advancing? But with regard to all this, the noble lord (Mornington) says he considers Mr. Hastings as not at all blameable; that he did all that was in his power to prevent Sujah Dowlah from behaving with cruelty; but that he could not turn his face against a prince whom he had engaged to assist. Why did he not? The principles of humanity and equity are paramount to all treaties and all ties. He ought to have made use of his power to prevent the violation of the sacred obligations of humanity. Sujah Dowlah and his troops were nothing. It was easily in the power of our people to have put an entire end to their violence, and to have prevented the ravage they made among the Rohillas. Whatever your engagements with any ally, you must never forget the rights of mercy and humanity; and when you find those who are with you unwilling to act their part, you ought to prevent them from making a bad use of the rod you have put into their hands. It is a greater motive for opposing their violence, that you have contributed to put it in their power to abuse victory. But at all times, and on every occasion, you are obliged to do all that is possible for you to do to prevent cruelty.

"I refer not to Puffendorf and Grotius; every man who has the feelings of a man is capable of judging. Does it require any investigation of minute relations in points of justice and equity to decide that you ought to put a stop to cruelty and barbarity whenever it is in your power so to do? These cruelties are not, indeed, chargeable on Mr. Hastings personally; but when I state that he levied an unjust war, he is guilty of the consequences that follow. In the prosecution of a war founded on justice, it cannot be said that we draw upon ourselves the guilt of all the evils that may happen; but it is far otherwise in an unjust war. Having departed from rectitude and justice in the outset, every further deviation, even without our immediate act, is additional guilt heaped upon our heads.

"But it has been said that Mr. Hastings is not liable to be charged with it, as he was at a distance, and could not remedy the evil. Neither is this a true representation. Mr. Hastings had intelligence of the cruelties that were practised, and he did not take the means to put a stop to them which were entirely in his power; he even refused, at the requisition of Colonel Champion, to give relief to the severities which were suffered by that unhappy people; and the reason he gives is, that Sujah Dowlah, if they were to control him, might make that a pretence of refusing the stipulated sum he had agreed to pay. The whole transaction, from beginning to end, was carried on for the purpose of acquiring these forty lacs of rupees—for that sum the character, the dignity, the honour of the English nation, were basely and treacherously exposed to sale."

Mr. Dundas, who spoke after Mr. Fox, maintained that while he still saw reason to blame Mr. Hastings for his conduct to the Rohillas, he saw no sufficient ground for a criminal charge. Since the period of the Rohilla war, Mr. Hastings had been re-appointed Governor-General of India by Act of Parliament, and that act might be considered as a Parliamentary pardon. The recent conduct of Mr. Hastings entitled him to be considered as the saviour of India. After a reply by Mr. Burke, the motion was rejected by 119 to 67.

Mr. Hastings appeared now to be secure. The attack on the Rohillas, their extermination, and the destruction of their country, was a part of the systematic policy of the late Governor-General: it was inconsistent with humanity, subversive of justice, but conducive to the immediate advantage of the Company, and profitable to their pecuniary interests. If such reasons failed to condemn, and such excuses were sufficient to absolve, it might be expected that the remaining charges, founded on similar acts, would meet with a similar rejection. But it was not to be so.

On the 13th of June, Mr. Fox, in a Committee of the whole House, brought forward what was called the Benares charge, and at the close of his speech moved, "That this Committee having considered the third article of charge of high crimes and misdemeanours against Warren Hastings, Esquire, late Governor-General of Bengal, and examined evidence thereupon, is of opinion that there is ground for impeaching the said Warren Hastings, Esquire, of high crimes and misdemeanours, upon the matter of the said article."

The matter of the charge may be thus related:—

Cheyt Sing was Rajah of Benares, a populous, wealthy, and above all a holy city of the Hindus. He had in 1770, through the influence of the Presidency of Calcutta, succeeded to his father as Zemindar upon paying tribute to the Nabob Vizier of Oude, of whom he held in feudal dependence. Afterwards the suzerainty, or sovereignty paramount, was transferred from the Vizier of Oude to the Governor and Council of Bengal. Upon this transfer the privileges of a separate mint, and the judicial power of life and death, were conferred upon the Rajah; Mr. Hastings at the same time proposing, "That the perpetual and independent possession of the Zemindary of Benares and its dependencies be confirmed and guaranteed to the Rajah Cheyt Sing and his heirs for ever, subject only to the revenue paid to the late vizier, &c. That no other demand be made on him, either by the Nabob of Oude or this Government." Afterwards Mr. Hastings obtained the assent of the Council to another article in these terms:—"That while the Rajah shall continue faithful to these engagements, and punctual in his payments, and shall pay due obedience to the authority of this Government, no more demands shall be made upon him of any kind, nor on any pretence whatever shall any person be allowed to interfere with his authority, or to disturb the peace of his country."

These articles seem to have been interpreted by the Rajah as freeing him from all obligations except the payment of the stipulated tribute, and this obligation he punctually discharged. Hastings, on the other hand, looked upon Cheyt Sing as a feudal vassal, liable to any demands of men or money which the exigencies of the lord paramount might enforce. Accordingly he twice demanded fifty thousand pounds to be paid immediately, and at another time a contingent of 2000 cavalry. Upon these demands Cheyt Sing demurred, supplicated, and submitted. He even offered a sum of 200,000*l.* to free himself from these constant exactions. But Hastings told Major Palmer, one of his agents, that he rejected the offer of 200,000*l.* made by the Rajah for the public service; that he was resolved to convert the faults committed by the Rajah into a public benefit, and would exact 500,000*l.* as a punishment for his breach of engagements.

At length, being pressed by the danger of the Mahratta war, Mr. Hastings went himself with a small escort to

Benares. Cheyt Sing hastened on board the pinnace of
the Governor-General, addressed him in a lowly and sup-
pliant manner, and taking off his turban, placed it on the
lap of Hastings. The Governor, no way softened, sent
him away, and the next morning ordered his arrest. The
timid Prince quietly submitted, but the people rose, killed
the Sepoys who guarded the Rajah, and placed the person
of Hastings in great danger. But the Rajah had even at
this moment no other thought than how to escape, and
this he effected by means of turbans tied together, from
the window of his palace. Hastings, on his side, was glad
to escape by night out of the town. But resuming his
pride with his freedom, his exactions did not end here. He
sent an officer to seize a fortress called Bidgigur, where the
wife and mother of the Rajah resided, and where his treasure was kept.

" The castle aforesaid," the charge went on to say,
" being surrendered upon terms of safety, and on express
conditions of not attempting to search their persons, the
women of rank aforesaid, their female relations, and
female dependents, to the number of three hundred,
besides children, evacuated the said castle ; but the
spirit of rapacity being excited by the letters and other
proceedings of the said Hastings, the capitulation was
shamefully and outrageously broken;" the women were
plundered of the effects they carried with them, and their
persons rudely and inhumanly dealt with by the licentious
followers of the camp. The articles of charge proceeded to
recount a second, third, and fourth revolution of Benares,
by which Mr. Hastings set up and deposed at pleasure the
instruments on whose subserviency and servility he thought
he could depend. Mr. Fox having commented on these

various transactions, and concluded with his motion of impeachment, every one was anxious to know the part which Mr. Pitt would take upon the charge.

Mr. Pitt commenced by saying that he would gladly abstain from giving any vote on these proceedings; but as his public situation forbade his taking this course, he had studied carefully the questions involved in the present motion which so deeply concerned the honour and the justice of the House. He then went at length into the relations of feudal dependence both in Europe and in Asia, and concluded that besides the ordinary tribute, Cheyt Sing. was bound to furnish any extraordinary aid which the circumstances of his superior lord might require. So far Mr. Pitt was warmly cheered by the supporters of Warren Hastings, and the majority expected that he would resist the motion. But, to the inexpressible astonishment of the House, he went on to say that all demands of the lord paramount must be limited by reason, and that he thought a fine of 500,000*l.* for not paying a subsidy of 50,000*l.* was exorbitant, unjust, and tyrannical, and he therefore declared his intention to vote for the motion. He made some reserve, however, as to the final vote of impeachment. Major Scott, after this unexpected blow, in vain endeavoured to rally the friends of Mr. Hastings. The Attorney-General and Lord Mulgrave indeed declared their intention to oppose the resolution, but on a division it was carried by 119 to 79.

No further proceedings of consequence took place in this session, but in the commencement of the year 1787, Mr. Sheridan brought forward the Oude charge. This charge was, in the estimation of Mr. Burke, the gravest of all, and he had at first intended to reserve it for himself, but finding

Mr. Sheridan very desirous to have it entrusted to him, he surrendered it without hesitation.

Mr. Sheridan did full justice to the subject. For many weeks he prepared the matter of accusation. He tracked Mr. Hastings through every incident; he guarded every thrust by a refutation of every possible defence.

The charge was in itself a very serious one. The substance of it was that Mr. Hastings, having been disappointed in the amount of money he was able to collect at Benares, made a treaty at Chunar with the Nabob of Oude, by which his mother and grandmother were to be despoiled of their landed property and treasure, in violation of a solemn guarantee given by the Government of Calcutta. This iniquitous object was accomplished by starving two un-happy old eunuchs who guarded the zenana of the Begums. As soon as this robbery was effected, Mr. Hastings shame-lessly violated one of the chief articles of the treaty by which the interests of the Nabob were apparently secured.

On the day fixed for his motion of impeachment, Mr. Sheridan for five hours and a half entranced the attention of the House of Commons. When he sat down an un-usual sign of applause was shown by clapping of hands, not only on the part of members, but of strangers. The testi-mony borne to the merits of this speech by men of the highest authority was no less extraordinary and surprising.

Mr. Burke declared it to be " the most astonishing effort of eloquence, argument, and wit united, of which there was any record or tradition." Mr. Fox is reported to have said that " all that he had ever heard, all that he had ever read, when compared with it, dwindled into nothing, and vanished like vapour before the sun." Mr. Pitt is alleged to have admitted " that it surpassed all the eloquence of ancient and modern times, and possessed everything that genius or art could furnish, to agitate and control the human mind." The Parliamentary history contains neither these tributes, nor any adequate report of this wonderful speech. The following extract will show, however, in what manner Mr. Sheridan could lighten the weight of an elaborate chain of legal argument.

Having referred to an extra-judicial opinion of Sir Elijah Impey: "The Begums being in actual rebellion, might not the Nabob confiscate their property? 'Most undoubtedly,' was the ready answer of the friendly judge. Not a syllable of inquiry intervened as to the existence of the imputed rebellion, not a moment's pause as to the ill purposes to which the decision of a chief justice might be perverted. . . . . It was curious to reflect on the whole of Sir Elijah's circuit at that perilous time. Sir Elijah had stated his desire of relaxing from the fatigues of office, and unbending his mind in a party of health and pleasure; yet wisely apprehending that very sudden relaxation might defeat its object, he had contrived to mix some objects of business to be interspersed with his amusements. He had, therefore, in his little airing of nine hundred miles, great part of which he went post, escorted by an army, selected those very situations where insurrection subsisted or rebellion was threatened; and not only delivered his deep and curious researches into the laws and rights of nations, in the capacity of the Oriental Grotius, but likewise in the humbler and more practical situation of collector of *ex parte* evidence; in the former quality his opinion was the premature sanction for plundering the Begums; in the latter character he became the posthumous supporter of the expulsion and pillage of Cheyt Sing. Acting on an unproved fact, he had not hesitated in the first instance to lend his authority as a licence for unlimited persecution. In the latter he did not disdain to scud about India."*

After a defence of Hastings by Mr. Burgess, Sir W. Dolben proposed an adjournment of the debate, which, although opposed by Mr. Fox, was obviously reasonable. On the next day the debate was resumed by Mr. Francis, who enforced the arguments against the conduct of Mr. Hastings. After Major Scott had spoken in his defence, Mr. Pitt rose. He considered the matter in a light serious beyond description, involving not only the honour and character of the House, but the integrity and reputation of the party accused. He looked upon the charge relative to the princesses of Oude as that which of all others bore the strongest marks of criminality, and he had therefore compared the charge, article by article, with the evidence brought in support of each, and the minutes and papers before the House. With respect to the seizure of the Jaghires, Mr. Pitt thought it was lawful in certain cases to resume landed estates, just as in Scotland the heritable jurisdictions had been resumed. But in regard to the seizure of the treasures of the Begums, on two grounds only could it be justified—that of a legal conviction, or of State necessity. But with regard to the first ground, it must be observed there was no process and no form of trial. With regard to the second, the ground of State necessity, there was no proof; and it was remarkable that the order for seizing the treasure was sent at the same time as the order for inquiry into the facts whereby it might be justified. Mr. Pitt, however, saw no sufficient reason for imputing to Mr. Hastings the cruelty by which the treasures had been obtained from the Begums. He

* " Parliamentary History," vol. xxvi. p. 285.

concluded by blaming some of the means of defence resorted to as unworthy of a great man.

Mr. Fox disagreed only on two points with Mr. Pitt. He thought the false accounts sent home to the Directors by Mr. Hastings, in 1781, highly criminal. Nor could he acquit Mr. Hastings of the charge of cruelty practised by his agents. Mr. Hastings gave order for the plunder of the Begums; he directed it to be carried into effect, and was liable for all that followed. Whoever, in Great Britain, directed a felony to be committed, was answerable for the consequences.

Thus supported, the Oude resolution was carried by 175 to 68. It was now clear that Mr. Hastings was to be impeached.

The subsequent conduct, both of Mr. Pitt and Mr. Dundas, gave strength to the accusers. Mr. Pitt spoke and voted in support of several of the articles of charge; and Mr. Dundas, though he affected to defend Mr. Hastings, suggested to Mr. Burke that he should report the resolutions to the House, so that the impeachment might go to the House of Lords in the beginning of May. This was the sensible suggestion of a practical man of business to an impetuous orator, who might be lost in the wanderings of his imagination, or be carried out of his way by the fervour of his passion. Mr. Dundas' hint was gladly taken.

But Mr. Pitt went a stage further in forwarding the impeachment; for at the beginning of April he suggested that, as the articles of charge contained particulars on which he and others considered Mr. Hastings free from guilt, a select committee should be appointed to prepare articles of impeachment on the articles of charge which had been the matter of debate. This suggestion, though objected to by Mr. Fox, was adopted by Mr. Burke, and on the following day (April 3rd) the House agreed to the resolutions of the Committee of the whole House, that there is ground for impeaching Mr. Hastings on the 3rd, 4th, 5th, 7th, 8th, 10th, 11th, 12th, and 22nd articles of charge. A select committee, consisting of all those who had taken an active part in these proceedings, was appointed to draw up the articles of impeachment.

The world was busy in conjectures upon this turn of affairs.

Such conduct could not fail to excite the anger of Mr. Hastings, and provoke the resentment of his powerful protectors.

The King was known to sympathize with a Governor-General whose arbitrary conduct harmonized so well with his own native disposition. It was believed that the Court had gone so far as to countenance a project for placing Mr. Hastings at the head of the Board of Control, and thus giving to him the government of India, with the private ear of the Sovereign. It was supposed that Mr. Dundas, afraid of this growing partiality, had contrived to throw the weight of Mr. Pitt's influence into the scale of impeachment. He thus, it was said, closed the gateway of power to an inconvenient colleague, or, it might be, a formidable rival. Mr. Dundas, who was certainly very obnoxious to the Court at this time, afterwards gave the stamp of authority to these suspicions, by a declaration he made voluntarily to Lord Maitland, at the bar of the House of Lords. The story is thus told by Lord Bulkeley, in a letter to the Marquis of Buckingham :—" On one of the adjourned questions on Hastings' trial in the House of Lords, Lord Maitland, standing next to Dundas, asked him what he thought would be the result of the inquiry; to which he replied in these words : 'I don't care what is done with him, for you and your friends in Opposition have done our business by keeping him out of the Board of Control.' Lord Maitland on this called up Colonel Fitzpatrick and Dudley Long, in whose presence Dundas actually repeated his words," &c.*

That Mr. Pitt turned the scale against Hastings, and that very suddenly, is a fact which is proved by abundant evidence. Mr. Addington, an attached friend of Mr. Pitt, writing before the Benares charge, tells his brother, " I am convinced Hastings is not blameless ; but I think I see enough to satisfy me that, if there is a bald place on his head, we ought to cover it with laurels."† Yet Mr. Addington afterwards voted in favour of the impeachment.

The suspicion entertained of Mr. Pitt acquires weight from the speeches he delivered on the Benares and the Oude charges. In the eyes of Mr. Fox, Mr. Burke, and Mr. Sheridan, the spoliation of Cheyt Sing and the Begum of Oude were acts of barefaced robbery, which no circumstances could justify. In the eyes of Mr. Pitt, Cheyt Sing was justly required to pay large sums ; but the sum of 500,000*l.* was an excessive and exorbitant fine. Nor did Mr. Pitt deny that the Jaghires of the Begum might lawfully be resumed ; and he entirely acquitted Mr. Hastings of the cruelties by which the women of the zenana were induced to surrender their treasure. Yet, if these topics of defence might be justly urged, were not the friends of Hastings entitled to plead the real and almost overwhelming dangers which surrounded the Governor of

* "Court and Cabinets," vol. ii. p. 154.
† "Life of Lord Sidmouth," vol. i. p. 41.

Bengal, as an excuse for much that was irregular and even violent? Was it not enough to justify Mr. Hastings, that at a moment when a French and Indian alliance had shaken the British power to its foundations, he had restored the tottering edifice, and made it a secure and formidable citadel? Nay, if Mr. Hastings had justly earned the title which Mr. Dundas had given him, of Saviour of India, could he be impeached of high crimes and misdemeanours without a departure from that equitable consideration of great services, shaded by grave faults, which becomes the government of a great empire, and ought to guide the conduct of an impartial House of Commons?

Mr. Hastings had been Governor of Bengal at a critical period. His advocates said truly, that while America, the West Indies, and the Mediterranean beheld the multiplied defeats and losses of Great Britain during the American War, her empire in the East alone was maintained, and even extended, during the progress of that disastrous warfare. Could it be right, then, as a recompense for such services, to impeach him of high crimes, to brand him with the denunciation of the House of Commons, to hold him up as the great delinquent of the age? The man who had lost an empire in the West was an accuser, he who had saved one in the East was a culprit.

> "Ille crucem sceleris pretium tulit, hic diadema."

Notwithstanding this defence, I cannot but think the impeachment of Warren Hastings to have been founded in justice. Had Mr. Hastings, in the course of the struggle, forced Cheyt Sing and the Begums to surrender their treasure in order to prosecute the war, and had he acknowledged the receipt of the money as a ground for future compensation, a generous indemnity and even a national reward might have been the fitting recompense of his conduct. But his whole policy was conceived in an Indian spirit of trick, perfidy, cruelty, and falsehood. His means were violent, his end was subversive of morality. The reputation and power of the British empire were not to be upheld by crimes.

Such was in fact the gravamen of the charges against him; and Mr. Pitt, who had long hesitated and wavered, put the question truly and forcibly on the 9th of May, when the House, on the second reading of the resolution, agreed to in Committee, had to decide whether Mr. Hastings should be impeached.

" The chief point of this mass of delinquency was all which he would touch upon; nor would he go into the articles at any length, having already delivered his sentiments at large upon such of them as he was not anticipated in by gentlemen who thought as he did. In one part of the charge of Benares there was great criminality; in that of the Princesses of Oude there was still more; and that, indeed, he looked upon as the leading feature in the whole accusation. In the charges concerning Furruckabad and Fyzula Khan, there was also much criminal matter. In all of these there were instances of the most violent acts of injustice, tyranny, and oppression; acts which had never been attempted to be vindicated, except on the plea of necessity. What that necessity was had never been proved, but there was no necessity whatsoever which could excuse such actions as those, attended with such circumstances. He could conceive a state, compelled by the necessity of a sudden invasion, an unprovided army, and an unexpected failure of supplies, to lay violent hands on the property of its subjects; but.

then, in doing so, it ought to do it openly—it ought to avow the necessity, it ought to avow the seizure, and it ought unquestionably to make provision for a proper compensation as soon as that should become practicable. But was this the principle on which Mr. Hastings went? No; he neither avowed the necessity nor the exaction; he made criminal charges, and under the colour of them he levied heavy and inordinate penalties, seizing that which, if he had a right to take it at all, he would be highly criminal in taking in such a shape, but which having no right to take, the mode of taking it rendered it much more heinous and culpable. He certainly had no right to impose a fine of any sort on the Princesses of Oude, for there was not sufficient proof of their disaffection or rebellion. And the fine imposed on Cheyt Sing, in a certain degree, partook of a similar guilt, though not to so great an extent; for there the crime was, in his opinion, not so much in the fine itself, as the amount of it, and its disproportion to the circumstances of the person who was to pay it, and the offence which he had committed. But this vindication from one part of the charge, in itself so weak, became, when coupled with other parts, a great aggravation, for when a person on the one hand commits extortion, and on the other is guilty of profusion, if he attempts to screen himself under the plea of necessity for his rapacity, it follows that he is doubly criminal for the offence itself, and for creating the necessity of that offence by his prodigality. And a still higher aggravation arises from the manifest and, indeed, palpable corruption attending that prodigality; to what else could be attributed the private allowances made to Heyden Beg Khan, the minister of the Nabob Vizier, and the sums paid to the vakeel of Cheyt Sing, when it was remembered that the one led the way to the Treaty of Chunar, and the other to the revolution in Benares?"

The motion was carried by 175 to 89, and on the 10th a resolution to impeach Mr. Hastings of high crimes and misdemeanours was carried without a division. It is well observed by Mr. Moore, in his "Life of Sheridan," that "whether Mr. Pitt, in the part which he now took, was actuated merely by personal motives, or (as his eulogists represent) by a strong sense of impartiality and justice, he must at all events have considered the whole proceeding at this moment as a most seasonable diversion of the attacks of the Opposition, from his own person and Government, to an object so little connected with either. The many restless and powerful spirits now opposed to him would soon have found or made some vent for their energies, more likely to endanger the stability of his power, and as an expedient for drawing off some of that perilous lightning which flashed around him from the lips of a Burke, a Fox, and a Sheridan, the prosecution of a great criminal like Mr. Hastings, furnished as efficient a conductor as could be desired."*

How far Mr. Pitt was actuated by such motives as have been alleged, how far he spoke his own sentiments when he condemned Mr. Hastings, cannot be determined. That his censure, and that of the House of Commons, was only equivalent to the finding of a grand jury cannot be maintained. A grand jury hears only *ex parte* evidence against the supposed criminal; his means of defence are reserved for the trial. In the case of Mr. Hastings, the accused made his defence before the House of Commons; Major Scott and others of his friends brought forward every cir-

* Moore's "Life of Sheridan," 4to, p. 322.

cumstance which could justify his policy or palliate his fault. It was after an inquiry spreading over several years, and debates extending through the greater part of two sessions, that Mr. Burke and Mr. Fox, Mr. Pitt and Mr. Sheridan, with the great majority of the House of Commons, came to a resolution to impeach Warren Hastings of high crimes and misdemeanours. There seems no sufficient reason to doubt the justice of a decision by which crimes committed in the East were subjected to a prosecution founded on the general maxims of law, and the eternal precepts of morality.

 THE LIFE AND TIMES OF

CHAPTER XXIII.

AFFAIRS OF INDIA TO 1793.

So much has been said in reference to the government of India, that it may be convenient to pursue the subject to the period of the renewal of the Charter in 1793.

The policy of Mr. Pitt, in respect to the government of India, has been well described by Mr. Mill. In speaking of Mr. Pitt's India Bill, he says, " In passing that law two objects were very naturally pursued. To avoid the imputation of what was represented as the heinous guilt of Mr. Fox's bill, it was necessary that the principal part of the power should *appear* to remain in the hands of the Directors. For ministerial advantage it was necessary that it should in *reality* be all taken away. Minds drenched with terrors are easily deceived. Mr. Fox's bill threatened the Directors with evils which, to them at any rate, were not imaginary; and with much art, and singular success, other men were generally made to believe that it was fraught with mischief to the nation. Mr. Pitt's bill professed to differ from that of his rival chiefly in this very point—that while the one destroyed the power of the Directors, the other left it almost entire. The double purpose of the Minister was obtained by leaving them the forms, while the substance was taken away. In the temper into which the mind of the nation had been artfully brought, the deception was easily passed, and vague and ambiguous language was the instrument. The terms in which the functions of the Board of Control were described implied, in their most obvious import, no great deduction from the former power of the Directors. They were susceptible of an interpretation which took away the whole."*

Whatever might be the motives of the Minister, it was on this foundation that his measures for extending the operation and enlarging the scope of his India Bill were erected.

In 1786 Mr. Pitt proposed that the Governor-General in Council should have the power of ordering any measure to be adopted in spite of the opposition of the whole of his council; who were, however, to be at liberty to record their dissent—in other words, to protest against the decision. He also proposed to enable the Directors and the Crown to give to the same person the powers of Governor-General and Commander-in-Chief. It cannot be denied that these powers gave additional vigour to the Indian Government; but as the Crown would have the nomination of the Governor-General and Commander-in-Chief, they *pro tanto* diminished the influence of the Directors, and their servants in India. It is true that this measure was adopted in accordance with the opinion of Lord Cornwallis, who had recently arrived in India as Governor-General.

A bolder step was taken in 1787. As the Directors hesitated to place on the Indian establishment three regiments, whose services they did not require, Parliament was asked to sanction a measure by which the Board of Control would have the power of adding at will to the military force of

---

* Mill's "British India," vol. v. p. 85.

the Crown in India, and of appropriating every rupee of Indian revenue to such services as they might think useful. It was proposed to do this by a bill declaratory of the meaning of the Act of 1784. It was in vain that Mr. Baring and others declared that the Directors would not have agreed to the Act of 1784 if they had so understood it. The mask had been worn long enough; Mr. Pitt was in haste to throw it aside, and to appear in the character of dictator, which he had unjustly attributed to Mr. Fox. As his followers, however, demurred to taking a road the very reverse of that by which they had been led to victory, the Minister consented to limit his power by three restrictions :—1st. The number of the King's troops in India was not to be increased beyond a certain amount without the consent of the Directors. 2nd and 3rd. No salary and no new pecuniary burthen was to be imposed on the finances of the Company by the Crown without a similar consent. Thus amended the bill passed.

In 1793 the period for the renewal of the Charter arrived. The application of the existing law had been found too convenient to admit, in the opinion of the Ministers, of fundamental change. Mr. Dundas, with an eloquence far inferior to that of Mr. Fox, Mr. Burke, or Mr. Pitt, but with a worldly sagacity superior to that of any one of the three, marshalled in order all the objections, difficulties, obstacles, and complications that lay in the way of either separating the trade from the government, or depriving the Company both of the exclusive trade and of the government. No writer on politics, he said, has thought that an empire can be well governed by a commercial association; no writer on commercial economy has thought that trade ought to be shackled by exclusive privilege. But the wisdom of

Parliament would hardly surrender practical advantages for benefits that may be imaginary, or relinquish a positive good in possession for a probable one in anticipation. The separation of the trade from the government might let in rivals who would disturb our empire; the substitution of Imperial rule for that of the Company might alarm the natives, who, though subject to the supreme sway of the Directors, still obeyed the nominal sovereignty of their own princes. "Would the attempt to unhinge their opinions be liberal, or would it be just? Lord Clive, to whom we owe our empire in India, with a discernment and a wisdom equal to his valour, laid the foundations for consolidating the British power in Asia by entwining his laurels round the opinions and prejudices of the subjugated natives." Whatever may be thought of the metaphors of unhinging opinions and entwining laurels round prejudices, there was much practical sense in this objection to change. He had consulted, he went on to say, Mr. Hastings, Mr. Barwell, Sir John Clavering, Mr. Francis, Col. Monson, Sir William Chambers, and Sir Elijah Impey on the subject of the executive, the judicial, and the legislative powers. Had he found that these able men agreed in opinion, it would have been an inducement to build a system upon them; but from their differences he drew the conclusion that it was safer to rest on the existing system. Proceeding to the Home Government, he frankly avowed that the Court of Directors had often listened to the recommendations of the Executive Government; but he thought that, if the Indian patronage were vested in the Crown, the weight of it would be too great in the balance of our Constitution. Thus cunningly did this sagacious Minister contrive to secure indirectly the patronage of India to himself and his party, while he still frightened the nation with fear of the phantom which had made it rush for safety into the arms of Mr. Pitt. He pointed out the advantages of the Act of 1784: "The Company could no longer oppress the natives by an unjustifiable augmentation of revenue, because the affairs of India were under the immediate control of the Executive power. The Company could no longer augment their investments by despoiling the natives of the fruits of their industry, because the tenures on which the lands were held were rendered permanent, and the taxes on the produce of arts and manufactures were known and fixed. The Company could no longer make war to gratify the avarice and ambition of their servants, because their servants were now made responsible to their superiors, and these to the decisions of a British Parliament. The present system of governing India, both abroad and at home, has been found adequate to the objects both of war and peace."

The rest of this very able speech was devoted to the development and enforcement of these views. Instead of a member of Privy Council, holding some other lucrative office, he now proposed that there should be a permanent head of the Board of Control.

Mr. Francis, in the course of a long speech in opposition to the plan, said, "Look through the whole of the right honourable gentleman's system, and you will see that the pervading essence and principle of it is, in every instance, to divide the ostensible from the real power, and to make one of them a cloak and shelter for the other." These few words convey the whole substance and meaning of the scheme of power of Mr. Pitt and Mr. Dundas.

On the third reading, and on the question that the bill do pass, Mr. Fox opposed it on the ground stated by Mr.

Francis. But the bill was carried, and so long as Mr. Dundas presided over the Board of Control a very effective government was established. Mr. Dundas, by his influence with the Directors, filled up vacancies in the Board from the list of his political friends in Scotland; his political friends become Directors, filled up appointments in India from their own relations and adherents in Scotland. Thus a very able and very harmonious Government was provided; Mr. Dundas could always influence the Directors; the Directors found their authority supported and maintained by Mr. Dundas. The cloak of an independent authority was still worn, but beneath that cloak was the dictatorial power, of which the reality belonged to Mr. Pitt, and of which the odium still clung to Mr. Fox.

In one very important point, however, the system of Mr. Dundas seems to me to have been preferable to that of Mr. Fox. It had been always contended by Mr. Fox that the seat of power must be at home; Mr. Dundas, on the other hand, as early as 1782, had maintained that the appointment of a Governor-General, at once able and honest, was the most efficient mode of correcting the disposition to unjust conquest and corrupt administration in India. When we consider the influence which a local authority must possess at a distance of five months' voyage from the seat of empire; when a decision made at Calcutta in January could hardly be reversed before the following December, if at all, we shall see reason to think that Mr. Dundas was right in his opinion. Nor did experience contradict his theory. In 1785 the office of Governor-General was offered to Lord Cornwallis, a man whose integrity was generally respected, whose military knowledge was considerable, and whose administrative talents were of a very high order. Lord Cornwallis at first refused the office; but early in 1786 he accepted it, and, proceeding to India, remained there till 1793.

Lord Cornwallis acted upon the pacific policy recommended in the Act of 1784; but in 1790 he found it impossible to avoid a war with Tippoo, whose ambition led him to imagine that he could drive the English out of India. General Meadows, who was placed at the head of the army, attempted to signalize himself by a victory; but failing in his management of the war, he was replaced in the following year by Lord Cornwallis himself, who marched to Scringapatam, and signed a treaty under its walls. By this treaty Tippoo agreed to surrender half his dominions, to pay 3,600,000*l.*, to release all his prisoners, and deliver two of his sons as hostages for the due performance of the conditions.

In his internal government Lord Cornwallis detected and punished the peculation and corruption of the Company's servants, especially in the matter of contracts. He set the example of a plain and frugal manner of living. "I am doing everything I can," he says, "to reform the Company's servants, to teach them to be more economical in their mode of living, and to look forward to a moderate competency; and I flatter myself I have not hitherto laboured in vain."*

This is not the place to speak of the Zemindarry settlement, a vast and intricate subject, upon which Lord Cornwallis legislated in a manner which has by turns been lauded as the wisest, and blamed as the most improvident of all modes of dealing with great interests.

Upon the whole, however, there is some reason for the boast

* "Life and Correspondence of Lord Cornwallis," vol. i,

of Mr. Dundas, so far as the Indian administration was concerned. "We never before," he writes to Lord Cornwallis in 1787, "had a Government of India, both at home and abroad, acting in perfect unison together on principles of perfect purity and integrity; the ingredients cannot fail to produce their consequent effects."*

* "Life and Correspondence of Lord Cornwallis," vol. i. p. 280. I should be glad to make many more extracts from this valuable work. Two passages from a letter of Lord Cornwallis I will, however, add :—

"The splendid and corrupting objects of Lucknow and Benares are re-moved; and now I must look back to the conduct of former Directors, who knew that those shocking evils existed, but, instead of attempting to suppress them, were quarrelling whether their friends or those of Mr. Hastings should enjoy the plunder."

"I sincerely believe that, excepting Mr. Charles Grant, there is not one person in the list who would escape prosecution."—Vol. i. p. 306. Such were the evils which Mr. Fox was imprudent enough to endeavour to correct.

CHAPTER XXIV.

PARLIAMENTARY REFORM.

1785.

In 1785 Mr. Pitt brought forward a specific plan of Parliamentary Reform. In the King's speech were these words, which were supposed to allude to that subject: "You may at all times depend on my hearty concurrence in every measure which can tend to alleviate our national burthens, to *secure the true principles of the Constitution,* and to promote the general welfare of my people."* But when called upon to explain the words in question, Mr. Pitt declared they were intended to guard against the introduction of such a measure as Mr. Fox's India Bill. He stated, however, that the Government business of the session would consist of three great measures: 1st. The Irish Commercial Propositions. 2nd. Parliamentary Reform. 3rd. Measures of Finance.

On the 18th of April Mr. Pitt proceeded to explain his plan. It was afterwards more fully developed in a memorandum circulated by Mr. Wyvill and the reformers of Yorkshire. It may be thus described :—

1. That a million sterling should be placed in a fund for the purpose of purchasing seventy-six of the smallest boroughs. Should that number of boroughs not accept the sum assigned as their price, the fund to accumulate at com-

* "Parliamentary History." Journals of the House of Commons.

pound interest till the temptation should be sufficient to ensure sellers.

2. Other sums to be applied to induce ten corporations to surrender their exclusive privileges, and four other boroughs to be induced to give up their privilege of returning members.

3. The seats thus obtained, amounting to one hundred, to be thus distributed. The first seventy-two to be given to counties and to the metropolis. The other eight, derived from small boroughs, to be transferred to Manchester, Birmingham, and other manufacturing towns. The twenty seats in the hands of corporations to be thrown open to the towns to which such corporations belonged.

4. The right of voting in counties to be extended to copyholders. The right of voting in the ten corporate towns, and the new manufacturing boroughs, to be vested in householders.

Such was the plan of Mr. Pitt, framed and matured in concert with the Yorkshire Reformers. It was not a very perfect plan; but was suited to a period when there was little excitement on the subject, when the nation was content with the county representation, and the manufacturing towns were yet insignificant in wealth and population in comparison to their present importance.

Mr. Pitt, in bringing forward his plan, thus defined a representative body: "An assembly freely elected, between whom and the mass of the people there was the closest union and most perfect sympathy." He concluded by asking "leave to bring in a bill to amend the representation of the people of England in Parliament."

Mr. Fox, in supporting the motion, said he should have preferred a general resolution to a specific plan.

Lord North, as usual, opposed any change in the representation. He again called for the petitions from Birmingham and other large towns, and triumphed in the want of any such proof of the wish of the people at large for reform. The old Tories, and a large portion of the Whigs, including the Duke of Portland and Lord Fitzwilliam, threw their weight into the scale against reform.

The motion was defeated by 74, the numbers being 248 against, and 174 for Mr. Pitt's bill.

The most remarkable thing in Mr. Pitt's conduct is that, after having united the members of his Ministry in favour of this plan of reform, having the assistance of Mr. Dundas and the Attorney-General on his own side, and of Mr. Fox and Mr. Sheridan on the other, he never again brought the subject forward. Indeed, no Minister, for forty-six years from this time, introduced any measure of reform. The French Revolution and the panic it caused operated over the larger portion of this period; but how is Mr. Pitt's silence from 1785 to 1792 to be accounted for? The only explanation that can be given is that the country was indifferent, his opponents divided among themselves, and Mr. Pitt himself sufficiently satisfied with the merits of his own Ministry to believe that, so long as he presided over the State, he was himself a security for good measures and popular rights. It will be seen afterwards how Mr. Fox turned this negligence against him. But Mr. Fox and the Whig party are not without their share of blame. Had the Whigs been zealous in the cause of reform, Mr. Pitt would have had no excuse for remaining silent and inactive. It is probable that in that case he would have carried a plan of reform before 1792.

CHAPTER XXV.

MARRIAGE OF THE PRINCE OF WALES.

WE have seen that the Prince of Wales, much to the displeasure of his father, attached himself personally and politically to Mr. Fox. The advantage to Mr. Fox was a very equivocal one, for as the Prince's character developed itself, the qualities of falsehood and duplicity which had been so conspicuous in his grandfather, became but too apparent. His dissolute morals and extravagant expense were common to him with the young men of fashion of the age, and did not impair the popularity in society which his lively conversation and finished manners, added to his youth and rank, were sure to acquire for him.

In the summer of 1784 the Prince fell desperately in love with Mrs. Fitzherbert, a lady whose character was irreproachable, whose beauty was generally admired, and whose disposition was most amiable. She had been twice married, but was still very young. She was a Roman Catholic, sincerely attached to her religion, and not likely to change . her faith from worldly motives. The Prince showed his attachment by every kind of extravagant demeanour. Mrs. Fox, then Mrs. Armistead, who was living at St. Anne's, assured Lord Holland that the Prince often came there to speak with Mr. Fox and her on the subject of

Mrs. Fitzherbert; that he cried by the hour, and testified the vehemence of his passion by rolling on the floor, striking his forehead, tearing his hair, falling into hysterics, and swearing that he would abandon the country, forego the crown, sell his jewels and plate, and scrape together a competency to fly, together with the object of his affections, to America.*   He actually went so far as to stab himself, inflicting a real wound on his breast.   Keit the surgeon, Lord Southampton, Lord Onslow, and Mr. Edward Bouverie went to Mrs. Fitzherbert, told her what had occurred, and said that her presence was necessary to save the Prince's life.   Thus urged, she prevailed on the Duchess of Devonshire to accompany her, and proceeded to visit the Prince at Carlton House.   There she saw the Prince, bleeding from his wound; he put a ring on her finger; but, on leaving him, she protested that she was not a free agent, and on the same day went to Holland, and remained on the Continent for a year.   While abroad the Prince continually wrote to her; and one of his letters alone contained thirty-seven pages of entreaty that she would marry him.   She seems at length to have relented, and to have left the Continent with the intention of consenting to the marriage.

In December, 1785, she returned, and it being rumoured that the Prince intended to marry her, Mr. Fox, unasked, wrote a letter, of which a draft was found among his papers in his own handwriting.   The following is its tenor:—

" Dec. 10th, 1785.

" Sir,—I hope your Royal Highness does me the justice to believe that it is with the utmost reluctance that I trouble you with my opinion unasked at any time, much more so upon a subject where it may not be agreeable to

* " Memoirs of the Whig Party," vol. ii. p. 126.

your wishes. I am sure that nothing could ever make me take this liberty but the condescension which you have honoured me with upon so many occasions, and the zealous and grateful attachment that I feel for your Royal Highness, and which makes me run the risk even of displeasing you for the purpose of doing you a real service.

"I was told just before I left town yesterday, that Mrs. Fitzherbert was arrived; and if I had heard only this, I should have felt the most unfeigned joy at an event which I knew would contribute so much to your Royal Highness's satisfaction : but I was told at the same time that, from a variety of circumstances which had been observed and put together, there was reason to suppose that you were going to take the very desperate step (pardon the expression) of marrying her at this moment. If such an idea be really in your mind, and it be not now too late, for God's sake let me call your attention to some considerations which my attachment to your Royal Highness, and the real concern which I take in whatever relates to your interest, have suggested to me, and which may possibly have the more weight with you when you perceive that Mrs. Fitzherbert is equally interested in most of them with yourself. In the first place, you are aware that a marriage with a Catholic throws the Prince contracting such marriage out of the succession of the Crown. Now, what change may have happened in Mrs. Fitzherbert's sentiments upon religious matters I know not; but I do not understand that any public profession of change has been made : and surely, sir, this is not a matter to be trifled with; and your Royal Highness must excuse the extreme freedom with which I write. If there should be a doubt about her previous conversion, consider the circumstances in which you stand.

The King not feeling for you as a father ought; the Duke
of York professedly his favourite, and likely to be married
agreeably to the King's wishes; the nation full of its old
prejudices against Catholics, and justly dreading all disputes about succession; in all these circumstances your
enemies might take such advantage as I shudder to think
of; and though your generosity might think no sacrifice
too great to be made to a person whom you love so entirely,
consider what her reflections must be in such an event, and
how impossible it would be for her ever to forgive herself.
I have stated this danger upon the supposition that the
marriage would be a real one : but your Royal Highness
knows as well as I, that, according to the present laws of
the country, it *cannot;* and I need not point out to your
good sense what a source of uneasiness it must be to you,
to her, and above all to the nation, to have it a matter of
dispute and discussion whether the Prince of Wales is or is
not married.   All speculations on the feelings of the public
are uncertain; but I doubt much whether an uncertainty
of this kind, by keeping men's minds in perpetual agitation upon a matter of this moment, might not cause a
greater ferment than any other possible situation.   If there
should be children from the marriage, I need not say how
much the uneasiness, as well of yourselves as of the nation,
must be aggravated.   If anything could add to the weight
of these considerations, it is the impossibility of remedying
the mischiefs I have alluded to; for if your Royal Highness should think proper, when you are twenty-five years
old, to notify to Parliament your intention to marry (by
which means *alone* a *legal* marriage can be contracted), in
what manner can it be notified ?   If the previous marriage
is mentioned or owned, will it not be said that you have

set at defiance the laws of your country; and that you now come to Parliament for a sanction for what you have already done in contempt of it? If there are children, will it not be said that we must look for future applications to legitimate them, and consequently be liable to disputes for the succession between the eldest son and the eldest son after the legal marriage? And will not the entire annulling the whole marriage be suggested as the most secure way of preventing all such disputes? If the marriage is not mentioned to Parliament, but yet is known to have been solemnized, as it certainly will be known if it takes place, these are the consequences: first, that at all events any child born in the interim is immediately illegitimated; and next, that arguments will be drawn from the circumstances of the concealed marriage against the public one. It will be said, that a woman who has lived with you as your wife without being so, is not fit to be Queen of England; and thus the very thing that is done for the sake of her reputation will be used against it: and what would make this worse would be, the marriage being known (though not officially communicated to Parliament), it would be impossible to deny the assertion; whereas, if there was no marriage, I conclude your intercourse would be carried on, as it ought, in so private a way as to make it wholly inconsistent with decency or propriety for any one in public to hazard such a suggestion. If, in consequence of your notification, steps should be taken in Parliament, and an act passed (which, considering the present state of the power of the King and Ministry, is more than probable) to prevent your marriage, you will be reduced to the most difficult of all dilemmas with respect to the footing upon which your marriage is to stand for the future; and your children will be born to pretensions which must make their situation unhappy, if not dangerous. These situations appear to me of all others the most to be pitied; and the more so because the more indications persons born in such circumstances give of spirit, talents, or anything that is good, the more will they be suspected and oppressed, and the more will they regret the being deprived of what they must naturally think themselves entitled to. I could mention many other considerations upon this business, if I did not think those I have stated of so much importance that smaller ones would divert your attention from them rather than add to their weight. That I have written with a freedom which on any other occasion would be unbecoming, I readily confess; and nothing would have induced me to do it but a deep sense of my duty to a Prince who has honoured me with so much of his confidence, and who would have but an ill return for all his favours and goodness to me, if I were to avoid speaking truth to him, however disagreeable, at so critical a juncture. The sum of my humble advice, nay, of my most earnest entreaty, is this —that your Royal Highness would not think of marrying till you can marry legally. When that time comes you must judge for yourself; and no doubt you will take into consideration both what is due to private honour and your public station. In the meanwhile, a mock marriage (for it can be no other) is neither honourable for any of the parties, nor, with respect to your Royal Highness, even safe. This appears so clear to me that, if I were Mrs. Fitzherbert's father or brother, I would advise her not by any means to agree to it, and to prefer any other species of connexion with you to one leading to so much misery and mischief.

"It is high time I should finish this very long and,

perhaps your Royal Highness will think, ill-timed letter;
but such as it is, it is dictated by pure zeal and attachment
to your Royal Highness. With respect to Mrs. Fitzherbert, she is a person with whom I have scarcely the honour
of being acquainted, but I hear from everybody that her
character is irreproachable and her manners most amiable.
Your Royal Highness knows, too, that I have not in my
mind the same objection to intermarriages of princes with
subjects which many have. But under the present circumstances a marriage at present appears to me to be the most
desperate measure for all parties concerned that their worst
enemies could have suggested."*

It has been said with truth that this letter, while it discouraged an illegal marriage, tended to favour an illicit
connexion. It must be confessed that Mr. Fox and his
friends were not at all more scrupulous on this head than
Henry IV. of France, Charles II., the Duke of Graf-
ton, Lord Sandwich, and other statesmen of the preceding
age, or the Prince of Wales and the Duke of York of his
own time. The answer of the Prince began in these
words :—

" Carlton House, Dec. 11th, 1785,
Two o'clock, Sunday morning.

"MY DEAR CHARLES,—Your letter of last night afforded
me more true satisfaction than I can find words to express,
as it is an additional proof to me, which I assure you I did
not want, of your having that true regard and affection for
me which it is not only the wish, but the ambition of my
life to merit. Make yourself easy, my dear friend; believe
me, the world will now soon be convinced that there not

* " Memoirs of the Whig Party," vol. ii. pp. 127–135.

only is not, but never was, any ground for these reports which of late have been so malevolently circulated."*

The Prince, as if anxious to avoid the subject, then made an abrupt transition to the apostacy of Eden, and concluded with declaring that he would sink or swim with his friends, and that he would meet Mr. Fox at dinner on Tuesday.

While the Prince was thus practising on the honest credulity of Mr. Fox, he was devising the means of accomplishing his proposed marriage. Mr. Johnes, a clergyman known and respected by Mr. Fox and his friends, received about this time, while he was at dinner with Lord North at Bushy, an invitation to sup with the Prince that evening at Carlton House. Lord North took him aside, and told him the Prince would probably ask him to perform the marriage ceremony. Such turned out to be the fact; but Mr. Johnes, forewarned not only by Lord North, but also by Colonel Lake, with whom he supped that evening in London, refused to comply with the Prince's request.

Nevertheless, on the 21st of December, 1785, Mrs. Fitzherbert was married by a Protestant clergyman to the Prince of Wales. Her uncle Harry Errington, her brother Jack Smythe, Lord Onslow, Lord Southampton, Mr. Edward Bouverie, and Mr. Keit were present. Two witnesses signed their names to the certificate of marriage.

It should be here stated that, by the decrees of the Council of Trent, which are the law of the Roman Catholic Church, marriage is valid in countries where the authority of the Council of Trent is not acknowledged, even

---

* " Memoirs and Correspondence." " Memoirs of the Whig Party," vol. ii. p. 136.

when not performed by a Roman Catholic priest. Thus, although the marriage of Mrs. Fitzherbert was void by the English law, it was sanctioned by the law of her own church, and she could without scruple live with the Prince of Wales as her husband.

In the spring of 1787 it was announced in the House of Commons by Alderman Newenham that application would be made to Parliament for the payment of the Prince of Wales's debts. Mr. Rolle (the hero of the "Rolliad") rose and declared that, if such a motion were made, he would move the previous question, as the proposal "involved matter by which the Constitution, both in Church and State, might be injuriously affected." These words were supposed to allude to a report of the private marriage of the Prince, which had appeared in the newspapers. On a succeeding day, Mr. Fox, who had not been in the House when Mr. Rolle spoke, took an opportunity of noticing the report in question, the truth of which he denied *in toto*, "in point of fact as well as law. The fact not only never could have happened legally, but never did happen in any way whatsoever, and had from the beginning been a base and malicious falsehood." On being further questioned, he declared that "he had direct authority for what he said."

When we reflect that Mr. Rolle had made his allusion some days before, his speech being on the 24th, and Mr. Fox's on the 30th of April—when we consider Mr. Fox's strict veracity and singular caution regarding all matters of fact,—we cannot but arrive at the conclusion that between the 24th and the 30th of April Mr. Fox had received from the Prince the direct authority he asserted himself to have received. We have already seen the terms in which the Prince had contradicted by letter the report of his intended marriage just before its celebration, and he could have little scruple in repeating his falsehood by word of mouth, when the marriage had already taken place.

On the morning after the denial of the marriage by Mr. Fox, the Prince called at the house where Mrs. Fitzherbert was living with a relation. He went up to her, and taking hold of both her hands and caressing her, said, " Only conceive, Maria, what Fox did yesterday: he went down to the House, and denied that you and I were man and wife." Mrs. Fitzherbert made no reply, but changed countenance and turned pale.*

On the same day the Prince saw Mr. Grey, and endeavoured to persuade him to say something in Parliament to satisfy Mrs. Fitzherbert, and take off the edge of Fox's declaration. This Mr. Grey positively refused, saying no denial could be given without calling in question Mr. Fox's veracity, which no one, he presumed, was prepared to do. After some time, the Prince, with prodigious agitation, owned the marriage. He at length put an end to the conversation by saying abruptly, " Well, if nobody else will, Sheridan must." Sheridan accordingly went to the House of Commons, and paid some vapid compliments to Mrs. Fitzherbert, which took away nothing from the weight of Mr. Fox's denial.

On the day after Mr. Fox's declaration, a gentleman of his acquaintance went up to him at Brooks's, and said, " I see by the papers, Mr. Fox, you have denied the fact of the marriage of the Prince with Mrs. Fitzherbert. You have been misinformed. I was present at that marriage."

Mr. Fox now perceived how completely he had been duped. He immediately renounced the acquaintance of

* "Memoirs of Mrs. Fitzherbert," by the Hon. Charles Langdale.

the Prince, and did not speak to him for more than a
year.

The late Lord Leicester (Mr. Coke), who related this
fact to me, told me another anecdote on this subject. Mr.
Fox, as was usual with him, paid a visit at Holkham in the
autumn. Just after his departure, Mr. Coke received a
letter from the Prince of Wales, telling him the Prince
would be at Holkham that day. Accordingly, about seven
o'clock he arrived, and towards eight the company in the
house assembled for dinner. As soon as the dessert was on
the table, the Prince rose, and begged to give a bumper
toast, "The health of the best man in England—Mr. Fox."
Much wine was drunk, and just before leaving the dining-
room, it being then near one o'clock, the Prince again rose,
and again gave, as a bumper toast, "The health of the best
man in England—Mr. Fox." At nine o'clock the next
morning he left Holkham, on his return to London. It
was obvious that the object of the Prince was to find Mr.
Fox at Holkham, and to seek a reconciliation.

Some time after this, when Mrs. Fitzherbert was sitting
down to dinner at the Duke of Clarence's, she received a
note from the Prince, plainly showing that his affections
were estranged from her. He was, in fact, under a new
influence.

The rest of this history : his marriage, the payment of
his debts, his separation from the Princess, the renewal of
his connexion with Mrs. Fitzherbert, and his second deser-
tion of her, are but too well known. Mrs. Fitzherbert
never afterwards spoke to Mr. Fox. Mr. Fox, on his side,
again frequented, again acted with, but never again believed
the Prince of Wales.

There can be no doubt that Mr. Fox had confided too

easily in the asseverations of the Prince. Unfortunately, his declaration in the House of Commons could not be re-tracted without exposing the Prince to the risk of losing his succession to the Crown. Although the marriage was void, the penalty might still attach. Thus Mr. Fox became un-knowingly the organ of an injury to Mrs. Fitzherbert, which he could not afterwards repair.

Mr. Pitt behaved with his usual coolness during these transactions. When Mr. Fox made his declaration, he repeated to his neighbour on the Treasury Bench a well-known line of " Othello."* Mr. Pitt afterwards was a party to the payment of the Prince's debts on condition of his marriage. The Princess Caroline of Brunswick was the victim of these heartless transactions.†

Fortunately for the nation, the marriage of the Prince of Wales and Mrs. Fitzherbert was not cursed with issue. Had a son been born from this marriage, a disputed, or at least a doubtful succession must have been the result; for the Roman Catholic subjects of the Crown were bound to believe in the validity of the marriage, and they might have disputed the binding nature of an Act of Parliament which set aside the legitimate issue of a reigning king. Mr. Fox had done no more than his duty in pointing out these perils to the Prince of Wales; but he did it at the risk of losing the favour of the Prince, and of incurring the lasting re-sentment of his victim.

* " Villain, be sure thou prove my love a whore."
† See " Memoirs of the Whig Party," vol. ii.; and the " Malmesbury Correspondence," for the origin of this marriage.

CHAPTER XXVI.

1788.

In 1788 Mr. Fox made a tour in Switzerland and Italy. Mr. Gibbon notices his visit to Lausanne in these terms: "In his tour to Switzerland (September, 1788), Mr. Fox gave me two days of free and private society. He seemed to feel and even to envy the happiness of my situation, while I admired the powers of a superior man, as they are blended in his attractive character with the softness and simplicity of a child. Perhaps no human being was ever more perfectly exempt from the taint of malevolence, vanity, or falsehood."*

Mr. Gibbon, like Dr. Johnson and Mr. Burke, retained his admiration of Mr. Fox in spite of the most serious differences of opinion; thus, in 1783 he wrote: "I am not sorry to hear of the splendour of Fox; I am proud, in a foreign country, of his fame and abilities, and our little animosities are extinguished by my retreat from the English stage."†

Thus, again, during the storm of the French Revolution, while he dreaded and abhorred the principles professed by Mr. Fox, he writes to Lord Sheffield: "I hope that

* " Miscellaneous Works," vol. i. p. 252.   † Ibid. vol. ii. p. 338.

your abjuration of all future connexion with Fox was not quite so peremptory as it is stated in the French papers. Let him do what he will, I must love the dog."*

On this occasion, after leaving Switzerland, Mr. Fox made a tour in Italy. It appears, from letters written some years afterwards, that he studied the great works of the Italian painters with intense but discriminate admiration.

It was said by his friends, that while on this tour he only once took up a newspaper, and that was to see which horse had won at Newmarket, in a race in which he took an interest.

While engaged in the delights of his Italian journey, and in admiration of Italian pictures and poetry, an express reached him, requiring his immediate presence in England. The occasion was one of pressing and unusual importance.

At the end of the session of Parliament it had been observed that the King's health was visibly impaired. Quiet, abstinence from business, and the medicinal waters of Cheltenham, were prescribed, but without success. His disorder increased, and was perceived to affect his intellects; his public receptions at St. James's were interrupted, and when on the 24th of October he appeared at a levee, his conversation and demeanour left no doubt of the nature of his malady. A violent fever supervened, and for several days his life was in imminent danger. Letters of Mr. Grenville to Mr. Addington, of the 7th, 10th, and 13th of November, represented the state of the King as "most alarming, and giving room for the utmost apprehensions of incurable disorder." "These particulars," Mr. Grenville

* "Miscellaneous Works," vol. i. p. 392.

added, "have been as much as possible concealed from the public."* However, the time was at hand when they could no longer be concealed. Parliament had been prorogued only till the 20th of November, and there was no authority competent to postpone the meeting. When the two Houses met, an adjournment for a fortnight was agreed to, and in the mean time a Privy Council was summoned, at which men of all parties were present, and the physicians who had attended his Majesty were examined upon oath. The physicians all agreed that the King's indisposition rendered him incapable of attending to public affairs. They attributed his illness to a scrofulous habit, which he had driven from his feet to his head by the mode of life he had pursued—too violent exercise, too rigid abstinence, and too little repose. Dr. Addington, Sir Lucas Pepys, and Dr. Willis all expressed a strong expectation of his recovery, on the ground that his illness had not been preceded by melancholy, but declined to fix the time when the cure might be expected. Six weeks was the shortest, two years the longest duration of similar maladies, in cases within their experience.

The course which Parliament ought to pursue in such a case seemed sufficiently clear. The Prince of Wales was now more than twenty-five years of age, and fully competent to exercise the powers of the Regency. The care of the King's person ought evidently to be confided to the Queen, with such a retinue as became his royal state, and such attendance as his melancholy condition required. Instead, however, of making the simple and natural provisions which the inability of the Executive power and the respect due to the Sovereign still on the throne appeared

* "Life of Lord Sidmouth." "Court and Cabinets," &c.

urgently to require, the able men who led the two Houses of Parliament prolonged for three months, while they debated on restrictions, the vacancy of the Executive.

Mr. Pitt's first step was to appoint a committee to search for precedents. It was well known that there was no precedent applicable; various cases had occurred in the disturbed reign of Henry VI., in which each side, as it triumphed in the field, disposed of the royal authority by the law of the strongest. The only case which bore any analogy to the present was that of the Revolution of 1688; and the policy pursued at that time was, as Mr. Grenville justly argued, no guide for the present emergency, it being then the object of Parliament to exclude the former occupant of the throne, and the object of the present time being to secure the resumption of the throne by its acknowledged and lawful possessor.

Mr. Fox, who had now arrived from Italy, at once pointed out that the search for precedents "would prove a loss of time, for there existed no precedent whatever that would bear upon the present case." There was then a person in the kingdom different from any person that any precedents could refer to—an heir-apparent of full age and capacity to exercise the royal power. He went on to declare his opinion in these precise terms :—

"In his firm opinion, his Royal Highness the Prince of Wales had as clear, as express a right to assume the reins of government, and exercise the power of sovereignty during the continuance of the illness and incapacity with which it had pleased God to afflict his Majesty, as in the case of his Majesty's having undergone a natural demise: And as to this right, which he conceived the Prince of Wales had, he was not himself to judge when he was entitled to exercise it, but the two Houses of Parliament, as the organs of the nation, were alone qualified to pronounce when the Prince ought to take possession of, and exercise this right."*

It is said that while Mr. Fox was delivering and enforcing this opinion, the countenance of Mr. Pitt assumed a triumphant smile, and that, slapping his thigh, he exclaimed to a colleague sitting near him, "I'll *unwhig* the gentleman for the rest of his life."

In his public reply Mr. Pitt affirmed that, except by the decision of Parliament, the Prince of Wales had no more right to assume the government than any other individual in the kingdom. Yet Mr. Pitt afterwards allowed that Parliament could not overlook or deny the claim of the Prince of Wales.

It would seem, to common understandings, that, between a claim of right in the Prince of Wales, which could not be exercised by him until the two Houses of Parliament should have pronounced in his favour, and a right of the two Houses of Parliament to name a Regent, which could only be exercised in favour of a Prince of Wales of full age, there was no great difference. Those who concurred in point of constitutional law with Mr. Fox might have admitted that the two Houses should not pronounce in favour of the Prince of Wales until they had secured the King on the throne from any obstacles to the resumption and full exercise of his royal powers in case of his recovery. Those who agreed with Mr. Pitt, on the other hand, might have allowed that, if the choice of the Prince of Wales as Regent was unavoidable, it was expedient not to prolong without

* "Parliamentary History."

necessity the abeyance of the constitutional powers of the Sovereign.

Mr. Fox and Mr. Pitt, however, were both very eloquent, each exceedingly jealous of the other, each leading a great party, and each contending for supremacy.

When the report of the Committee had produced only, as Mr. Sheridan afterwards said, "some bad Latin and bad French," Mr. Pitt proposed to create a power of giving the royal assent by fiction, the Great Seal being the shadow or phantom of the Sovereign. He then brought forward resolutions by which the Regent was prohibited from creating peers, from granting any office in reversion, or for any other term than during pleasure, and from disposing of the King's real or personal property.

Although it was obvious that the object of these restrictions was to secure to Mr. Pitt his Parliamentary position in case of the King's recovery, yet it was equally obvious that such restrictions could be only temporary, and that, were the Prince of Wales once installed as Regent, with Mr. Fox as his Minister, there would be little difficulty in repealing such of them as should prove actual hindrances to the free movements of the Executive. It was equally clear that it was the interest of the Prince to leave to the Queen the entire guardianship of the King's person, and not to incur a suspicion that he either neglected any point of ceremonial respect, or exposed to risk the chances of recovery of his royal father.

These suggestions of common sense were set aside by Mr. Fox and his friends. In one respect, indeed, they showed prudence and good sense. It was rumoured, on the authority of one or more of the Royal Princes, that the Prince of Wales would refuse the Regency if hampered with restrictions. But when the scheme was presented to him in a letter from Mr. Pitt, he indeed protested against the restrictions, but accepted the Regency. On this occasion his answer was drawn up by Mr. Burke, in language simple, but at the same time full of dignity and stately severity. In this answer, the plan proposed by Ministers was represented as "a scheme for disconnecting the authority to command service from the power of animating it by reward, and for allotting to the Prince all the invidious duties of Government without the means of softening them to the public by any one act of grace, favour, or benignity. . . . . The Prince, however, holding as he does that it is an undoubted and fundamental principle of this Constitution that the powers and prerogatives of the Crown are vested there, as a trust for the benefit of the people, and that they are sacred only as they are necessary to the preservation of that poise and balance of the Constitution which experience has proved to be the true security of the liberty of the subject, must be allowed to observe that the plea of public utility ought to be strong, manifest, and urgent, which calls for the extinction or suspension of any one of those essential rights in the supreme power or its representative, or which can justify the Prince in consenting that in his person an experiment shall be made to ascertain with how small a portion of the kingly power the Executive Government of this country may be carried on."

In 1811, when the Regency question was again debated, Mr. Canning, speaking in his own name, gave free scope to those powers of fancy which Mr. Burke, writing in the name of the Prince of Wales, had so strictly restrained. He exclaimed with energy :—

" What! if Lord Wellington, who has displayed so eminently, during the late campaign, those distinguished qualities of a general which he was supposed, but falsely supposed, not to possess, should before the conclusion of the present year exhibit to his admiring and grateful country-men another specimen of those more shining qualities for which he has been uniformly acknowledged to be conspi-cuous, and should terminate a campaign signalized by such consummate · prudence and skill by an achievement more congenial, perhaps, to his nature and habits—a brilliant victory—would I be the man to deny him the well-merited reward of a more exalted rank in the peerage? Or if a gallant admiral, with the characteristic enterprise of his profession, should rush into battle with that animating exclamation with which Nelson led on the battle of the Nile—' a Peerage or Westminster Abbey!'—would I be the man to contend for closing against his hopes one part of that glorious alternative? for leaving him, indeed, the monument to cover his remains if he should fall, but for shutting the ranks of the peerage against his living glory?"*

These are eloquent illustrations of the dicta of Mr. Burke, and yet *pace tantorum virorum,* the restrictions were neither entirely destructive of the power of reward, nor would they have permanently weakened the just prero-gatives of the Crown. Experience, indeed, has proved how vain were these constitutional alarms and these gloomy anticipations. In 1789 the King recovered, and exercised all his royal powers; in 1811 he did not recover, and the

* " Canning's Speeches," vol. iii. p. 93.

Regent, after an interval of suspense, succeeded to the full authority of the Crown. The Regency question affords a pregnant instance of the magnifying power of oratory in the mouths of such men as Fox, Burke, and Canning. The little insects in a drop of water, which fight and perish unknown and unperceived, become, when seen through the glass of the optician, terrific monsters, as fierce as tigers and as large as elephants.

The violence with which Mr. Burke and Mr. Sheridan had urged the claims of the Prince of Wales, disturbed the minds of the sober public. The King began to show symptoms of amendment. At length, after three months of suspense and of contest, news of the complete recovery of the use of his faculties was announced, and the ancient authority of the monarch was re-established amid the general and sincere joy of the whole nation.

Mr. Fox had, as we have seen, made a hurried journey from Bologna to England at the commencement of these transactions; his health suffered from the journey, and from the fatigue of the debates. He added nothing to his reputation, and did not regain popular confidence by the mode in which he put forward the claims of a Prince whose public conduct inspired no respect, and whose private morals were the theme of national reprobation. In reviewing the contest, it must be allowed, that if Mr. Fox had some superiority in point of abstract argument, Mr. Pitt had greatly the advantage in practical results.

The abstract argument of Mr. Fox is thus stated by himself, in his " History of James II. :" " The Whigs, who consider the powers of the Crown as a trust for the people, a doctrine which the Tories themselves, when pushed in argument, will sometimes admit, naturally think it their duty rather to change the manager of the trust than impair the subject of it; while others, who consider them as the right or property of the King, will as naturally act as they would do in the case of any other property, and consent to the loss or annihilation of any part of it, for the purpose of preserving the remainder to him whom they style the rightful owner." Further on he adds: "The royal prerogative ought, according to the Whigs, to be reduced to such powers as are in their exercise beneficial to the people; and of the benefit of these they will not readily suffer the people to be deprived, whether the Executive power be in the hands of an hereditary or of an elective king—of a regent, or of any other denomination of magistrate; while, on the other hand, they who consider prerogative with reference only to royalty, will, with equal readiness, consent either to the extension or the suspension of its exercise, as the occasional interests of the Prince may seem to require." When Mr. Fox had composed these sentences, walking in his garden, he brought them to Mr. Adam, who was then on a visit at St. Anne's, and said, " Here is our case on the Regency."

I confess, however, it does not appear to me that the questions of the Exclusion Bill and of the Regency have that close analogy which in the mind of Mr. Fox they appeared to have. The Duke of York, in the former case, was either to be excluded altogether from the throne, or admitted to reign with limitations and restrictions during the whole period of his life. The disability was permanent, so was the remedy. In the case of the Prince of Wales, the professed object was to impose temporary restrictions for a temporary purpose : if the King were to recover, the Regency would expire ; if he should not recover, the restrictions would fall to the ground.

Mr. Pitt, on the other hand, had the advantage of a practical, and, in the eyes of the country, a laudable, object in view; nor was this all. The broad assertion of a right to the Regency, although qualified by the admission that it could not be exercised without the consent of Parliament, created much apprehension. An expression of Mr. Burke's, that the King had been hurled from his throne by the decree of the Almighty, shocked the loyal feelings of the nation. An assertion of Mr. Sheridan's, that the Prince showed great forbearance and moderation, in not at once assuming the title and powers of Regent, alarmed the friends of legal government. An intrigue by which Lord Thurlow was supposed to be secured to the interests of the Prince, was most distasteful to Mr. Fox. " I have swallowed the pill," he says, in a letter to Mr. Sheridan, " a most bitter one it was; and have written to Lord Loughborough, whose answer of course must be assent. . . . . Pray tell me what is to be done; I am convinced, after all, the negotiations will not succeed, and am not sure that I am sorry for it. I do not remember ever feeling so uneasy about any political thing I ever did in my life."* Mr. Fox was quite right to feel uneasy, and quite right to doubt of the success of this underhand negotiation.

After this discreditable business had proceeded some length, and the Chancellor was supposed to be secured to the interests of the Prince, Lord Thurlow found reason to believe that his safest position was on the side of the King.

* "Life of Sheridan," by Thomas Moore.

He accordingly rose in the House of Lords, and, expressing in solemn terms his gratitude to the Sovereign on
the throne, he ended with the pious ejaculation, " When I
forget my King, may my God forget me !"   Wilkes, who
was standing under the throne, exclaimed to his neighbour,
" He'll see you d——d first !"   Burke, with more decency,
and equal wit, said " The best thing that can happen to
you."   Mr. Pitt was of course informed of the intrigue
which had preceded this pious exclamation, and from this
time had no trust in his Lord Chancellor.

CHAPTER XXVII.

FOREIGN AFFAIRS—INVASION OF HOLLAND BY PRUSSIA—ARMAMENT
AGAINST RUSSIA.

1786 — 1792.

THE Prussian march into Holland in 1786, and the dispute
with Russia respecting Otchakoff are events which have
nearly lost their interest in our times; I shall only notice
them in connexion with the part taken by Mr. Fox in
reference to these transactions.

The French party in Holland, encouraged by the Court
of Versailles, had attained, in 1786, a great pitch of influence, which was exerted against the authority of the
House of Orange, the interests of Prussia, and the friendly
alliance with Great Britain. Fortunately for these Powers,
the French, or democratic party, insulted the Princess of
Orange by stopping her carriage as she was travelling
without an escort from Loo to the Hague. After some
hours' detention, she was allowed to proceed on her journey.
But the King of Prussia felt the insult offered to his sister.
The Minister of England, Sir James Harris, was a man of
singular activity in combining resources, and of remarkable
boldness in making use of them when acquired. Having
the entire confidence of Mr. Pitt, he acted with little scruple,
and no fear.

Instigated by him, the King of Prussia, who had just succeeded to Frederick the Great, demanded four conditions as reparation for the insult to his sister, and means of security for the future. These conditions being peremptorily and even insolently refused, twenty thousand men, under the command of the Duke of Brunswick, invaded Holland. The Duke marched, accompanied by popular favour, to the Hague, and in a short time made himself master of Amsterdam, and dictated terms of arrangement, by which the authority of the Stadtholder was restored and the democratic party effectually restrained. The French Government, finding resistance at an end, submitted, and by a convention with Great Britain, both Powers, all dispute being over, agreed to disarm.

When these transactions were referred to in the King's speech, Mr. Fox warmly and cordially expressed his approbation of the conduct of the British Government. He said he considered the statements made to amount to a public avowal from the Throne, and as public an acknowledgment on the part of the House of Commons, that those systems of politics which had on former occasions been called romantic, were serious systems established on that sound and solid political maxim, that Great Britain ought to look to the situation of affairs on the Continent, and take such measures as should tend best to preserve the balance of power in Europe. Upon that maxim he had founded all his political conduct.

"It was now," he observed, "confessed by Government that it was necessary to come to the lower orders of people, those who were labouring under the heaviest burthens, those who paid for their candles, their windows, and all the various necessaries of life, and say, ' Severely taxed as we know you are, you must nevertheless contribute something towards the expense of keeping political power upon a balance in Europe.' This was open and manly; it was dictated by sound policy. . . . . He took the beginning of the Address, containing an avowal that the situation of affairs in the Republic of the United Provinces seemed likely, in its consequences, to affect the security and interest of the British dominions; and that his Majesty had acted with success upon that circumstance to be the essential substance of the Address, and to that he gave his full assent."*

It will be seen from these extracts how fully Mr. Fox recognised the doctrine of the balance of power as a guarantee for the security and interests of Great Britain. In fact, there are but few and short steps between the maintenance of that balance and the insecurity of our national independence. The balance of power can only be overthrown by the preponderance of one great State; a great preponderant State would threaten the independence of all its neighbours, and Great Britain would only have a choice between submission and war. So that the words " balance of power," which appear to many minds to convey an idle theory, or a flimsy disguise, do in fact mean the maintenance of the liberties and independence of the British people.

Mr. Fox was soon to show how different from support and approbation would be his course when Government interfered in a case in which, in his opinion, the security and interests of the British dominions were not involved. But before we refer to that case, I must not omit to mention, that in the affair of Nootka Sound Mr. Fox

* " Fox's Speeches," vol. iii. pp 331-333.

cordially supported the Minister by voting for the naval armament which was prepared in order to defend British pretensions. Of this dispute with Spain and its conclusion I need say no more. I now turn to the graver affairs of the East.

The Empress Catherine entertained views of ambition in the East which extended to the entire conquest of Turkey in Europe. In a progress she had made to the Crimea, upon an arch under which she passed was placed the inscription, " The road to Constantinople." One of her sons was baptized Constantine. Her conduct towards Turkey was always haughty and aggressive.

The Turks, on their side, apprehensive of attack, had demanded the restoration of the Kuban, which by treaty had been annexed to Russia.

These opposite pretensions led to war between the two empires. The Empress, in 1789, took the fortress of Oczakow, on the Dniester, and proposed to add it to her dominions. At this stage of her conquests Mr. Pitt, interfered, pretended that Oczakow was essential to the security of the Turkish empire, and in conjunction with Prussia prepared armaments to prevent the annexation of that fortress to the Russian dominions.

Mr. Fox viewed the subject in a different light. He considered that the Turks had been in the wrong in the commencement of the war; and he regarded the possession of Oczakow as a matter of indifference to Great Britain.

In pursuance of the policy of his government, Mr. Pitt, at the end of March, 1791, brought to the House of Commons a message from the Crown, stating that the King had hitherto been unable to restore peace between Russia and the Porte; that the consequences which might arise from the prosecution of the war might be highly important to the interests of Great Britain and her allies, and proposing an augmentation of our naval force.

Mr. Fox opposed the address. He maintained that in the war between Russia and Turkey, Turkey had been the aggressor; he suspected that British influence had been used to induce Turkey to attack Russia. He pointed out, that when aggression failed, the party attacked had a right to make conquests in the territories of the aggressor. He considered the terms proposed by the Empress Catherine—namely, to give up everything between the Bug and the Danube, and to retain only her conquests between the Dniester and the Bug—extremely moderate. That country was barren and unprofitable; it contained only one possession of value, which was the fortress of Oczakow, taken by Russia in 1789. We had assisted Russia in 1771, in entering the Mediterranean; how absurd to stop her now, when she was gathering the legitimate fruits of policy we had supported! The advances of Russia towards the south could never, he thought, be injurious to our commerce.

Mr. Burke, supporting Mr. Fox, maintained that the attempt to bring the Turkish empire into the European system was extremely new, and contrary to all former systems of the balance of power.

The address was carried, on a division, by 228 to 131.

On a subsequent division upon resolutions moved by Mr. Grey, the Opposition divided 162 to 254; majority 92.

The unusual strength of the minority induced Mr. Pitt to modify his policy; he instructed Mr. Whitworth not to deliver a menacing note, which had been prepared in the Foreign Office, and in the course of the summer a treaty between Russia and the Porte was concluded, by which the disputed fortress of Oczakow was given up to the Empress Catherine. In the following year this change of policy became the theme upon which the Opposition taunted the Ministry on their feebleness and vacillation. Mr. Fox put the argument with his usual force.

"If it was so important to recover Oczakow, it is not recovered, and Ministers ought to be censured; if unimportant, they ought never to have demanded it. If unimportant, they ought to be censured for arming; but if so important as they have stated it, they ought to be censured for disarming without having gained it. . . . Thus it seems Oczakow was worth an armament, but not worth a war; it was worth a threat, but not worth carrying that threat into execution. Sir, I can conceive nothing so degrading and dishonourable as an argument such as this. To hold out a menace, without ever seriously meaning to enforce it, constitutes in common language the true description of a bully; applied to the transactions of a nation, the disgrace is deeper, and the consequences fatal to its honour.

"I cannot conceive any case in which a great and wise nation, having committed itself by a menace, can withdraw that menace without disgrace. The converse of the proposition I can easily conceive—that there may be a demand, for instance, not fit to be made at all, but which being made, and with a menace, it is fit to insist upon. This undoubtedly goes to make a nation, like an individual, cautious of committing itself, because there is no ground so tender as that of honour. How do Ministers think on this subject? Oczakow was everything by itself; but when they added to Oczakow the honour of England, it became nothing. Oczakow by itself threatened the balance of Europe; Oczakow and honour weighed nothing in the scale. Honour is, in their political arithmetic, a *minus* quantity, to be subtracted from the value of Oczakow."*

Mr. Pitt had brought himself to this dilemma by attaching an exaggerated value to Oczakow, and then parting with this precious jewel for a merely nominal consideration. He cried up the importance of Oczakow, in order to get votes for his armament; and he cried down the importance of Oczakow, because he could not get votes for a war. Lord North, now Lord Guildford, in arguing this question, in answer to Lord Hawkesbury, put this absurdity in a very ludicrous light.

"The noble lord," he said, "with that love of method which distinguishes him, has divided his speech into two parts. The first part was intended to prove that, for the sake of Oczakow, it was right to make great armaments, to incur great expense, and to risk a rupture with an ally. The second part was intended to convince us that, having made great armaments, incurred great expense, and risked a rupture with an ally, it was right to abandon without an equivalent the object for which we had made these costly and hazardous efforts. I admire the method of the noble lord, but I disagree with both propositions."†

But although Mr. Pitt was mistaken in the value he attached to Oczakow, we can hardly assent to the doctrine of Mr. Fox, that the advances of Russia towards the south could never be injurious to our commerce. Even supposing our commerce to comprehend all British interests, which is manifestly not the case, the conquest of Turkey in Europe by Russia would manifestly enable Russian commerce to exclude British trade from some of the fairest and most

* "Fox's Speeches," vol. iii. p. 339.
† From Lord Holland. "Parliamentary History," vol. **xxix.** p. 856.

fruitful territories in the world. But in fact the possession of Constantinople would give to Russia the command of the Mediterranean, and a preponderance in Europe.

It has been absurdly said, that Mr. Fox's opposition to the armament against Russia contributed to the partition of Poland. How can it be shown that if Oczakow had been given up to Turkey, Poland would have been saved? In case of hostilities between Russia and Prussia, indeed, the partition might have been delayed; but that tempting prey would probably have been seized to furnish indemnity for the expenses of the war. If even the terrors of the French Revolution, and the employment of his troops in the invasion of France, did not induce the King of Prussia to let go his hold of Poland, how is it possible to believe that a contest about Oczakow would have prevented that iniquitous bargain?

There is one more topic connected with the Russian armament which bears a relation to Mr. Fox's conduct. Mr. Adair, his friend and follower, had projected at this time a journey on the Continent. He determined in the first place to go to St. Petersburg. Mr. Fox seems to have endeavoured to dissuade him, but finding him resolved, said, " Well, if you are determined to go, send us all the news." Mr. Adair remarked, that his letters would be opened; on which Mr. Fox told him he might use Burgoyne's cypher, and to puzzle them the more, put the figures in red ink. Burgoyne's cypher was a book-cypher used by General Burgoyne and Mr. Fox during the American War. While abroad, Mr. Adair saw some of the principal Ministers of different States, especially at St. Petersburgh, where he was treated with signal honour by the Empress Catherine. He spoke everywhere of the value of an alliance between Austria, Russia, Holland, and Great Britain, as a counterpoise to the power of the House of Bourbon. In short, his foreign politics were those of King William, Lord Godolphin, and the Duke of Marlborough.

From these simple circumstances Mr. Burke built up a charge against Mr. Fox, amounting nearly to high treason. He supposed Mr. Fox to have sent Mr. Adair on a secret mission to Petersburg, without the knowledge of his party or of the Minister. He supposed that Mr. Adair had thwarted some of the objects of a mission of Mr. Fawkener, who was sent to Petersburg about this time. This charge, coined in the umbrageous fancy of Mr. Burke, was revived some thirty years afterwards by Bishop Tomline, who said he could prove the truth of it from authentic documents. But when called upon by Mr. Adair for his proofs, he had none to give. Having no predilection for truth, he had picked up the false charge, and thought to corroborate it by a bold but groundless assertion. Mr. Adair was afterwards employed by Lord Grey and Mr. Canning in confidential missions of high importance, requiring the utmost knowledge, discretion, and prudence. The disordered imagination of Mr. Burke, and the inventive malice of Bishop Tomline, have affixed no stain on a reputation too pure to be affected by such improbable slander.

CHAPTER XXVIII.

THE FRENCH REVOLUTION.

1789 — 1791.

WE approach the portentous period of the French Revolution, and the gigantic wars which were its offspring.

Lord Chesterfield, in a letter written upon Christmasday, 1753, after describing the state of the Court, the Church, and the army in France, uses these memorable words: "In short, all the symptoms which I have ever met with in history, previous to great changes and revolutions in government, now exist, and daily increase in France."*

What were these symptoms? What were the causes which produced the most horrible murders and the most destructive wars at the close of that century, which appeared a few years before to be flowing smoothly on to an age of reason, humanity, and universal benevolence? How came it that the primrose paths of refined society and literary wit should have led to frightful scenes of brutality, massacre, and pillage?

The Court of Louis XIV. had veiled profligacy of moral conduct by a certain decency, much elegance of

* " Chesterfield's Letters."

manners, a noble and polished taste, and, above all, by sincere Catholic faith and a constant outward respect for religion.

The Regent Duke of Orleans and Louis XV., in contrast to this example, abandoned themselves to the coarsest habits of sensuality, and, with cynical contempt for opinion, exposed to the world their own vices and the baseness of their courtiers.

The nobility, too prone to imitate their princes, consumed their lives in scandalous intrigues; and while they maintained privileges that were odious, exhibited to the people conduct that was contemptible. At Paris they passed their time in frivolous dissipation; in their country seats they were seldom seen; in the army alone, when the occasion arose, they showed spirit and courage.

The administration of the country was centralized at Paris. Nothing could be worse than the collection of the taxes and the local distribution of justice. There were no provincial checks of any avail to save the farmer from excessive imposts or the labourer from grievous oppression.* The feeling among the people at large was that of hopeless slavery and interminable poverty.

Among the vices of Louis XV., there were two great scandals—one degraded his society, and the other led to his death. The position of King's mistress was almost an office of state. The prostitute who attained that object of ambition had her place at Court, her part in the politics of the State, her seat at mass and the solemn functions of the Church. Louis raised to that rank one of the most

---

* "L'Ancien Régime et la Révolution," par A. Tocqueville. Alas! no more to be continued. The premature death of this able and virtuous man is a loss for France and for the world.

abandoned women of an infamous class. She was married by his desire to a certain Du Barry, and did the honours of Versailles.

The other favourite and long-continued scandal was the maintenance of a harem, where young girls were secluded for the indulgence of the King's pleasures. One of these young girls, not more than fourteen years old, gave him the smallpox. He became the subject of loathsome disease, and, as his body putrefied, his room was left solitary. He died deserted and despised.

While the courtiers flocked to worship the rising sun, the Dauphin and his young wife, appalled by the magnitude of the task before them, fell on their knees, and prayed, "Help us, O God! for we are too young to govern!"*

Yet the task imposed on Louis XVI., had he been endowed with a mind to imagine great things, and a heart to perform them, was a glorious one. It was true the finances were disordered, the administration corrupt, the manners of the time depraved; but the authority and the example of a virtuous Court, retrenching expenses, punishing corruption, and exhibiting pure moral conduct, might have restored vigour to the monarchy, and effected change without convulsion. The force of public opinion was strong enough to defeat any clamours of the nobility, any resistance of the clergy; and, indeed, the better portion of these bodies —a minority in numbers, but strong in reputation—were anxious to co-operate in just and beneficial reforms.

The King, unfortunately, was born to obey and not to govern. Sometimes following his own benevolent impulses, he favoured a virtuous Minister; then again, deterred

* Madame Campan.

by the interested alarm of the courtiers, he abruptly dismissed the wise reformer, and gave all his confidence to the worthless intriguer. Turgot, an honest economist, was driven away; Necker, a skilful financier, could not hold his ground; Calonne, Lomenie de Brienne, the favoured empirics of the Court, tried in vain, by hollow delusions, to conceal the bankruptcy of the State.

At the end of the American War the finances of Great Britain and France were seriously deranged. In five years William Pitt, by judicious retrenchment, by imposts cheerfully borne, and by allowing the energy of the nation free scope, had restored public credit and confirmed public order. A popular sovereign reigned over a contented people, who filled the public coffers and supported a monarchy which they loved.

In the same five years the Government of Louis XVI., after many changes, and amidst increasing impatience, was brought to the verge of bankruptcy. It was resolved, as a last resource, to summon the States General. This was in effect to call upon the representatives of the people to reconstruct the monarchy. Who in this emergency were the advisers of the monarch? Who were the persons to frame the plan of this vast work? What was the character and state of the nation, whose labour was to raise the edifice?

The Minister of most influence was Necker, placed for the second time in the post of honour and of danger. It was obvious that, after three centuries of disuse, it was the business of a statesman to mark carefully every precedent, and to trace minutely the lines in which the States General were to move. In conformity to the direction given would be the motion of the body now to be stirred from its long repose. If a steady movement towards a defined object could be impressed, the action itself would be smooth and happy; if, on the contrary, a wavering hand and a wandering eye should give the first impulse, the course would be that of a misdirected rocket, deviating to the right hand and to the left, carrying destruction in its path and spreading its flames to those who should preside over its projection.

M. Necker was a respectable banker of Geneva, a philosopher, and a man of business, replete with ingenious schemes of finance, pure in his private life, benevolent in his ends. He might have shone at Geneva as the Minister of Finance of that small republic, but he was not the man to restore and save the monarchy of France. He had neither the imperious will of Richelieu nor the supple dexterity of Mazarin. In counselling Louis he appeared only as the wavering adviser of an irresolute sovereign. Two questions were agitated among the public. Should the representatives of the people be twice as numerous as the members for the nobility and clergy? Should the Commons sit in the same Chamber with the nobility and clergy, or should there be two or three separate orders?

The last of these questions was obviously the most important. The balance of the State depended upon it. Yet Necker left this cardinal problem without a solution. The authority thus abandoned was lost for ever. The National Assembly hastened to seize the sceptre which the absolute King had let fall upon the ground.

We have now arrived at the question, "What was the character and state of the nation whose skill, labour, and patience were to raise the new edifice?"

From the day of the death of Louis XIV., writers of

acknowledged genius and incredible industry had employed themselves in shaking the throne which he had sustained, and undermining the altar which he had revered. Montesquieu proved epigrammatically the evils of despotism and the folly of foreign conquest. Voltaire kept up for fifty years a harassing warfare of essays and jokes against the religion of the State. The lessons of deism which he taught were ridiculed as too narrow by bolder sceptics. Diderot and the whole tribe of Encyclopædists taught their readers to believe nothing, to fear nothing, to hope nothing. The courtiers, the aristocracy, and the higher clergy found an agreeable amusement in reading these light works, and an excuse for their profligate lives in the disbelief of the Divine authority by which their vices were rebuked. They admired Voltaire, they flattered Hume, and took every opportunity of showing their contempt for the religion of Christ. They aimed to be daring and free while the people should continue ignorant and submissive.

Thus the statesmen, the philosophers, and the poets of Pagan Rome derided the belief in the immortal gods. Thus the priests of Catholic Rome whispered, in the days of Luther, in the celebration of the Eucharist, *"Panis es et panis manebis, vinum es et vinum manebis."** Thus Leo X. endeavoured to render the Pontifical Court an academy for the philosophy of Plato.

Following such examples, Voltaire, Hume, and D'Alembert could conceive no better Utopia than a state of society in which the higher classes should enjoy Epicurean contempt of religious obligations, and the lower classes should believe and tremble. But such a partition of the community is happily impossible: that which is to the instructed portion

* D'Aubigné's " History of the Reformation."

of a nation an object of contempt and ridicule, will not long
continue to be to the uneducated portion of it an object of
reverence and of worship.   But the mighty question now
arose, What was to be put in the place of the crumbling faith
of the people?   When the temples of Rome were deserted,
a pure religion and a sound morality took the place of the
ruined shrines and corrupt manners of the heathen world.
When Germany and Great Britain broke the images of
saints and renounced the doctrines of Popery, the Holy
Scriptures were opened to the multitude as the rule of faith
and the guide of life.   But France?

The influence of Voltaire and his coadjutors had been
exerted for no other purpose than to root out what they
considered as the weeds of the social garden—the Christian
religion and its establishments.   The only man who had
attempted to plant a new faith was Jean Jacques Rousseau.
In the indulgence of his speculative talent he had sown the
seeds of a new theory of government, logical, symmetrical,
and impracticable.   Profound reason and unblemished
virtue were presumed to be the probable qualifications of
every man in a vehement, unreasoning, and depraved community.   Yet, to do him justice, he more than once pointed
out that his theories were not suited to France.   He said
they were not suited to a society essentially corrupt and
vicious.   His disciples imbibed his doctrine and neglected
his warning.

Thus led, the multitude followed the guidance of writers
who had no faith in any religion, no experience of any
tolerable government, no principles to direct their reason,
no restraints to curb their passions.   No wonder that
leaders and followers became, as Mr. Burke called them,
the greatest architects of ruin that the world ever saw.

Their very patriotism only led to anarchy. On the night of the 4th of August, 1789, one member of the nobility rose after another to give up some ancient right or some established property. At last some one proposed to give up the privilege of pigeon-houses, and this grave matter of legislation ended in a ridiculous farce. That which might have been done, and ought to have been done with decency and order, became a riotous and precipitate destruction. No gratitude was inspired and no stability was attained.

There was one man, however, who might have reconstructed the monarchy—Mirabeau. Madame de Staël has described him, in her " Considerations," as she saw him on the first day of the meeting of the Assembly :—

" Some nobles had got themselves elected Deputies of the Third Estate, and among them Mirabeau was particularly remarked. The opinion entertained of his talents was singularly augmented by the fear caused by his immorality; and yet it was this very immorality which diminished the influence which his astonishing abilities ought to have obtained for him. It was difficult not to keep one's eyes fixed on him a long time, when he was once seen; his immense head of hair distinguished him from all the other deputies; one would have thought his strength, like that of Samson, depended on it; his face derived expression even from his ugliness; and his whole person gave the idea of power, of irregular power indeed, but still such as one should expect to find in a tribune of the people."* He was marked by the smallpox, which added to his uncouth appearance.

Mirabeau was a man of violent passions, of debauched

* " Considérations sur la Révolution Française," tome i. p. 191.

habits—the product of a despotic court and a corrupt state of society; often imprisoned in the Bastille, constantly involved in debt, running from one mistress to another, the slave of his necessities and his impulses, without fixed principles of any kind, no sense of personal dignity, no scruples, no integrity. But he was a man of genius; he had conceived the idea of a monarchy tempered by liberty, and he was eager to adapt the institutions of England to his own country. He was bold in council, eloquent in the Assembly; he had a natural mastery over the minds of those whom he addressed, and he soon obtained a wonderful ascendency over the people of France. He never yielded his opinion to the vague theories of philosophers, or the senseless clamour of a mob. In his speeches he defended, with admirable reason and force, the royal prerogative of peace and war. He marked with ability and precision the outlines of a representative constitution. He was the true apostle of monarchy as it is understood in England.

The only resource which remained to the King, therefore, when the Assembly had wrested all authority from him, was to make Mirabeau his Minister, and to give him without reserve the confidence of the Crown. Mirabeau alone could have stayed the Revolution. His position as Minister would have been assailed; but his readiness, his eloquence, his intuitive sense of political science, his presence of mind, his boldness, his vast superiority over his rivals, his great popularity, would have sustained him. Unhappily the Court was capable of intrigue, of plots and counterplots, of sudden concessions, and secret reaction; but was totally incapable of a wise and manly resolution. They consulted Mirabeau; they sometimes took his advice; they gave him money to pay his debts; but full and fair confidence they never gave him.

Mirabeau himself aimed at the place of Prime Minister. In describing to M. de Talleyrand the person required for that post, he portrayed exactly a man with his own qualities and powers, eloquent, daring, popular, — "and marked with the smallpox?"—rejoined that subtle wit.

The impediments which prevented the adoption of Mirabeau as Minister lay partly in the characters of the King and Queen, and partly in the circumstances of the time.

Louis XVI. was benevolent in his general views, but without sympathy in his individual nature. He was gross in his habits, low in his appetites, indifferent or irresolute when the moment of a great crisis arrived. When he was stopped at Varennes, and destined to the loss of his crown and his life, he made a hearty meal in the house of the postmaster, and declared that the Burgundy wine was the best he had ever tasted.* When, on the 10th of August, he took refuge from the assaults of the mob in the box of the shorthand writer of the Assembly, while his brave and too faithful Swiss were paying with their lives for their fidelity and his forgetfulness, he was seen eating a copious luncheon, unaffected by the unceasing sound of the cannon and musketry by which his defenders perished.†

The Queen was of another temperament, and of a more lofty nature. The early part of her reign saw her intimate and affectionate with her friends; gay at the small supper, graceful in the ball-room; bright with joy and pleasure; fit to preside over the splendid society she adorned. But

* Carlyle. † Lamartine.

her intimate friends were in their tastes frivolous, and in all grave concerns ignorant; her own reading was confined to novels and romances, and she loved but too well the brilliancy of a sparkling court. When called upon by the dangers of the time to take part in council, it was as if the boat of Cleopatra, with its silken sails and silver oars, had been suddenly carried down the Cydnus into a roaring sea amid the darkness of the tempest, and without a pilot. Her pride of birth and her magnanimous heart would have taught her to perish rather than submit; events she could not control led her to imprisonment, to indignity, and to a scaffold.

The circumstances of the time were unfavourable to the peaceable establishment of a free constitution. A sovereign who has inherited absolute power, and a people who are determined to submit to absolute power no longer, can with difficulty agree, or, if they agree, continue to act in harmony together. A king thus placed considers every concession either as a free grant which ought to produce gratitude and content, or as a robbery to which he is only bound to submit while his hands are tied and his weapons taken from him. In the one case he is disappointed and irritated by fresh demands; in the other, he is always attempting, by secret intrigue, to recover the power which he has publicly surrendered. In the same spirit of uneasiness the people are pushed on by fresh agitators to ask for fresh concessions, and are led by inevitable circumstances to suspect the sincerity of those which have already been made. The necessary prerogatives of a constitutional monarch, the command of the army, the nomination of ministers the appointment of diplomatic agents, the power of peace and war, become so many objects of temptation to the prince, and of alarm to the people.   In fact, the constitutional powers of a limited monarch are too great to be trusted to any one who is likely to abuse them. Confidence in the sovereign, jealousy of his ministers, are the cardinal principles of a representative monarchy.   When confidence cannot be felt, the whole fabric falls to the ground.

It is not a matter of wonder, therefore, that both in England and in France the attempt to convert an absolute sovereign into a constitutional king should have failed. Nor, when we see similar resistance, similar concessions, similar secret protests on the part of princes so different in character as Charles I. and Louis XVI., can we avoid the conclusion that the transition from arbitrary power to limited authority can hardly be accomplished peacefully in the person of the same sovereign.   We see in both instances that the first concessions made led to fresh demands on the part of the people; that the next surrender of pre-rogative was accompanied by a secret intention to with-draw it when the Crown should recover its authority; that this secret intention, known or suspected by the popular party, led to confirmed distrust; and that confirmed distrust produced its natural fruit, in the deposition and death of the sovereign.

Yet there is more than one remarkable difference between Charles I. and his Parliament and Louis XVI. and his Assemblies. The nobility or aristocracy of England carried on the struggle upon the soil of England; some, like the Earl of Sunderland and Lord Falkland, fell in the cause of royalty; others, like the Earl of Essex and Lord Fairfax, aided by such country gentlemen as Hampden and Vane, took up arms for the Parliament. But neither party appealed to foreign aid; and when the royal standard disappeared from the field, the greater part of the Cavaliers returned to their homes, and obeyed, sullenly, perhaps, but quietly, the authority *de facto* of the Commonwealth. The widow of the Earl of Sunderland dwelt undisturbed at Althorp; the Earl of Bedford remained at Woburn Abbey; even the Earl of Derby retained part at least of his great estates; and the widowed Countess, after her glorious defence of the Isle of Man, lived in tranquil retirement. The Earl of Northumberland, not concealing his abhorrence of the trial and execution of the King, yet remained unmolested at Petworth. The Marquis of Hertford and the Duke of Richmond bravely demanded the body of Charles, after his death, and paid the last rites to their unfortunate master. Few followed Charles II. to Madrid, or his mother to Paris. The Ministers of France and Spain remained in London to attend and recognise the Court of Cromwell.

Not so the nobility of France. Although they numbered one hundred and fifty thousand—although they had the monopoly of commissions in the army—although they had vast estates, and the advantage of legality when the King was forcibly removed from Versailles to Paris, and again when he was forcibly prevented from going to St. Cloud,— yet they never raised the royal standard on French territory. They fled early from the contest, and sought at Coblentz the aid and the protection of the ancient rivals and enemies of France. They appeared in the field, not as at Naseby or Worcester, to oppose their own arms to the Jacobin levies, but in the van of the Prussian army, or as the followers of an English admiral.

As I do not pretend to give even an outline of the French Revolution, I shall notice here only some of those events which immediately preceded the great struggle between the stormy surge of Jacobin democracy and the established monarchies of Europe. The madness exhibited on the one side, and the stupidity evinced on the other, left no room for prudence and moderation to prevent the calamities of civil strife and foreign war, which for twenty-three years, with little interval, consumed the energies and wasted the resources of the contending States.

Jan. 28th, 1791.—The King informs the Assembly that the emigrants foment the hostile dispositions of some of the German Princes upon the frontier. The Assembly makes provision for an addition of 100,000 men to the army.

. April 2nd.—Honoré Riquetti, Comte de Mirabeau, dies, exhausted by the disorders of his dissolute life and the labours of his gigantic ambition, at the early age of forty-two. Few men have played so conspicuous a part in the great drama of European history. He was endowed with great talents for government; an eloquence which persuaded, astonished, terrified; a courage which was prompt, firm, invincible; a capacity for the highest positions; a daring will, which was equally fitted to annihilate the petty intrigues of courtiers, and to withstand the rude assaults of the Jacobins. Unhappily, his excesses made him poor, his poverty made him venal, his mind raised him to the skies, his moral character chained him to the earth. The Court, ready to pay him for his services, did not use these services where alone they would be useful, in the highest posts of administration.

On a day in January, after applying leeches, he presided at an evening sitting of the Assembly, bandaged, feverish, and suffering. Dumont, his friend and secretary, says: "At parting he embraced me with an emotion I had never seen in him. 'I am dying, my friend; dying as by slow fire; perhaps we shall not meet again. When I am gone, they will know my value. The miseries I have held back will burst from all sides on France.'"* On the 27th of March he went to the Assembly, spoke five times, loudly and eagerly, and returned to die. Amid wild dreams and frequent delirium, the light of his genius threw its fitful gleams: "I carry in my heart the death-dirge of the French monarchy; the remains of it will be the spoil of factions." When some friend was propping up his head: "Yes, support that head; would I could bequeath it to thee!" He died, and with him the last attachment of the French people, and the last hope of the French monarchy. After him all was suspicion, doubt, fear, panic, cruelty, on the part of the people; degradation, struggle, submission, servitude, agony, on the part of the monarchy.

June 21st.—The flight to Varennes. The King left a declaration, protesting against all acts "emanating from him during his captivity." This captivity was dated by him from the 6th of October, 1789; so that the King disavowed all the acts which he had sanctioned during a period of a year and three quarters. The ostentation with which this secret journey is conducted betrays its purpose, and the King is brought back in triumph to Paris.

It is obvious that there was now but one course for the King and the nation to pursue—that course was for the King to abdicate, and for the nation either to appoint a regency, or to constitute a republic. The virtue of a constitutional monarchy, as we have said, consists in the confidence existing between the sovereign and his people. From the moment when the assent given by the King to

* Dumont, p. 269.

the acts of his parliament or assembly is a feigned assent, to be retracted when opportunity allows, the whole fabric falls to pieces. The King uses the power still left him in preparing means for overthrowing the constitution; and his subjects, in order to deprive him of those means, impose upon him conditions inconsistent with the very existence of monarchy. Such were the relative positions of Charles I. and his parliament after the proclamation of Nottingham; such was the relation of Louis XVI. to his Assembly after the flight to Varennes. The various negotiations between Charles I. and his adversaries could lead to no good result, because the Parliamentary party knew that Charles would not observe the conditions. The decrees passed by the National Assembly could not lead to any real living constitution, because the people of Paris were made aware, by the flight to Varennes, that, in the opinion of the King, the most solemn asseverations were invalid, and the only object on both sides was to be strong. A fair and honest abdication on the part of the King was the only manly part left him; unfortunately, a new party of so-called King's friends had now arisen in the Assembly. Barnave, an eloquent but rash orator, had exclaimed, when the first murders were announced, "Was the blood that has flowed so very pure?" As if the life of the most prejudiced or corrupt citizen were not as much under the protection of the law as that of the purest patriot! This very reckless demagogue had been sent to Varennes to accompany the King to Paris, and had been so much touched by the dignified sorrow of the Queen, that he devoted himself to the defence of a monarch who was no longer defensible. These varying currents of audacity and pity, of ferocity and sentiment, carried the vessel of the State upon the rocks, and finally caused her total shipwreck.

Sept. 3rd.—The Constitution of 1791 is decreed; it rests upon primary assemblies, composed of all men of twenty-five years of age paying three days' wages in taxes. These assemblies elect the electors. A single assembly of 745 deputies, elected every two years, form—with a king, hereditary and irresponsible—the legislature and government of the State.

Sept. 14th.—The King proceeds to the Assembly, and takes an oath to maintain the Constitution. It is neither in his will nor in his power to do so.

Sept. 30th.—The National Assembly, called the Constituent, has its last sitting. It has abolished many abuses, decreed 2500 laws, done much to promote anarchy, and entirely failed in combining liberty with order; neither liberty nor order exists in France.

CHAPTER XXIX.

THE FRENCH REVOLUTION AND THE CONTINENT.

1792.

THE Constitution of 1791 was not made to endure. It was sure to fall either by the will of the King, recovering his power, and unable to bear its restraints, or by the impatience of the people, eager to break down the barrier which still separated the mock monarchy from a republic. In either case, foreign powers might have awaited in security the ultimate development of these mighty throes. If the King had regained some of his authority, a limited or absolute monarchy might have been the result. If he had been set aside, the republic would have been too weak to endure or to have given confidence at home or abroad. A Cromwell would probably have seized the rule of the State, and restored order to the nation and vigour to the Executive power.

Besides these obvious probabilities, other reasons should have inclined the great European Powers to refrain from interference in the affairs of France. A high pitch of enthusiasm inspired twenty-five millions of her people; a menace by foreign governments, and still more an invasion by foreign troops, would be sure to inflame, to excite, and to madden their minds. The axe and the sword would both be sharpened—the one against the domestic, the other against the foreign enemy. Neutrality would lead to suspicion, suspicion to proscription, and proscription to death. Any one who spoke of moderation and reason would be denounced as an accomplice of the hated foe. On the other hand, disaffection would cease on the appearance of a German manifesto; those most averse to democracy would prefer a national republic to subjugation by the arms of Austria and Prussia. Between anarchy and foreign conquest the choice might be hard, but the high-spirited and courageous people of France would never hesitate. In the fervour of vindicated freedom, in the belief that they were the first country in the world, the nation would haughtily refuse to be trampled under the feet of Croat hussars and Prussian grenadiers.

Nor were there wanting historical examples to deter the absolute sovereigns of Europe from attacking France. Machiavel, in his admirable " Discourses," has thus referred to one of these examples: "There was such disunion in the Roman republic between the people and the nobility, that the inhabitants of Veii, together with the Etruscans, thought they could extinguish the Roman name." He goes on to relate that the Romans "who were disunited became united, and engaging the enemy, defeated and routed them." He ends with the prediction, "And so for the future will be deceived whoever in a similar way and for a similar cause shall think to oppress a nation."*

On the other hand, a contrary conduct had been successful. In the seventeenth century, the people of England went to war with their King, defeated him, and put him to death on the scaffold. No foreign powers attempted to

* " Discorsi."

espouse the cause of monarchy—on the contrary, France and Spain, the two most powerful of the States of Europe, vied with each other in courting the chief of the Commonwealth,* and the English nation, left to themselves, at their own time, by their own army and their own Parliament, restored hereditary monarchy.

Deaf to the counsels of reason and experience, the Emperor of Germany and the King of Prussia determined to extinguish with a few buckets of water the great conflagration which overspread France.   The French emigrants who had left their native country assembled at Coblentz, and raised among themselves an armed body of 20,000 men. The Government of France informed the Elector of Trèves that the King would consider as hostile to himself any collection or assembling of troops on the French frontier.

But the whole provocation did not arise from the conduct of the emigrants or of the German princes.   At the beginning of December, 1790, Louis had written a letter addressed to the Emperor of Germany, the Empress of Russia, the King of Prussia, the King of Spain, and the King of Sweden, suggesting the convocation of a Congress of the principal sovereigns of Europe, supported by an armed force, as the best means of establishing order in France, and preventing the contagion of dangerous principles.

This step, so much at variance with the public declarations of the King of France, justifies in a great degree the suspicions of his sincerity entertained by his people.   The declaration he left behind him on his flight to Varennes was a more patent proof that his assent to the laws of the Assembly was considered by him as violent and void.

* Guizot's " Histoire de la Révolution d'Angleterre."

In August, 1791, the Emperor of Germany and King of
Prussia met at Pilnitz to consider the affairs of France and of
Poland.   With regard to Poland, the penalty for her maintenance of independence was partition; with regard to France,
the inclination was similar, but the power not so clear. The
two Sovereigns therefore contented themselves with issuing
a declaration to the effect that they were desirous to co-
operate in efficacious measures to enable the King of France
to consolidate in perfect liberty a monarchical government
suited to conciliate the rights of sovereigns and the welfare
of the French people.

. In February, 1792, a treaty, miscalled defensive, was
signed by Austria and Prussia, with the view, it was alleged,
of putting an end to the troubles of France and Poland.
The Empress of Russia was invited to accede to this
treaty.

The pretext of this alliance was to restore the King of
France to liberty, that he might confer upon his subjects
the constitution he might think fit.   But it was clear that
the King, who was at that time the helpless tool of the
Jacobin club, would not have regained his liberty by being
made the instrument of the emigrant nobility and of two
German sovereigns.   The nation was not to be consulted.

France could not await patiently such a fate.   Accordingly, on the 20th of April, 1792, the King, by the advice
of his Ministers, proposed to the National Assembly a
declaration of war against Francis I., King of Hungary and
Bohemia.   After two hours' debate in an evening sitting,
the decree was adopted, almost with unanimity.

From this date began the fearful struggle between the
democracy of France and the despotic sovereigns of Ger-

many, which first deluged France with blood, and then overspread all Europe with its fearful devastations. The minor causes of war alleged by the two parties, the confiscation of the feudal property of German princes in France, the opening of the Scheldt, the seizure of Avignon, the conquest of Savoy, the withdrawal of ambassadors, were mere pretexts. France had resolved to have a Republican Constitution, with or without a Royal President; the absolute sovereigns of Europe determined to put down by force the popular will of France. Hence the war terminated by the treaty of Luneville and the peace of Amiens. France, in her turn, having won that wager of battle, endeavoured to impose her will upon all Europe. Hence the war, which was closed by the abdication of Napoleon and the Treaty of Paris.

It is melancholy to consider that the blood which flowed and the treasures which were expended in this double war might have been saved, and the people of Europe during this period might have advanced in all the arts, comforts, and enjoyments of civilized life. Kings and nations alike engaged in a contest which the event proved to have been unnecessary.

Hitherto the leaders of the working population of Paris had contented themselves with prescribing indirectly through the Legislative Assembly, the Municipal Council, and the Jacobin Club, the measures to be adopted. But as the danger approached, a more direct dictation was thought necessary; accordingly, on the 20th of June an immense crowd marched towards the Palace of the Tuileries. The King directed that no resistance should be made, and when the masses approached his own apartments, he ordered the door to be thrown open, and presented himself unarmed

before them.   For six hours the collected mob marched
through the Royal presence-chamber; one of them offered
him a red cap, the uniform of the Jacobins, which the King
accepted and wore.   Seated at a table, he saw the multitude pass before him, himself the humiliated and degraded
image of a royalty which had departed.

One of the cries of the day was " Down with the *veto !*
Sanction the Decrees!"   Among the many absurdities of
the Constitution of 1791 was the suspensive veto given to
the Sovereign.   With harmony between the King and the
Legislative Assembly, a veto would be a vain form, but in
times of revolution it was a mode of arming the King with
a foil to enable him to contend against an adversary with
a sword.   The moment the unfortunate Louis attempted
to exercise his constitutional right, the moment he showed
his sincerity and honesty, he was denounced as a traitor to
the nation by the press and the clubs of Paris.

La Fayette at this crisis attempted to save the King
by offering to conduct him to Compiègne, to surround him
with a faithful army, and to call for obedience to the Sovereign in the name of the Constitution and the law.   But
the courtiers could not bear the name of the Constitution,
and vainly flattering themselves with emancipation from all
ties, all promises, and all restrictions, prevailed on the
wavering monarch to reject this manly and patriotic
advice.   The last chance of safety was thrown away by
the Court.

June 26th, 1792.   Manifesto of Prussia.—In making
war upon France, the King justified himself by alleging
the general anxiety which prevailed in regard to a
kingdom which formerly had been so considerable a
weight in the balance of power, but had now fallen into a

state of anarchy, which destroyed its political existence. If this had really been the case, Frederick William might surely have waited while France remained in a condition which gave her no weight and no importance inconsistent with the welfare of her neighbours.

This declaration reached Paris at the time when a number of petitions and addresses from the departments, protesting against the insult offered to the Throne on the 20th of June, were presented to the Assembly. The menace of foreign war neutralized all these proofs of remaining loyalty; the armed attitude and the threats of the German powers hastened the fall of the monarchy, gave vigour to the cut-throats of Paris, and produced the horrors of August and September.

On the 25th of July, with a vanguard of 20,000 emigrants thirsting for vengeance, 30,000 infantry and 10,000 cavalry, the Duke of Brunswick set out from Coblentz, on his march to the invasion and conquest of France. On the same day was dated his celebrated proclamation, intended to terrify and reduce to submission the French people. By this proclamation the inhabitants of France were exhorted to yield themselves to the will of the King, who had promised three years before that he would himself make them happy. It was also declared, "that the French National Guards, if they should fight against the allied troops, and were taken with arms in their hands, should be punished with death as rebels; that the members of municipalities should be responsible, on pain of losing their heads, for all crimes which they should not in a public manner have attempted to prevent; that the inhabitants of towns and villages, who should dare to defend themselves against the allied forces, should be punished with all the rigours of war, and that their houses should be demolished; that their Imperial and Royal Majesties made personally responsible for all events, on pain of losing their heads, pursuant to the sentences of court martial, without hope of pardon, 'all the members of the National Assembly, of the departments, of the districts, of the municipalities, the National Guards of Paris, justices of the peace, and others whom it may concern;' further, that if any the least outrage were done to the royal family, if they were not immediately placed in safety and set at liberty, their Imperial and Royal Majesties will inflict on those who shall have deserved it 'the most exemplary and ever-memorable vengeance and punishment, by giving up the city of Paris to military execution, and exposing it to total destruction, and the rebels who shall be guilty of illegal resistance shall suffer the punishments which they shall have deserved.' "*

This proclamation, declaring the final intentions of Austria and Prussia, left the people of France only the alternative of submission to foreign enemies or a contest for independence. For the will of Louis, when made to conform to the dictates of Francis, Frederick William, and the emigrants, would in fact have been the arbitrary decree of the enemies of France. The royal will was, in fact, as different from the will of the Count d'Artois, as it was from the will of the Jacobin club. But how would that will have found any place to act when the seat of authority was changed from the mob of Paris in the streets assembled to the head-quarters of the Duke of Brunswick?

All hope of a peaceful issue to the struggle vanished before this atrocious proclamation. Robespierre, Danton,

* Adolphus's " History of George III."

and Collot d'Herbois rejoiced. The manifesto declared what would be done by the Allies, when Paris should fall into their power. But the Jacobin club had Paris already in its power; and speedily did they consummate their triple work of abolishing the monarchy, murdering their opponents, and rousing the people to defend the soil of France.

With a view to the first of these objects, the sections of Paris, to the number of forty-seven out of forty-eight, were impelled to require the abolition of monarchy. Petion, Mayor of Paris, made this demand at the bar of the Assembly, in the name of his constituents. To expedite and insure this result, a committee of insurrection was formed. On the 9th of August all the preparations were complete. No attempt was made by the authorities to prevent this insurrection. In the night the tocsin was sounded from all the steeples of Paris. At daylight the Carrousel was filled with the populace of the fauxbourgs, and the Mayor urged the National Guards to keep themselves strictly on the defensive. At five o'clock in the morning the King passed in review his few troops, and eight hundred gentlemen who had come to the palace to aid in his defence. Unfortunately, when the attack began, upon the advice of Rœderer, Attorney General of the department, and a violent democrat, the King resolved to take refuge in the hall of Assembly. When there, he sent an order to the Swiss not to defend the palace, and to the remainder of the body, which was at Courbevois, not to come up to Paris. For two hours the unfortunate Swiss were sought out, pursued, and murdered by the mob. The palace was sacked and set on fire.

. A new party had lately arisen in the Assembly, called,

from the department in which they had been chiefly elected, the Girondins. It appeared to them that this was the right moment to attack the monarch, and aim at the abolition of the monarchy. While Louis sat helpless in the seat of the reporter of the Assembly, and his guards were being shot by the ruthless mob, Vergniaud, the mouth-piece of the Girondin party, made a most eloquent invective against the prostrate and fallen King. The great majority of the Assembly took courage against a throne already subverted, and sent the unhappy Louis and his family to the prison of the Temple. Before the King left the Assembly, a decree ordered that he should be sus-pended from his functions, and a National Convention summoned.

It is said that Louis XVI. studied constantly the history of Charles I. of England, and that he hoped for safety by making his conduct a contrast to that of the English sovereign. But in times of revolution courage and deter-mination, if they do not disarm and vanquish enemies, serve at least to rally and protect friends; nay, considering the unwarlike habits of the middle and lower classes in France, Louis might have succeeded where Charles failed. His apathy and forbearance passed for weakness and treachery.

From this time, however, deprived of all will, the good and even great qualities of the King shone forth. Inex-haustible patience, unbounded charity, firmness combined with meekness, were conspicuous in all he said and did from the day of his imprisonment to that of his death.

The first object of the Jacobin leaders was attained on the 10th of August. The monarchy was abolished. Their next object was to rid themselves of their enemies. This was ac-complished in the four days from the 2nd to the 6th of September, by murdering all the accused and suspected persons detained in nine of the principal prisons of Paris. The horrible atrocities which accompanied these murders, the pretended trials, the ferocious assassinations, the apathy and stupor of the people of a great capital, the criminal connivance of the pretended ministers, and the wretched legislature, may be found related in the histories of this dreadful period.

The third, and the only legitimate object of the Jacobin chiefs was the organization of the country to resist the invaders. It seemed to those who weigh only appearances to be a desperate undertaking. The King of the French was suspected, and with reason, to be an accomplice of the invaders. An agent of his, Mallet du Pan, had gone to Berlin to communicate to the Allied Sovereigns the wishes of his master. The best chivalry of France was assembled at Coblentz under the Prince of Condé. An army of one hundred and thirty-eight thousand men, well disciplined, obedient to their officers, under a chief of experience in war, were prepared to enter France. On the other hand, the dissolving tendencies of the Revolution had destroyed all subordination in the French army. Two or three repulses and defeats had led, in each instance, to a rout and a disorderly flight. Dillon, one of their generals, had been put to death by his soldiers. La Fayette, after some vain attempts to inspire the King with energy, and the Assembly with moderation, had fled from his army across the frontier. The Emperor of Germany exercised a mean revenge against a disarmed enemy by putting him in the dungeons of Olmutz, where he remained three years.

The Allies were beyond measure elated by these symptoms of weakness and disunion among their adversaries.

Bischofswerder, a Prussian much trusted, said to several officers of distinction : " Do not waste your money in buying too many horses; the comedy cannot last long. The fumes of liberty are evaporating in Paris; the army of lawyers in Belgium will soon be annihilated; and towards the autumn we shall all be at home again."* But while these gentlemen officers were relying on manœuvres and drill and pomatum, other spirits, more formidable, were invoked by the daring magicians who had assumed the direction at Paris.

It is remarkable that, at the commencement of the Revolution, whether it were foresight or national instinct, the Constituent Assembly had decreed the formation of a great force, to be called the National Guard, and to comprise a million of men. When the Sovereigns of Germany began to prepare by concert for war with France, the whole country was covered with a network of Jacobin clubs, and every village had its demagogue, ready to spread false rumours, to make unfounded accusations, and to put to death every aristocrat and every priest who might oppose the rule of unmitigated democracy. When the war was actually declared, the same means were used to send off recruits, to furnish arms, to supply magazines. In August a decree was passed declaring " the country in danger." This decree, transmitted to the eighty-five departments, produced a wild and supernatural activity. At Paris persons of all ages and both sexes worked at the fortifications of Montmartre. The churches were filled with women making uniforms for the soldiers. While such were the means furnished by patriotic and civic ardour, military skill and valour were not wanting. The Allies proceeded leisurely,

* " Mémoires d'un Homme d'Etat," vol. i.

towards the end of August, to the capture of Thionville and Verdun. A difference of opinion seems to have then arisen among their chiefs. The emigrants, backed by the Austrians, wished to march at once to Paris, and put out the fire of straw, as they called the Revolution. The Duke of Brunswick, taking a totally different view of France and his own means, proposed to make a regular campaign, to take Sedan and other fortresses, and thus obtain a base of operations. His views did not prevail, but in adopting a plan adverse to his own opinion, he advanced sluggishly, took no measures for the supply of provisions for his army, and appeared to invite defeat.

Dumouriez, on the other hand, who commanded the French army, like himself, eager for distinction, saw with a glance the advantages of his position. The forest of Argonne, a branch of the Ardennes, stretches for thirteen leagues, with unequal breadth, across Champagne. Intersected by rocks and marshes, only five practicable roads led to Paris. When Dumouriez found that the Prussians had delayed to occupy it, "This," he said to a confidential officer, "will be the Thermopylæ of France; if I reach it before the Prussians, all is safe."

Yet his first operation was not successful. In retiring from Grandpré to St. Menehould, a body of 10,000 French infantry were put to flight by 1500 Prussian hussars. Dumouriez was called a traitor, and the Allies exulted in their approaching conquest. This action took place on the 14th of September. But on the 20th, Kellerman, at the head of 22,000 troops of the Army of the Rhine, during a long and well-fought day, repulsed all the attacks of the Prussians, and forced them to retire. The Prussian army was now reduced to the distress which the genius of Dumouriez had foreseen. Unable to force the passes of the forest, ill furnished with provisions, finding no resources in the country, and no support from the people, scrambling through rain and mud, over rocks, and in the midst of morasses, having, above all, no vigour to cope with difficulties, the Duke of Brunswick and his forces thought only of retreat. After some negotiation and an idle attempt to induce the French to set their King at liberty, it was agreed between the two generals that no attack should be made upon the Prussians, and that they should be allowed to retire unmolested. On the 30th they began their retreat, and in a few days reached the frontier.

Such, then, was the result of this rash and unjustifiable invasion. The sanguinary Republic of Paris was not fated to endure, but the independence of France was secured. As the people of Veii had failed in conquering Rome, so Francis and Frederick William failed in conquering France by means of her divisions. The Allies had no feats to boast of save and except the massacres of September.

The rest of the autumn was consumed in acts of atrocity committed by the new authority in France, and counsels of weakness on the part of the Allies, which will properly find a place hereafter. We now propose to review the proceedings, intentions, and opinions of the statesmen of England on this new state of affairs in Europe.

CHAPTER XXX.

THE FRENCH REVOLUTION AND GREAT BRITAIN.

BEFORE we relate the part taken by Mr. Fox and Mr. Burke in regard to the portentous events which were daily occurring, it may be well to remember the opinion prevailing in England respecting the old political institutions of France.

The arbitrary nature of the French monarchy, the corrupt character of the Court, and the degraded condition of the peasantry, were generally subjects of contemptuous comment among the enlightened classes of Great Britain. Among the people at large, the phrase " slavery and wooden shoes" expressed the sense entertained by them of the state of the French nation.   Cowper pretty accurately represented the feelings of his country when he thus spoke of the Bastille :—

> " Then shame to manhood, and opprobrious more
> To France than all her losses and defeats,
> Old or of later date, by sea or land,
> Her house of bondage, worse than that of old
> Which God avenged on Pharaoh—the Bastille!
> Ye horrid towers, the abode of broken hearts;
> Ye dungeons and ye cages of despair,
> That monarchs have supplied from age to age.
> With music, such as suits their sovereign ears,
> The sighs and groans of miserable men!
> There's not an English heart that would not leap

> To hear that ye were fallen at last; to know
> That ev'n our enemies, so oft employ'd
> In forging chains for us, themselves were free.
> For he who values Liberty, confines
> His zeal for her predominance within
> No narrow bounds; her cause engages him,
> Wherever pleaded. 'Tis the cause of man." *

It was the peculiar quality of Mr. Burke's mind to dress up the images of his idolatry in the gorgeous habits with which the wardrobe of his fancy amply furnished him. Thus he had clothed in divine attributes the filthy objects of Hindu superstition. Thus he threw a splendid light of rhetoric upon the palace of Versailles, and converted the court where Pompadour and Du Barry had carried on their obscene rites, into a temple where "vice itself lost half its evil in losing all its grossness." While, therefore, he chastised with just severity the errors and the presumption of the French reformers, he applied with evident impropriety the maxims of Somers to the new Assembly of France. Philippe de Comines had pointed out in his own time the vast difference between England and France. That difference had in three centuries been greatly aggravated. The different classes in England had been knitted together by the bonds of a free constitution; the different ranks in France had been separated into a court and clergy enervated by unchecked depravity, and a people exasperated by unmitigated suffering.

Mr. Fox, on the other hand, knowing better the state of France, hailed with joy the fall of the Bastille, and was full of hope of the success of the French Revolution. Nor did he wait for events to correct his judgment. In a speech

* "The Task."

made on the 5th of February, 1790, in opposition to the army estimates, Mr. Fox said " He had never thought it expedient to make the internal circumstances of other nations the subject of much conversation in that House, but if there ever could be a period in which he should be less jealous of an increase of the army, from any danger to be apprehended to the Constitution, the present was that precise period. The example of a neighbouring nation had proved that former imputations on armies were unfounded calumnies, and it was now universally known throughout Europe that a man, by becoming a soldier, did not cease to be a citizen."

Mr. Burke was not slow in taking up the glove thus imprudently thrown down by Mr. Fox. On the 9th of February he thus stated his opinions regarding the state of France:

" That France was at this time, in a political light, to be considered as expunged out of the system of Europe. Whether she could ever appear in it again, as a leading power, was not easy to determine, but at present he considered France as not politically existing, and most assuredly it would take much time to restore her to her former active existence. *Gallos quoque in bellis floruisse audivimus* might possibly be the language of the rising generation. . . . In a political view France was low indeed. She had lost everything, even to her name.

" Jacet ingens littore truncus,
Avulsumque humeris caput, et sine nomine corpus."

" He was sorry that his right honourable friend [Mr. Fox] had dropped even a word expressive of exultation on that circumstance, or that he seemed of opinion that the objection from standing armies was at all lessened by it. He attributed this opinion of Mr. Fox entirely to his known zeal for the best of all causes—liberty. That it was with a pain inexpressible he was obliged to have even the shadow of a difference with his friend, whose authority would be always great with him and with all thinking people. *Quæ maxima semper censetur nobis, et erit quæ maxima semper.* His confidence in Mr. Fox was such, and so ample, as to be almost implicit. That he was not ashamed to avow that degree of docility. That when the choice is well made, it strengthens instead of oppressing our intellect. That he who calls in the aid of an equal understanding doubles his own. He who profits of a superior understanding, raises his powers to a level with the height of the superior understanding he unites with. He had found the benefit of such a junction, and would not lightly depart from it. He wished almost, on all occasions, that his sentiments were understood to be conveyed in Mr. Fox's words: and that he wished, as amongst the greatest benefits he could wish the country, an eminent share of power to that right honourable gentleman; because he knew that to his great and masterly understanding he joined the greatest possible degree of that natural moderation which is the best corrective of power, that he was of the most artless, candid, open, and benevolent disposition, disinterested in the extreme, of a temper mild and placable, even to a fault, without one drop of gall in his whole constitution."*

Mr. Burke proceeded to make the contrast between the Revolution of 1688 and the Revolution in France. He expatiated on the wisdom of the legislators of the former period, the folly and the wickedness of the agitators of France. He concluded in this manner:—"Mr. Burke said he should have felt very unpleasantly if he had not de-

* "Fox's Speeches," vol. iv. p. 46.

livered these sentiments. He was near the end of his natural, probably still nearer to the end of his political career; that he was weak and weary, and wished for rest. That he was little disposed to controversies, or what is called a detailed opposition. That at his time of life, if he could not do something by some sort of weight of opinion, natural or acquired, it was useless and indecorous to attempt anything by mere struggle. *Turpe senex miles.* That he had for that reason little attended the army business, or that of the revenue, or almost any other matter of detail for some years past. That he had, however, his task. He was far from condemning such opposition; on the contrary, he most highly applauded it where a just occasion existed for it, and gentlemen had vigour and capacity to pursue it. Where a great occasion occurred, he was, and while he continued in Parliament would be, amongst the most active and the most earnest, as he hoped he had shown on a late event. With respect to the Constitution itself, he wished few alterations in it; happy, if he left it not the worse for any share he had taken in its service." As soon as Mr. Burke had concluded,

"Mr. Fox declared, that he rose with a concern of mind, which it was almost impossible to describe, at perceiving himself driven to the hard necessity of making at least a short answer to the latter part of a speech, to which he had listened with the greatest attention, and which, some observations and arguments excepted, he admired as one of the wisest and most brilliant flights of oratory ever delivered in that House. There were parts of it, however, which he wished had either been omitted, or deferred to some other and more fit occasion. His right honourable friend, in alluding to him, had mixed his remarks with so much personal kindness towards him, that he felt himself under a difficulty in making any return, lest the House should doubt his sincerity, and consider what he might say as a mere discharge of a debt of compliments. He must, however, declare, that such was his sense of the judgment of his right honourable friend, such his knowledge of his principles, such the value which he set upon them, and such the estimation in which he held his friendship, that if he were to put all the political information which he had learned from books, all which he had gained from science, and all which any knowledge of the world and its affairs had taught him, into one scale, and the improvement which he had derived from his right honourable friend's instruction and conversation were placed in the other, he should be at a loss to decide to which to give the preference. He had learnt more from his right honourable friend than from all the men with whom he had ever conversed.

" His right honourable friend had grounded all which he had said on that part of a speech made by him on a former day, when he wished that his right honourable friend had been present, in which he had stated, that if ever he could look at a standing army with less constitutional jealousy than before, it was now; since, during the late transactions in France, the army had manifested, that on becoming soldiers they did not cease to continue citizens, and would not act as the mere instruments of a despot. That opinion he still maintained. But, did such a declaration warrant the idea that he was a friend to democracy? He declared himself equally the enemy of all absolute forms of government, whether an absolute monarchy, an absolute aristocracy, or an absolute democracy. He was averse to all extremes, and a friend only of a mixed government, like our own, in which, if the aristocracy, or indeed either of the three branches of the Constitution, were destroyed, the good effect of the whole, and the happiness derived under it, would, in his mind, be at an end. When he described himself as exulting over the success of some of the late attempts in France, he certainly meant to pay a just tribute of applause to those who, feelingly alive to a sense of the oppressions under which their countrymen had groaned, disobeyed the despotic commands of their leaders, and gallantly espoused the cause of their fellow-citizens, in a struggle for the acquisition of that liberty, the sweets of which we all enjoyed.

"He begged, however, not to be misunderstood in his ideas of liberty. True liberty could only exist amidst the union and co-operation of the different powers which composed the legislative and the executive government. Never should he lend himself to support any cabal or scheme, formed in order to introduce any dangerous innovation into our excellent Constitution; he would not, however, run the length of declaring, that he was an enemy to every species of innovation. That Constitution, which we all revered, owed its perfection to innovation; for, however admirable the theory, experience was the true test of its order and beauty. His right honourable friend might rest assured that they could never differ in principles, however they might differ in their application. In the application of their principles they more than once had experienced the misfortune of differing, particularly in regard to the representation of the people in Parliament, and they might occasionally continue to differ in regard to other points, which depended rather on the application of their principles, than on their principles themselves. The scenes of bloodshed and cruelty which had been acted in France no man could have heard of without lamenting; but still, when the severe tyranny under which the people had so long groaned was considered, the excesses which they committed, in their endeavour to shake off the yoke of despotism, might, he thought, be spoken of with some degree of compassion; and he was persuaded that, unsettled as their present state appeared, it was preferable to their former condition, and that ultimately it would be for the advantage of this country that France had regained her freedom."

When Mr. Fox had done, "Mr. Burke answered, that he could, without the least flattery or exaggeration, assure his right honourable friend, that the separation of a limb from his body could scarcely give him more pain than the circumstance of differing from him, violently and publicly, in opinion. It was not even in his idea to insinuate that his right honourable friend would lend his aid to any plan concerted for the support of dangerous and unconstitutional procedures. He knew the contrary. His motive for the remarks which he had made was to warn those who did not possess the brilliant talents and illumined penetration of his right honourable friend, whose moderation was one of the leading features of his political character, from entertaining sentiments which he conceived to be adverse to good government. He was exceedingly glad, however, that he had delivered himself so plainly in his former speech, since what he had said had drawn from his right honourable friend an explanation not more satisfactory to his mind, than he was persuaded it was to the House, and all who had heard it."*

* "Fox's Speeches," vol. iv. pp. 51–54.

The debate might well have ended here. But Mr. Sheridan, who seems to have been anxious to widen the breach, rose at the end of Mr. Burke's speech, made an apology for the cruelties of the French populace, on the ground that the accursed system of the former Government had stripped the people of the feelings of justice and humanity, and charged Mr. Burke with being an advocate for despotism.

Mr. Burke rejoined that, henceforth he and his honourable friend were separated in politics. He had been cruelly misrepresented. "All who knew him could not avoid acknowledging that he was the professed enemy of despotism in every shape, whether it appeared as the splendid tyranny of Louis XIV., or the outrageous democracy of the present Government of France, which levelled all distinctions in society."

Colonel Fitzpatrick, speaking of this debate and alluding to Burke and Sheridan, said "it was a fine race over the Curragh."

In the course of the year appeared that brilliant and memorable work of Mr. Burke, known as "Reflections on the Revolution in France." To all who wish to know the spirit of the British Constitution, its due subordination of orders, its temperate solution or avoidance of difficulties, the study of this book, by day and by night, is invaluable. To those who wish to learn the spirit of the ancient monarchy of France, its vices and defects, Mr. Burke is a guide better fitted to mislead than to furnish a clue to its perplexities.

The Revolution in France was a portent more likely to affright than to enlighten the nations of Europe. Like the horses of the Sun, under the direction of Phaeton, when they felt the reins thrown upon their backs,—

> " Quæ postquam summum tetigere jacentia tergum
> Expatiantur equi: nulloque inhibente per auras,
> Ignotæ regionis eunt; quâque impetus egit
> Hâc sine lege runnt; altoque sub æthere fixis
> Incursant stellis, rapiuntque per avia cursum."*

The truth is, Mr. Burke looked only at one side of the French Revolution. He perceived clearly the presumption, the shallowness, and the incapacity of the popular leaders, the fury, the cruelty, and the madness of the Parisian populace. But he never gave any weight in the scale to the shameless immorality of Louis XV.'s Court; the corruption of the administration, the speculative infidelity and practical vices of the nobility and clergy. He never enumerated the occasions upon which, by summoning foreign soldiers to the palace, by intriguing with foreign sovereigns, and with leaders in the Assembly, by purchasing writers in the press and applauders in the populace, the Court had convinced the most moderate of the lovers of liberty that a re-action in favour of despotism and the punishment of the friends of a free constitution, was the only result with which the courtiers would be satisfied. It was the Court itself which, by the distrust it showed of La Fayette, of Mirabeau, of the Duke of La Rochefoucault, of Lally Tolendal, and other patriots, had made impossible that middle form of constitutional monarchy which Mr. Fox desired no less than Mr. Burke.

Fourteen months elapsed before the difference between Mr. Fox and Mr. Burke led to an open rupture in politics and a termination of friendship. At the end of a speech on

* Since I wrote down these lines, I find that Moore, in his "Life of Sheridan," has made the same quotation.

the Russian armament, Mr. Fox pronounced his opinion on the French Revolution in the following enthusiastic terms : "With regard to the change of system which had taken place in that country [France], he knew different opinions were entertained by different men, but he, for one, admired the new Constitution of France, considered altogether, as the most stupendous and glorious edifice of liberty which had been erected on the foundation of human integrity in any time or country."*

Mr. Burke's opinion differed so widely from that expressed by Mr. Fox, that no one could expect he would refrain from a declaration of his views in the House of Commons. Unfortunately, he was stopped, and hence, probably, the bitterness which he infused into the discussion. Mr. Fox regretted that he was not allowed to proceed. In the debate upon the Quebec Bill Mr. Fox objected to the duration of the Canadian parliaments, the reserves for the clergy, and the hereditary honours intended for the members of the Legislative Council. With regard to the general purport of the bill, however, he had said, on its introduction, "that he was willing to declare that the giving to a country so far distant from England a legislature, and the power of governing for itself, would exceedingly prepossess him in favour of every part of the plan. He did not hesitate to say that, if a local legislature was liberally formed, that circumstance would incline him much to overlook defects in the other regulations, because he was convinced that the only means of retaining distant colonies with advantage was to enable them to govern themselves."

Such was the simple wisdom of Mr. Fox. The scheme

* "Fox's Speeches," vol. iv. p. 200. It is remarkable that the Constitution of France was not completed till the September following.

of Mr. Pitt for the government of Canada was unhappily a complex contrivance for separating the English from the French race; for creating in the New World a special church establishment and a special nobility, unsuited to the people of Canada, and only calculated to bring on a contest between the Upper and Lower Province, and between both and the mother country.

Our present purpose, however, is not the government of Canada. When Mr. Fox, on the 8th of April, opposed the Quebec Bill, Mr. Burke was not in the House. On the 15th Mr. Fox made his panegyric on the French Constitution. On the 21st the Quebec Bill was to be re-committed. On the morning of that day Mr. Fox called upon Mr. Burke, and Mr. Burke opened to his friend very fully and particularly the plan of the speech he intended to make, stated what restrictions he meant to impose upon himself, and showed Mr. Fox the books, pamphlets, and reports to which he intended to refer. Mr. Fox differed from Mr. Burke, but entered into no quarrel with him; and they walked down to the House together, conversing upon the subject the whole way.

It is clear from this statement, made publicly by Mr. Burke, that Mr. Fox at least never intended to make his difference of opinion on the French Revolution a subject of personal quarrel. Mr. Fox had differed both with Mr. Burke and with Lord North on the great subject of Parliamentary Reform; but the difference existed without any breach of personal friendship. His placability and kindness of temper were undeniable.

For some reason or other, Mr. Fox was desirous that the discussion on the French Constitution should not take place on the Quebec Bill, and his friends going beyond his wishes, endeavoured to prevent Mr. Burke from taking the occasion of that bill to explain and enforce his opinions. Hence the extreme irritation of Mr. Burke; hence, perhaps, the melancholy termination of their friendship. On the 21st, however, before Mr. Fox and Mr. Burke entered the House, Mr. Sheridan had moved to postpone the re-commitment till after the holidays. Mr. Fox, therefore, contented himself with saying that he had alluded perhaps too often in the course of the session to the French Revolution, that his opinion was, on the whole, much in its favour, and although he should be sorry to differ from some of his friends, on account of the great respect he entertained for them, he should never be backward in delivering his opinion, and he did not wish to recede from anything which he had formerly advanced.

Mr. Burke, after a few remarks, finished by saying that, should he and his friend differ, he desired it to be recollected that, however dear he considered his friendship, there was something still dearer in his mind—the love of his country; nor was he stimulated by Ministers, for they had learned from him, not he from them.

On the 6th of May the Quebec Bill was re-committed, and the Chairman put the usual question, "That the Bill be read paragraph by paragraph." Mr. Burke now rose, and went at once into the consideration of the "Rights of Man," lately imported from a neighbouring country. He was proceeding to describe the French Revolution, and was denouncing the violence used towards the King on the occasion of his desiring to go to St. Cloud, when he was called to order by Mr. Baker. Mr. Fox said ironically, that this was a day of privilege, when any member might abuse any government he pleased: the Gentoo government or the government of Turkey were as apposite to the question as the French Constitution. Mr. Burke said he understood his right honourable friend's irony, but his conclusions were not rightly drawn from his premises. Mr. Burke attempted to proceed, but was four times called to order by members of the Opposition. Mr. Burke was so much irritated by these vexatious interruptions from inferior men, that he exclaimed with the grief, and somewhat, perhaps, of the insanity of Lear,—

> "The little dogs and all,
> Tray, Blanch, and Sweetheart, see they bark at me." *

On the fifth occasion, when Mr. St. John called him to order, Mr. Burke said an attempt was now made by one who had formerly been his friend to bring down upon him the censure of the House. It was unfortunate, he said, for him to be hunted sometimes by one party, sometimes by another. He was again proceeding, when Lord Sheffield rose to order, and moved that dissertations on the French Constitution were not regular or in order.

Mr. Pitt now interposed in favour of Mr. Burke, and said that, when the constitution of a colony was the question, any other constitution might properly be referred to in debate. Mr. Fox, on the other hand, maintained that Mr. Burke was out of order.

"On the French Revolution he did indeed differ from his right honourable friend : their opinions, he had no scruple to say, were wide as the poles asunder. . . . On that revolution he adhered to his opinion, and never would retract one syllable of what he had said. He repeated that he thought it on the whole one of the most glorious events in the history of mankind. But when he had on a former

* "Life of Lord Sidmouth."

occasion mentioned France, he had mentioned the Revolution only, and not the Constitution; the latter remained to be improved by experience and accommodated to circumstances. The arbitrary system of government was done away, the new one had the good of the people for its object, and that was the point on which he rested."

Had Mr. Fox stopped there, the ground would have been cleared for mutual explanation. Unfortunately, he went on to taunt Mr. Burke with the opinion that " Minute discussion of great events without information did no honour to the pen that wrote or the tongue that spoke the words." He was sorry Mr. Burke had learnt to draw an indictment against a whole people, and he alluded to his doctrine that revolts always were provoked. These were galling recollections, and, together with the repeated interruptions he had received, seem to have driven Mr. Burke to a final and fatal decision. He no longer called Mr. Fox his friend. He began in a grave and restrained tone of voice, but the matter was beyond measure bitter.

" The speech," he remarked, " to which he was to reply was perhaps one of the most disorderly ever delivered in that House. His public conduct, words, and writings had not only been misrepresented and arraigned in the severest terms; but confidential conversations had been unfairly brought forward, for the purpose of proving his political inconsistency. Such were the instances of kindness which he had received from one whom he always considered as his warmest friend; but who, after an intimacy of two-and-twenty years, had at last thought proper, without the least provocation, to commence a personal attack upon him."

" For a variety of reasons he confessed that he wished to introduce the subject of the French Constitution, which he thought that he might have done perfectly in order. In the first place, he felt desirous of pointing out the danger of perpetually extolling that preposterous edifice upon all occasions, and in the highest strain. Mr. Fox had himself termed it 'the most stupendous and glorious edifice of liberty which had been erected on the foundation of human integrity in any time or country.' A second motive, which had, indeed, some little influence over him, was of a more personal nature. He had been accused both of writing and speaking of the late proceedings in France rashly, unadvisedly, and wantonly. This charge he was certainly anxious to refute; but at the very time when he was about to produce facts in corroboration of his assertions, blended with private information and respectable authorities, he was stopped in the most unfair and disorderly manner. Had he been permitted to continue his speech, he would have shown, that the issue of all that had been done, and of all that was then doing in France, could never serve the cause of liberty, but would inevitably tend to promote that of tyranny, oppression, injustice, and anarchy.

"But what principally weighed with him, and determined him in his conduct, was the danger that threatened our own Government, from practices which were notorious to all the world. Were there not clubs in every quarter, who met and voted resolutions of an alarming tendency? Did they not correspond, not only with each other in every part of the kingdom, but with foreign countries? Did they not preach in their pulpits doctrines which were dangerous, and celebrate at their anniversary meetings proceedings incompatible with the spirit of the British Constitution? Did they not everywhere circulate, at a great expense, the most infamous libels on that Constitution? At present he said that he apprehended no immediate danger. The King was in full power, possessed of all his functions; his Ministers were responsible for their conduct; the country was blessed with an Opposition of strong force; and the common people themselves seemed to be united with the gentlemen in a column of prudence. Nevertheless he maintained there was still sufficient cause for jealousy and circumspection. In France there were 300,000 in arms, who at a favourable moment might be happy to yield assistance; besides, a time of scarcity and tumult might come, when the greatest danger was to be dreaded from a class of people, whom we might now term low intriguers and contemptible clubbists.

" He again adverted to the unkindness with which he had been treated by Mr. Fox, who had ripped up the whole course and tenour of his public and private life, with a considerable degree of asperity. The right honourable gentleman, after having fatigued him with skirmishes of order, which were wonderfully managed by the light infantry of Opposition, then brought down upon him the whole strength and heavy artillery of his own judgment, eloquence, and abilities, to overwhelm him at once. In carrying on the attack against him, the right honourable gentleman had been supported by a corps of well-disciplined troops, expert in their manœuvres, and obedient to the word of their commander. [Mr. Grey here called Mr. Burke to order, conceiving that it was disorderly to mention gentlemen in that way, and to ascribe improper motives to them.] Mr. Burke proceeded to remark, that he had frequently differed from Mr. Fox in former instances, particularly on the subject of a Parliamentary Reform, of the Dissenters' Bill, and of the Royal Marriage Act; but that no one difference of opinion had

ever before for a single moment interrupted their friendship. It certainly was indiscreet at his time of life to
provoke enemies, or give his friends occasion to desert him;
yet if his firm and steady adherence to the British Constitution placed him in such a dilemma, he would risk all;
and as public duty and public prudence taught him, with
his last breath exclaim, ' Fly from the French Constitution!'
[Mr. Fox whispered, that there was no loss of friendship.]
Mr. Burke replied, *Yes, there was—he knew the price of his
conduct—he had done his duty at the price of his friend—
their friendship was at an end.* Afterwards, addressing
himself to the two right honourable gentlemen who were
the great rivals in that House, he expressed a hope that,
whether they hereafter moved in the political hemisphere
as two flaming meteors, or walked together like brethren
hand in hand, they would preserve and cherish the British
Constitution; that they would guard against innovation,
and save it from the danger of those new theories. In a
rapturous apostrophe to the infinite and unspeakable power
of the Deity, who, with his arm, hurled a comet like a
projectile out of its course—who enabled it to endure the
sun's heat, and the pitchy darkness of the chilly night; he
said, that to the Deity must be left the task of infinite
perfection, while to us poor, weak, incapable mortals, there
was no rule of conduct so safe as experience. . . ."

Mr. Fox rose to reply; but his mind was so much
agitated, and his heart so much affected by what had fallen
from Mr. Burke, that it was some minutes before he could
proceed. Tears trickled down his cheeks, and he strove in vain
to give utterance to his feelings. The sensibility of every
member in the House appeared excited by his emotion. Re-

covered at length from the depression under which he had
risen, Mr. Fox proceeded to answer the assertions which
had caused it.

"He said that, however events might have altered the
mind of his right honourable friend, for so he must call
him, notwithstanding what had passed,—that, grating as
it was to any man to be unkindly treated by those who
were under obligations to him, it was still more grating
and painful to be unkindly treated by those to whom they
felt the greatest obligations, and whom, notwithstanding
their harshness and severity, they found they must still
love and esteem—he could not forget that, when a boy
almost, he had been in the habit of receiving favours from
his right honourable friend, that their friendship had grown
with their years, and that it had continued for upwards of
five-and-twenty years, for the last twenty of which they
had acted together, and lived on terms of the most familiar
intimacy. He hoped, therefore, that, notwithstanding what
had happened that day, his right honourable friend would
think on past times, and, however any imprudent words or
intemperance of his might have offended him, it would
show that it had not been at least intentionally his fault.
His right honourable friend had said, and said truly, that
they had differed formerly on many subjects, and yet it did
not interrupt their friendship. Let his right honourable
friend speak fairly and say, whether they could not differ
without an interruption of their friendship, on the subject
of the French Revolution, as well as on any of their former
subjects of difference. He enumerated, severally, what
those differences of opinion had been, and appealed to his
right honourable friend whether their friendship had been

interrupted on any one of those occasions. In particular,
he said, on the subject of the French Revolution, the right
honourable gentleman well knew that his sentiments differed
widely from his own ; he knew also, that as soon as his
book on the subject was published, he condemned that book
both in public and private, and every one of the doctrines it
contained.

" Mr. Fox again said, that he could not help feeling that
his right honourable friend's conduct appeared as if it
sprung from an intention to injure him, at least it produced
the same effect, because the right honourable gentleman
opposite to him had chosen to talk of republican principles
as principles which he wished to be introduced into the new
constitution of Canada, whereas his principles were very far
from republican in any degree. If, therefore, his right
honourable friend had thought it necessary to state to the
House his sentiments on the French Revolution, he might
have done it on any other occasion, with less injury to him,
than on the Quebec Bill; because his doing it then, confirmed and gave weight to the misrepresentation of the
right honourable gentleman opposite to him ; and not only
that, it put it out of his power to answer him properly.
Besides he had, as every other man must have, a natural
antipathy and dislike to being catechised as to his political
principles. It was, he said, the first time that ever he had
heard a philosopher state, that the way to do justice to the
excellence of the British Constitution was never to mention
it without at the same time abusing every other constitution
in the world. For his part, he had ever thought that the
British Constitution in theory was imperfect and defective,
but that in practice it was excellently adapted to this
country. He had often publicly said this ; but because he

admired the British Constitution, was it to be concluded that there was no part of the constitution of other countries worth praising, or that the British Constitution was not still capable of improvement ?   He, therefore, could neither consent to abuse every other constitution, nor to extol our own so extravagantly as the right honourable gentleman seemed to think it merited. As a proof that it had not been thought quite perfect, let the two only reforms of it be recollected that had been attempted of late years—reform relative to the representation in Parliament of the Chancellor of the Exchequer, in 1783, and the reform in the Civil List by his right honourable friend. Was it expected that he should declare the Constitution would have been more perfect or better without either of those two reforms ?   To both had he given his support, because he approved both; and yet one went to retrench the influence of the Crown, the other to enlarge the representation in that House; and would his right honourable friend say that he was a bad man for having voted for both?   He was, Mr. Fox said, an enemy to all tests whatever, as he had hitherto thought the right honourable gentleman was, and therefore he objected to any man's being expected to have his political principles put to the test, by his being obliged to abjure every other constitution but our own. Such a mode of approving one's zeal for the latter reminded him of the man who signed the Thirty-nine Articles, and said he wished there were a hundred and thirty-nine more, that he might have signed them too, to prove his orthodoxy.

"Nothing but the ignominious terms which his right honourable friend had that day heaped on him. [Mr. Burke said loud enough to be heard, that he did not recollect he had used any.]   'My right honourable friend,' said Mr. Fox, 'does not recollect the epithets: they are out of his mind: then they are completely and for ever out of mine. I cannot cherish a recollection so painful, and, from this moment, they are obliterated and forgotten.'   .   .   .

" He lamented the difference that had happened, but he hoped that, when his right honourable friend came to turn in his mind all the circumstances that had occasioned it, he would forget what was past. His right honourable friend had said, that if he were to quote some of his expressions on particular occasions, he could prove his inconsistency. Mr. Fox acknowledged that no member of that House was more apt to let expressions fall which, perhaps, were rash and imprudent, than he was. He knew he had done so; but his right honourable friend never let anything fall but what did him honour, and might be remembered to his credit. Mr. Fox now proceeded to speak of the reasons which had induced his right honourable friend and himself to enter into a systematic opposition to the present administration. This was not, he said, for the purpose of obtaining power and emolument by the means of a faction, but he had ever understood that they and their friends had formed a party for supporting the true principles of the British Constitution and watching the prerogative. After expatiating on this, Mr. Fox said, 'Let the right honourable gentleman maintain his opinions, but let him not blame me for having mine.' He then noticed the cruel and hard manner in which his right honourable friend had used him, and spoke feelingly of the pain it had given him. The course he should pursue, he said, would be to keep out of his right honourable friend's way, till time and reflection had fitted his right honourable friend to think differently upon the subject; and then, if their friends did not contrive to unite them, he should think their friends did not act as they had a right to expect at their hands. If his right honourable friend wished to bring forward the question of the French Revolution on a future day, in that case he would discuss it with him as temperately as he could; at present he had said all that he thought necessary, and let his right honourable friend say what he would upon the subject, he would make him no farther reply.

"Mr. Burke again rose. He began with remarking, that the tenderness which had been displayed in the beginning and conclusion of Mr. Fox's speech was quite obliterated by what had occurred in the middle part. He regretted, in a tone and manner of earnestness and fervency, the proceedings of that evening, which he feared might long be remembered by their enemies to the prejudice of both. He was unfortunate to suffer the lash of Mr. Fox, but he must encounter it. Under the mask of kindness, a new attack, he said, was made upon his character and conduct in the most hostile manner, and his very jests brought up in judgment against him. He did not think the careless expressions and playful triflings of his unguarded hours would have been recorded, mustered up in the form of accusations, and not only have had a serious meaning imposed upon them, which they were never intended to bear, but one totally inconsistent with any fair and candid interpretation. Could his most inveterate enemy have acted more unkindly towards him? The event of that night's debate, in which he had been interrupted without being suffered to explain, in which he had been accused without being heard in his defence, made him at a loss to understand what was either party or friendship. His arguments had been misrepresented. He had never affirmed that the English, like every other constitution, might not in some points be amended. He had never maintained that to praise our own Constitution, the best way was to abuse all others. The tendency of all that had been said was to represent him as a wild, inconsistent man, only for attaching bad epithets to a bad subject.

" With the view of showing his inconsistency, allusions had been made to his conduct respecting his economical reform in 1780, the American War, and the questions of 1784; but none of these applied. If he thought, in 1780, that the influence of the Crown ought to be reduced to a limited standard, and with which Mr. Fox himself at the time seemed to be satisfied, it did not follow that the French were right in reducing it with them to nothing. He was favourable to the Americans, because he supposed they were fighting not to acquire absolute speculative liberty, but to keep what they had under the English Constitution; and as to his representation to the Crown in 1784, he looked back to it with self-gratification, still thinking the same. Yet he knew not how to devise a legislative cure for the wound then inflicted, as it came from the people, who were induced to decide for the Crown, against the independence of their own representatives. The inconsistency of his book with his former writings and speeches had been insinuated and assumed, but he challenged the proof by specific instances; and he also asserted that there was not one step of his conduct nor one syllable of his book contrary to the principles of those men with whom our glorious revolution originated, and to whose principles, as a Whig, he declared an inviolable attachment. He was an old man, and seeing what was attempted to be introduced instead of the ancient temple of our Constitution, could weep over the foundation of the new.

" He again stated, still more particularly, the endeavours used in this country to supplant our own by the introduction of the new French Constitution; but he did not believe Mr. Fox at present had that wish, and he did believe him to have delivered his opinions abstractedly from any reference to this country; yet their effect might be different on those who heard them, and still more on others through misapprehension or misrepresentations. He replied to the grounds on which Mr. Fox explained his panegyric. The lesson to kings, he was afraid, would be of another kind. He had heard Mr. Fox own the King of France to be the best-intentioned sovereign in Europe. His good-nature and love of his people had ruined him. He had conceded everything, till he was now in a jail. The example of the confusions, on the other hand, would have very little operation, when it was mentioned with tardy and qualified censure, while the praises of the Revolution were trumpeted with the loudest blasts through the nation. He observed that Mr. Fox himself had termed the new French system a most stupendous and glorious fabric of human integrity. He had really conceived that the right honourable gentleman possessed a better taste in architecture, than to bestow so magnificent an epithet upon a building composed of untempered mortar. He considered it as the work of Goths and Vandals, where everything was disjointed and inverted.

" Mr. Burke again expressed his sorrow for the occurrences of that day; yet if the good were to many, he said that he would willingly take the evil to himself. He sincerely hoped that no member of that House would ever barter the Constitution of his country, that eternal jewel of his soul, for a wild and visionary system, which could only lead to confusion and disorder.

"Mr. Pitt, after having made some remarks upon the singular situation in which the House then stood with respect to the question before it, and having declared his own opinion to be, that Mr. Burke had not been, even in the first instance, at all out of order, suggested the propriety of withdrawing the motion which had been made by Lord Sheffield. This being agreed to, the Chairman reported progress, and asked leave to sit again."*

The debate was not renewed till the 11th, when the House again went into Committee on the Canada Bill. On this occasion Mr. Fox made a speech on the subject of the Legislative Council of Canada, which well deserves to be remembered. He thus defined and explained his notions as to the proper constitution of the Council as a second chamber :—

" First, he laid it down as a principle never to be departed from, that every part of the British dominions ought to possess a government, in the constitution of which monarchy, aristocracy, and democracy were mutually blended and united; nor could any Government be a fit one for British subjects to live under which did not contain its due weight of aristocracy, because that he considered to be the proper poise of the Constitution, the balance that equalized and meliorated the powers of the two other extreme branches, and gave stability and firmness to the whole. It became necessary to look what were the principles on which aristocracy was founded, and he believed it would

* "Fox's Speeches," vol. iv. pp. 218–28.

be admitted to him that they were twofold—namely, rank and property, or both united. In this country the House of Lords formed the aristocracy, and that consisted of hereditary titles, in noble families of ancient origin, or possessed by peers newly created on account of their extended landed property.

"Mr. Fox said that prejudice for ancient families, and that sort of pride which belonged to nobility, was right to be encouraged in a country like this, otherwise one great incentive to virtue would be abolished, and the national dignity, as well as its domestic interest, would be diminished and weakened. There was also such a thing to be remembered as long-established respect for the persons and families of those who, in consequence either of their own superior talents and eminent services, or of one or both in their ancestors, constituted the peerage. This, he observed, was by no means peculiar to pure aristocracies, such as Venice and Genoa, nor even to despotic or to mixed governments. It was to be found in democracies, and was there considered as an essential part of the constitution; affection to those whose families had best served the public, being always entertained with the warmest sincerity and gratitude. Thus in the ancient republics of Athens and of Rome, they all knew the respect paid to those who had distinguished themselves by their services for the commonwealth.

"Upon every ground of consideration, therefore, it would be wise, and what was more, indispensably necessary, that an aristocracy should make a branch of the Constitution for Canada; it was undoubtedly equally important with either the popular or the monarchical. But then the nature of the case must be considered; and he should therefore not advise the giving Canada a servile imitation of our aris-

tocracy, because we could not give them a House of
Lords like our own. . The Chancellor of the Exchequer
appeared to be aware of this, and therefore he had
recourse to a substitute for hereditary nobility. It was,
however, he must contend, a very inadequate substitute—it
was a semblance, but not a substance. Lords, indeed, we
might give them, but there was no such thing as creating
that reverence and respect for them on which their dignity
and weight in the view of both the popular and monarchical
part of the. Constitution depended, and which alone could
give them that power of control and support that was the
object of their institution. If Canada should grow into a
great and flourishing colony (and he trusted that it would),
as it was removed at such a distance from the principal
seat of Parliament, it was the more necessary to make the
· Council in a considerable degree independent of the
governor and the people; because the province being so far
off, the power of control could not be properly exercised by
that House, with a view to the calling upon the responsibility of Ministers, and punishing them for any abuse of
the prerogative, by giving wrong advice to the Council,
through the medium of the Governor. This was, he said,
a clear argument why the Council ought not to be appointed
by the Crown.

"Property, Mr. Fox said, was, and had ever been held
to be the true foundation of aristocracy. And when he used
the word aristocracy, he did not mean it in the odious sense
of aristocrat, as it had been lately called—with that he had
nothing to do. He meant it in its true sense, as an indispensably necessary part of a mixed Government under a
free Constitution. Instead, therefore, of the King's naming

the Council at that distance—in which case they had no security that persons of property, and persons fit to be named, would be chosen—wishing as he did to put the freedom and stability of the Constitution of Canada on the strongest basis, he proposed that the Council should be elective. But how elective? Not as the members of the House of Assembly were intended to be, but upon another footing. He proposed that the members of the Council should not be eligible to be elected unless they possessed qualifications infinitely higher than those who were eligible to be chosen members of the House of Assembly, and in like manner the electors of the members of Council must possess qualifications also proportionably higher than those of the electors to representatives in the House of Assembly. By this means, Mr. Fox said, they would have a real aristocracy chosen by persons of property from among persons of the highest property, and who would thence necessarily possess that weight, influence, and independency from which alone could be derived a power of guarding against any innovations that might be made, either by the people on the one part, or the Crown on the other.

"In answer to this proposition, Mr. Fox observed, it might possibly be said to him, if you are decidedly in favour of an elective aristocracy, why do you not follow up your own principle, and propose to abolish the House of Lords, and make them elective? For this plain reason, because the British House of Lords stood on the hereditary, known, and acknowledged respect of the country for particular institutions; and it was impossible to put an infant constitution upon the same footing. It would be as ridiculous to say, you shall have a House of Lords like that in

England, as for a person in his closet to say what degree of reverence and respect should belong to them. From what he had said, Mr. Fox remarked, that he might possibly be deemed an advocate for aristocracy singly; he might, undoubtedly, with as much reason as he had been called a Republican. Those who had pretended that he was a favourer of democratical principles, had surely read very little, and little understood the subject. He mentioned the American governments, and said he thought they had acted wisely, when upon finding themselves reduced to the melancholy and unfortunate situation of being obliged to change their governments, they had preserved as much as they possibly could of the old form of their governments, and thus made that form of government which was best for themselves; most of which consisted of the powers of monarchy, aristocracy, and democracy blended, though under a different name. In order to show that his idea of an elective council was not a new one, he said that, before the Revolution, more of the councils of our colonies were elected by the people than the King. . . .

"In the province of Canada, Mr. Fox continued to observe, the introduction of nobility was peculiarly improper, for a variety of reasons. In fact, there was a sort of nobility there already—namely, the Seigneurs, who were utterly unfit, and were not respected enough, to be made hereditary nobles. And yet would Ministers, he asked, pass by the real nobility of the country, the Seigneurs, and create a set of people over them, whom the world called nobility, and invest them with hereditary honours? By the bye, the sort of titles meant to be given were not named in the bill; he presumed the reason was, that they could not be named without creating laughter. Having thus gone through his proposition, Mr. Fox remarked, that so necessary was aristocracy to all governments, that in his opinion the destruction of all that had been destroyed could be proved to have arisen from the neglect of the true aristocracy, upon which it depended whether a Constitution should be great, energetic, and powerful. He explained that he was so far a Republican, that he approved all governments where the *res publica* was the universal principle, and the people, as under our Constitution, had considerable weight in the Government. Mr. Fox concluded with declaring emphatically, that true aristocracy gave a country that sort of energy, that sort of spirit, and that sort of enterprise which made a country great and happy."*

Mr. Burke commenced by asking for the protection of the House in the situation in which he stood. He found that sentence of banishment from his party had been pronounced against him. The House he hoped would not consider him as a bad man, although he had been banished by one party, and was too old to seek another. Being thus, without any just cause, separated from his former friends, he confessed that he severely felt his loss, but that what he felt like a man he would bear like a man. He objected to the Council for Canada, which he thought belonged to a democratic constitution. He complained of being obliged to stand upon his defence by Mr. Fox, who when a young man, at the age of fourteen, had been brought to him, and evinced the most promising talents, which he had used his best endeavours to cultivate; and this man, who had arrived at the maturity of being the most brilliant and powerful debater that ever existed, had accused him of having deserted his principles!

* "Fox's Speeches," vol. iv. pp. 228–232.

"In saying what he had upon the subject, he was conscious that he had done his duty, and hoped that he had in some measure arrested what might otherwise have effected the downfall of our justly boasted Constitution. Supported by such reflections, he was not deprived of consolation, although excluded from his party; a gloomy solitude might reign around him, but all was unclouded sunshine within."

There was something extremely melancholy in this speech of Mr. Burke. He seemed in some respects to have lost that irritation which had made him renounce with ostentatious publicity the friendship of Mr. Fox. That great man could not fail to be touched with the situation of his early instructor, with whom, for twenty-two years, he had been on terms of intimate friendship. But he also had a public principle to maintain. He had explained and almost retracted his sentence respecting France, by declaring it to apply not to the Constitution of 1791, but only to the popular basis which had been given to the French Government. He had been marked out as a republican for expressing a wish that France might prosper in her search for freedom. He, therefore, at the commencement of his speech, could not help adverting to the fact that Mr. Burke, "the right honourable gentleman," as he now styled him, had been unkind in imputing to him democratical or republican sentiments. He compared his own situation to that of Cordelia in " King Lear." Others, like Regan and Goneril, had indulged in fulsome praises of the Constitution; for his own part, he could only say he loved it as he ought. He defended himself against an insinuation of Mr. Pitt's that his sentiments were republican; he said his opinions only went so far that he wished to give the Crown less power, and the people more. But such he contended had been the object and purport of various bills supported both by Mr. Pitt and Mr. Burke.

Mr. Burke shortly replied, accepting the position of a man publicly disgraced by his party, and declared that he did not solicit the right honourable gentleman's friendship, nor that of any man, either on one side of the House or the other.

It is worthy of remark that the Quebec Bill of Mr. Pitt led in the end to rebellion, and that Canada has at length been pacified and made prosperous by restoring the union Mr. Pitt destroyed, and adopting the principles Mr. Fox recommended.

On the 12th of May, the day following this debate, the following paragraph appeared in the *Morning Chronicle:* " The great and firm body of the Whigs of England, true to their principles, have decided on the dispute between Mr. Fox and Mr. Burke; and the former is declared to have maintained the pure doctrines by which they are bound together, and upon which they have invariably acted. The consequence is that Mr. Burke retires from Parliament."

The separation of Mr. Burke from his party was a natural consequence of the position he had assumed in his book. The breach of friendship with Mr. Fox was an effect of his own wilful intemperance. But it was no momentary passion which confirmed and widened the breach. Mr. Burke did not rest till he had estranged from Mr. Fox many of his best friends, and broken into fragments " the great and firm body" of the English Whigs.

CHAPTER XXXI.

POLICY OF GREAT BRITAIN.

1791 — 1792.

On the last day of January, 1792, the King opened the session of Parliament in person. In the course of his speech he said: "The friendly assurances which I receive from foreign powers, and the general state of affairs in Europe, appear to promise to my subjects the continuance of their present tranquillity. Under these circumstances I am induced to think that some immediate reduction may safely be made in our naval and military establishments; and my regard for the interests of my subjects renders me at all times desirous of availing myself of any favourable opportunity of diminishing the public expenses."

In another part of the speech the reduction of taxes, and the lowering of the rate of interest of part of the public debt were recommended from the Throne. It is clear from this announcement that Mr. Pitt had not at this time any intention of taking part in the impending war. At a still later period, namely, on the 17th of February following, Mr. Pitt spoke with still more precision than in the King's speech. After stating that, in 1808, the Sinking Fund would amount to four millions, he proceeded to observe :—

"I am not, indeed, presumptuous enough to suppose,

when I name fifteen years, that I am not naming a period in which events may arise which human foresight cannot reach, and which may baffle all our conjectures. We must not count with certainty on a continuance of our present prosperity during such an interval; but *unquestionably* there never was a time in the history of this country when, from the situation of Europe, we might more reasonably expect fifteen years of peace, than we may at the present moment."*

Having quoted this passage, I cannot refrain from adding to it the peroration of this celebrated speech, both on account of the true, though brilliant picture which it gives of the state of the country before we entered upon the war of 1793, and, also, because it is perhaps the most perfect specimen that can be given of the stately and majestic flow of Mr. Pitt's eloquence.

After alluding to the principle of the accumulation of capital, he observed that it had never been fully developed but in the writings of Adam Smith, " whose extensive knowledge of detail, and depth of philosophical research will, I believe, furnish the best solution to every question connected with the history of commerce, or with the systems of political economy." He then proceeded: " The great mass of the property of the nation is thus constantly increasing at compound interest; the progress of which, in any considerable period, is what at first view would appear incredible. Great as have been the effects of this cause already, they must be greater in future; for its powers are augmented in proportion as they are exerted. It acts with a velocity continually accelerated, with a force continually increased :—

* " Parliamentary History," vol. xxix. p. 826.

'Mobilitate viget, viresque acquirit eundo.'

It may, indeed, as we have ourselves experienced, be checked or retarded by particular circumstances—it may for a time be interrupted or even overpowered—but, where there is a fund of productive labour and active industry, it can never be totally extinguished. In the season of the severest calamity and distress its operations will still counteract and diminish their effects; in the first returning interval of prosperity, it will be active to repair them. If we look to a period like the present, of continued tranquillity, the difficulty will be to imagine limits to its operation. None can be found while there exists at home any one object of skill and industry short of its utmost possible perfection; one spot of ground in the country capable of higher cultivation and improvement; or while there remains abroad any new market that can be explored, or any existing market that can be extended. From the intercourse of commerce, it will in some measure participate in the growth of other nations, in all the possible varieties of their situations. The rude wants of countries emerging from barbarism, and the artificial and increasing demands of luxury and refinement, will equally open new sources of treasure, and new fields of exertion in every state of society, and in the remotest quarters of the globe. It is this principle which, I believe, according to the uniform result of history and experience, maintains on the whole, in spite of the vicissitudes of fortune, and the disasters of empires, a continued course of successive improvement in the general order of the world.

. "Such are the circumstances which appear to me to have contributed most immediately to our prosperity. But these, again, are connected with others yet more important. They are obviously and necessarily connected with the duration of peace, the continuance of which, on a secure and permanent footing, must ever be the first object of the foreign policy of this country. They are connected still more with its internal tranquillity and with the natural effects of a free but well-regulated government. What is it which has produced, in the last hundred years, so rapid an advance beyond what can be traced in any other period of our history? What but that, during that time, under the mild and just government of the illustrious Princes of the family now on the throne, a general calm has prevailed through the country, beyond what was ever before experienced; and that we have also enjoyed in greater purity and perfection the benefit of those original principles of our Constitution which were ascertained and established by the memorable events that closed the century preceding? This is the great and governing cause, the operation of which has given scope to all the other circumstances which I have enumerated. It is this union of liberty with law which, by raising a barrier equally firm against the encroachments of power and the violence of popular commotion, affords to property its just security, produces the exertion of genius and labour, the extent and solidity of credit, the circulation and increase of capital, which forms and upholds the national character, and sets in motion all the springs which actuate the great mass of the community through all its various descriptions. The laborious industry of those useful and extensive classes (who will, I trust, be in a peculiar degree this day the object of the consideration of the House), the peasantry and yeomanry of the country, the skill and ingenuity of the artificer, the experiments and improvements of the wealthy proprietor of land, the bold speculations and successful adventures of the opulent merchant and enter-prising manufacturer — these are all to be traced to the same source, and all derive from hence both their encouragement and their reward. On this point, therefore, let us principally fix our attention, let us preserve this first and most essential object, and every other is in our power. Let us remember that the love of the Constitution, though it acts as a sort of natural instinct in the hearts of Englishmen, is strengthened by reason and reflection, and every day confirmed by experience; that it is a Constitution which we do not merely admire from traditional reverence, which we do not flatter from prejudice or habit, but which we cherish and value because we know that it practically secures the tranquillity and welfare both of individuals and of the public, and provides, beyond any other frame of government which has ever existed, for the real and useful ends which form at once the only true foundation and only rational object of all political societies.

" I have now nearly closed all the considerations which I think it necessary to offer to the Committee. I have endeavoured to give a distinct view of the surplus arising on the comparison of the permanent income (computed on the average which I have stated) with what may be expected to be the permanent expenditure in time of peace, and I have also stated the comparison of the supply and of the ways and means of this particular year. I have pointed out the leading and principal articles of revenue in which the augmentation has taken place, and the corresponding increase in the trade and manufactures of the country, and finally I have attempted to trace these effects to their causes, and to explain the principles which appear to account for the striking and favourable change in our general situation.

From the whole result, I trust I am entitled to conclude that the scene which we are now contemplating is not the transient effect of accident, not the short-lived prosperity of a day, but the genuine and natural result of regular and permanent causes. The season of our severe trial is at an end, and we are at length relieved not only from the dejection and gloom which a few years since hung over the country, but from the doubt and uncertainty which, even for a considerable time after our prospect had begun to brighten, still mingled with the hopes and expectations of the public. We may yet, indeed, be subject to those fluctuations which often happen in the affairs of a great nation, and which it is impossible to calculate or foresee; but as far as there can be any reliance on human speculations, we have the best ground from the experience of the past to look with satisfaction to the present and with confidence to the future. 'Nunc demum redit animus, cum non spem modo ac votum securitas publica, sed ipsius voti fiduciam et robur assumpserit.' This is a state not of hope only, but of attainment; not barely the encouraging prospect of future advantage, but the solid and immediate benefit of present and actual possession.

" On this situation and this prospect, fortunate beyond our most sanguine expectations, let me congratulate you, and the House, and my country! And, before I conclude, let me express my earnest wish, my anxious and fervent prayer, that now, in this period of our success, for the sake of the present age and of posterity, there may be no intermission in that vigilant attention by Parliament to every object connected with the revenue, the resources, and the credit of the State which has carried us through all our difficulties, and led to this rapid and wonderful improvement; that, still keeping pace with the exertions of the Legislature, the genius and spirit, the loyalty and public virtue of a great and free people, may long deserve and (under the favour of Providence) may ensure the continuance of this unexampled prosperity, and that Great Britain may thus remain for ages in the possession of these distinguished advantages under the protection and safeguard of that Constitution to which, as we have been truly told from the throne, they are principally to be ascribed, and which is indeed the great source and the best security of all that can be dear and valuable to a nation !"

Mr. Fox took occasion, at the commencement of his speech on this day, to pay a compliment to the eloquence of Mr. Pitt, and to subscribe to the philosophical principles of government on which he had argued. He fully agreed with Mr. Pitt that the prosperity of the country and of the revenue were above all to be attributed to the happy form of our Constitution.

Yet it was at the very time when these two great men were exulting in the prospect of peace and the enjoyment of freedom that the seeds were sown of the most destructive war and the most extensive misery which had befallen Europe since the Middle Ages.

For a short period, indeed, Mr. Pitt pursued his plan of retrenchment at home and neutrality abroad. The army was reduced from 30,000 to 25,000 men, and the invitation of foreign Powers to join against France was positively declined. The private correspondence of Lord Grenville and Mr. Dundas shows that neutrality was the sincere purpose of the Government.

Mr. Burke however, fanatical in his hatred of the French Revolution, and unforgiving towards his former friend

turned to accomplish his object. Lord
Windham, and Sir Gilbert Elliot listened
his vehement harangues. Mr. Windham
; favourable to the revolution in France,
at Mr. Grey, who he said was " bit by that
lurke's."* Mr. Windham, strange to say,
e the most furious adherent of Burke, while
ed the faithful friend of Mr. Fox.
himself added greatly to Mr. Fox's diffi-
it consulting his leader, he became a
Association of the Friends of the People.
ociation of which the objects were to pro-
qual representation of the people and more
;. The list of its members comprised Mr.
irskine, Mr. Lambton, Mr. Francis, Lord
'. Tierney, and other men of liberal opinions.
he representation, temperately undertaken,
;he removal of notorious defects, and the
creased confidence in the House of Com-
rt of the people, would have been a wise
measure. But the formation of a society
addressing itself rather to the people than
t, was sure to alarm the great body of men
her societies had been formed with a view
ie doctrines of the French Revolution, and
ntercourse with the French Assembly. The
vould evidently be confounded with these
ds. Indeed, some of the members of
ng Society belonged to the Association.
ore disapproved of the formation of the
ie Friends of the People. But when Mr.

* From the late Lady Spencer.

Grey announced his intention in Parliament, Mr. Fox resolved not to desert a cause which in the hands of Mr. Pitt he had always supported.

Mr. Pitt, on the other side, was compelled to take a part at variance with all his former conduct. He first asked the Speaker, in private, whether he meant to allow Mr. Grey to make a speech on giving his notice. The Speaker said it would certainly be out of order to make a speech without a motion, but he should be guided by the wishes of the House. Mr. Pitt said, that for his part he was too ill to speak. Dundas, on being told this, said Pitt must speak.* Accordingly, when Mr. Grey, after a short speech, gave his notice for the next year, Mr. Pitt vehemently denounced the mode and the time of agitating this question. His own former exertions in the cause compelled him to speak with a certain moderation against any change in the representation; but he implied very clearly that the state of the finances at the end of the American War furnished the only motive for his repeated efforts for reform, and that when the finances were flourishing, the state of the representation ought not to be altered.

Mr. Fox said, that if he had been informed by Mr. Grey of his intention to join the Association, he would have advised him to hesitate; that he had not joined the Association himself because, though he saw clearly the existing defects, he did not see his way to a remedy. But he had always supported Mr. Pitt in his proposals, and he should give his support to Mr. Grey. He avowed that, while he was strongly attached to our form of government, he thought the power of the Crown too great, and he wished to diminish it.

* "Life of Lord Sidmouth."

Mr. Burke, who had attended very little since his separation from Mr. Fox, eagerly embraced this opportunity of attacking Reform and the French Revolution. As he had never supported reform, he gave himself free scope in his warnings, his invectives, and his denunciations.

Mr. Sheridan, Mr. Erskine, and Mr. Francis spoke in favour of reform. Lord North spoke, as usual, against it, but expressed himself desirous to maintain his friendly relations with Mr. Grey. Mr. Grenville spoke strongly against any reform at this time.

It was evident from the tone of this grave though irregular debate, that a separation of the Whig party was impending. That portion of it which had followed Lord North felt alarm at the new complexion of affairs; others were ready to catch this prevailing complaint. Mr. Grey, Mr. Sheridan, and Mr. Erskine were, on the contrary, disposed to consider Reform of Parliament no longer merely wholesome diet, but a specific remedy for the disorders of the State.

The views of Mr. Fox on the subject are expressed in a letter to Mr. Adair, dated in the month of November following. "I do not think I said a word respecting Parliamentary Reform which I had not said months ago to the Duke of Portland and Lord Fitzwilliam, and years ago to Lord Rockingham. And upon that subject let me observe, that though it was not, as Burke says, in the original contract, yet neither was opposition to it in that contract; and that Grey, &c., had good reason to be surprised at so violent a storm arising from his undertaking what the Duke of Richmond, when he was upon the most cordial terms with the party, what Sir George Savile, and so many of us had done before him; what was supported by the Rockingham Administration; what was voted for by Lord John Cavendish, and assented to by some of Lord Rockingham's best friends (mixed, I grant, with some of his wickedest enemies) in Yorkshire. . . . Now as to the question of Parliamentary Reform, I never had even a wish that the Duke of Portland should recede from his former opinion on the subject. He and Lord Fitzwilliam were always against it; but what I want them to do is, to adhere to their former line of conduct, and to oppose it without any hostility to the supporters of it, or any friend-ship with those who resist it. If this is said to be a difficult line, I answer it was theirs in '82, '83, '84, and '85. Indeed, instead of my making strides forwards towards new opinions, or even leaning to them, they are adopting systems of conduct entirely *new*, and in so doing are, I am convinced, the dupes of those who have the worst intentions."*

The intention of Mr. Burke was evidently to separate a great portion of the Whig party from Mr. Fox. In the pursuit of this object he was active, rancorous, and unrelenting. Circumstances favoured his purpose. Various societies, formed in London, in Birmingham, and in Scotland, composed generally of obscure men, without weight or influence, acquired a bad notoriety by their pompous admiration of the French Revolution. Two or three of them went so far as to present extravagant addresses to the National Convention, and received from them in return turgid and unwarrantable compliments.

It was thought right by the Ministers to issue a proclamation, warning the people against seditious writings, pointing out the mischievous activity of the disseminators

* "Memorials and Correspondence of Fox," vol. iii. p. 262.

of French principles, and declaring that the law should be enforced. In ordinary cases of public ferment, this proclamation might have been thought useful by some, and needless by others, but would hardly have excited any serious difference of opinion. All that is connected with the French Revolution, however, is exceptional. An attempt was made to bring the Duke of Portland to the Council, when an order for the proclamation was to be given by the King; and although this attempt failed, the Duke's previous approbation was secured to the substance of the document.

When the proclamation was laid before Parliament by Mr. Dundas, it occasioned a violent debate. Mr. Grey made it the occasion of a powerful invective against Mr. Pitt; he declared that he considered the step taken by Government as intended to mark for reprobation the Association of the Friends of the People, and framed with a view to separate the Opposition. He denounced Mr. Pitt as a man whose whole political life was an act of apostacy.

On the other hand, Lord North, Lord Tichfield, Mr. Windham, and Mr. Powis approved of the proclamation. Mr. Fox on this occasion neither lost his temper, nor forgot his principles. He did not share in the alarm which affected one part of his friends, nor in the anger which excited the other. He said he stood in a very serious predicament; he had not signed the declaration upon which the Friends of the People had associated, and he could not subscribe to the principles upon which others of his friends supported this proclamation. In 1782 there was a meeting at the Thatched House, attended by Mr. Pitt, the Duke of Richmond, Major Cartwright, and Mr. Horne Tooke. Now some of his friends had got into company with the two former of these gentlemen, and some with the two latter. The Association of the Friends of the People had disavowed the doctrines of Major Cartwright and Mr. Horne Tooke; but there had been no disavowal of the others (meaning Mr. Pitt and the Duke of Richmond). In reply to Mr. Pitt, who had reproached him with not seeing danger in the writings attacked, he avowed he did not see danger because he knew that the good sense and the constitutional spirit of the people of this country were a sure protection against the absurd theories which had been alluded to. Nor did Mr. Pitt see danger till he saw, or thought he saw, in these writings, the means of stirring up division among the friends of freedom.

Unhappily, these divisions grew more and more marked. Yet, after the debate on the proclamation, an attempt was made to form a coalition between Mr. Fox and Mr. Pitt. Mr. Dundas, who always had the highest opinion of Mr. Fox's talents, and Lord Malmesbury, who was still personally attached to him, appear to have made the first overtures. Lord Malmesbury represented that, unless Mr. Fox accepted this offer, he could only expect to come into office by some violent outbreak, which would almost change the form of government. Mr. Dundas hinted that the offices of Secretary of State for Home affairs, two or three other cabinet offices—those of Lord President and Lord Privy Seal included, two or three Privy Councillor's places in the House of Commons—and several minor offices might be at the disposal of Mr. Fox.

Mr. Fox was at first favourably disposed to this junction. He said "It was so right a thing, it must be done."* He made no stipulation of Mr. Pitt's leaving the Treasury, but spoke of fair and even conditions to share equally all power

* Lord Malmesbury, vol. ii. p. 432.

and patronage; he evidently looked himself to the conduct
of foreign affairs.   Presently, however, he began to hesitate;
he doubted Mr. Pitt's sincerity; he said the honour, indeed
the pride, of the party must be consulted. Mr. Pitt, on
his side, found great difficulty with his friends, and probably with the King; he could not at once, said Mr.
Dundas, give the foreign office to Mr. Fox, owing to his
language in Parliament on the French Revolution; he
suggested, desired union, but made no direct acceptable
offer.

It is probable that no favourable issue to these negotiations could have been attained, unless the two principal
persons concerned had been far more in earnest than they
were.   Mr. Fox was at no time fond of office; he did not
like either the devotion of his time or the restraint upon his
freedom of speech which office required. Mr. Pitt, on the
other hand, greedy of power, reigned without a rival, and
feared no abilities, except those of Mr. Fox, which he might
find more formidable in the Cabinet than in the House of
Commons.

But whatever may have been the inclinations of these
two statesmen, there was a third politician, who looked
with dread to any additional influence to be allotted to
Mr. Fox. Lord Malmesbury gives us an account of a
meeting at his house, which was attended by Lords Loughborough and Porchester, Burke, Windham, Sir Gilbert
Elliot, Anstruther, Dr. Lawrence, and Elliot of Wells.
"Burke, with his usual eloquence, talked for an hour. He
said the Duke of Portland was riding in a ship with two
anchors, one cast in the Palais Royal, the other in Berkeley-
square; that he was the instrument of Fox's schemes, or
rather of Fox's abettors; that these had seduced Fox's

principles, had made him believe that a government like ours was not a proper one for great talents to display themselves in; that by working on his ambition, which, carried to excess, becomes wickedness, they had made him from these reasons approve and praise the French Revolution; that if he was to renounce them, it was because he must become a convert or a hypocrite; that he saw little of the first, that he dreaded we should be the dupes of the latter." Nothing can be more unlike Mr. Fox than this representation; his adherence to the principles of the Constitution had always been open and consistent; he had never gone the lengths of the Duke of Richmond, who was now in the Ministry; and he had given to Reform of Parliament only a general and guarded support. As to Mr. Fox's becoming a hypocrite, nothing can show the insanity of Mr. Burke more than such an insinuation.

That Mr. Pitt and Mr. Fox should not have been able to form a junction at this time is a circumstance calculated to excite more regret than surprise. It is true there did not exist any such difference of political opinion as should have forbidden the union. On Parliamentary Reform Mr. Pitt had gone further than Mr. Fox, but both statesmen were agreed that no Ministry could be formed on the basis of proposing Reform as a measure by which the Government should stand or fall. They both voted in favour of the abolition of the slave trade. Both had a dislike of penalties on religious dissent; both were cautious in the steps they took for removing those penalties. Mr. Pitt, indeed, had supported the maintenance of the Corporation and Test Acts. On the great question of France, the Revolution had now taken a shape which inspired disgust in Mr. Fox as well as in Mr. Pitt; Mr. Fox was averse to war, and Mr. Pitt, pledged to financial economy, was determined to maintain neutrality as long as he thought it possible.

But while Mr. Pitt was thwarted by followers jealous of a great intellect obscuring their scanty light, Mr. Fox was bound to obtain for his friends an influence in the Government which neither the King, nor the Tory party, nor the Burke Whigs would have seen without alarm. Lord Holland mentions a story, that Mr. Fox had a personal interview with Mr. Pitt, in which an objection was raised to Mr. Sheridan by Mr. Pitt, and that Mr. Fox honourably adhered to his political friend. But this obstacle, if it ever arose, was only a small part of the difficulty. Had Mr. Pitt consented to place in the Cabinet Mr. Fox and three of his friends, whom would he have named? The Duke of Portland and Lord Fitzwilliam would have opposed his views. Lord Spencer, Mr. Grey, Mr. Sheridan, and Mr. Windham would have differed in the Cabinet as they had done in Parliament.

Thus the position of public affairs made the union of Mr. Fox with Mr. Pitt impracticable. The absurd condition that Mr. Pitt should leave the Treasury, suggested by Lord Fitzwilliam, served to make that impossible which, in the opinion of all Mr. Burke's friends, nearly all Mr. Pitt's, and more than half of Mr. Fox's, was undesirable. Mr. Pitt, therefore, was left in sole possession of the Government.

CHAPTER XXXII.

GREAT BRITAIN—WAR WITH FRANCE.

MR. PITT, thus left without a rival in the Cabinet, was forced to choose a policy. His temper was pacific; his plan of government no less so; he had already built up a great fame by financial economy, domestic reforms, and a commercial alliance with France. Was the whole work to be overthrown? Was he to undertake to restrain and bring to reason the madmen who had already broken loose from their home and were roaming over the Continent? We may be sure that Mr. Pitt's inclination was averse to such a risk; that he would gladly have avoided war, and maintained a position of neutrality. But neither in the disposition of the French Assembly, nor in the inclinations of the governing classes at home, did he find support for his pacific wishes. There was in the Convention a party which, in the period between the King's deposition and his death, exercised great power, and which, equally with Mr. Burke, was bent on war. This was the party of the Girondins, led by M. Brissot, and often called by his name. This party, as soon as they saw that the King was helpless, sought his destruction. They conceived that a war with all Europe would tend to this result. But Robespierre, who was favourable to peace, pointed out another consequence not less certain, namely, that, in case of war, power would fall into the hands of a successful general, and not into those of a civil authority.* The Girondins, or Brissotines, who were the most short-sighted of all the parties in the Convention, were blind or indifferent to the loss of liberty which Robespierre so clearly foresaw: they argued that every provocation given in France would stimulate the Allied Sovereigns, and that every threat uttered by the Allied Sovereigns would hasten the fate of the unfortunate King. In this calculation they were but too well justified. But they looked no further.

The arms of the Republic were at this time crowned with brilliant success. Dumouriez now commenced that course of military tactics which consisted in giving free space to French impetuosity, careless of the lives he squandered, provided he could gain the victory he sought. Thus, at the battle of Jemmappes he carried, at the point of the bayonet, the strong entrenchments of the Austrian general, at the expense of a loss four or five times as great as that of his enemy. But his audacity was in some measure justified both by the nature of the war and the success of his operations. The French, wrought up to the highest pitch of enthusiasm, were hardly sufficiently disciplined to execute punctually the learned manœuvres of military tactics. Their energy was irresistible. The victory of Jemmappes was immediately followed by the conquest of Flanders. Tournay, Menin, Courtray, Ypres, Antwerp, Bruges, Ghent, and Malines fell into their possession, and Dumouriez himself entered Brussels in triumph. He gave the explanation of his policy in these words: "I can go very far with my

* Lamartine: "Histoire des Girondins."

Carmagnoles, but I do not spare them, and I shall want a great many recruits."

In pursuance of this plan he soon quitted Brussels, defeated the Austrians at Tirlemont, and entered Liége. Forbidden by the Convention to besiege Maestricht, he took up his winter quarters at Aix-La-Chapelle. The Low Countries had been conquered in a month; and the Convention, ready to throw down the gauntlet to Europe, decreed the opening of the Scheldt, and the annexation of the Belgian Provinces to France.

While these events happened on the Continent, societies in England sprung up like exhalations, to darken and disturb the prospect. The Revolution Society congratulated societies in France on the deposition of a tyrant and the enlightened philanthropy which had already accomplished so many great murders. The society was proud to observe: "Our enemies call us 'a society for revolutions;' we glory in the title; so long as a despotic government exists, we shall endeavour to deserve it."* Another society, called a Society for Constitutional Information, had been originally founded by the Duke of Richmond and Mr. Wyvill, and had counted Mr. Pitt among its members. It was now under the direction of Mr. John Horne Tooke and Major Cartwright, and was verging towards the great luminary of France. Another body, called the London Corresponding Society, was a ridiculous copy of the French models; they affected to introduce the terms "citizen" and "citizeness," and ardently desired that England might follow in the brilliant career of putting aristocrats to death without trial, and burning their houses without law, of

* Adolphus, vol. v. p. 212.

which France had given so happy, so wise, and so fraternal an example.

Yet this society, like its fellows, had little support. It held meetings in about thirty public houses situated in obscure lanes, and communicated with about thirty other societies, connected or affiliated.

On the 9th of November the Constitutional Society framed an address to the National Convention of France, congratulating them on their victories, and the prospect of a constitution founded on reason and nature. Lord Semphill and Dr. Towers signed this address.

The sense of the people seems to have revolted, as Mr. Fox said it would, against all this disgusting balderdash. An information having been filed against Paine's " Rights of Man," the author, though defended by Erskine, was found guilty by a jury without a moment's hesitation. A debating society in the city was suppressed by a strong body of constables, and the Court of Common Council unanimously voted their thanks to the Lord Mayor for suppressing the seditious society, and passed resolutions declaring their steady determination to support the Constitution.

Some riots occurred in Scotland, especially at Edinburgh and Dundee, but they were easily suppressed, and were not renewed.

Nor did the rational advocates of Parliamentary Reform afford any countenance to these frantic proceedings. In May the Society of the Friends of the People expressed, through Lord John Russell, their refusal to co-operate with the Constitutional Society. They condemned the addresses of the Constitutional Society as " the indefinite language of delusion, which, by opening unbounded projects of political adventure, tends to destroy that public opinion which is the support of all free government, and to excite a spirit of innovation, of which no wisdom can foresee the effects, and no skill direct the course." They thought it "their bounden duty to propose no extreme changes, which, however specious in theory, can never be accomplished without violence to the settled opinions of mankind, nor attempted without endangering some of the most estimable advantages which we confessedly enjoy. Associations formed in the face of power, in opposition to the interests of our present legislators, evince that individual security and personal independence are already established by our laws."*

Thus it appeared that, although the great volcano had sent some of its shower of ashes into our atmosphere, and its murky vapour had hovered over England, her fields were not destroyed, nor her bright sun of freedom obscured. A man of serene mind would have exclaimed :—

> "Fond impious man, thinkest thou yon sanguine cloud
> Thy hand has raised can quench the orb of day?
> To-morrow he renews his golden flood,
> And warms the nations with redoubled ray."

There can be little doubt that so late as the beginning of November, Lord Grenville, then Secretary of State, was still inclined to peace. On the 7th of November he wrote to his brother: "I bless God that we had the wit to keep ourselves out of the glorious enterprise of the combined armies, and that we were not tempted, by the hope of sharing the spoils in the division of France, nor by the prospect of crushing all democratical principles all over

---

* "Report of Committee of Secresy," 1794.

the world with one blow." Again, on the same day, "The Emperor must feel that he has now got an enemy whom he must devour, or be devoured by it. And the governing party at Paris have very many very obvious reasons for continuing the war. The rest of the empire will give their contingent, unless they have been wily enough to be forced to sign a capitulation of neutrality. The King of Sardinia and Italy will defend themselves as they can, which will probably be very ill. What Spain will do she does not know, and therefore certainly we do not. *Portugal and Holland will do what we please. We shall do nothing.* . . . . All my ambition is, that I may at some time hereafter, when I am freed from all active concern in such a scene as this, have the inexpressible satisfaction of being able to look back upon it, and to tell myself that I have contributed to keep my own country at least a little longer from sharing in all the evils of every sort that surround us. I am more and more convinced that this can only be done by keeping wholly and entirely aloof, and by watching much at home, but by doing very little indeed; endeavouring to rouse up in the country a real determination to stand by the Constitution, when it is attacked, as it most infallibly will be, if these things go on; and, above all, by trying to make the situation of the lowest orders among us as good as it can be made."*

A week after this Lord Grenville still seems to have entertained little or no apprehension. In a familiar letter to his brother he observes truly, that our laws suppose magistrates and grand juries to do their duty; he explains the origin of an absurd story called Cooper's " Ass's Feast;" states that the riot said to have happened at Sheffield did not

---

* " Court and Cabinets of George III."

deserve that name, even in the opinion of Lord Loughborough ; that the riot supposed to have taken place at Perth
he never heard of; and concludes with saying that it was
not unnatural that the body of landed gentlemen, who were
thoroughly frightened, should exaggerate these reports.*

The alarms of the country gentlemen, however, were increased to a panic by the insane provocations of the Convention. On the 19th of November they decreed, in the
name of the French nation, that they would grant fraternity and assistance to all people who wished to recover
their liberty; they charged the executive government to
send the necessary orders to the generals to give assistance
to any such people.

This decree naturally caused much indignation in England.
Had its terms been limited to the subjects of sovereigns
who had endeavoured to excite a civil war in France, it
might have been considered as fair retaliation; but as there
was no such limitation, and it was ordered that the decree
should be translated into all languages, the proceeding was
justly deemed an offence to all neutral powers.

Still, a step from peace to war had not yet been made
by either nation. The Ministry of Mr. Pitt had hitherto
professed the utmost desire to maintain their neutral position; but from the time of the decree of November they
seem to have made up their minds that such a position was
no longer tenable, and that they must throw in their lot
with the coalition of the Powers who had invaded France
and endeavoured to destroy her independence. The several
reasons which brought on this determination may be ex-
tracted from a correspondence between M. Chauvelin, the
agent of France, and Lord Grenville, now Minister of

* Lord Grenville : Nov. 14th, 1792. "Court and Cabinets of George III."

Foreign Affairs.   These reasons were afterwards stated and amplified in the proceedings of Parliament.   They may be thus summed up :—

1. The conquest of Flanders by the French, with the subsequent decree of the Convention, thus violating treaties and aggrandizing France.

2. The opening of the Scheldt, contrary to an express treaty.

3. The decree of November, inviting all nations to rise against their governments.

' 4. The danger to Holland.

1. On the 12th of May, 1792, M. Chauvelin, who had been sent with M. de Talleyrand to assist him to represent France at the Court of St. James's, addressed a note to Lord Grenville on the subject of the war which had been declared by France against the Emperor of Germany.   In that note M. Chauvelin said that he hoped the British Government would see the justice and necessity of the war in which France was engaged against the King of Hungary and Bohemia, and " moreover find in it that common principle of liberty and independence of which they ought not to be less jealous than France.   For England is free likewise because she determined to be so, and assuredly she did not suffer other powers to compel her to alter the Constitution she had adopted, to lend the smallest assistance to rebellious subjects, or to pretend to interfere under any pretence in her interior disputes."

In a subsequent letter of the 18th of June, M. Chauvelin pointed out the marks of a conspiracy against free states, which threatened universal war, and he called upon his Britannic Majesty " to stop while it is yet time the progress of that confederacy which equally threatens the peace, the liberty, the happiness of Europe," &c.

But the Government of England, so far from being jealous of a design to conquer and despoil France, secretly wished it success.   Lord Grenville therefore replied, on the 8th of July, that "the same sentiments which have determined him [the King] not to take a part in the internal affairs of France, ought equally to induce him to respect the rights and the independence of other sovereigns, especially those of the Allies; and his Majesty has thought, in the existing circumstances of the war now begun, the intervention of his counsels, or of his good offices, cannot be of use unless they are desired by all the parties interested."

It is obvious that Lord Grenville in this answer confounded two things essentially distinct.   It is one thing to decline to interfere in the internal affairs of another country, it is a totally different thing not to interfere with an external war which is intended to effect the conquest and share the spoils of one of the great members of the European confederacy.   The first is a due homage to the independence of another nation, the second is a culpable indifference to the peace of Europe and the treaties upon which that peace was founded.   Moreover, in the particular position of England, such indifference was nearly impossible.

Accordingly, the Government, which had looked on with complacency when the soil of France was invaded, became restless and menacing when Flanders was conquered. Remonstrance was loud, and complaint incessant.   It became obvious, therefore, to the French Government that a fair and honest neutrality was not the policy of the Cabinet of England.   Their intention evidently was to let the Allies conquer as much as they could; but if the fortune of war should turn in favour of France, to throw the sword of England into the balance.

2. The opening of the Scheldt.

Lord Grenville complained that the opening of the Scheldt was contrary to the treaties between the Emperor and Holland, to which England was a party, and that this abrogation of treaties at the will of a single Power shook the whole system of Europe.

The French Government replied that such a stipulation was contrary to the rights of Belgium and the laws of nature. That every country ought to have the use of rivers running through it, and that the Belgians had been deprived of this legitimate advantage without their consent. They added that the measure was only temporary, that France did not covet Belgium, and that at the general peace her liberty and independence might be secured on such conditions as might be agreed upon.

In this case, as in the former, the interference of England was too late. A great revolution was running its course, and as the war had not been prevented, the only wise course that remained was to make peace with events which had been completed, and accept a state of affairs against which no foresight had guarded.

In 1831 the independence of Belgium was acknowledged; the free navigation of the Scheldt had been previously sanctioned by the Powers of Europe.

" Ibi omnis
Effusus labor."

In fact, the closing of the Scheldt was a measure inspired by the commercial jealousy of the Dutch, and unjustly acquiesced in by a sovereign of the Low Countries, indifferent to their prosperity, and only anxious to shift from his own shoulders the burthen of defending them.

3. The decree of November.

M. Chauvelin maintains that this decree was only intended to apply to nations which had shaken off their old governments and required assistance in maintaining their independence.　But he does not say, nor could he say, that England was not one of the nations which might be expected to shake off its government and establish freedom in the French sense of the word.　In fact, the Monarchy, the House of Peers, and the Established Church constituted, in the eyes of the French Convention, a feudal tyranny. Nor did they hesitate to express to the various societies which appeared at their bar their sympathy with the sufferings of the people of Great Britain.

Here, then, a great question arises.　The French, from being the defenders of their own internal government, had become aggressors against the institutions of Europe, all marked more or less with the odious brands of royalty, aristocracy, or church.　How was peace to be kept with such a nation?

Yet here, again, we must revert to the situation of the preceding spring.　Austria and Prussia had maintained a large body of armed Frenchmen on the frontier of France, with the avowed intention of overthrowing the Constitution to which the King of the French had pledged his faith, and which the French people had accepted.　The King of Great Britain had professed his inability to interfere with the designs of the Allies.　Who could wonder, then, that the French should proclaim their principles as loudly as the Allies had proclaimed theirs, and should offer the assistance of their arms to all nations which should accept those principles?

The only real cure for such an evil, if cure was still possible, was a just interposition between the contending parties. If Austria and Prussia had been called upon to renounce all interference in the internal affairs of France, the Convention might, on such a pledge being given, be called upon to repeal its decree of November. The hostility of England might well have been proclaimed as the penalty of the power which should refuse to comply with so impartial a decision.

The genius and benevolence of Fox, the calmness and sagacity of Washington might, in such a spirit, have found the means of sparing to Europe rivers of blood and heaps of treasure. But Mr. Pitt, never very strong upon foreign affairs, and taken unawares by this fearful portent, found no solution of the difficulty but in yielding to the timid alarms of the commercial classes, and the ignorant fears of the " thoroughly frightened" landed gentry. Yet, on the 27th of the month of December, when it was too late, Mr. Pitt directed a dispatch to be written to the British Minister at Petersburg, which, until 1800, remained unknown. The dispatch contained an explanation of our policy, which the Court of Russia had requested us to give :—

" The two leading points on which such explanation will naturally turn," said the dispatch, " are the line of conduct to be followed previous to the commencement of hostilities, and with a view, if possible, to avert them ; and the nature and amount of the forces which the powers engaged in this concert might be enabled to use, supposing such extremities unavoidable. With respect to the first, it appears, on the whole—subject, however, to future consideration and discussion with the other Powers—that the most advisable step to be taken would be, that sufficient explanation should be had with the Powers at war with France, in order to enable those not hitherto engaged in the war to propose to that country terms of peace. That these terms should be, the withdrawing their arms within the limit of the French territory; the abandoning their conquests; the rescinding any acts injurious to the sovereignty or rights of any other nations, and the giving, in some unequivocal manner, a pledge of their intention no longer to foment troubles or to excite disturbances against other governments. In return for these stipulations, the different Powers of Europe who should be parties to this measure, might engage to abandon all measures or views of hostility against France, or interference in her internal affairs, and to maintain a correspondence and intercourse of amity with the existing Powers in that country with whom such a treaty may be concluded. If, on the result of this proposal so made by the Powers acting in concert, these terms should not be accepted by France, or being accepted, should not be satisfactorily performed, the different Powers might then engage themselves to each other to enter into active measures for the purpose of obtaining the ends in view, and it may be to be considered, whether, in such case, they might not reasonably look to some indemnity for the expenses and hazards to which they would necessarily be exposed."

Mr. Fox, when this dispatch was quoted for the first time in 1800, praised it as " a proper, wise, and legitimate course of proceeding." But he made two very just remarks upon it. The one, that it had never been communicated to France, and therefore had, in fact, never been acted upon. The other, that, in respect to conquests made by France, the language of M. de Witt to the confederates against the ambition of Louis XIV. was worthy of imitation. "When it was said that the French monarch had made unprincipled conquests and that he ought to be forced to surrender them all, what was the language of that great and wise man? 'No,' said he, 'I think we ought not to look back to the origin of the war, so much as to the means of putting an end to it. If you had united in time to prevent these conquests, well; but now that he has made them, he stands upon the ground of conquest, and we must agree to treat with him, not with regard to the origin of the conquest, but with regard to his present posture.'"

There can be little doubt that if, instead of waiting till the end of December, Mr. Pitt had by that time obtained the co-operation of Russia; if this concert had been notified at Paris, and if part of the Low Countries had been ceded to France, or the whole of Belgium erected into an independent State, as was done forty years afterwards, peace might have been restored to Europe. Possibly the life of Louis XVI. might have been spared; that of the Queen would in all probability have been saved. M. Chauvelin was instructed to say that Belgium should be free to choose her own form of government as an independent State. Austria, indeed, would have objected, but on the principle of the *uti possidetis*, she would have had no right to complain.

4. In regard to Holland, the French Government gave the most positive assurance that its conquest should not be attempted, so long as that *country* should confine itself within the bounds of an exact neutrality. These last words led to some cavils on the part of Lord Grenville; but Holland would of course have been secured by the shield of

England, had her views been friendly to French independence. Holland herself seems to have been only anxious to
be neutral, and was dragged by England, most reluctantly,
into the war.

Yet there was another reason, not consigned to state
papers, nor much dwelt on in Parliament, which, with the
landed gentry, and the majority of the two Houses of Parliament, had greater weight than any other. A fear crept
upon persons of property that the democratic principles of
France might take root in England, and it was thought
that by turning the minds of the people to foreign war this
danger might be averted. This reason has actually been
assigned as the prevailing motive of Mr. Pitt by an able
historian of our own day.*

This view of the question shows very little trust in the
attachment of the people of England to their institutions,
and very little disposition to do justice to the French nation.
If the Government of France had given us just cause of
war, we were entitled to repel the aggression upon our rights;
but if she had not done so, we could justify ourselves by
saying that her Revolution afforded so tempting an example, that we would go to war with her to quench that
example in blood. But, in fact, the English were becoming
more and more shocked by French crimes, and were so far
from being prone to revolutions, that they were becoming
averse to the most temperate reforms from dread of ulterior
consequences. Yet that the war was a war of panic I do
not mean to deny. Mr. Pitt loved above all things to be
Minister, and he could hardly have remained Minister had
he not yielded to the prevailing sentiment. It must have
been with a pang that he renounced economy for extrava-

* Sir A. Alison.

gance, commerce for armaments, and the hopes of reform for the prejudice against innovation which he had hitherto combated.

I have now gone over and examined the reasons in favour of the war. There were other reasons for a pacific policy which remain to be stated.

In the first place, it was difficult to contemplate war with France without at the same time contemplating intimate alliance with the Powers which were already belligerent. Their objects had been truly stated by Lord Grenville in the letter already quoted; they were "sharing in the spoils of the division of France," and "crushing all democratical principles all over the world with one blow." Now, it could not be the policy of England to achieve either the one object or the other. The division of France, if effected, would have destroyed one of the great members of the European family; the "crushing of all democratical principles" would have crushed at the same time the vital principles of the British Constitution.

In the next place, the same powers, Austria and Prussia, had, together with Russia, recently combined in the most nefarious project which the States of Europe ever beheld. Poland had lately revived and amended her Constitution. Prussia had congratulated her in the warmest terms on the consolidation of her Government. But Catherine, Empress of Russia, who had murdered her husband, and set at nought all the moral obligations which bind mankind together, had seen with anxiety the completion of this work. She dreaded lest Poland, in the enjoyment of freedom and independence, might thenceforth be happy and prosperous. She therefore proposed to Prussia the bait of Thorn and Dantzic as her part of the plunder in case of a partition.

Prussia eagerly gorged the hook, and gave as a reason for her perfidy the very constitution upon the inauguration of which she had been so loud in her congratulations!

Pretexts, indeed, were not wanting. Russia pretended a concern for some dissentient nobles, called the Confederates of Torgewitz, whom she afterwards denounced and disavowed. Prussia, in a manifesto of January, 1793, complained of the principles of French Jacobinism and the spread of revolutionary clubs. Mr. Fox treated with becoming scorn this scandalous pretext. "And how did he [the King of Prussia] cure them of these abominable principles? Oh! by an admirable remedy!—invading their country and taking possession of their towns! Are they tainted with Jacobinism? Hew down the gates of Thorn, and march in the Prussian troops! Do they deny that they entertain such principles? Seize upon Dantzic, and annex it to the dominions of Prussia!"*

By a treaty imposed by the combined Russian and Prussian arms, and signed on the 20th of August, 1793, Prussia obtained Thorn and Dantzic, and extended her frontier to the banks of the rivers Pilica and Skiernewka. Russia added to her dominions half of Lithuania, the palatinate of Podolia, Poloska, Minsk, a portion of Vilna, and the half of Volhinia, besides other territories. By a very needless piece of hypocrisy the contracting Powers guaranteed to Poland her remaining territory.

It was in union and close alliance with Powers such as these that Great Britain made war on France. The King made war, as the Royal Message to Parliament avowed, "for supporting his Allies; and for opposing views of aggrandizement and ambition on the part of France, which

* "Fox's Speeches," vol. v. p. 44.

would be at all times dangerous to the general interests of Europe, but are peculiarly so when connected with the propagation of principles which lead to the violation of the most sacred duties, and are utterly subversive of the peace and order of all civil society."*

It is difficult to see what principles would be more in violation of the most sacred duties, or which would lead more surely to the subversion of the peace and order of society than those which were acted upon by the authors of the partition of Poland.

There remained this further consideration—the Allies were united to dictate a government to France; George III. disavowed any such intention. How could Great Britain send subsidies to aid Prussia? How could she despatch troops to join her armies without sharing in the pursuit of her objects? And if sharing in her objects, then we should be at war to impose on France a government not of her choice but of ours. In this inextricable dilemma Mr. Pitt involved his country. He held sometimes one language and sometimes another; he sent money without inquiring how it was spent; he sent troops, which returned defeated; he burthened his country with an immense debt, and he aggravated all the evils he deplored.

There was another probability, although, in the estimate of sanguine politicians, it was hardly a possibility. The Emperor of Austria, or the King of Prussia, if not immediately successful in the partition of France and the suppression of democracy, might make peace with the sanguinary republic, and leave to England the cost and the danger of continued war. It was a contingency a wise Minister would have admitted into his calculations.

* " Parliamentary History," vol. xxx. p. 239.

In spite of all these grounds for a policy of peace, the Government, between the 19th and the 30th of November, seem to have resolved on a course which could not fail to bring on hostilities with France. · On the 1st of December a proclamation was issued stating that the utmost industry was still employed by evil-disposed persons within the kingdom, acting in concert with persons in foreign parts, to subvert the laws and established Constitution, and to destroy all order and government; and that a spirit of tumult and disorder, so excited, having lately shown itself in acts of riot and insurrection, his Majesty thought it necessary to embody the Militia. Parliament was summoned to meet on the 13th.

At the same time, or soon afterwards, a determination was taken to augment the land and sea forces. The explanations offered by M. Chauvelin regarding the decree of the 19th of November, the opening of the Scheldt, and the neutrality of Holland, were at the end of the month refused as utterly unsatisfactory.

It was plain that war with France was the deliberate choice of the British Cabinet. The extreme parties in France rejoiced exceedingly at this determination. The trial of the King was urged on with haste, and the flag of democratic propagandism was hoisted with exultation. The die was cast.

CHAPTER XXXIII.

THE confidence of the enemies of France was not less than that of her defenders. Great Britain, the German Empire, Russia, Spain, Sardinia, were about to marshal their forces to restore the French monarchy. At home Mr. Pitt saw his opponents divided, and he could now reckon on the support of the Duke of Portland, Lord Spencer, Lord Fitzwilliam, Sir Gilbert Elliot, many of the old Whig, and nearly the entire of the North party. Mr. Burke was about to contribute his powerful eloquence in support of the Minister he had so often and so vehemently denounced. While Mr. Pitt thus saw his Government immensely strengthened, he was not bound to admit any man into his cabinet who, like Mr. Fox, would have had a power of his own, derived from splendid abilities and the palm of many a debate. The country gentlemen were " thoroughly frightened;" the nation, averse to French theories, and attached to its own Constitution, was quite ready to resent any insult to the majesty of the Throne or the institutions of the country.

Thus everything seemed to prosper with the happy Minister; nor could his followers be induced to doubt that a few months of war would bring the French to their senses, and induce them to supplicate for peace. Their finances were disordered; their troops were recruits; their generals without experience; their Government in conflict with the Convention; their party contests ending invariably in the guillotine. How was it possible to suppose that such a country could withstand such a coalition?

Mr. Fox, though disheartened by the conduct of his friends, was not dismayed. He had made up his mind that peace might be preserved, and that it was his duty to lay before the country his own opinions. His friends might leave him—his party be broken up—his name become a mark for the finger of scorn—but at all hazards his duty must be done. Nobly did he perform it.

The Parliament met on the 13th of December. The King was advised to inform Parliament that not only a spirit of tumult and disorder had shown itself in acts of riot and insurrection, but that the industry employed to excite discontent had appeared to proceed from a design to attempt, in concert with persons in foreign countries, the destruction of our happy Constitution, and the subversion of all order and government.

As these persons in foreign countries were clearly the members of the National Convention of France, so likewise it was evident that war had now been resolved upon.

This resolution not being yet fully avowed, however, and Mr. Pitt having vacated his seat on his acceptance of the sinecure office of Lord Warden of the Cinque Ports, Mr. Fox did not think it necessary to discuss at length the subject of the impending hostilities. But he did not disguise his sentiments, or refrain from expressing boldly his opinions both on the state of Great Britain and the invasion of France. With regard to the first of these subjects, he said that there was not one statement in his Majesty's speech which was not false.

"An insurrection! Where is it? Where has it reared its head? Good God! an insurrection in Great Britain! No wonder that the Militia were called out, and Parliament assembled in the extraordinary way in which they have been. But where is it? Two gentlemen have delivered sentiments in commendation and illustration of the speech; and yet, though this insurrection has existed for fourteen days, they have given us no light whatever, no clue, no information where to find it. The right honourable magistrate tells us that, in his high municipal situation, he has received certain information, which he does not think proper to communicate to us. This is really carrying the doctrine of confidence to a length indeed. Not content with Ministers leading the House of Commons into the most extravagant and embarrassing situations, under the blind cover of confidence, we are now told that a municipal magistrate has information of an insurrection, which he does not choose to lay before the Commons of England, but which he assures us is sufficient to justify the alarm that has spread over the whole country! The honourable gentleman who seconded the motion tells us that the 'insurrections are too notorious to be described.' Such is the information which we receive from the right honourable magistrate and the honourable gentleman who have been selected to move and second the address. I will take upon me to say, sir, that it is not the notoriety of the insurrections which prevents those gentlemen from communicating to us the particulars, but their non-existence."*

With respect to the invasion of France, he said:—

* "Fox's Speeches," vol. iv. pp. 445-6.

"I do not wish to enter at length into the affairs of France, which form the next prominent passage in his Majesty's speech; but though I do not desire to enter at length into this part, I cannot conceal my sentiments on certain doctrines which I have heard this night. The honourable gentleman who seconded the motion thought proper to say, as a proof that there existed a dangerous spirit in this country, that it was manifested 'by the drooping and dejected aspect of many persons, when the tidings of Dumouriez's surrender arrived in England.' What, sir, is this to be considered as a sign of discontent and of a preference to republican doctrines? That men should droop and be dejected in their spirits, when they heard that the armies of despotism had triumphed over an army fighting for liberty? If such dejection be a proof that men are discontented with the Constitution of England, and leagued with foreigners in an attempt to destroy it, I give myself up to my country as a guilty man, for I freely confess that when I heard of the surrender or retreat of Dumouriez, and that there was a probability of the triumph of the armies of Austria and Prussia over the liberties of France, my spirits drooped, and I was dejected. What, sir, could any man who loves the Constitution of England, who feels its principles in his heart, wish success to the Duke of Brunswick, after reading a manifesto which violated every doctrine that Englishmen hold sacred, which trampled under foot every principle of justice and humanity and freedom and true government; and upon which the combined armies entered the kingdom of France, with which they had nothing to do; and when he heard or thought that he saw a probability of their success, could any man possessing true British feelings be other than dejected? I

honestly confess, sir, that I never felt more sincere gloom
and dejection in my life, for I saw in the triumph of that
conspiracy not merely the ruin of liberty in France, but the
ruin of liberty in England, the ruin of the liberty of man.
But am I to be told that my sorrow was an evident proof
of my being connected with the French nation or with any
persons in that nation, for the purpose of aiding them in
creating discontents in England, or in making any attempt
to destroy the British Constitution? If such a conclusion
were to be drawn from the dejection of those who are hostile
to the maxims of tyranny, upon which the invasion of
France was founded, what must we say of those men who
acknowledge that they are sorry the invasion did not
prosper? Am I to believe that the honourable gentleman,
and all others who confess their sorrow at the failure of
Prussia and Austria, were connected with the courts in
concert, and that a considerable body of persons in this
country were actually in the horrid league formed against
human liberty? Are we taught to bring this heavy charge
against all those whose spirits drooped on the reverse of
the news, and when it turned out that it was not Dumouriez,
but the Duke of Brunswick who had retreated? No; he
would not charge them with being confederates with the
invaders of France, nor did they believe, nor could they
believe, that the really constitutional men of England, who
rejoiced at the overthrow of that horrid and profligate
scheme, wished to draw therefrom anything hostile to the
established government of England."*

. Mr. Fox avowed openly, that instead of taking steps to
suppress opinion, he would, if called upon to advise, take
steps to redress grievances.

* " Fox's Speeches," vol. iv. pp. 447-9.

"But it may be asked," he said, "what would I propose to do in times of agitation like the present? I will answer openly. If there is a tendency in the dissenters to discontent, because they conceive themselves to be unjustly suspected and cruelly calumniated, what would I do?—I would instantly repeal the Test and Corporation Acts, and take from them, by such a step, all cause of complaint. If there were any persons tinctured with a republican spirit, because they thought that representative government was more perfect in a republic, I would endeavour to amend the representation of the Commons, and to show that the House of Commons, though not chosen by all, should have no other interest than to prove itself the representative of all. If there were men dissatisfied in Scotland or Ireland, or elsewhere, on account of disabilities and exemptions, of unjust prejudices, and of cruel restrictions, I would repeal the penal statutes, which are a disgrace to our law books. If there were other complaints of grievances, I would redress them where they were really proved, but, above all, I would constantly, cheerfully, patiently listen. I would make it known that if any man felt, or thought he felt a grievance, he might come freely to the bar of this House and bring his proofs, and it should be made manifest to all the world that where they did exist they would be redressed, where they did not, that it should be made evident. If I were to issue a proclamation, this should be my proclamation:— 'If any man has a grievance, let him bring it to the bar of the Commons' House of Parliament with the firm persuasion of having it honestly investigated.' These are the subsidies that I would grant to Government."*

Mr. Fox moved an amendment promising inquiry into.

* "Fox's Speeches," vol. iv. pp. 459-60.

the causes of " measures adopted by the Executive Government, which the law authorizes only in the case of insurrection within the realm."   Mr. Fox was supported by Mr. Grey, Mr. Sheridan, and Mr. Erskine; but he was opposed by Mr. Windham and Mr. Burke, who followed the lead of Mr. Dundas. The division was 290 to 50. Mr. Fox must have been reminded of the commencement of the American War.

It can hardly be denied that the assertion of an insurrection was a mere pretext to enable Ministers to call out the Militia. The nation was overflowing with loyalty, and the tumults which had occurred were by no means formidable. That which took place at Manchester was caused by a Church and King mob, and was directed against a Mr. Walker, who distributed Jacobin pamphlets. There can be no doubt that in the whole country, in point of numbers, as well as of property and intelligence, the majority in favour of the British Constitution, of King, Lords, Commons, as against a French Republican Constitution of a single Convention chosen by universal suffrage, and absorbing all the powers of the State, was overwhelming.

The most intelligent members of the Convention knew this fact, and admitted it in their State Papers.

The British Government, however, taking advantage of the panic, introduced a bill to place certain restrictions on aliens coming into the country. They were to register their names, to give up their arms, not to travel unless provided with passports, and to be subject to the discretion of the Secretary of State.

This was a very unworthy admission of fear of foreign propagandism. It was objected to by the French Minister as directly contrary to the articles of the commercial treaty of 1786. He was, however, hardly entitled to make such a remonstrance while the decree of the 19th November remained in force. The bill was resisted by the Opposition on the broader grounds of reason and of policy.

It seemed good to the friends of the Duke of Portland to take this occasion to force him to a public separation from Mr. Fox. This rupture must have been painful to the Duke of Portland. From a position of splendid insignificance he had been raised by Mr. Fox to the headship of the great Whig party, in disregard of the claims of the Duke of Richmond and of Mr. Fox himself, to that high position.

He had scarcely any of those qualities which gave Lord Rockingham, though not an effective speaker, a commanding influence in the councils of his party. He had no art in reconciling differences, he had no great public virtues which made him an object of reverence to the nation. The Duke of Portland bore a fair character, and that was all. Yet, as he was the recognised leader, it became a matter of extreme consequence to the alarmists to bring him to their side. Their visits to him were continual. One night three of their chiefs passed with him two hours of incessant importunity, dragging from him only monosyllables, and beholding his silent, dejected face.* At length, on a subsequent day, they obtained from him authority to Sir Gilbert Elliot to express his sentiments in the House of Commons in opposition to those of Mr. Fox.

* Lord Malmesbury, Sir Gilbert Elliot, and Elliot of Wells were the three Job comforters. Lord Malmesbury thus describes his political leader: "I, although I have often seen him *benumbed* and *paralysed*, never saw him, or any one else, so completely so before. All was one dead silence on his part; he seemed in a trance, and nothing could be so painful as those two hours, for our conversation lasted as long as that, reckoning intervals of ten and fifteen minutes' silence."—"Malmesbury Correspondence," vol. ii. p. 445.

On the second reading of the Alien Bill this authority was used. Sir Gilbert Elliot, on this occasion, expressed his regret at a difference of opinion from some of his honourable friends whom he highly respected and esteemed. He had received distinguished marks of friendship from Mr. Fox. The difference of opinion he now entertained he had felt since the close of the last session. It was not a difference regarding a particular measure—it was a difference which affected their whole course of conduct, and their whole turn of thinking. He was happy to think he did not stand alone; he spoke the sentiments of many honourable friends with whom he had been accustomed to act, and who still continued to act upon their ancient principles, and under their ancient leader, the Duke of Portland—that illustrious personage whose character was so highly respected, and whose sentiments could not fail to have the greatest weight. He went on to say that the Duke of Portland was favourable to the present Alien Bill.

This speech was a severe, nay, a cruel blow to Mr. Fox. Two persons, one of whom was the recognised leader of the Whig party, and the other a prominent member, had concurred in discarding Mr. Fox and creating themselves into a separate party; and all this without notice of any kind to him!

Mr. Fox laid the whole blame of this novel proceeding on Sir Gilbert Elliot. Yet it appears that Sir Gilbert had been authorized by the Duke of Portland to make a declaration in favour of the Alien Bill; and to the Duke of Portland's timidity and want of openness the chief fault must be attributed.

Mr. Fox rose after Sir Gilbert Elliot, and expressed his surprise that a difference of opinion should have existed between the honourable baronet and himself since the close of the last session, and yet that this should be the first occasion on which he had the least reason to suppose the existence of that difference. He had hoped, although some of his friends might differ from him on particular measures, their difference with the Ministry remained the same—a difference which had been formerly called fundamental and irreconcilable. He had heard, in this and other places, that the Administration ought to be systematically supported in the present situation of affairs. He blamed not those who said so; but with regard to himself, and those who entertained that opinion, union and co-operation were at an end. "The honourable baronet had alluded to the Duke of Portland, with whom he had lived sixteen or seventeen years on terms of friendship, and for ten of those years in habits of the greatest intimacy and affection. He had long acted, and continued to act, with persons whose characters he esteemed and loved, but if he should be driven, which God forbid! to the situation of acting without, or even against, those persons, he hoped and trusted he should have sense enough to perceive his duty, and fortitude to perform it."

An allusion to Mr. Burke as having banished his friends to Sinope, brought on a vehement speech from that great orator, in the course of which he alluded to the manufacture of three thousand daggers at Birmingham; and producing one from his breast, threw it with great violence on the floor.

Thus was dissolved that great party which had been formed in 1783 by the coalition of Mr. Fox and Lord North. Scarcely an adherent of that Minister, says Lord Holland, remained with Mr. Fox, except his son George North, now Lord Guildford, and Mr. Adam.

It appears to me that this falling off when a question relating to the principles of liberty arose, is an additional presumption against the original coalition. A similar case occurred about 1818-19, when the Grenville branch of the Grey and Grenville party in like manner abandoned Opposition to support the Government. The reason of these separations was that the previous alliance had been founded on concurrence of opinion on a particular occasion, and not identity of principle. Lord Loughborough was the first of the North party to lead the deserters; when in an interview of an hour he had endeavoured to obtain the approbation of the Duke of Portland and had failed in eliciting a single word, he said at last, with the handle of the door in his hand, "Then I am to understand that your Grace disapproves of this step?" The Duke answered dryly: "Most certainly."* For some time the language of Burlington House was that of severe censure on the new Lord Chancellor.

Far more important was the defection of the Duke of Portland himself, Lord Spencer, Lord Fitzwilliam, Mr. Windham, and Mr. Thomas Grenville, the leaders and the props of the Whig party. There can be no question that an honest difference of opinion led to this secession. It was futile to say that the manner in which Mr. Pitt had first assumed office formed an eternal barrier between him and the Whig chiefs. The people, in the election of 1784, had given him absolution for that offence, and had that condonation been less complete, the circumstances of 1792 were too grave to admit of so pedantic a punctilio. It was a convenient watchword while no other public differences existed; but it would have been a sacrifice

* Lord Holland: " Memoirs of the Whig Party."

(in their view) of the public interests, if those who thought the country in danger from French principles, had kept up a systematic opposition to a Government which shared in their apprehensions, and was about to enter into war with their approbation.

Mr. Fox received some atonement for Sir Gilbert Elliot's abrupt attack on a subsequent day in a speech of Lord Tichfield, who, while he supported the Alien Bill, declared his opinion of the Ministry to be as adverse as it had ever been. Mr. Fox in a short speech declared himself satisfied, and Sir Gilbert Elliot himself owned that he was the organ of the Duke of Portland's sentiments only as respected the Alien Bill.

This speech of Lord Tichfield seems to have been produced by the following letter of Mr. Fox to the Duke of Portland, dated December 31, 1792:—

" MY DEAR LORD,—Though I mean to call upon you in the course of the morning, yet as it may be uncertain whether I shall have an opportunity for a full conversation with you, I think I owe it to our long and uninterrupted friendship, to tell you plainly and directly my thoughts upon the state of this last unpleasant business; and especially with respect to what may pass to-day. That Sir G. E.'s speech was made with the intention to force you in some way or other to a declaration which might undo the effect of your speech in the House of Lords, I have no doubt, and I certainly suspect that in this project he was the agent of those who wish, at all events, to widen the breach, if they can find one, or to make one, if they cannot find it, between you and me. His indelicacy in delivering an opinion from you, which, from what has since passed,

.I must think you never authorized him to do in public, and his pertinacity in so doing, when he knew that Lord Titch-field was to speak, leave me, I own it, in no doubt of his unfair intentions,—full as unfair, if not more so, towards you as to me. I hope he will not have succeeded in making any breach between us, but he has in my judgment succeeded in making it necessary for you, either by yourself or Lord Titchfield, to declare yourself fully; and it is with regard to this declaration to be made to-day, as I understand, by Lord Titchfield, that I feel myself incredibly anxious. If it should be in the smallest degree ambiguous, if it should not be as perspicuous and explicit as language can make it, the consequences to *me* will be very unpleasant indeed, but to *you* much worse; if after to-day it should remain a question, whether you are or are not a supporter of the Ministry—whether you still remain the head of that Opposition which has so long considered you as such, I must speak the truth and tell you, that your name will be bandied about in a manner which I cannot bear to think of, and possibly it may become necessary for you. to make another explanation and to have the repetition of these scenes, in which, if I am to judge from myself, you must have felt much more than is commonly understood by the words " anxiety" and " distress." My fears upon this head are the stronger on account of some expressions, particularly two, which, from what I heard from you and others who have seen you, I think Lord Titchfield may possibly use. The first is, *relaxing from the severity of Opposition.* These words, when I heard them first, did not strike me to be so objectionable as they appear to me now upon reflection. They certainly convey the idea of the system of *opposing* more than I understand you to have done; because, to what do they apply? Certainly not to this bill, and others of a similar complexion, because, with respect to such measures, you do not relax in opposition to them, but you actually support them. They will therefore be not unreasonably applied to the other measures, or general conduct of Administration, and in fact be considered as tantamount to Mr. Burke's *dulcification* and *neutralization*. This sense I take to be directly repugnant to your speech. You say you consider the present mischiefs as in part owing to the misconduct of Ministers. Surely, then, though it may be necessary to support particular measures which the safety of the country may require, it is a time with regard to the men rather to redouble your vigilance and jealousy, than to relax in your severity. The other expression which I heard of with alarm, was a hope that we (meaning you and me) might soon *meet again*. If anything of this sort is said, it will give great credit to those who give out with so much industry that we are separated, and great discredit to me who maintain everywhere the contrary. I feel the impropriety of suggesting expressions to you, and still more to Lord Titchfield; but I own I think he ought to be, for your sake, still more than for mine, very distinct and explicit, and that he ought to declare directly either that he is a supporter of Ministry, and separated from me, or the direct contrary—that he remains in his former sentiments and conduct with respect to both them and me. If, as I hope, the last is nearest to his opinion, I need not say that the present bill and other measures formed upon the ground of the dangers in which you believe, and I do not, may be made an exception without any inconsistency. To support individual measures of Administration, while we act in general opposition to the

Ministers, is no new conduct to us, and though I own that, if such measures become more important, and are more frequently the subjects of discussion, in such case the union of those who differ upon them will become more lax, and the opposition to those with whom we so often concur more feeble; yet this is an evil which may arise, but ought not to be anticipated. Indeed, in the present case, I am the more sanguine, because I know so few points upon which you and I do actually differ. However, this is matter for future consideration, and rather a digression from the immediate object of this letter, which is to press you by every consideration both of friendship for me, and regard for yourself, as well as wish for the preservation of the Whig Party, to think justly of the importance of this day; to see the necessity of being completely explicit.

"Yours most affectionately,

"C. J. Fox."

Notwithstanding the anxiety expressed in this letter for a maintenance of the connexion, it was evident that the chasm was too deep to be filled up. A difference of opinion in the policy to be pursued towards France was a difference affecting every question of urgent importance which could be brought before Parliament. Exclusion of foreigners deemed dangerous—provocations to war—a refusal to negotiate until France changed her Government,—were the inevitable consequences of the policy which Mr. Pitt had now adopted. Opposition to reform, extravagant subsidies, enormous loans, must form part of the same system.

This was the system which the Duke of Portland, Mr. Burke, Lord Fitzwilliam, and Mr. Windham agreed to support, and which Mr. Fox was determined to resist. There could be no concert or sympathy between them.

I have mentioned the chief persons who left the banner of Mr. Fox to follow that of Mr. Pitt. Of those who remained by his side the leaders were Charles Grey, whose manly eloquence fitted him to reach the highest eminences of the State; Richard Brinsley Sheridan, the most brilliant orator and most sparkling writer of his time; Thomas Erskine, the most powerful advocate who ever addressed a jury; Samuel Whitbread, the intrepid and consistent friend of all liberal and enlightened views. With them sat Mr. Coke and Mr. Lambton, two of the richest of the country gentlemen; Lord John and Lord William Russell, brothers of the Duke of Bedford, who himself was firm in his support of Mr. Fox. Lord George Cavendish voted with Mr. Fox on his amendment to the Address, but I do not find his name either in the minority on his resolutions against the war nor on Mr. Grey's motion for reform. The minority, which in the first division was 50, sunk to 44 and then to 41 on Mr. Grey's resolutions.

Yet, few as they were, the principles they maintained, their powers of debate, and the truly patriotic sentiments they enunciated, gave them great means of keeping alive the lamp of constitutional liberty, though its light often flickered in the wind, or was scarcely perceptible in the surrounding darkness. To them we owe, perhaps, the maintenance of our free Constitution.

On the report of the committee on the Alien Bill the discussion took a wider range than it had hitherto done, and Mr. Fox explained and enforced his views on the state of the country. "To what purpose was a military force prepared?—to repel opinions? Opinions were never yet driven out of a country by pikes and swords and guns. How then were they to be met if they existed? By contempt, if they were absurd; by argument, if specious; by prosecutions, if seditious. . . . . Could not Ministers have prosecuted Paine without an army? Was any apprehension stated that the trial would not be allowed to go on in the usual course? . . . . He knew not how to fight an opinion, nor did history furnish him with instruction. The opinions of Luther and Calvin had been combated by arms; there was no want of war, no want of blood, no want of confederacies of princes, to extirpate them; but were they extirpated? No; they had flourished through bloodshed and persecution." Yet, while Mr. Fox disapproved of a war of opinion, of which Mr. Burke was the advocate, he said much to prove to his old friends that he was not the friend of peace at any price. He admitted that if the Dutch called upon us to resent the opening of the Scheldt as a *casus fœderis*, we were bound by treaty to respond to the call. "He thought the same national spirit which, under Louis XIV., had threatened the liberties of all Europe, might influence, and had influenced, the conduct of the French at present;" nay, it was more likely to collect and act now than at the former time. He thought the danger great and imminent, and he had voted for the increase of the army and navy because he never knew a Minister so bad that he would not trust him with a fleet and army rather than expose the country to danger. He spoke with just abhorrence of "the detestable massacre of the 2nd of September," and observed that the fact "that the crime was not prevented or followed up by striking examples of punishment would be an indelible disgrace to Paris and to France."

The course that Mr. Fox would have advised, had he at this time been Secretary for Foreign Affairs, would evidently have been that of armed negotiation. As Holland was ready to do what England wished, he probably would have counselled her not to insist on the perpetual closing of the Scheldt; but he would have taken ample security for her independence. He would have required France to refrain from further conquests, upon securing an assurance that England would guarantee her against another invasion, on the ground of her internal affairs. He would have interposed the good offices of Great Britain to save the life of the King, and he would have openly recognised the French Republic. How far such a policy might have succeeded no one can say; but it would have been just, fearless, and magnanimous. Let us now see what a contrary course produced.

The party which had organized the insurrection of the 10th of August had apparently succeeded in their object. They had forced the King to fly from his palace; they had murdered his defenders; they had deposed him and confined him in a prison. A republic had been proclaimed, and the monarchy was abolished. But whether their thirst of blood led them to choose the most illustrious victim—whether they delighted in immolating a life which their enemies had declared to be sacred—or whether they were merely actuated by the vanity of showing themselves the equals of the judges of Charles I. in boldness and vigour—in short, whatever was the motive for so useless an act of cruelty, the Convention determined to proceed to the public execution of Louis, with the previous form of a judicial proceeding.

On the 7th of November it was resolved by the

Convention that Louis should be tried, and from a day in December till the middle of January the pretended trial was prolonged. In vain Lanjuinais and others protested that the Convention was not a court of justice; in vain Diseze, his advocate, quoted the article of the Constitution by which, in case of the most manifest treason, deposition was the utmost penalty to which the sovereign could be subjected. Robespierre, scorning any pretence to do justice, called for the execution of Louis as a measure of public safety.

During the interval between the middle of December and the day of condemnation, some attempts were made to save the King's life by the intervention of England. Mr. Pitt, however, when applied to, thought it beneath the dignity of England to make an application which was not likely to be successful.* Mr. Burke, looking to the effect to be produced by the King's death, thought it was not worth while to save the carcass of the monarch, if the monarchy was to perish. Mr. Fox alone seems to have been zealous and sincere in his efforts to save the King's life. But he was not in a position to interfere with effect.

It was decreed by a great majority that Louis was guilty of conspiracy against liberty, and of attempts, crimes and offences against the general safety of the State. It was likewise decreed, by a majority of 424 against 283, that there should be no appeal to the people. At length, on the 16th of January, at eight o'clock in the evening, the question was put, "What punishment has Louis incurred?" In this sitting every one pronounced his opinion, standing at the tribune, at such length or with such brevity as he might choose.

* Villemain.

At the end of twenty-four hours it appeared that, of 714 who voted, those who voted simply for death were 361; for detention in prison, banishment, or other punishment, 286. But 67 voted for death with some delay, or precedent condition, such as the invasion of French territory. These were vain or cowardly pretences. But, considering that ferocious bands of assassins filled all the avenues to the Chamber, and that the memory of the days of September was raw enough to give a cold shudder to all present, it is surprising that so many as 286 refused to sanction the sentence of death. After this vote the Assembly adjourned till the 18th. On that day the question was put, " Shall the execution of the sentence on Louis Capet be postponed ? Yes or no."

Number of voters, 690. For delay, 310; against, 380.

There was, therefore, a majority of 70 in favour of immediate execution. The sentence was carried into effect on the Place de la Revolution on the 21st. The King mounted the scaffold with a firm step, went to the left of the · platform and said, with a loud voice, " Frenchmen, I die innocent; I pardon my enemies. I wish that my death may be ——" The beating of drums, ordered by Santerre, interrupted and stifled his voice; and at twenty minutes past ten his head fell from the guillotine.

If the conduct of Louis as King of France were to be impartially reviewed, many parties might blame him. The friends of the monarchy might justly reproach him with abandoning the reins when guidance was most required. The friends of Constitutional government might reasonably complain that, instead of placing a Ministry composed of Mirabeau and his friends at the head of his affairs, he wasted his influence in corruption and fruitless intrigues. The authors of the Constitution of 1791 might arraign him for endeavouring to overthrow, by means of foreign armies, the institutions he had sworn to maintain. England, too, might have recollected that when her revolted sons were pressing her hard, Louis took advantage of her distress, and broke her western dominion into fragments. But all such reflections were cast aside at the sight of the appalling catastrophe. Men called to mind that Louis mounted the throne at twenty years of age; that absolute power was placed in his hands; and that he willingly divested himself of his prerogatives that he might the better provide for the welfare of his people. They contrasted his virtuous domestic life with the unbounded sensuality of his predecessor. They reflected on the bright dawn, the tempestuous day, and the dark evening of his reign. They sobbed with pity over his meek endurance of calumny and outrage; the calm piety he opposed to brutal blasphemy; and the Christian resignation with which he submitted to ruffian insolence. The very absence of all struggle on his part made the victory of his enemies more odious, more despicable, more sacrilegious.

Amid the general feeling of sorrow and indignation which shook the bosoms of men with unusual and almost overpowering emotions, Mr. Pitt brought down a message from the Crown, accompanied by the diplomatic correspondence of Lord Grenville, and two days afterwards proposed a vote which was rightly interpreted as the prelude to war with France. It was no wonder that, in the storm of passion which swept over the political horizon, few could be found to weigh the reasons, or calculate the hazards, or estimate the cost of this new crusade. Those who did so were nearly overwhelmed by the scorn of indignant patriotism. We are in a position to examine somewhat more closely the arguments by which Mr. Pitt urged his country to a war for life or death with a numerous, warlike, and enthusiastic people.

The Minister, on the 1st of February, moved an Address to the Crown expressing condolence on the death of the King, and pledging the House to resist the aggrandizement of France. His speech displayed the highest qualities of an experienced orator. He began by pathetic lamentations over the execution of Louis, as an event unexampled in history, and he applied to it the quotation in which De Thou reproached his countrymen for the Massacre of St. Bartholomew :—

> "Excidat ille dies ævo, neu postera credant
> Secula : nos certe taceamus et obruta multâ
> Nocte tegi nostræ patiamur crimina gentis."

Yet he dwelt for some time upon this act as a natural consequence of the principles the French had adopted, and which, he said, must shake the security of life, and rob the humblest individual in every country of that which was most dear to him. Having thus wound up his hearers to a due pitch of horror and indignation, he proceeded to refer to the correspondence of M. Chauvelin with Lord Grenville. He read the assurance given in the preceding month of May, that the King of France did not seek aggrandizement, would not foment insurrections, and would respect the rights of his Majesty and his Allies. He then argued that the conquest and annexation of Savoy was a breach of the first of these engagements ; that the decree of November was a violation of the second ; and that the opening of the Scheldt was in contravention of the third. He pointed out the conduct pursued by Dumouriez in Flanders as a proof that France meant to impose her notions of liberty upon all nations, whether they wished it or not; and he gave the somewhat lame proof of this assertion that the tree of liberty had been planted at Brussels in the midst of a square formed by French troops. He concluded a very able and masterly speech in these words—"If France is really desirous of maintaining friendship and peace with England, she must show herself disposed to renounce her views of aggression and aggrandizement, and to confine herself within her own territory without insulting other Governments, without disturbing their tranquillity, without violating their rights; and unless she consent to these terms, the final issue must be war." After stating that explanation was not yet precluded, he added—"But I should disguise my sentiments to the House if I stated that I thought it *in any degree probable.* This country has always been desirous of peace. We desire it still; but such as may be real and solid, and consistent with the interests and dignity of Britain, and with the general security of Europe. War, whenever it comes, will be preferable to peace without honour, without security, and which is incompatible either with the external safety or the internal happiness of this country."

If this speech left any doubt whether war was meant, the terms of the Address moved by Mr. Pitt were fitted to dispel any such doubt. The execution of Louis was deplored as "an outrage on religion, justice, and humanity; and as a striking and dreadful example of the effect of principles which lead to the violation of the most sacred duties, and are utterly subversive of the peace and order of all civilized society." The House went on to declare themselves "sensible of the views of aggrandizement and am-

bition, which, in violation of repeated and solemn professions, have been openly manifested on the part of France,
and which are connected with the propagation of principles
incompatible with the existence of all just and regular
government." The House then, for the purpose of opposing
these views of aggrandizement, went on to promise a
further augmentation of the King's forces by sea and
land.

Notwithstanding Mr. Pitt's great art as an orator, and
the ascendency he had acquired over the assembly he inspired and ruled, there was one question which must have
struck all men not blinded by passion.   Mr. Pitt had declared that the only terms of peace he would listen to would
be that the French should retire within their frontiers, and
renounce all attempts to carry their principles into foreign
countries.   But it is manifest that, if the French had complied with these conditions, the Allies would have been at
liberty to renew their attempts to conquer and divide
France, and to inculcate their principles of government
at Paris.   Was it possible for the French to agree to such
conditions?   Could they withdraw their troops from Savoy
and Flanders, quench the enthusiasm they had excited,
and leave the members of the National Convention to be
sent to the dungeons of Olmutz and Spandau, if not to the
scaffold?   Mr. Pitt had himself felt so forcibly the iniquity
of such conditions that he had proposed to the Empress of
Russia to impose upon the Allies the condition, that they
should not interfere in the internal affairs of France.   But
neither in the correspondence with M. Chauvelin, nor in
the present speech of Mr. Pitt, is any trace of such a condition to be found.

After Lord Wycombe and Mr. Whitbread had opposed

the Address, Mr. Fox rose. He felt it a duty to speak out frankly and fairly; if he were deterred by calumny from delivering his opinions because they might be unpopular, he should basely betray his trust to his constituents and his country.

He pronounced the condemnation and execution of the King to be an act as disgraceful as any that the page of history recorded. Not only were the rules of criminal justice —rules that more than any other ought to be strictly observed—violated with respect to him; not only was he tried and condemned without any existing law to which he was personally amenable, and even contrary to existing laws, but the degrading circumstances of his imprisonment, the unnecessary and insulting asperity with which he had been treated, the total want of republican magnanimity in the whole transaction, added every aggravation to the injustice and inhumanity of those acts.

Having said this as the genuine expression of his feelings and his conviction, he saw neither propriety nor wisdom in that House passing judgment on any act committed in another nation which had no direct reference to us. The general maxim of policy was, that the crimes perpetrated in one independent State were not cognizable by another.

With respect to Holland, the conduct of Ministers afforded a fresh proof of their disingenuousness. They could not state that the Dutch had called upon us to fulfil the terms of the alliance. In the order for a general fast, issued by the States-General in the month of January, it was expressly said, "That their neutrality seemed to put them in security amidst surrounding armies, and had hitherto effectively protected them from molestation." This he by no means construed into giving up the opening of the Scheldt on their part, but it pretty clearly showed that they were not disposed to make it a cause of war unless forced to do so by us.

The decree of the 19th of November he considered as an insult, and he was ready to admit that a tacit repeal would not be a sufficient reparation; but we were bound to say what reparation we required.

"Next it was said, they must withdraw their troops from the Austrian Netherlands, before we could be satisfied. Were we, then, come to that pitch of insolence as to say to France, 'You have conquered part of an enemy's territory who made war upon you; we will not interfere to make peace, but we require you to abandon the advantages you have gained, while he is preparing to attack you anew.' Was this the neutrality we meant to hold out to France? 'If you are invaded and beaten, we will be quiet spectators, but if you hurt your enemy, if you enter his territory, we declare against you.' If the invasion of the Netherlands was what now alarmed us—and that it ought to alarm us if the result was to make the country an appendage to France, there could be no doubt—we ought to have interposed to prevent it in the very first instance, for it was a natural consequence which every man foresaw, of a war between France and Austria. The French now said they would evacuate the country at the conclusion of the war, and when its liberties were established. Was this sufficient? By no means; but we ought to tell them what we would deem sufficient, instead of saying to them, as we were now saying, 'This is an aggravation, this is nothing, and this is insufficient.' That war was unjust which told not an enemy the ground of provocation and the measure of atone-ment—it was as impolitic as unjust, for without the object of contest clearly and definitively stated, what opening could there be for treating of peace? Before going to war with France, surely the people who must pay and must suffer ought to be informed on what object they were to fix their hopes for its honourable termination. After five or six years' war, the French might agree to evacuate the Netherlands as the price of peace. Was it clear that they would not do so now, if we would condescend to propose it in intelligible terms? Surely in such an alternative, the experiment ,was worth trying. But then we had no security against French principles! What security would they be able to give us after a war which they could not give now?

"With respect to the general danger of Europe, the same arguments applied, and to the same extent. To the general situation and security of Europe we had been so scandalously inattentive; we had seen the entire conquest of Poland, and the invasion of France, with such marked indifference, that it would be difficult now to take it up with the grace of sincerity; but even this would be better provided for by proposing terms before going to war.

"He had thus shown that none of the professed causes were grounds for going to war. What, then, remained but the internal Government of France, always disavowed, but ever kept in mind, and constantly mentioned? The destruction of that Government was the avowed object of the combined Powers whom it was hoped we were to join; and we could not join them heartily if our object was one thing while theirs was another, for in that case the party whose object was first obtained might naturally be expected to make separate terms, and there could be no cordiality nor confidence. To this, then, we came at last, that we were ashamed to own our engaging to aid the restoration of despotism, and collusively sought pretexts in the Scheldt and the Netherlands. Such would be the real cause of the war, if war we were to have—a war which he trusted he should soon see as generally execrated as it was now thought to be popular. He knew that for this wish he should be represented as holding up the internal government of France as an object for imitation. He thought the present state of government in France anything rather than an object of imitation, but he maintained as a principle inviolable, that the government of every independent State was to be settled by those who were to live under it, and not by foreign force."*

The people of this country loved their Constitution. They had experienced its benefits, they were attached to it from habit. Why, then, put their love to any unnecessary test? . . . If there were any danger from French principles, to go to war without necessity was to fight for their propagation.

The justifiable grounds of war were injury, insult, danger. For the first satisfaction, for the second reparation, for the third security was the object. Each of these was the proper object of negociation, which ought ever to precede war, except in case of an attack actually commenced. If we did but know for what we were to fight, we might look forward with confidence, and exert ourselves with unanimity; but while thus kept in the dark, how many might there be who would believe that we were fighting the battles of despotism! If Mr. Pitt would but save the country from a war—above all, a war of opinion—he would gladly give

* "Fox's Speeches," vol. v. pp. 19–21.

him a general indemnity, and even a vote of thanks. Let not the fatal opinion go abroad, that kings have an interest different from that of their subjects !

This speech of Mr. Fox, though very able and striking, wanted the method of Mr. Pitt, and was not equal to many of his own speeches in sustained and pressing argument.

In fact, the insane conduct of the French Convention, now that all hope of assistance or mediation from England had been destroyed, precipitated the impending rupture. On the 1st of February, the same day upon which Mr. Pitt made his warlike speech, the Convention actually declared war against Great Britain and Holland. Had they not taken this course, Mr. Pitt must have demanded the evacuation of Flanders, and on the refusal of France, he must have advised a declaration of war. The Convention saved the Minister from this necessity, and in the eyes of those who looked only at the surface, made Great Britain appear the aggrieved party. In point of fact, the French Convention were eager to make war, and the insufficient reasons they gave for it showed how willing they were to take up the gauntlet thrown down by Mr. Pitt.

On the 12th of February, a message from the Crown was brought to the two Houses, informing them of the French declaration, and calling upon Parliament to support the Crown, not only in resisting France, but in conjunction with the King's allies, in preventing the extension of anarchy and confusion.

Mr. Pitt, in the House of Commons, in moving an address to the Crown, discussed the reasons for war alleged by France. These were :—1st. That since the 10th of August, the ambassador of Great Britain had been withdrawn from Paris, and that the Minister of the Republic had not been acknowledged in London. 2ndly. That in violation of the Treaty of Peace of 1783, and the Treaty of Commerce of 1786, the exportation of corn to France had been prohibited, French citizens were not allowed freely to enter England, as provided by the treaty of 1786, and that money had been given to chiefs and officers in arms against the Government of France, in violation of the Treaty of Peace of 1783. 3rdly. That Great Britain had armed both by sea and land, and that it was obvious, from the language used in Parliament, that these armaments were intended to be used against France.

It is obvious that all these steps were consequences of the extraordinary position of France and of Europe; of the deposition of the King and the provisional character of the French Government; of the language held by the Convention to the English societies who came to denounce the British Constitution at their bar; of the opening of the Scheldt and the conquest of Flanders. They might have been fair subjects of negotiation and arrangement, had there been the least disposition on either side to negotiate and to arrange. But the British Government was happy to seize the opportunity offered by the French declaration. Mr. Dundas, who was more open than Mr. Pitt, confessed that the proclamation prohibiting the sending corn to France did not originate from any necessities of this country, but was a necessary measure of precaution for the purpose of crippling the French. This was done, be it observed, while we professed to be neutral! Mr. Dundas said that, although there had been no treaty with the Emperor in January, his Majesty's Ministers would now endeavour to bring down every power on earth to assist them against France. This clearly implied interference in the internal government of France. To the same purport, he said, he would leave it to the feelings of gentlemen to determine whether, after the atrocious act committed in France, M. Chauvelin could be allowed to remain as accredited from the Republic. He meant, of course, that after the execution of the King, no relations of amity could be maintained with France. He ended with saying :—" They were going to war with France, to secure the best interests of the country, by effectually opposing *a set of principles which, unless they were crushed, would necessarily occasion the destruction of this and every other country.*" Mr. Dundas thus openly proclaimed a war of opinion in concert and alliance with the abettors of despotic power against the asserters of democratic license.

Mr. Fox had spoken before Mr. Dundas. He admitted that he was now called upon to support his Majesty in the war, for the war was begun, and he would do it. But he disclaimed all the crooked reasonings and unfounded pretences upon which the war had been founded. The admitted evils of war were sufficient to prove that war should never be undertaken, when peace could be maintained without breach of national faith, injury to national honour, or hazard to future security. " We complained of an attack on the rights of our ally, we remonstrated against an accession of territory, alarming to Europe ; but we proposed nothing that would be admitted as satisfaction for the injury, we pointed out nothing that would remove our alarm. Lord Grenville said something about withdrawing the French troops from the Austrian Netherlands ; but if by that was understood a requisition to withdraw their troops while they were at war with the Emperor, without any condition that such evacuation of territory conquered from the enemy was to be the price of peace, it was such an insult as entitled France to demand satisfaction. The same argument would apply to their conquest of Savoy from the King of Sardinia. . . . . Yet on this the whole question of aggression hinged; for that the refusal of satisfaction, and not the insult, was the justifiable cause of war, was not merely his opinion, but the opinion of all writers on the law of nations. . . . . He felt great respect for monarchy, and it was neither his practice nor his inclination to speak harshly of kings. He had already said that monarchy was the corner or rather the keystone of the British Constitution, which was limited and not unlimited monarchy. But was it not possible that the limited monarchy attempted to be set up in France was the true cause of the combination of some of the crowned heads of Europe? If we joined the Emperor and the King of Prussia, we must make common cause with them, or act always with jealousy and suspicion of parties, either of whom might secure their own views by a separate peace."

This is exactly what happened. In 1795, Prussia made a separate peace, and we were left with all the burthen and expense of the war we had begun to support her independence.

Mr. Fox moved an amendment to assure his Majesty, that his Majesty's faithful Commons will exert themselves with the utmost zeal in the maintenance of the honour of his Majesty's crown, and the vindication of the rights of his people :—"That nothing should be wanting on their part in repelling every hostile attempt, and any other exertions that might be necessary to induce France to consent to such terms of pacification as may be consistent with the honour of his Majesty's Crown, the security of his allies, and the interest of his people." This amendment was negatived without a division.

Among the delusions by which Mr. Burke had deceived himself, there was none so contrary to fact as the dream that France had been governed by a religious clergy, a virtuous aristocracy, and a pure Administration. Mr. Sheridan, in supporting Mr. Fox, exposed these fictions admirably:—" The philosophers had corrupted and perverted the minds of the people; but when did the precepts or perversions of philosophy ever begin their effect on the root of the tree, and afterwards rise to the towering branches? . . . . He contended that the general atheism of France was, in the first place, no honour to the exertions of the higher orders of the clergy against the philosophers, and in the next place, that it was notorious that all the men and women of rank and fashion in France, including possibly all the present emigrant nobility, whose piety the right honourable gentleman seemed to contrast with republican infidelity, were the genuine and zealous followers of Voltaire and Rousseau; if the lower orders had been afterwards perverted, it was by their precept and example. The atheism therefore of the new system, as opposed to the piety of the old, was one of the weakest arguments he had yet heard in favour of this mad political and religious crusade."*

A curious illustration of this just remark of Mr. Sheridan occurs in a little work of La Harpe, entitled " Prophecy of Carnotte." He represents a gay supper of the highest nobility and most choice philosophers, at which the Duchess of Grammont amuses the company by quoting some of the least decent verses of Voltaire. Carnotte, a sullen and sar-

* " Parliamentary History," vol. xxx. p. 394.

castic man of letters, breaks in and predicts that most of the party will die by the hands of the executioner, and that Condorcet will destroy himself to escape that fate. "What!" they say, "is there to be an irruption of Vandals and Tartars into France?" "No, madam, the persons who will commit these atrocities will be the disciples of your own beloved philosophers." "And, La Harpe? you have not predicted his destiny." "La Harpe will turn Christian." On which there is a general laugh, and the Duchess cries out, "Oh! if we are not to lose our lives till La Harpe turns Christian, our heads are safe enough!" And thus the supper breaks up amid general gaiety and security. Such, indeed, was the general irreligion of the higher orders, that the Vicar-General of the Bishop of Autun (Talleyrand) is reported to have said of him—"The bishop is a very weak man; he believes in God."

But, to return to Mr. Sheridan, in the speech already referred to he remarked :—"It was a mean and narrow way of viewing the subject, to ascribe the various outrages in France to any other cause than this unalterable truth, that a despotic Government degrades human nature, and renders its subjects in the first recovery of their rights, unfit for the exercise of them."

Mr. Fox's amendment was negatived without a division.

On the 18th, Mr. Fox moved resolutions with a view of putting on record his opinions. The debate contained little that was new ; Mr. Fox was supported by Mr. Grey, Mr. Adam, and Mr. Lambton, and opposed by Mr. Burke in one of his wildest orations. The previous question being moved, the numbers were—Yeas 44, Noes 270.

The first three resolutions contain Mr. Fox's deliberate opinions on the subject of the war. They are :—

1. "That it is not for the honour or interest of Great Britain to make war upon France on account of the internal circumstances of that country, for the purpose either of suppressing or punishing any opinions and principles, however pernicious in their tendency, which may prevail there, or of establishing among the French people any particular form of government.

2. "That the particular complaints which have been stated against the conduct of the French Government are not of a nature to justify war in the first instance, without having attempted to obtain redress by negotiation.

3. "That it appears to this House, that in the late negotiation between his Majesty's Ministers and the agents of the French Government, the said Ministers did not take such measures as were likely to procure redress, without a rupture, for the grievances of which they complained; and particularly that they never stated distinctly to the French Government any terms and conditions, the accession to which, on the part of France, would induce his Majesty to persevere in a system of neutrality."*

It has been untruly said, that the purport of these resolutions was to declare that in the recent transactions Great Britain had been in every case wrong, and France right and just.† The doctrine of Mr. Fox, as we have seen, was that the opening of the Scheldt was a violation of treaty, and the decree of the 19th of November an insult to Great Britain, but that it behoved the British Government not merely to complain, but to state what reparation she would accept. Moreover, that if our terms were that France should deprive herself of her means of offence against her invaders, but that her enemies should be left in full pos-

* "Fox's Speeches," vol. v. p. 45.   † Adolphus.

session of the means to attack, to conquer, and to dismember the French territory, such terms would not be just or equal. It is difficult to resist the force of this reasoning now that the passions of that day have in great measure subsided.

It seems singular that so little reference was made to the events which occurred in England in 1649. The English had made war upon their King, they had imprisoned him, they had beheaded him; yet no statesman in Europe then proposed to make war on England to root out the abominable principles of the levellers of those days; on the contrary, the two principal Powers of those days, France and Spain, hastened to conciliate the good-will of the Commonwealth.

In reviewing the speeches of these two great men, it is a duty to do justice to the motives of Mr. Pitt. French historians of the greatest eminence, such as M. Mignet and M. Thiers, have not hesitated to declare as certain that Mr. Pitt desired war, that he wished for it to strengthen his own Cabinet, and to establish the maritime and colonial preponderance of Great Britain. I believe, on the contrary, that his most anxious desire was to preserve neutrality, and that he hoped amidst the storms of the Continent, by a wise system of economy and a judicious repeal of taxes affecting industry, to place the prosperity of Great Britain on a sure basis.

The progress of events, the horror caused by the crimes of the Revolution, the fear of French conquests in Belgium and Holland, and the influence of Mr. Burke and the Whig peers, drove him from this position. The question remains, how far was he right in resolving upon war at the time and in the manner he did?

It can hardly be denied, I think, that the tacit consent

and secret favour given to the invasion of France in the spring of 1792 was a serious mistake. Great Britain, as experience has shown, can scarcely be long a stranger to the convulsions of the Continent of Europe. In the case before us, the attempt of the Allies could not by possibility lead to a peaceable and definitive settlement. If the Allies had reached Paris, if they had liberated Louis, if they had hung the majority of the Convention, and shot thousands of mayors, magistrates, and peasantry, according to their own declared intentions, how would such proceedings have tranquillized France? How could Louis, restored to liberty at the head-quarters of the Allies, have conferred upon his subjects institutions which would have satisfied his people? How could the French be expected to submit to the loss of their independence while they were in the first fervour of a jealous love of liberty and exaggerated antipathy to monarchy? If, aware of this difficulty, the Allies had proceeded to weaken, to disarm, and even to dismember France, how fierce would have been the struggle and how uncertain the result!

If, on the other hand, as it actually fell out, the march to Paris should not only be a difficulty, but a failure, who could believe that the wild leaders of the Assembly, the republican Brissotine, and the ambitious Dumouriez, would adhere to the promise of refraining from conquest and intervention which had been held out to Great Britain as an inducement for her interference?

Here, then, was the first serious error of Mr. Pitt. If in answer to the request of the King of France, conveyed by M. Chauvelin, he had advised the King to declare that he would not allow any interference in the internal government of France, nor any conquest by France under whatever pretext it might be covered, he would probably have saved the King's life, and prevented a war in Europe. He committed the mistake of thinking that England could remain an unconcerned spectator of a war against all liberty on the one side and all monarchy on the other.

In order to excuse this error, Mr. Pitt afterwards pretended that the war had been from the first one of aggression on the part of France. The private letter of Lord Grenville, his Foreign Secretary, tells a very different tale :—

" I bless God," he says, " that we had the wit to keep ourselves out of the glorious enterprise of the combined armies, and that we were not tempted by the hope of sharing the spoils in the division of France, nor by the prospect of crushing all democratical principles all over the world with one blow."

Such, then, were in Lord Grenville's opinion the views of the Allies. But to divide France and crush democratical principles, even supposing such objects to have been legitimate, were evidently unattainable ends.

Let us now listen to the same Lord Grenville, when this nefarious attempt was in progress :—

" September 20th, 1792. — The Duke of Brunswick's progress does not keep pace with the impatience of our wishes," &c.

Then again, when it failed, he writes :—

" October 11th, 1792.—We are all much disappointed with the result of the great expectations that had been formed from the Duke of Brunswick's campaign." Then, after attributing the retreat to a flaw in the Prussian army, he concludes : " Whatever be the cause, the effect is equally to be regretted."

It was in such a temper that the Government of Great Britain viewed the failure of the attempt to divide France and crush democracy. It was obvious that nothing like fair arbitration was to be expected from such a Government. Accordingly, while Lord Grenville insisted that all the conquests of France should be evacuated, and the decree of the 19th of November repealed or disavowed, he never offered to protect, secure, or guarantee France against a renewal of the Duke of Brunswick's march, and the execution of the majority of the Convention as traitors and murderers. It was quite impossible that any Government of France should accept such unequal terms. Here, then, was the second error of Mr. Pitt. He made his country clearly the aggressor in the war.

In the next place, the British Government, having thus brought on the declaration of war by France, immediately joined the Allies, and, with profuse liberality, gave troops, money, and concert for objects which Mr. Pitt disavowed. To interfere in the internal affairs of France was the declared purpose of Austria and Prussia; to interfere in the internal affairs of France was inconsistent with all the declarations made by Mr. Pitt and Lord Grenville in the name of their sovereign. In order to cover this inconsistency Mr. Pitt, with a vagueness of language in which he frequently indulged, attributed the execution of Louis XVI. to principles which he called upon Parliament and the country to resist. That the execution was an atrocious murder all men felt, but, taken by itself, it was purely an act of the internal Government of France. The principles upon which the act was perpetrated were the same principles upon which Charles I. and Mary Queen of Scots were beheaded—namely, considerations of the security of

the governing power in defiance of the rules of justice and
law. Elizabeth and Cromwell had acted upon the same
principles which Robespierre had avowed in the Convention.

When the further question arose what was the security
for the future which was to be required as a condition of
peace, this vagueness of purpose was still more apparent.
We shall see presently how wide was the difference between
Mr. Pitt and the Allies. Mr. Pitt, at Toulon, was willing
to accept Louis XVII. with the Constitution which Mr.
Burke had so loudly disavowed. The Sovereigns of Austria
and Prussia sought their own aggrandizement, and the
suppression of democracy all over the world.

Let us now, with the knowledge of subsequent events
which we possess, see what have been the fruits of Mr.
Pitt's policy. In the first place the war, which his supporters did not expect to last two years, lasted upwards of
twenty. The National Debt of Great Britain increased
from two hundred and fifty millions to eight hundred millions. Battles were fought in which the prowess of two
brave and mighty nations was conspicuous to the whole
world, and memorable to all history.

The French, of whom Mr. Burke's successors were to
say, "Gallus quoque audivimus olim in bello floruisse,"
gained the battles of Gemappes, Fleurus, Rivoli, Marengo,
Hohenlinden, Austerlitz, Jena, Friedland, and Wagram.
The English have to boast of victories both by sea and
land at Camperdown, St. Vincent, the Nile, Trafalgar,
Vimiera, Talavera, Salamanca, Vittoria, and Waterloo.
But what was the result of all this bloodshed? What
object was attained which might not have been otherwise
secured? The pressure of war furnished victims to the

guillotine, and the Reign of Terror was prolonged by the Allies.

The question remains, whether the policy of Mr. Fox —that of armed arbitration abroad, and the redress of grievances at home—would not have preserved Europe from the devastation of conquest, and Great Britain from a weight of taxes which still enhances to every man and woman in the United Kingdom the price of ordinary articles of comfort, and aggravates the task of industry by an addition to the hours of labour? To this question every one must furnish an answer for himself.

On the 6th of May, Mr. Grey made his promised motion for Parliamentary Reform. He first presented a petition from the Society of the Friends of the People, which deserves to be considered as an historical document. He then proceeded to argue on the very imperfect state of the representation, and moved that the several petitions be referred to a select committee.

Mr. Pitt could hardly insist, after the course he had himself pursued, on the abstract perfection of the state of the representation. His strongest argument for opposing the motion was, that the great majority of the people were opposed to any change at that time. His weakest was derived from the French Revolution. Taking advantage of an admission of Mr. Grey, that he proposed to refer all the petitions on the table to a select committee, he pointed out that some of these petitioners prayed for universal suffrage, and then declaimed at great length on all the horrors produced, as he said, by that suffrage in France.

Mr. Fox made a powerful exposure of the inconsistency of Mr. Pitt's arguments, and a candid statement of his own views on Reform. He reminded the Minister that his

own motion had been for a select committee; and that he
had thereby induced Mr. Fox himself, who objected to his
plan, to vote with him.   Nay, more, if Mr. Horne Tooke
and Major Cartwright were now friends to universal
suffrage, that principle had been first put forward by the
Duke of Richmond, with whom, upon this very question,
Mr. Pitt acted.

With regard to any plan of Reform, Mr. Fox was con-
sistently cautious.   He said he believed that if the wisest
men of all countries were brought together, they could not
form even a tolerable political constitution.   He used the
familiar illustration of building a house, and said that the
most skilful architect could not build, in the first instance,
so commodious a dwelling as one that had been gradually
improved by successive alterations.   If, then, so simple a
structure as a commodious house was so difficult in theory,
how much more difficult the structure of a government!
The American Constitution formed no exception to this
remark; they had not a Constitution to build from the
foundation; they had ours to work upon, and adapt to their
own wants and purposes.   This was what the present
motion recommended; not to pull down, but to work upon,
our Constitution, to examine it with care and reverence, to
repair it where damaged, to amend it where defective, to
prop it where it wanted support, to adapt it to the purposes
of the present time, as our ancestors had done from generation to generation, and always transmitted it not only
unimpaired, but improved, to their posterity.   In the same
spirit he objected to universal suffrage; not from a distrust
of the decision of the majority, but because by the operation of hope in some, fear in others, and all the sinister
means of influence that would so certainly be exerted,

fewer individual opinions would be collected than by an appeal to a limited number.

He was equally frank with regard to the Monarchy and the House of Lords. " But it was said a House of Commons so chosen as to be a complete representation of the people would be too powerful for the House of Lords, and even for the King; they would abolish the one and dismiss the other. If the King and the House of Lords were unnecessary and useless branches of the Constitution, let them be dismissed and abolished; for the people were not made for them, but they for the people. If, on the contrary, the King and the House of Lords were felt and believed by the people, *as he was confident they were*, to be not only useful, but essential, parts of the Constitution, a House of Commons freely chosen by, and speaking the sentiments of the people, would cherish and protect both, within the limits assigned to them by the Constitution.

The motion was rejected by 282 to 41. Nor, although the sentiments of Mr. Fox would be styled in these days Conservative rather than otherwise, can it be said that the motion was one the House of Commons ought to have adopted. It was a time to adhere to old forms, rather than seek for improvements, however beneficial, in the constitution of Parliament; and Mr. Pitt placed himself on strong ground when he said truly, that the great majority of the people did not wish for any change.

Parliament was prorogued on the 21st of June.

CHAPTER XXXIV.

REIGN OF TERROR.

I PROPOSE here to make some remarks on that appalling course of events ending in what is appropriately called the Reign of Terror.

When Louis first assembled the States-General the wishes of the electors were recorded in the powers given to their representatives. The points on which these wishes were nearly unanimous were the following: 1. The Government of France is a monarchy. 2. The person of the King is inviolable and sacred. 3. The crown is hereditary in the male line. 4. The King is the depository of the executive power. 5. The agents of the royal authority are responsible. 6. The royal sanction is necessary for the promulgation of laws. 7. The nation makes the law with the royal sanction. 8. The consent of the nation is necessary for the imposition of taxes and the making of laws. 9. Taxes can only be granted for the period from one meeting of the States-General to the next. 10. Property is sacred. 11. Individual liberty is sacred.* In the royal sitting of the 23rd of June the King granted in effect all these demands, with the addition of the liberty of the press and provincial States. But he required that the

* See the various histories of the French Revolution, and especially "Abregé Chronologique."

three orders should meet separately, and that the consent of each order should be necessary for any future change of the law.

This was the first stumbling-block of the Revolution. Necker, by his awkwardness, raised it into immense importance; Mirabeau took up the quarrel, and in four days forced the King to surrender.

But Mirabeau was himself an admirer of representative monarchy; his speech in favour of leaving to the Crown the prerogative of peace and war is a masterpiece of reason and eloquence. The men who inherited his influence left to the Crown only a shadow of authority. The transfer of the royal family to Paris introduced the physical force of the mob as an element in framing the Constitution.

In the midst of these agitations, during which the democracy was always encroaching, and royalty always suspected, a new party arose called the Girondins, who, with much eloquence and little wisdom, denounced the monarch in whose feeble hands authority was already expiring. They succeeded in their object. The King was put to death. But they had wished for a republic of riches, of luxury, of literature, and the arts. They had founded a republic of rude force and woollen nightcaps. A member of the Convention said with truth, "These men during the monarchy were always calling out for a republic, and now that they have got a republic they want to restore something like a monarchy." They were, in the natural course of events, deposed, imprisoned, and guillotined.

Now arose the last struggle; what was to be the form and spirit of the new republic? The mind of France had been prepared for the revolution by two men entirely different in their understandings, their tastes, their wishes,

and their habits. Voltaire, "the spoiled child of the world,
which he spoilt," excelled in ridiculing the religion and
government of his country, while he favoured every licence,
indulged every vice, and looked forward to an age of
brilliant society, pleasant suppers, and general incredulity.
Rousseau, on the other hand, poor, sullen, and suspicious,
drew all his philanthropy from his imagination. He held
that man is a benevolent being till corrupted by institutions and arts; that despotic governments ought to be
overthrown, and every act of sovereignty ought to emanate
from the general will, which always means right, and
though it may be deceived, can never be corrupted. Liberty
and Equality are the great ends of civil society; liberty
consists in the possession of sovereignty by the people;
equality, in such a distribution of riches, as well as of
power, that no man shall be wealthy enough to buy his
neighbour, and no man poor enough to fall into dependence.
The sovereignty of the people is no mere abstract dogma;
man is by nature a benevolent being, and therefore fit to
exercise the sovereignty he possesses.

Hitherto, it may be said, the government of France had
been in the hands of the disciples of Voltaire. Loménie de
Brienne, Mirabeau, Dumouriez, Danton, were all men without faith, without morals, all greedy of getting money, and
profuse in spending it; bribed by the Court, faithless to
the power which bought them, democrats for interest;
selfish in their ends, unscrupulous in their means.

Another school—that of Rousseau—was now to arise.
These were men of ardent faith in themselves and in
human nature; ferocious and sanguinary in disposition;
ready to wade through slaughter in order to realize their
theory; hated deeply all that had preceded and now sur-

rounded them—court, clergy, nobility; and jealous, above all, of those who competed with them for the government of the State.

In his speech on the 7th of May, 1794, Robespierre proclaimed at once his antipathies and his idolatry. "The Encyclopedists contained some estimable characters; but a much greater number of ambitious rogues. Many of them became leading men in the State. Whoever does not study their influence and policy would form a most imperfect notion of our Revolution. It was they who introduced the frightful doctrine of atheism; they were ever in politics below the dignity of freedom; in morality they went far beyond the detraction of religious prejudices. Their disciples declaimed against despotism, and received the pensions of despots; they composed alternately tirades against kings and madrigals for their mistresses; they were fierce with their pens, and rampant in antechambers. That sect propagated with infinite care the principles of materialism, which spread so rapidly among the great and the *beaux-esprits*. We owe to them that selfish philosophy which reduced egotism to a system; regarded human society as a game of chance, where success was the sole distinction between what was just and unjust; probity an affair of taste or good breeding; the world as the patrimony of the most dexterous of scoundrels.

"Among the great men of that period was one distinguished by the elevation of his soul and the greatness of his character, who showed himself a worthy preceptor of the human race [Rousseau]. He attacked tyranny with boldness, he spoke with enthusiasm of the Deity. His masculine and upright eloquence drew in colours of fire the charms of virtue; it defended the elevated doctrines which

reason affords to console the human heart. The purity of his principles, his profound hatred of vice, his supreme contempt for the intriguing sophists who usurped the name of philosophers, drew upon him the hatred and persecution of his rivals and friends. Could he have witnessed our Revolution, of which he was the precursor, and which bore him to the Pantheon, can we doubt he would have embraced with transport the doctrine of justice and equality?
. . . . . What strange coalitions have we seen, in persons embracing the most opposite opinions, in favour of the doctrines which I combat! Have we not heard, in a popular society, the traitor Gaudet denounce a citizen for having pronounced the name of Providence? Have we not, some time after, heard Hébert accusing another of having written against atheism? Was it not Vergniaud and Geusonné who, in your very presence, descanted with fervour from your tribune on the propriety of banishing from the preamble of the Constitution the name of the Supreme Being, which you had placed there? Danton, who smiled with scorn at the words glory, virtue, posterity. Danton, whose system it was to vilify whatever can dignify the mind. Danton, who was cold and mute in the midst of the greatest dangers of liberty, was warm and eloquent in support of the same atheistical principles. Whence so singular a union on this subject among men so divided on others? Did they wish to compensate their indulgence for aristocracy and tyranny by their war against the Deity? No, it was because they all alike, though from different motives, strove to dry up the fountains of whatever is grand and generous in the human heart. They embraced with transport, to justify their selfish designs, a system which, confounding the destiny of the good and the bad,

leaves no other difference between them but the casual distinctions of fortune; no other arbiter but the right of the strongest or the most deceitful. . . . How different is the God of nature from the God of the church! The priests have figured to themselves a God in their own image; they have made Him jealous, capricious, cruel, covetous, implacable; they have enthroned Him in the heavens as a palace, and called Him to the earth only to demand, for their behoof, tithes, riches, pleasures, honours, and power. The true temple of the Supreme Being is the universe; his worship, virtue; his fêtes, the joy of a great people, assembled under his eyes to draw closer the bonds of social affection, and present to Him the homage of pure and grateful hearts."

If we compare these eloquent words of Robespierre with the frightful deeds of the time at which he spoke them, we shall be struck with amazement and horror. "The bonds of social affection" were drawn closer, "the homage of pure and grateful hearts" was paid by the daily murder of hundreds of innocent human beings, who were condemned to death for being related to aristocrats, for corresponding with their sons or their brothers, for being priests—nay, for a sigh, a tear, a gesture. The Queen, whose title to sympathy no one will deny, was brutally murdered; Malesherbes, the intrepid defender of the King, was condemned for sheltering a supposed emigrant; the prisons were filled with women of noble birth, whose rank, beauty, and name were their only crime. The Duchess of Grammont, when placed before the tribunal, said, pointing to Madame de Châtelet, who was placed beside her: "I know it would be useless to speak about myself, but what has this angel done? She who never took any part in political contests, who belonged to no party, was involved in no intrigues, but was devoted only to works of charity. There are others as innocent, none so little open to suspicion as she is."*

When the son of Buffon was accused of having conspired in the Luxembourg, he said simply: "I was confined in St. Lazare, and could not have conspired in the Luxembourg." "No matter," said Fouquier Tinville, "you conspired somewhere."

The very chiefs of the extreme party, those who had no mercy for the King, no pity for the victims of September, were among the chief sufferers in the Reign of Terror. Danton, Camille Desmoulins, Hébert, Ronciu, Anarcharsis Clootz, followed Marie Antoinette to the tribunal and the scaffold. Indeed, it seems strange that, while Moury, Cazalis, Bouilli, Lafayette, Dumouriez, and the orators of the Constituent Assembly, were safe from the guillotine, even-handed justice should have commended the poisoned chalice to the lips of those who had prepared its ingredients.

The decrees of the Convention erected into crimes a multitude of acts, or even accidents, in themselves innocent. Being an emigrant or a banished priest entailed the punishment of death in twenty-four hours.† Their agents and domestics who took part in any insurrectionary movement, a similar punishment. Those who had shown themselves partisans of tyranny or federalism, the wives, daughters, sisters, fathers, husbands, brothers of emigrants who had not shown their attachment to the Revolution, were declared suspected and liable to arrest, to be detained till duly acquitted.‡ More than 300,000 persons were arrested.

* Alison. Serac de Meilhan, p. 147.　　† Law of 18th March.
‡ Loi des Suspects, 17th Sept.

The worst of the Roman emperors, in the excess of their tyranny, had denounced and destroyed those of their subjects who by their riches, their character, or their sentiments made themselves odious to those cruel monsters. But these atrocities were confined to Rome and to a number comparatively small. In France, 500,000 of the most depraved wretches to be found among the dregs of society were formed into clubs, each of which exercised collectively and individually arbitrary and despotic power. The possession of fortune, relationship to an emigrant, having exercised the functions of a priest, the expression of pity for a person unjustly condemned, offence given in former days to some low scoundrel or ungrateful dependent—in short, any or no cause sufficed to mark the victim for the guillotine. Twenty-four millions of pounds sterling a year were distributed among these committees. At Paris some forty or fifty victims were brought out every day to be executed. The vile mob followed with their execrations the sacrifices of the day; whether it were the noble daughter of Austria, Marie Antoinette; Madame du Barry, the frivolous courtesan; Madame Roland, the ardent Republican; Bailly, the first Mayor of Paris; or Camille Desmoulins, the author of the tricolour cockade;—neither lofty virtue nor cowardly ruffianism afforded any immunity; neither the grey hairs of Malesherbes nor the bloody Jacobinism of Hébert gave safety to those whom Robespierre denounced. Danton, on the first proclamation of war, had said: " The coalesced kings threaten us, and we throw down at their feet, as our gage of battle, the head of a king." Within a year his own head was exhibited as that of a traitor who had conspired with Dumouriez and the foreign enemy.

Combined with this sanguinary terror was the most.

active, vigilant, unsparing application of all the means of war. Forty millions sterling of paper-money were issued on the credit of the confiscated estates of the emigrant clergy and nobility. That sum not sufficing, more millions were issued, and any one who ·declined to receive the depreciated assignats were punished with irons. Three hundred thousand men were called out to defend the territory, and that number not sufficing, twelve hundred thousand were ordered to join the army. Generals who failed, generals who paused, were sent to the revolutionary tribunal, and fell by the guillotine.

The cry of Danton in the days of September: " Il nous faut de l'audace, encore de l'audace, et toujours de l'audace." — " We must dare, and still dare, and always dare," was the war-cry of the new policy. All the benevolent pacific maxims of the makers of the first Constitution iu 1789 were entirely thrown aside.

Strange as it may appear, there is no reason to doubt that Robespierre and his immediate agents, who put this terrible system in operation, were blindly led by the vain abstractions and misanthropical invectives of Rousseau. If anything could humble the pride of human intellect, it would be to reflect on the accumulated knowledge and the logical philosophy of the eighteenth century, and then to observe the desolation, the tyranny, the misery in which it had its consummation.

As a singular instance of the difference between a French and an English understanding, it may here be mentioned, that when the " Social Contract" of Rousseau was quoted by Lord Mornington in the House of Commons, Mr. Fox said he had once begun the book, but he found it so extravagant, that he could not go on with it. The essay which Mr. Fox, a great reader, and no enemy to democracy, found it impossible to go on with, was the work from which the rulers of France drew their inspiration at the very climax of the Revolution! ·

There are other reflections which occur painfully to the mind. In the year 1788 nothing appeared easier than to reform the Government of France. The King was animated with the kindest regard to the welfare of his people, the nobles were ready to give up their exclusive privileges, the clergy to grant full religious liberty to all who dissented from the Church. The path to a free Constitution and a happy state of society seemed easy to find and smooth to pursue. Few, very few, wished to abolish the monarchy, scarcely any to break the bonds by which society was held together. But, as Mr. Burke has said, and as I have heard Sir James Mackintosh repeat after him, " Difficulty is good for man." The very facility of the triumph deceived the conquerors, and in the intoxication of their success, they carried blood ·and fire where no resistance was made and no opposition was possible.

CHAPTER XXXV.

1793.

Mr. PITT and his colleagues had now invited and accepted the war, let us see what measures they adopted in order to make it successful. The first duty of the British Government was to protect Holland, our complying but reluctant ally. For this purpose 20,000 men were landed at Rotterdam. The next object was to provide for Flanders and the general purposes of the campaign.

At the time when the British Government entered upon the scene, the French army had sustained some signal reverses. Beaten at Neerwinden, at Tirlemont, and Louvain, the new levies of France were retiring upon their own frontier with all the circumstances of panic, of dispersion, and distrust of their commanders, which are so certain to affect young troops in adverse fortune. The Prince of Coburg, however, instead of pushing forward and destroying the dispersed and dispirited enemy, entered into negotiation with General Dumouriez. It was agreed that Dumouriez should march to Paris with his army, dissolve the Convention, and restore the monarchy; he was to be assisted in this enterprise by Austrian troops. It was found, however, that the French army and the French garrisons indignantly refused to follow Dumouriez, and he himself, with Young

Equality and 1500 men, was obliged to seek for refuge in the Austrian head-quarters.

In these circumstances the Prince of Coburg, with Count Metternich on the part of Austria, Lord Auckland on the part of England, and Count Keller on the part of Prussia, met on the 7th of April, at Antwerp. It was speedily decided that the co-operation with Dumouriez having failed, no further step should be taken in that direction. Prince Coburg accordingly, on the 10th of April, revoked a proclamation he had issued on the 5th, promising his assistance in restoring the French monarchy.

It would evidently have been wise to modify rather than to revoke the proclamation. But the Allies went further. Now, for the first time, were heard the words of indemnity for the past, and security for the future. It was agreed that the fortresses taken by Austria were to be occupied in the name of the Emperor, with a view to form out of the French frontier a new frontier for Germany. As no similar security was provided for Prussia, Frederick William from this moment sought both his indemnity and his security from the spoils of unhappy Poland. The obvious plan of marching in force upon Paris, as soon as a base of operations could be secured, was now abandoned; and while Austria attempted to weaken and master France by land, England on the other sought to despoil her of her fleets and her colonies. Instead of sympathy with the cause of the murdered monarch, the two Governments sought only to share the riches and inherit the force of the torn and dismembered monarchy.

The forces of the Allies were now very considerable. The Prince of Coburg, having the Duke of York under his orders, advanced with 80,000 men to form the siege of

Valenciennes. The French army which covered that place was defeated, and forced to take post at a position called the Camp of Cœur. The Duke of York then laid siege to Valenciennes, and an Austrian division to Condé. Condé surrendered on the 13th, and Valenciennes on the 22nd of July.

Similar success attended the army of the Duke of Brunswick. Mentz was vigorously besieged, and surrendered on the 28th of July.

Thus the Allies found themselves, at the end of July, with armies amounting to nearly 300,000 men, in possession of strong fortresses, and masters of the road to Paris.* Leaving 100,000 men to keep open their communications, they might have marched with from 150,000 to 180,000 men upon Paris. No army of force and discipline sufficient to resist them lay between them and the capital of the Revolution. The fruits of Mantua and of Pilnitz seemed ready to be gathered by these champions of religion and of monarchy, of justice and of order. But their arms were paralysed by their own selfishness, jealousy, and timidity. The Duke of York, with a large division, besieged Dunkirk, a port which, since the Succession War, had always been a bugbear to English commerce. Over Valenciennes and Condé waved the flag of the Emperor, and the Prince of Coburg specially declared that he took possession of them by right of conquest. The King of Prussia, catching the example, authorized a cartel in his own name coupled with that of the French Republic; ordered his generals not to give any effective assistance to the Austrian army, and promptly returned home to complete and consolidate his new acquisitions in Poland. The garrisons of Mentz, of

* Adolphus, vol. v. p. 444.

Valenciennes, and of Condé were allowed to return to France, and enabled the Jacobin Government to perpetrate at Lyons, at Toulon, and in La Vendée the most horrible cruelties which were ever known even in the cruelty of civil war.

Yet all the sacrifices of the unhappy Royalists by the Allies to selfish objects did not avail to make Dunkirk cease to be French, or Valenciennes permanently Austrian. A new master of the art of war arose in the Committee of Public Safety, and scattered to the winds all these mean calculations. This was Carnot, who, seeing that the 100,000 men covering and besieging Dunkirk were scattered in positions distant from each other, ordered General Houchard to attack first Marshal Freytag, then the Dutch, and lastly the Duke of York. He hoped thus to encounter each with a superior force, and overwhelm all three. Houchard executed but partially this commission. He defeated Freytag, and was preparing to follow up his success, when the Duke of York, seeing his flank menaced, raised the siege of Dunkirk, leaving fifty guns in the hands of the enemy. This discomfiture had been much assisted by the annoyance his camp sustained from the French gunboats, while England had not been able to fit out any force appropriate to the service.

Yet Houchard soon himself committed the fault of which the Allies had been guilty. While one of his divisions attacked and defeated the Dutch, he was himself attacked at Courtray by General Beaulieu, and so thoroughly beaten, that his troops, in panic and disorder, took refuge under the walls of Lille. This was not a fault to be pardoned under the severe rule of the Committee of Public Safety. He was brought to trial, and Barrère, addressing him in their name, said, "For a long time the principle established by the great Frederick, that the best way to take advantage of the courage of troops is to accumulate them in large masses on particular points has been an established maxim in war. Instead of doing this, you have divided them into separate detachments, and the generals in command have had to combat superior forces. The Committee of Public Safety, fully aware of the danger, had sent the most positive instructions to the generals to fight in large masses; you have disregarded their orders, and reverses have followed." He was brought before the Revolutionary Tribunal, condemned, and executed. The principle of the Committee of Public Safety became the rule of war, and the star of victory. General Jourdan was placed in command of the army of Flanders. Twelve hundred thousand men were ordered to be raised to defend the French territory. The Allies, much discouraged, but not yet hopeless, now laid siege to Maubeuge, with a view of opening a road to Paris. But the French, fully roused to their danger, were making superhuman efforts to meet this new invasion. On the 15th of October Jourdan attacked in three columns the key of the Austrian position. After a brave defence the Prince of Coburg, afraid of having his flank turned, retreated from Wattignies, with the loss of six thousand men. The siege of Mauberge was raised, and the campaign on this side was decided in favour of France.

On the Rhine the differences between the Austrians and Prussians, now openly declared, neutralized any real advantage which might have been obtained from the overwhelming force of the Allies. Victories, it is true, were gained; the lines of Wiessenburg were forced by the Allies with great slaughter. But a proclamation of General

Wurmser, calling upon the people of Alsace to re-unite themselves to the Empire, and thus undo the work of Louis XIV., augmented the jealousy of Prussia. The Duke of Brunswick received orders from Berlin to thwart the efforts of Austria, and he willingly complied with this order. Presently the French under Hoche, with augmented forces, rushed upon Wurmser, forced him to repass the Rhine, and regained Landau.

In La Vendée the royalists sustained two very bloody defeats at Mons and Juvenay. Lord Moira, who was sent to assist them, arrived too late, and left the coast.

The fate of Toulon was the most disastrous of all the events which checked the Grand Alliance. The middle classes of that town declared in favour of Louis XVII., with a constitution; and the British Government, with sundry reserves, undertook to protect them till the general peace. But a young officer of artillery, sent by the Committee of Public Safety, called Napoleon Bonaparte, defeated all the efforts of Lord Hood and the Spanish admiral by making himself master of a post from which the harbour was commanded. Lord Hood and his advisers decided to evacuate the place and burn so much of the French fleet as they could not remove. The Spanish admiral remonstrated against this destruction; he said it was as contrary to the interests of Spain as it was consonant to the particular policy of Great Britain. This remonstrance was unavailing; but the remissness of the Spaniards saved seven sail of the line to the Republic. Eighteen sail of the line and nine frigates were destroyed or removed; of these, fifteen sail of the line were burnt and three added to the British navy. Fourteen thousand persons were carried away by the Allies. The vengeance of the Republicans was horrible. The guillotine executed the principal adherents of monarchy and the richest of the inhabitants. Large numbers were drawn out in line and shot down by musketry. As even this process was found too slow, Frounc, the Commissioner of the Republic, ordered the people of the town to assemble in the Champ de Mars. This order was generally obeyed; and even many country people joined the crowd, thinking a procession or some festive games were to be seen. When the crowd was assembled, grape shot was fired upon them; those who had fallen from terror or slight wounds were ordered to stand up, and when they did so, a second discharge of grape was the recompence of their obedience. Two thousand dead bodies were left on the field of carnage.

Thus ended the attempt to establish the monarchy of Louis XVII. at Toulon. The story of Lyons is still more dreadful, and is a reproach on the age in which such crimes could be perpetrated. The monsters who ordered the massacres exulted in the sight of these cold-blooded murders of their countrymen.

The end of the year beheld the indisputable triumph of the sanguinary monsters who ruled France. The hostility of Great Britain seemed only to have furnished an excuse for aggravated terrors in the interior, and a motive for un-exampled efforts to repel the foreign enemy. Mr. Carlyle says truly :—

"Whatsoever is cruel in the panic frenzy of twenty-five million men, whatsoever is great in the simultaneous death-defiance of twenty-five million men, stand here in abrupt contrast, near by one another. As, indeed, is usual, much more when a nation of men is hurled suddenly beyond the limits."*

* Carlyle: "French Revolution," vol. iii. p. 4.

In the meantime the year 1793 came to a close. Its day dawned on the murder of a king, its sun set on the horrible spectacle of a great nation slaying rich and poor, the brilliant and the obscure, the widow and the orphan. The monarchs and the statesmen of Europe had found no better remedy for these crimes than a league to light up the flames of war and add the slaughter of the battle and the siege to that of the street and the scaffold.

CHAPTER XXXVI.

REMARKS ON THE CONDUCT OF THE WAR.

In October, 1793, Mr. Burke, dissatisfied with the first-fruits of the war he had invoked, sat down to place on record his views of what ought to be done, and his reflections on what had been done. In these remarks there is, as usual, much that is striking, forcible, and true, mixed with much that is intemperate, extravagant, and false.

One passage is to the following effect: "If we consider the acting power in France, in any legal construction of public law, as the people, the question is decided in favour of the Republic, one and indivisible. *But we have decided for monarchy.* If so, we have a king and subjects; and that king and subjects have rights and privileges which ought to be supported at home; for I do not suppose that the government of that kingdom can, or ought to be regulated by the arbitrary mandate of a foreign confederacy."*

Nothing can be more unsound or contradictory than this paragraph. Who gave us the right to decide for monarchy in France? Why was it not as competent for the people of France, as for the people of Holland, of

* "Policy of the Allies."

Hamburg, of Genoa, of Venice, and of the United States in America, to constitute themselves into a republic? But if a foreign confederacy was competent for this decision in favour of monarchy, why was it not equally fit to regulate the government of the kingdom?

Mr. Burke goes on to argue that all which had been done in 1789, and since, must be undone. That the old clergy and nobility must be brought back; that property confiscated must be restored to its ancient owners, and the king or regent empowered to enter into all the rights which Louis XVI. possessed before the meeting of the Constituent Assembly. Mirabeau and Lafayette were no better in his eyes than Robespierre and Danton.

The plain answer to this project was, that it was impracticable. Not only was the place wanting where the lever could be placed, but the lever itself was insufficient for its work. Fifty thousand of the old nobles, even if assisted by two hundred thousand of the old priests, could not govern France when mad with enthusiasm for the destruction of monarchy and the abolition of the priesthood.

But while Mr. Burke utterly fails in showing that his plan could possibly be successful, he is powerful in proving that the scheme adopted by the Allies was sure to fail. Thus, speaking of the notion that the affairs of France would be better arranged by the Allied Powers than by the landed proprietors of the kingdom, he says, " It is of all modes of flattery the most effectual, to be told that you can regulate the affairs of another kingdom better than its hereditary proprietors. It is formed to flatter the principle of conquest, so natural to all men. It is this principle which is now making the partition of Poland. The powers concerned have been told by some perfidious Poles, and perhaps they believe, that their usurpation is a great benefit to the people, especially to the common people."

In describing the enemy with whom we had to deal, Mr. Burke was not blind to his strength. "The Jacobin revolution," he says, " is carried on by men of no rank, of no consideration, of wild, savage minds, full of levity, arrogance, and presumption ; without morals, without probity, without prudence. What have they, then, to supply their innumerable defects, and to make them terrible even to the firmest minds? *One* thing, and *one* thing only—but that one thing is worth a thousand—they have *energy*."* He goes on to show how a "languid, uncertain hesitation, with a formal official spirit, which is turned aside by every obstacle from its purpose, and which never sees a difficulty but to yield to it, or at best to evade it," is unfit to cope with this great quality of energy. In this opinion Burke and Danton were of the same mind.

In order to meet this distempered energy, Mr. Burke recommended a manly vigour, and the magnanimity of good faith. He said truly that, if we attempted sinister advantages, we should teach others the game, and be out-witted and overborne. That, instead of being at the head of a great confederacy, we should break into a thousand selfish little quarrels.

" I have Toulon in my eye. . . . . These ships are now so circumstanced that, if we are forced to evacuate Toulon, they must fall into the hands of the enemy, or be burnt by ourselves. I know this is by some considered as a fine thing for us ; but the Athenians ought not to be better than the English, nor Mr. Pitt less virtuous than Aristides.

* The italics are Mr. Burke's.

My clear opinion is that Toulon ought to be made, what we set out with, a royal French city."

Mr. Burke goes on to argue that, if we considered only our own selfish advantages, other Powers would fear our preponderance quite as much as the triumph of the French arms; that Prussia in the same way would dread the power of Austria, and the whole confederacy would melt away. "Nothing is so fatal to a nation as an extreme of self-partiality, and the total want of consideration of what others will naturally hope and fear. . . . . It signifies nothing whether we are wrong or right in the abstract; but in respect to our relation with Spain, with such principles followed up in practice, it is absolutely impossible that any cordial alliance can subsist between the two nations. If Spain goes, Naples will speedily follow. Prussia is quite certain, and thinks of nothing but making a market of the present confusions. Italy is broken and divided; Switzerland is Jacobinized, I am afraid, completely."

After declaring that this was a religious war, and that the clergy must be restored, Mr. Burke proceeds to make other observations more worthy of his great and comprehensive mind. He declares that, unless France remains a very great and preponderating power, the liberties of Europe cannot possibly be preserved. "The design at present evidently pursued by the combined potentates, or of the two who lead, is totally to destroy her as such a power. For Great Britain resolves that she shall have no colonies, no commerce, and no marine. Austria means to take away the whole frontier from the borders of Switzerland to Dunkirk." He then points out that the internal arrangements of France, prescribed "by force of the arms of rival and jealous nations," would produce in that government distraction and debility. " One cannot conceive so frightful a state of a nation. A maritime country without a marine and without commerce; a Continental country without a frontier, and for a thousand miles surrounded with powerful, warlike, and ambitious neighbours! It is possible that she might submit to lose her commerce and her colonies; her security she never can abandon. If, contrary to all expectations, under such a disgraced and impotent government, any energy should remain in that country, she will make every effort to recover her security, which will involve Europe for a century in war and blood. What has it cost to France to make that frontier? What will it cost to recover it? Austria thinks that without a frontier she cannot secure the *Netherlands*. But without her frontier France cannot secure *herself*."

Mr. Burke thus proves that the Executive Government of France, by whatever name it might be called, Committee of Public Safety, or Jacobin Club, was fighting on behalf of national interests—nay, of national existence. He proceeds to predict the failure which was sure to attend the iniquitous scheme of the Allies.

" But let us depend upon it, whatever tends, under the name of security, to aggrandize Austria, will discontent and alarm Prussia. Such a length of frontier on the side of France, separated from itself, and separated from the mass of the Austrian country, will be weak, unless connected at the expense of the Elector of Bavaria (the Elector Palatine), and other lesser princes, or by such exchanges as will again convulse the empire. Take it the other way, and let us suppose France so broken in spirit as to be content to remain naked and defenceless by sea and by land,

is such a country no prey? Have other nations no views?
Is Poland the only country of which it is worth while to
make a partition? We cannot be so childish as to imagine
that ambition is local, and 'that no others can be infected
with it but those who rule within certain parallels of lati-
tude and longitude. In this way I hold war equally certain. But I can conceive that both these principles may
operate : ambition on the part of Austria to cut more and
more from France; and' French impatience under her degraded and unsafe condition. In such a contest will the
other Powers stand by? Will not Prussia call for indemnity as well as Austria and England? Is she satisfied with
her gains in Poland? By no means. Germany must pay,
or we shall infallibly see Prussia leagued with France and
Spain, and possibly with other Powers, for the reduction of
Austria; and such may be the situation of things that it
will not be so easy to decide what part England may take
in such a contest."*

Again, let us listen to Mr. Burke in respect to France.
" However formidable to us taken in this one relation,
France is not equally dreadful to all other States. On the
contrary, my clear opinion is, that the liberties of Europe
cannot possibly be preserved but by her remaining a very
great and preponderating Power."†

Such were the views of Mr. Burke. It cannot be denied
that they were borne out by the events of 1793 and 1794.
Prussia naturally withdrew from a contest by which the
preponderance of Austria in Germany was to be increased.
Spain, jealous of the maritime power of England, felt no
wish to destroy the only equipoise to our weight. The
confederacy fell to pieces, leaving the Continent hum-

* " Policy of the Allies."   † Ibid.

bled, and Great Britain in debt. At length, however, the tide of conquest ebbed, and the Allies, after the victory of Leipzic, found themselves on the frontier of France. What did they then say of her? "They desire that France should be powerful and happy—that commerce should revive, and the arts flourish—that its territory should preserve an extent unknown under its ancient kings; because the French power great and strong is in Europe one of the fundamental bases of the social edifice," &c.* They thus echo Mr. Burke. But, although Mr. Burke was right in his objections to Mr. Pitt's mode of conducting the war, his own policy was even less practical and less promising· A King of the Bourbon race, placed by foreign arms upon the throne, must either have been kept there by foreign arms, or take his choice (if choice he should be allowed) beween exile and the scaffold. He would have found none to execute his orders, none to obey them. He would have been regarded as the degraded Viceroy of Austria, Prussia, Russia, and Great Britain. The old parliaments, the old clergy, the old aristocracy, had ceased to exist as powerful members of the political and social body. The Eurydice which Mr. Burke embraced as a reality was now no more than a phantom. To him, turning back to clasp her in his arms, and

"Prensantem nequicquam umbras,"

the fair vision never re-appeared. For

"Illa quidem Stygiâ nabat jam frigida cymbâ."

The fact is, the French Revolution was an epidemic disease for which war was not the remedy. The more violence was used, the more the patient raved—the more chains and

* Declaration of Frankfort, 1814.

straw, the more utter the failure in restoring reason. Nor did the spectacle of the physicians clutching greedily at fees give a favourable opinion of their skill.

The question in the end again recurs, Was it necessary, and consequently was it just, to swell the tide of blood by the addition of foreign invasion? The favourite charge against the victims of the Reign of Terror, the charge most easy to invent, the charge impossible to rebut, was that of wishing well to the foreign enemy, and being ready to open to him the gates of France. The sieges of Condé, Valenciennes, Dunkirk, and Maubeuge roused the spirit of patriotism, and bound together those who proudly asserted the cause of national independence with those who ruled in the name of a bloody, jealous, and implacable democracy. It is clear that the fearful tumult was incarnadined, and its period prolonged by the external war. The guillotine was fed with the heads of young women who had hailed with garlands the King of Prussia at Verdun, and of persons of all classes who had rejoiced in the successes of the Allies, in the capital, the country, and the provincial towns. The musketry and the cannon of the Republicans revenged at Toulon and La Vendée the cause of the Convention against the English. Wherever an innocent man was obnoxious for his wealth, his virtues, or his talents, the suspicion of wishing well to the Allies furnished a ready accusation, a speedy conviction, and a certain execution. Every evil influence was augmented, every bitter enmity was heightened, every ferocious clamour was made louder by the interference of hostile strangers.

Yet, if the aim of the Allies had been to march at once to Paris, to extinguish the raging fire of the Revolution, to place a constitutional King on the throne, and to proclaim a general amnesty for the past, we might have thought that, although the attempt was imprudent, and the end unattainable, yet that the generosity and greatness of the enterprise in some degree atoned for the rashness of the political crusade. The royal family, cruelly persecuted; the nobles, among the highest and most refined members of European society, reduced to poverty and proscribed; the clergy, many of whom were patterns of Christian patience and humility, sent to die by hundreds,—might pardonably have excited somewhat of the spirit of chivalry on their behalf. But when we find an Emperor of Germany appropriating a fortress, and a King of Great Britain conquering an island—when we find the emigrants, and Louis XVIII. in their name, protesting against the friendship of the Allies,—we are lost in amazement at the effrontery which could cover a scheme of plunder with the cloak of religion and humanity.

Mr. Burke observes, curiously enough, that the Convention did not contain one military man of name. But, although the reputation of Carnot was not then made, the organizer of victory has since been enrolled among the names of those who have in a critical moment decided the destiny of nations. It was his maxim that military talent ought not to be sought in the limited sphere of a single class; that a Turenne and a Condé are happy accidents; that by vigilant inquiry men fit to command may be found in any part of the army. Thus Jourdain, who had served as a private in the American War, and become by election colonel of his battalion in 1791, rose very speedily to command, raised the siege of Maubeuge in 1793, and gained the battle of Fleurus in 1794. Thus Pichegru, also a private during the American War, became, in 1794, the conqueror of Holland. In 1793 also, Davoust, one of the first marshals of the Empire, led a division. Lastly, in 1793, Napoleon Buonaparte, the son of a Corsican gentleman, a lieutenant of artillery, gave proof of his military genius at Toulon, and rose to a height seldom reached by mortal man.

The creation of these great generals, and the national fame of the French army, were the spawn of the wrong which Leopold and Frederick William, George III. and Catharine, had attempted to inflict upon France. Resisting invasion, defying conquest, they carried the sympathies of Europe with them when they marched over Germany, revolutionized Italy, and shook the thrones of half the princes of Europe. Peace seemed to confirm their conquests and ratify their supremacy.

The military ruler of France, however, in his turn, abused his strength. It seemed to be his object to extinguish the life of nations, and leave standing only one mighty despotism. In 1808 the Spaniards, first among the people of Europe, partly in ignorance of the means of their enemy, but also in the full knowledge that independence is the breath of life to a nation, took up arms from their own firesides to fight their invaders, not as soldiers, but as men; in villages, in defiles, in the darkness of the night, in small squadrons, in single spies, amid the feast of intoxication and the security of sleep. In 1813 the Prussians raised a similar cry, and as an armed nation revenged the defeats of disciplined armies.

Then, indeed, the popular feeling, which in 1793 had supported France, turned to the side of the Allied Sovereigns. Then the Emperors of Russia and Austria, using the words of Mr. Burke, proclaimed that France ought to be powerful and great. Then, indeed, a march to Paris became practicable and fruitful. The French nation, no longer enthusiastic for liberty and fraternity, had been exhausted in the effort to make the will of a single man the law and gospel of Europe. The war, then, at length became successful, not because Mr. Pitt had been endowed with wisdom and foresight in 1793, but because Napoleon had made the empire of 1804 incompatible with the independence of the nations of Europe.

END OF VOL. II.